THE JOCK

AN M|M SPORTS ROMANCE

TAL BAUER

PROLOGUE

IT WAS PARIS, and it was summertime.

Study abroad, his counselor had said. *We can make it work with your scholarship. Knock out a year of language. What do you say?*

Sounds great. As long as I can clear it with Coach Young.

He'd been careful to plan everything. Schedule his flights so he wouldn't miss the final week of football practice. Pick up extra shifts so he had a little more leeway in his budget. Work up a travel training routine so he could stay in shape away from the campus gym. So careful.

But he hadn't anticipated Justin.

AT NIGHT, the Eiffel Tower lit up every hour, a million dazzling lights twinkling off and on, off and on, and the glow played over Justin's face as he turned stared, eyes so full of wide-eyed wonder it stole Wes's breath away, made his lungs stutter and choke. The image crystallized, every flicker stilling as Wes's mind freeze-framed the moment.

Justin's smile, the lilt of his laugh, curled around Wes's heart.

He'd always thought kissing his first guy would be harder. That he'd be afraid, nervous. Shouldn't his heart be pounding? Shouldn't his hands be shaking? Where was the earthquake in his soul? Why wasn't his mind screaming at him to stop?

He didn't want to stop.

Everything felt right. Perfect. The moment, the man.

He stepped forward and cupped his hand around Justin's cheek, then stroked his football-calloused thumb over Justin's sharp jawline. He waited, watching the lights dance in Justin's eyes, in and out of the curve of his smile and the dimples in his cheeks.

And when Justin's gaze flicked to his, Wes leaned in, eyes open, until their lips were millimeters apart.

He was risking everything. His past, his future, and even his now, reaching for a kiss based on one week of stolen glances and sideways looks and a frisson underneath his skin he couldn't scratch away. A hum in his head, an itch beneath his fingers, and it didn't matter what he did, he couldn't get rid of this because it was already so deep inside him. Twenty-one years of ignoring himself, of looking down when he wanted to look up, drink a man's body like he was a cold glass of water under the Texas sun. Of turning away. Of not going there.

One week in Paris, with Justin, and here he was, ready for— aching for—his first kiss. Or, at least, the first one that counted. The first one he'd ever really wanted.

Wes waited, his vision dazzled by the lights winking in Justin's eyes, the glow tangling in the strands of his honey hair. It was like he was looking into the stadium lights.

But there was no route for this, no pattern. No timing. This was his Hail Mary.

CHAPTER ONE

One Week Earlier

THE FLIGHT to Paris was long and loud, the engines like a drill through his skull for the entire nine hours over North America and then the Atlantic. He'd been squished in the middle seat between two businessmen who both wanted to work on their laptops, and both shoved their elbows into his eighteen-inch seat space until he felt like he couldn't breathe. If he shifted at all, he jostled both men, from their shoulders to their knees and definitely their elbows, type-typing away. He'd apologized the first few times, but unless he held his damn breath for the entire flight, he was going to move now and then. A guy his size, well. He was born big, and he was destined to be big. Years of football and ranching had only hardened his raw strength. He'd been described as mountainous.

Halfway through the flight, one of the flight attendants had taken pity on him, or on the businessmen, and guided him to an empty row in the back. It was near the bathrooms, and he heard the toilet flushing every five minutes, but he could at least stretch out his arms and legs and not ruin another man's hard work. He could inhale and exhale without needing to apologize.

Paris was loud, too, and even though he was used to standing out, apparently they didn't make men his size in France, because Lord Almighty, he was stared at. He almost checked his face for food or snot or boogers, because that many people staring at him, conversations dying as he passed, as his boots clicked over the tile floor—well, that had to mean something, right? Maybe it was the boots and the hat. Maybe it was just him.

He took the train from the airport to the transfer hub before getting off in the seventeenth arrondissement, where the study-abroad group was staying. Everyone else had come in three days before, but he couldn't miss the last week of football practice. They were the final days to impress Coach Young before he decided the starting line for next year.

But an opportunity to spend three weeks in Paris covered by his scholarship? He'd grabbed that with both hands. Never in his life had he thought he'd ever be able to go to France.

Never mind that he wouldn't be able to do any of the add-ons, the day trips, the real moneymakers for the trip organizers. No, he would not be going up in a hot-air balloon or taking a weekend trip to the Riviera or out to the wineries. A day flight to Vienna. He'd be just fine walking the streets of Paris, taking in the sights. The online guide said he could feed himself for ten euros a day on a budget, which was what he was going to do. Pizza—they had that there, right?—French bread, cheese and ham. It was enough to be there.

Things like this didn't happen to West Texas farm boys. Paris, when he was growing up, was a town in Hill Country, foreign because it was a ten-hour drive to the other side of Texas, way out there near the city folk.

There were only two ways out of West Texas: on the gridiron or in shackles, bound for Huntsville. Even the oil jobs were evapo-rating, moving on to other fields, offshore or up north, where

West Texas boys froze as soon as they saw a flake of snow. Where he was from, kids sometimes waited years before they felt actual rain on their faces. It was hard and dry and bitter in West Texas, and most people quit, but his father was a rancher like his father before him. Their parcel of land was small, their herd modest, and they eked just enough out of the dust and the scrub to keep on living for the next year.

Boys like him grew up looking skyward, not to God, but to those Friday night lights, and the swarms of beetles and gnats and cicadas that swam in and out of the stadium lights at the high school. He'd looked up from the time he was as tall as his dad's boots. When he was four, he played dirt ball with other kids, tying kitchen towels to their belt loops to mimic flag football. He was fast even then, they said, and big. A boulder rolling one way. In middle school he was ranked in the top ten players in the state. In high school, the top five.

He earned his athletic scholarship with every torn muscle, every bruised bone, every hairline fracture, every black eye, every concussion of his youth. He'd seen his dad proud of him a lot of days in his life, but he'd never seen him as proud as when they opened that letter from the university together at Mama's grave. His old man had stared at Mama's headstone for a long time, the brim of his hat angled down so Wes couldn't see his eyes. But when he looked up again, there were tear tracks running down his leathery cheeks.

His DNA was in that dust, generations of Van de Hoeks who had worked the land with their sweat and blood and given their bones to the dirt. His dad had always told him, "You're gonna have a better life than this, son. Keep you playin', and you'll be able to create your own future."

The biggest city Wes had ever been in before was Austin, and that was for his pre–college athletics physical. He'd run five miles on a treadmill with an EKG hooked to his chest, breathed into what looked like an experiment from the space station, and stood patiently for X-rays of all his bones. He'd had to squat to fit in the machine's viewfinder.

Simply being in Paris was enough. It was enough to fly overseas for the first time, get his first stamp in his passport. Enough to take the subway for the first time, navigate the transfer, muddle through with his high school and college French.

He hefted his suitcase up the six flights of wooden stairs to the top floor. The staircase was so narrow he could touch both walls with his elbows. Eventually he made it to the landing, what used to be the rafters in ye olde times, probably around when his great-great-great-grandparents were setting down roots in Texas, and found the door to his shared room.

His metal key was like a Hollywood prop, something he'd only ever seen in old movies. But it fit in the lock and turned, and he shoved open the warped door with his shoulder before walking in.

Whatever the quaint little hotel lacked with its staircase and boring lobby, it more than made up for with the view. His first glimpse was through the south-facing windows, and he saw the Arc de Triomphe and the tip of the Eiffel Tower. Gauzy curtains blew on the hot summer breeze, ruffling into and out of his view. Spread before him were what seemed like all the rooftops of Paris, ceramic tiles and antique chimneys, delicate wrought iron scrollwork and Juliet balconies mingling as the city rolled on and on.

"Hello?"

Wes heard him before he saw him. His roommate, a guy he only knew as *Justin S.* from the paperwork he'd been emailed. There were no other details. "Hello?" he called back. His drawl, which always came in strong when he was tired, was thick as whiskey. He cleared his throat. A head popped around the corner. He lifted his hat from his head, held it over his chest. "You must be Justin."

Wide eyes set in an angular face stared. Justin looked him up and down, a long, slow rake that took in every inch of Wes's frame. He felt the burn of those eyes, felt them stutter and take a second look.

"Uhh, yeah." Justin appeared in full view, then, his body following his head until he was fully facing Wes. He was slender. A runner, a swimmer, maybe even a dancer. Wes had an eye for bodies, for musculature. Justin was as tall as he was, and his strength wasn't accidental. He worked at himself. Taut, wide shoulders—butterfly shoulders—and a trim waist, defined hipbones. Carved thighs, the muscles playing peekaboo with skintight denim. "You're the late guy?"

He held out his hand and nodded. "Wes."

Justin's touch was firm, his skin cool. "Justin. Sorry. You surprised me."

Wes didn't know what to say, so he said nothing. He waited, trapped in the entranceway, the rest of their room barricaded by Justin. They were in a staredown, it seemed, Justin's saddle-leather eyes locked on his own. Searching for something.

"Oh!" Justin finally peeled his eyes from Wes's and backed up. "Sorry. Again." He shook his head, rubbed his fingers over his temples. "It was a long night. I think I had too much wine." He gestured to the room, fluttering his wrist across the divide to the other single bed. The bed frames were pushed against the wall on either side of the hallway, set up so they could gaze out the windows over Paris at night. A tiny kitchenette, smaller than the one in Wes's freshman dorm, and a skinny door squatted in the far corner. "Bathroom, kitchen." Justin gave the grand tour with one point of his finger.

Justin checked his watch as Wes set his duffel on his bed next to his hat, crown down on the mattress. "Everyone is meeting up downstairs to take the shuttle to campus in twenty minutes. You got here just in time."

He'd taken the red-eye, planned his arrival for this morning, right before classes started. Time to change out of his T-shirt, maybe wash his face. Brush his teeth.

"There's coffee." Justin's voice came over his other shoulder, and from the corner of Wes's eye, he saw Justin leaning against the window frame with his arms folded, staring over the city. "And I picked up a baguette this morning, but I didn't finish it. Help yourself."

"Thanks." He shucked his shirt and dropped it on his bed, fished out his favorite Ariat tee, grabbed his toothbrush, and headed for the bathroom. He had to turn sideways to slide through the door, and there was no room at all to bend over. Clearly, indoor plumbing was a modern addition to the hotel, done sometime in the early 1900s and never updated.

Wes hesitated before he slid back into the room, his gaze sliding to Justin and stilling. Justin was still at the window, still staring over the Paris skyline, his head tilted against the frame. He wore skinny jeans, the ends tucked into untied boots. Fashion combat boots, not the working Ropers Wes wore. Justin wore a T-shirt and an unbuttoned plaid shirt, and his hair was somewhere between brown and blond, like honey left out in the sun too long. His eyes were pinched, his gaze fixed on the far distance, bottom lip slightly plump, as if he wanted to pout but was holding himself in. There was a coiled tension to him, a rattler drawing tighter around itself, readying to spit and fight.

Paris's morning glow caught on all the glass and concrete and bustle of the city. Wes could hear cars and buses and a thousand voices call out, bike chimes and tires and brakes, exhaust bellowing. Laughter. Radios, French rap and hip-hop and even Arabic music rising from the street.

At the open window, Justin, statuesque, stared out over the city like it had already disappointed him. There was something in his shoulders, in the hard line of his back.

Wes poured himself a cup of coffee from the French press next to the sink. Justin's mug was abandoned on the counter, and he refilled it, then brought it to Justin. Held it out and smiled.

Justin started, and he looked from the coffee to Wes then back to the coffee before he smiled back. It was a slow thing, like the unfurling of a sunrise, first his eyes and his cheeks crinkling, the hints of dimples appearing, and then his eyelids fluttering before his lips parted and curled, revealing perfectly straight, perfectly white teeth. "Thank you." He cupped the mug in both hands and sipped.

Wes's heart *thump-thump*ed. He toasted Justin silently, and hooked one thumb in his waistband, leaning against the window frame.

With every sip, Wes's eyes skittered sideways, sneaking glances at Justin.

"Right," Justin finally said, straightening. He rolled his neck, stretched, and set his mug on the windowsill. "Time for class. *Êtes-vous prêt à aller à l'école?*"

"*Oui.*" Wes mirrored Justin, setting down his cup on the windowsill. He grabbed his hat from the bed, a wide-brimmed, cream cowboy hat with a cattleman's crease, the edges turned up just the way he liked and the front tipped down to block the sun's glare. He brought it to his chest and then tried to let Justin go first, but there was no way two grown men could squeeze into that narrow entranceway. He scooted out but turned to hold the door open for Justin with his fingertips. A flush rose on Justin's cheeks, and he looked away as he locked their door.

They thundered downstairs, Wes's Ropers echoing on the worn wood of the stairs. Justin held the door as they hit the street, and Wes fitted his hat on his head as he stepped into the sunshine. Parisians stopped and stared, and one or two spun all the way around.

Wes shoved his hands in his pockets and waited at the curb, near the gaggle of other university students. They, too, stared, but he saw a few startled looks of recognition. Two of the girls took him in, starting at his feet and working their way up before turning sexy smiles loose when their eyes met his.

Justin cleared his throat as he waited beside Wes, his arms

once again crossed, his back to the rest of the students. "Everyone else has partnered up, and they've been in this group chat for months, preparing for this trip." He shrugged. "I didn't really decide to go on this trip until a month ago, so, I guess we're both the late ones."

Wes nodded. "Okay."

"Yeah." Justin bounced on the balls of his feet, rocked back on his heels. "I mean, if you'd rather be alone, I can—"

"No, it's fine." Wes spoke quickly, cutting Justin off. "It's good."

The bus arrived, covering whatever Justin would have said in squealing brakes and natural gas exhaust. Everyone clambered on, most heading in gaggles to the back of the bus. Justin stayed near the front, sliding into the second row next to the window. His eyes flicked to Wes as he followed, then back out the window.

Wes slid in beside Justin and set his hat in his lap. He smiled, a crook of his lips that only worked on the left side.

Justin stared at him for three long seconds.

"Do I smell?" Wes sniffed at his underarm. Deodorant running a little thin, but nothing offensive, he thought. "Do you want me to move?"

"No!" Finally, Justin smiled again. It was quick, but it was there. "No, you're fine. You don't smell. You just surprised me is all."

The bus doors shut with a hiss, and with a lurch and a rattle and a shake, they were off, merging into Parisian traffic and heading across the city.

Justin flicked the brim of his hat. "So, are you, like, a real cowboy? I know we're all from Texas, but..."

Wes turned over his hands, revealing his worn and leathery palms, roughened from years of working the ranch and then, later, football. His knuckles were gnarled at twenty-one. Cracks split his skin already, canyons that had scarred over into ditches and furrows and white lines. He nodded.

"You don't say much, do you?"

"*Non, monsieur.*"

Justin smiled again. "Your drawl with the accent... It's unique."

He ducked his head, tried to hide his own grin. "I've been trying to chisel that drawl out of me for years."

"Don't do that." Justin's fingers landed on his forearm. "It's nice. I like it."

He looked away, and Justin pulled back, and they spent the rest of the ride in silence, swaying into each other's shoulders with every brake and turn. Wes gnawed on the inside of his lip, his entire body aware of those few inches of skin Justin had touched.

When they got to the university, he stood and blocked the rest of the group from stampeding down the bus's aisle. "*Après vous, monsieur.*"

Justin's cheeks and the tips of his ears pinked. He shoved his hands into his pants pockets when he leaped off the bus, but he waited for Wes, falling into step with him as they made their way to the classroom. Inside, they found tables already arranged in pairs: two seats at each table, two workbooks side by side, one textbook to share.

"So," Justin asked. "Partners?"

Wes pulled out a chair for Justin. "*Oui.*"

ALL WES WANTED, after a red-eye flight and a full day of French class, was to pour himself into bed and sleep for three days. He barely kept his eyes open on the bus ride back to the hotel, and Justin had to flick his knee to pull him out of that woozy twilight space when they finally pulled up at the curb. He trudged up the stairs slowly, and this time, Justin pushed open the door for him when they got back to their cramped attic room.

He went face-first onto his bed, burying his head in the flat pillow and toeing off his Ropers. They dropped to the floor with two heavy thuds, and he dug his arms beneath the pillow, trying to merge himself with the old mattress. The ancient springs groaned beneath his weight. He hoped it held, at least long enough for him to catch a quick nap.

A presence hovered beside him. He rolled his head and peeled one eye open.

Justin ran his fingers through his hair, refreshing his thick pompadour in the mirror on the wall over his bed. He checked himself out, turning right and left and frowning before smoothing his hair again. The sides were cut short, but on top, he had enough hair for a man to lose his hands in. Wes blinked.

"Are you going out to dinner? The group has some kind of reservation at this restaurant." Justin pulled a tube of ChapStick from his pocket and slicked it over his lips. Rubbed them together.

"No." Wes blinked again. Swallowed. "I need sleep. I'm beat. You going?"

Justin snorted. He shook his head again. "Nah. I do my own thing."

"Going out?" He recognized the signs.

Justin's eyes darted to him and then away. "I might." His voice had dropped a few dozen degrees, hovering just over frigid. "Problem?"

"Nope." Wes buried his face in his pillow again, blanking his mind as he exhaled. He didn't need those thoughts, those images. Justin, lit by club lights, the twinkle of a disco ball and the flashing strobes. Justin, leaning against a bar top, laughing with a beautiful woman, making her smile and touch his arm, like Justin had touched Wes's arm earlier. He could still feel Justin's cool skin, those four fingertips, delicate as a ladybug landing on him.

Justin made a lot of noise getting ready to leave. He stomped into and out of the bathroom, washed his hands, dropped coins on his nightstand. Went to the window and then back to his bed.

There was quiet for a moment, save for the digital *whoosh* of messages passing back and forth on Justin's cell phone.

"'Kay, I'm out," Justin announced. "Have a good nap."

"Thanks," Wes grunted into his pillow. "Have a good time tonight."

Justin's footsteps hesitated by the door, but a moment later, it opened and closed, and the key slid into the lock.

Wes rolled to his side and stared at Justin's empty bed, at the rumpled sheets and the discarded plaid button-down. He'd changed. What was he wearing? Wes's eyes traveled over Justin's bulging duffel, half shoved under the bed, and skittered to a halt, frozen on a corner pocket. Condoms spilled onto the floor, as if Justin had grabbed a few in a hurry on his way out. Wes blanked his mind. No, no thoughts about that.

He bunched his pillow into a knot, like he was wrestling with the stuffing rather than trying to sleep on it, and curled up, half on his belly and half on his side. Car horns and bike bells and the warm breeze drifted into the room, and minutes later, he was asleep.

When his eyes popped open, it was dark, save for the lights of the city, Victorian streetlamps and globe lights strung between the buildings casting a golden glow that rose into the room. The night was quiet, the shops closed, the traffic tucked away save for an occasional siren in the distance.

Wes groaned, flipping to his back on the squeaky mattress before scrubbing his face. He peeked over at Justin's bed.

There was a body-shaped lump beneath the sheets, and a tumble of hair caught the light, like spun gold was spread out on Justin's pillow. Justin faced Wes with his eyes closed, his shoulders rising and falling steadily, gentle snores whispering out of him.

Wes's gaze caught on something a little closer. A bottle of water and a wrapped baguette sandwich rested on Wes's nightstand. He sat up and grabbed it, peeled back the paper wrapping, and sniffed. A *jambon beurre*, ham and salted butter. His stomach roared, a violent growl that he thought might wake Justin. But Justin didn't stir. "Thank you," he whispered to the quiet bedroom.

He rose and crept to the window, sitting on the sill and propping his bare foot on the ledge. Leaning back, he took his first bite of the sandwich, and he closed his eyes and groaned, *thunk*ing his head against the frame. God, how could something so simple be so damn delicious? He needed another five of these. He tried to eat slowly and savor it, but he was done too soon, licking his fingers clean of crumbs and butter before downing the bottle of water in one long gulp.

And then he watched, listening to Paris come alive in the early morning. Smelled the city, the sour-sweet smell of humanity and nature colliding, of concrete and exhaust and baked rubber, and trees sucking down carbon dioxide, and bakeries just beginning their day. The first glimpses of dawn were painting the sky, turning the indigo overhead to layered shades of bluebonnet and chicory and dayflower.

When dawn had turned the sky to a watercolorist's palette, Wes rose and returned to his bed, pulling out his duffel and grabbing his running shoes and shorts from the side pocket. He might be in Paris, but that didn't mean he was free from his obligations. He should have run yesterday, but he hadn't, so he'd have to add that mileage to today.

He changed right there, then grabbed his phone, dropped a pin on the hotel, and pulled up a five-mile run route from his jogging app. He didn't need to know where to go, as long as his phone kept feeding him directions. He popped his earbuds in, grabbed his metal key, and tiptoed out, trying not to wake Justin.

CHAPTER TWO

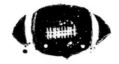

AS THE LOCK turned in the door, Justin's eyes opened. He stared at the empty space where Wes had just changed.

Just his damn luck. He came to Paris to escape: escape his life, and Texas, and, especially, Texans. Guys elsewhere, guys he met online who were in California or New York or Chicago, they all said he was lucky, he was surrounded by those sexy cowboys.

Yeah, sure, if you wanted your sexy with a side of snide, under-the-breath dismissal. Real cowboys, in his experience, were not the kind of men he wanted to hang around with, no matter how sexy they might be.

So, of course, he went five thousand miles and crossed an ocean to live in a cosmopolitan, progressive European city for three weeks… and ended up rooming with an honest-to-God Texan cowboy. Boots, buckle, hat and all.

Just his luck, he'd figured, when Wes walked in. Just his damn luck. He'd felt his dreams collapse as Wes had settled in, boots thumping on the old hardwood floors. Three weeks had seemed like freedom only moments before. How quickly it became a cage. When would the sneers start? The jeers? When would his roommate become aggressive? Act paranoid, like Justin was panting after his shadow? Justin wanted to tell his former roommates from freshman and sophomore year, *Don't think that highly of yourself.* He'd rather fuck a cowboy—and he never intended to do that—than either of them.

Justin grabbed his hair and groaned.

Could Wes be any more of a cowboy? He'd fit right in at Universal Studios, or Hollywood, or, hell, if he wore nothing but chaps, he could make ten grand a night at the gay clubs in Dallas. He'd look right at home driving the herd down Main in Fort Worth, too, tipping his hat to women in sundresses and giving them that shy little grin. God, did women hurl their thongs at Wes every day? What about men? How many men saw him and wanted to hit their knees, run their fingers up the those tight, denim-covered thighs?

Justin fumed, glaring at the ceiling. His cock was rock hard, flat against his belly. Why did Wes have to change right there?

Well, why wouldn't he, if he thought Justin was sleeping? That would change soon, of course. Maybe Wes would tack up a sheet to separate the halves of their room, like his second freshman roommate had.

He wasn't going to jack off to his roommate. His straight cowboy roommate.

But it wasn't like he was getting any other action, either. Four days now, he'd been in Paris, and he'd yet to find his dreamy Parisian summer fling.

His sultry, pouty look that worked wonders in Texas didn't seem to translate in Paris. He wasn't used to the men here, how they flirted, what they said. Sure, he could whip out the apps, but... His mom said he would end up dead in a ditch someday if he wasn't careful, and he didn't want to prove her right. Meeting a stranger on a hookup app in a foreign country seemed like the kind of reckless that turned boys like him into missing-persons posters. He wasn't pretty enough to get worldwide attention if someone abducted or offed him.

Why did Wes have to be his roommate? Why couldn't they put him with a nerd, one of the IT majors who smelled like Doritos and Mountain Dew? Or a hipster who was cool enough to scope out guys with him at the Louvre and Tuileries, as long as Justin was cool enough to play the part of the gay bestie when he wanted to pick up chicks?

The sun was over the horizon now, reflecting shards of light off every window and rooftop and into their room. Delivery vans were making their rounds, collecting wine bottles and dropping off milk bottles, and the smell of fresh-baked bread perfumed the city. Well, he wouldn't be sleeping any more now. He flung his blanket back and stood, glaring down at his crotch before heading for the bathroom.

The water pressure wasn't great enough to really enjoy, and the shower was smaller than the cubicles back in the dorms. But he showered, shaved, and brushed his teeth, ran his hands through his hair, wrapped his towel around his waist, and opened the door—

Wes, back from his run, looked up. He was in the kitchenette, pouring coffee into two mugs, and he froze when he saw Justin, the coffee continuing to pour and pour until it overran the top of the mug and spilled over his hand.

"Shit." Wes backed away, searching for a dish towel, shaking his hand. Drops of coffee spattered the front of his sweat-soaked shirt.

"Here." Justin whipped off the towel draped over his shoulders and handed it to Wes. Wes grabbed it, his eyes darting over Justin's bare chest and down to the knot of his white towel wrapped low around his hips, then away. He wiped his hand, then squatted and wiped the counter, the cupboard, the floor.

"I didn't know you were back. Sorry." What Justin was apologizing for, he didn't know, but it was reflex now to apologize to his straight roommates. *I'm sorry I bother you. I'm sorry you're so fucking fragile that my existence threatens your masculinity. I'm sorry I breathe in and out. Don't worry, others have thought about changing that, too.*

Wes grunted. "My fault." He wiped again at the dried counter, not looking as Justin slipped on an undershirt and slid his boxers up under his towel. Finally decent, he turned back to Wes, pasting a smile on his face.

A smile that froze as Wes held out a cup of coffee and a chocolate-filled croissant. There was an open box of pastries behind Wes, half a dozen croissants: chocolate, plain, almond, raisin, and more. "Thank you for the sandwich," Wes said. His voice was like gravel, something deep and rich and rumbling that reminded Justin of cabins and backwoods. He felt Wes's voice in the center of his chest.

He took the coffee, careful not to brush Wes's fingers, and the croissant. "You're welcome. You didn't have to."

Wes smiled, and Justin nearly hit the floor, nearly sank to his knees and wept like his mom's friends did on Sundays at their church. That smile, Christ almighty. That smile could melt his bones. It was an *aw-shucks* grin, a grin that said, *I'm trouble,* with Wes's head tilted forward, hiding his open-sky eyes. How many girls had he led to his bed with that little smile?

"Well, I was starving, and it's rude to eat in front of others."

Rude. Sure. His luck, again. He got the cowboy with the manners. "Your mother teach you that?" He took a bite of the croissant. It was still warm. The chocolate oozed out, coating his tongue. He almost groaned.

Wes was still grinning. "She did, in fact."

"Well, thank you, Mom." Justin toasted Wes's imaginary mother with the croissant and took a sip of coffee. "Good run?"

Wes nodded, biting half of his croissant off and chewing before downing a gulp of coffee. "Ran to the Arc de Triomphe, then to the park. It was nice. You, uh. You run?"

"I do."

"Thought so. You have runner's legs." Wes shoved the rest of his croissant in his mouth and turned away, crossing the room to the open window and parking himself in front of it, his back to Justin. Justin looked from Wes's back to his own legs and then back to Wes's shoulders.

The rest of the morning was quiet, Wes figuring out the shower and banging his knees and elbows into the old tile every time he tried to move, and Justin finishing another croissant and trying not to imagine how water looked running down Wes's spine or around his corded biceps. Wes finished the rest of the pastries, chugged another coffee, and then they were off, down to the street to wait for the bus. By unspoken agreement, they settled into the same seats.

Justin eyed Wes as he brushed dust and lint from his cowboy hat. When Justin gazed out the window, watching Paris roll by, he caught Wes's reflection gazing at him.

"WHAT ARE YOU DOING FOR DINNER?" Justin asked after class. "You going out with the group?"

Wes shook his head. He spun his hat in his hands, stared down at the cream wool. "No. I won't be going on any of the outings. My scholarship is paying for this trip, and they didn't include any of those. I'll grab something simple."

Justin blinked. There were a few questions he wanted to ask, all at once. Simple was usually a euphemism for cheap, for one. "Scholarship?"

"Athletics."

"Make sense." He waved his hand at Wes's body, his massive muscles. "Which sport?"

Wes finally looked up. They trotted down the stairs inside the school, strode across the glass-and-marble lobby. The rest of the class was already on the bus. "I play a little bit of football."

The bus driver glared, waving at them to hurry up. Justin stopped, his boots skidding on the pavement. Wes halted with him, setting his hat on his head and turning to Justin, his face a question mark. "Forget them," Justin said. "Want to walk back? We can grab something to eat on the way."

"*Oui.*" Wes grinned. "*Oui, s'il te plaît.*"

THEY WALKED the banks of the Seine, past Notre Dame and the Tuileries, past the Place de la Concorde and toward the Arc de Triomphe. Along the way, Justin pulled them into a bar for beers and sandwiches, insisting that he pay because Wes had brought back half the bakery that morning. Wes ordered the cheapest thing on the menu, so Justin ordered double appetizers and ate slowly, pushing the rest toward Wes. Wes was a big boy. He needed a lot of calories.

He found out they both attended the same campus in the University of Texas system, they were both going into their junior year, and that, when Wes said he played "some football," he meant he was a tight end on Texas's team and, had Justin ever turned on a game, he would have seen Wes on the field most Saturdays for the past two years.

"Football… that's with the baskets, right? Orange ball?"

Wes stared.

"No, no, don't tell me. They're called goals?"

"Not quite."

"I'm kidding. I'm Texan, I was born knowing football. And football is obviously played on a diamond. You're the tight infielder, right?"

Wes laughed as Justin pretended to toss his hair and smirk. "Football isn't my thing, but if you've ever scored a touchdown, I'm sure my dad loves you."

Wes chuckled into his beer. The arches of his cheeks were dusted with burgundy. "I've scored a few." He changed the subject, though, suddenly asking Justin about his major and his family. Where he was from.

Justin had been born and raised in a "best places to live" suburb outside Dallas, shuttled to school and camp and Little League by his mom in her SUV. His earliest memories were of hymns sung at church and the Sunday-best shoes that pinched. His childhood was a patchwork quilt of Bible studies, bake sales, and bicycles zooming up and down the block, little kids laughing away the hours under the Texas sun as their moms and dads drank margaritas in their driveways, condensation dripping down the glasses and onto their fingers, so that when one of them checked for bumps and bruises after a spill, their touch was as cold as the bag of frozen peas that would be offered for the boo-boo. He tasted salt and lime in his memories, heard laughter in the background, smelled fresh-baked cookies and cakes and pies. Football played on a TV in the garage. Dads from up and down the block would move from driveway to driveway, peering into car engines and changing tires. Tossing footballs and softballs back and forth. It was a storybook life. Until he turned sixteen.

Until he stopped faking it, stopped pretending he was going to bring home a sweet girl, stopped acting like he was crushing on the cute blonde in the choir loft. He was tired of the questions and the assumptions and, most of all, the pressure, the way his mom and dad looked at him like his life was already planned out, like they already saw him with his Texas bombshell wife and their two-point-five kids. *Your future wife is praying to the good lord about you right now, Justin,* his mom used to say to him every night. *I can't wait to meet the woman who will make you happy.*

His parents always knew he was exceptional. Every finger painting he'd done in kindergarten was put up on the fridge, every macaroni necklace lovingly saved, every glitter ornament for the tree hauled out each year. His Little League photos and school portraits lined the hallway. He was taken to Aspen, Vail, Bermuda, San Diego. Nothing held back.

How were they to know he'd be one of the 10 percent of the population who was gay? He'd always been an overachiever. Exceptional in every way.

One night he sneaked out, took the DART to the gayborhood in downtown Dallas, faked his way into one of the clubs, and made out with every boy he could. He took selfies kissing guys, grinding with them against the dirty club walls and in the bathroom stalls, got an outrageous picture of an older man licking his bare chest as he threw his head back in ecstasy. And he sent them all to his parents.

His father wouldn't speak to him for three weeks, and his mother burst into tears whenever she saw him. He was grounded for a year—no car, no outings, no going anywhere except school and church—but he didn't care. He was finally free from their pressure.

His mother almost didn't let him go to college four hours away. Almost insisted that he live at home and commute to a local campus every day, but he told her he was an adult and he was going, and if she wanted to see him ever again, she would be happy for him. "Of course we're happy for you," his mother had said. "We're proud of you. I'm just so scared." Scared for his soul, scared for his life. He'd seen the panic pamphlets her pastor had given her: gays and AIDS, the homosexual lifestyle, gays and drugs, gays and disease.

His father, though, surprised him. "You broke her heart when you sent those photos," he'd said, talking to an engine block in the garage instead of to his son. "Why didn't you sit her down and look her in the eyes and tell her? She deserved to hear the truth from you like you loved her, not have it thrown in her face like you hated her."

So family was complicated. He didn't hate his mom, and he didn't hate his dad, and they didn't hate him. He wanted to rip his hair out if he was around them for more than a few hours, and there were still times he caught his mom looking at him, something indecipherable and heavy in her long, silent gazes. But he called regularly, sent photos of him smiling and happy and, most importantly, alone, and told them about the tests he'd passed. They sent birthday and Christmas cards, care packages of cookies, fresh socks and underwear. They paid his tuition and told him they loved him, always.

"Family's okay." Justin shrugged. "I'm a nursing major." Not prelaw, like his mother had planned. Or even business. His father was in sales, vice president of something, and he brought home a bonus every year that had Justin's mother thumbing through the Porsche catalog and planning month-long trips to Italy for the two of them. His dad had sent him a check for five grand for these three weeks in Paris.

He studied Wes. "Football scholarship... You're a general studies major?" He winked.

It was a joke how the star athletes graduated. Most of them, at least. Some really studied. But the ones who were going to the NFL and who saw college as a speed bump in the path to their destiny? General studies, GPA 2.5. Every class taught by one of the coaching staff. How much English and history was really imparted in those classes, or was it more like the verb tense of a tackle, and the point of view of a blitz? How to diagram a handoff to the running back?

Wes smiled again, batting the beer glass between his hands. "Public health."

Justin's eyebrows crawled up his forehead. "I have never met an athlete in public health."

Wes stared out the bar's windows overlooking the street,

watched crowds of Parisians mingle. They were in an older neighborhood, and cobblestones faded in and out of asphalt. Tires clacked and rumbled as vehicles drove by, winding through the clumps of pedestrians clogging the road.

"I'm surprised we haven't had any classes together." He would have noticed Wes. He would have remembered him. "Some of our early health classes could have overlapped."

"*Nous pouvons être en français ensemble.*"

Justin laughed. "You're taking another year of French after this summer? Shouldn't you have what you need to graduate?"

"Yeah. But I think I'll take another year. Maybe go all the way." Wes shifted. "If you want to work overseas with a lot of the medical relief organizations, you have to know French. And if you want to work for the UN, you need to be fluent."

"You want to work for the UN?" And overseas medical relief?

Wes drained his beer and looked outside again. "Maybe."

Justin studied him, the hard lines of his features, the bulge of his jaw. The corded muscles along his neck. The way his shoulders tremored, ever so slightly. "Guess you don't make that many touchdowns," he finally said. "Not trying to go pro, huh?"

Wes tipped his head back and laughed.

IN THE MORNING, Justin rolled over in bed as Wes slid on his running shoes. He wasn't trying to catch a peek at Wes changing, not really. He wanted Wes to know he was awake, though, so if he wanted to change in the bathroom or under the covers or out in the hallway, he could. The worst part of imploding friendships was always the accusations, the looks of betrayal. As if he'd been a predator all this time, fiending for a flash of hip or bare chest. Straight guys could be so Victorian when it came down to the nuts and bolts. As if any of his roommates had been his type, anyway.

Wes, though...

They weren't friends, not yet, but there was potential there. Shockingly. He liked the guy. Wes was more than his cowboy hat and his bulging muscles. He had that *still waters run so very, very deep* vibe, which was so foreign to Justin's life it was basically just a movie trope. Strong, silent cowboys didn't actually exist, right? Apparently they did. And they played some football, too. And took French. And had a shy, killer smile that tied Justin's intestines up into curly little bows.

"Did I wake you?" Wes whispered. He was sitting on the edge of his bed in his running shorts but no shirt. His muscles rippled, his biceps and triceps and trapezius all moving beneath his skin as he hiked up his foot to the mattress and tied his shoelaces.

"No," Justin croaked. He shouldn't have rolled over.

Wes stood, grabbed his shirt, and tugged it over his head. "I have to work out every day. I'm still in training, even though I'm here."

"It's fine." Every morning, like this. He might not survive. He really should have gone out last night, tried to find a Parisian fling again, but… he was having too good of a time with Wes to end things. Dinner turned into wandering the streets, which turned into sharing a half bottle of wine as they people-watched at a sidewalk café until almost midnight. Damn it.

Wes fiddled with his phone. He didn't look at Justin when he spoke. "You wanna come with? I can show you the park."

Justin blinked. "Yeah, sure. Give me a minute to get dressed."

"Take your time." Wes went to stretch by the window as Justin pawed through his duffel, pulling out his running shorts and shoes, which he'd thrown in optimistically, laughing at himself as he did. Running in Paris was half romantic and half ridiculous. He'd hoped for a different type of cardio on this trip. A minute later, he was laced up and ready to go, and he did a few stretches as Wes tapped at his phone and plugged one earbud in his ear.

"Ready."

THEY ONLY HAD three days of classes a week, which left long, empty weekends for everyone to pack in the optional extra outings. Justin had flicked through the catalog of options before he left, dog-earing the pages on wine tasting in the countryside, short trips to Vienna and Prague and an overnight in Rome, a weekend in Marseille and Monaco. The first long weekend loomed before them, and if he was going to catch the shuttle to the airport for the short hop to the coast, he needed to leave soon.

But Wes, at lunch, fed the birds at the pond in the university's quad, and when Justin wandered over to watch, he saw Wes smiling as he tossed food into the water for the ducks and ducklings and the few swans joining the feeding frenzy.

All his weekend plans screeched to a halt.

Wes was bathed in the French sunlight, his cowboy hat shadowing his face, his plain white T-shirt clinging to his thick chest and his cut biceps and his trim, slender waist. His jeans that were too tight for decency. Sure, Justin wore skinny jeans, but Wes wasn't wearing them by choice. They just fit him like a second skin because he had the body of Adonis. Thick, tree-trunk thighs. What would they feel like if Justin had his own thighs wrapped around them? If he was perched on Wes's lap, grinding their hips together? If he got his fingers on Wes's jeans and ran his palms over them?

Wes smiled, that lopsided, shy grin, when Justin ambled across the lawn to join him. He'd thought Wes was throwing a baguette to the ducks, but no, he was throwing seed and nuts. There was a feed dispenser behind him, up on the trail that ran through the quad.

"If you feed 'em bread, it hurts the ducklings' development," Wes said. His voice rumbled through Justin, vibrating his bones. "Too many empty calories, not enough nutrients, gives them angel wing. They can't fly." He tossed another small handful of feed, scattering the ducklings across the pond.

"I never knew that."

Wes squinted at the water. "I know a thing or two about animals."

"What are you doing this weekend?"

Wes shrugged, looking down. His hat shielded his face, hiding his expression from Justin. "Exploring the city. It's Paris. There's a million things to see. I'll try and scratch a few off the list." He looked up, this time squinting at Justin as he tossed the last of his seed to the ducklings. "You going with the group to the coast?"

The French Riviera, sun-drenched beaches, golden sunshine. Perfect, tanned bodies lying on the sand. More gay clubs than he could count. Nightlife more famous than Vegas. His French lover might be down there, just waiting for his Texan summer fling. "No," Justin said, shaking his head. He shoved his hands in his jeans pockets. "I was going to explore the city, too. Want company?"

HE WAS BEING all kinds of stupid, sacrificing his plans to tag along with Wes, a straight cowboy from Texas. Straight cowboys were a dime a dozen back home, and football players? Every guy had a jersey in his closet, dreams of his glory days running on a loop in his mind. Wes wasn't special. Justin knew the kind of guy Wes was. So what was he doing? He'd come half a world away to fall for the same guy he saw every day at home? What Texan came to Paris and fell for a cowboy? There was something Freudian in that. There had to be.

He berated himself in the bathroom mirror at the university, shaking his head at his foolishness.

But they walked home together again, a different route this time, wandering past the Palais Garnier, the home of the Paris

Opera and, more importantly in Justin's mind, the Paris Opera Ballet. He veered away from Wes, drawn to the playbills, the posters of this production and that. *Swan Lake. Romeo and Juliet. La Bayadère*. The opera house rose over him, its gothic opulence somehow a perfect contrast to the delicate illusion of ballet.

Wes hovered behind him, eyeing the posters of dancers, delicate ballerinas *en pointe* and danseurs hoisting them sky high, leaping across the stage in full extension, arms and legs thrown wide, muscles taut, heads tilted back. Pure focus. Pure ecstasy. "You like ballet?"

Usually, there was more of a sardonic edge to that question, turning it into an accusation, an indictment. Usually, Justin's hackles rose. But not today. "I do," he breathed, trailing his fingers down the advertisement for *Swan Lake*. The production was going for the next month. Maybe he could find a way to see it. "It's beauty and power wrapped together. It may look delicate, but it's not. At all. I love the absolute rawness of ballet."

Wes blinked. His eyes scanned the posters again. Raw was not a word used to describe ballet very often, but it was true. Raw power, iron control. Ballerinas were cheetahs, so much capacity and potential and skill constrained into each fine movement. "Never thought of it that way," Wes rumbled. "But yeah. Look at him." He jerked his chin to the danseur in the midst of his leap. "That's a lot of power right there. I know football players that would be jealous of that jump."

Justin beamed. His heart fluttered. "Exactly. The athleticism, it's..." He sighed.

"Do you dance?" Wes eyed him, his gaze running down Justin's body, lingering at his hips and thighs. "You have the strength."

He turned away. Paced down the row of posters, letting the dancers' faces swim in front of him. "Not seriously. I love ballet, but I'm not any good at it. Not enough to really chase it. I'm a better modern dancer. I was on the drill team in high school."

He'd joined his junior year, after he'd finally burst the bubble of his parent's fantasies. He wasn't going to play baseball anymore. He was one of four guys on the drill team, and they were all very, very gay. He'd lost his virginity to one in the back of the bus on the way to an out-of-town football game.

Wes was quiet. "Our drill team was the color guard," he finally said. "They did both. Color guard girls were usually the ones the cheerleading captain didn't pick at tryouts."

"It was pretty serious in Dallas. More than a few girls went to try out for the Cowboys cheerleaders and made it after being on the drill team."

"You must have been good, then, to be on the team." Wes bumped his shoulder. When did he get so close? "And you do know a little bit about football if you were on the drill team. You were at the games for your school."

Justin laughed. "I spent most of my time in the stands gossiping, but yeah, I guess I know a bit." He knew which of the running backs had the best butt, and which quarterback had gotten drunk over spring break and let a guy give him a blow job.

Halfway back to their hotel, Justin ducked into a restaurant and came out with a bottle of wine. Wes tried to protest, tried to dig out some euros from his pocket, but Justin waved him off. There was something swimming in his veins, some kind of electricity that he needed to bleed off. Thoughts he shouldn't be thinking. Hopes he shouldn't be pinning to the sky. Getting drunk was a tried-and-true way to erase his mind.

They tipped wine into the same coffee mugs they drank from each morning, sitting cross-legged in front of their window and watching the Paris night come to life. The Eiffel Tower lit up across the city, twinkling like a thousand fireflies had come together for a brilliant show. He sighed, sipping his merlot, and slumped against the windowsill. Paris in summertime, and his heart was pitter-pattering. His eyes slid sideways, to Wes, the cowboy football player he could have met any other day in

Texas, on campus, even, but who he'd met here. In the city of love.

He was so screwed. This was going to come crashing down, like it always did. This was going to end in pain, and regret, and wishing he'd never, ever tried. *Don't do it,* his mind whispered. *You can't be friends with him.*

And another part of him whispered back, *I'm not sure what I want with this man is friendship. Not anymore.*

CHAPTER THREE

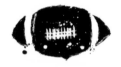

WES SPLASHED water on his face, washing away the remnants of shaving cream. Droplets ran down his neck and the valley between his pecs. He felt the cool touch like fingers on his skin, skittering all the way to his waist. Like Justin's fingers, stroking—

He squeezed the edge of the porcelain sink, hard enough his arms trembled. He tipped his head forward, closing his eyes as water dripped from his nose, his chin. All his life he'd fought this. He'd choked this want, this desire, ever since the day he declared to his father he was going to marry the ranch foreman or one of the cowboys down from Montana. He'd been young enough to get away with it, get called hilarious instead of a freak. He'd been laughed at.

He kept his crush on the foreman secret after that. Stopped watching the hands work shirtless as they fed the horses, changed the hay, cleaned the stalls. Kept his mouth shut and waited, and waited, and waited for his eyes to start wandering to the girls and their bouncy ponytails at school, to focus on curves and skirt hems instead of happy trails and tight asses and bulges. It never happened. He stared at the inside of his locker when everyone changed, memorizing the same square inches of battered metal and balled-up socks. Maybe he could fake it, he thought. Or force himself to like girls.

In high school, sophomore year, he'd dated Lisa. She broke up with him when he wouldn't go all the way in her back seat on the fourth date. Senior year, Marietta got him into a bedroom at a house party, when he was a few beers past common sense, and got his pants down and her mouth on him before he found that sense again. She was trying to get her own pants off when he pushed her back gently, told her no, and then held her when she cried. She was one of the desperate girls his senior year, looking at grades that weren't good enough for a scholarship and no money in the bank to afford college tuition. Her only hope out of that town was to hitch her wagon to a boy on his way up, and who better than the top tight end in the state with a full-ride scholarship in the big city? "I'm sorry," he'd told her in that dark room. "I'm sorry, but I can't."

He couldn't force it. And he didn't want to try.

But he couldn't go out and find a boyfriend, either. He could count the number of out pro NFL players on one hand, and the number of out football players currently at the Division I-A level in college was zero. Coming out, at his level? The guys who had worked their way up dreamed of that NFL contract, hungered for it so deeply it gnawed at their bones, filled their veins with poisonous hope. An entire team of dreamers, each one fixated on a shared goal: winning. Championships. Scouts. One team, one purpose.

Who the hell was he to break that focus? Strike out from the team, be himself? The selfishness of that thought made his stomach turn inside out, made his lungs stop and his heart stutter. There were all kinds of platitudes, pretty talk on posters about being yourself and embracing who you were, but when a hundred other guys depended on you, being yourself wasn't an option. He was part of a team, part of a machine, and he was helping every one of those guys achieve their dreams, scrape stars from the sky as they reached for futures hidden behind the moon. All their lives, they'd been told if they worked hard enough, they could get there. But they couldn't do it on their own—none of them could.

He'd be damned if he was going to be the one who shattered everyone's dreams because he was different. Different didn't work on the team.

What happened to teams when guys tried to come out? When it went ten kinds of sideways and everything collapsed? When everything was different, suddenly, and what was out of the closet couldn't get wrestled back in?

His life wasn't awful. He had his friends—hell, he had best friends. His teammates. He had his dad. They had each other, after Mama. He had the team, and Coach Young. He had a scholarship and a plan for the future. He wasn't quite sure his future was filled with the same brightly lit NFL dreams as his teammates'. Maybe, once all his friends were set in their star-studded futures, when they were living in the worlds they drew on their bedroom ceilings every night, he could raise his eyes and take a look at the things he'd stiff-armed away.

Later. In the future. Not now. Not here. Not when he was on the verge of being named the starting tight end, when the rumors were he'd been a serious consideration for the Heisman Trophy last year—and if he had the same kind of season this year, he would be a shoo-in and an obvious first-round draft pick if he tossed his name into the great NFL draft hat.

He'd worked too hard to get here. Too many people were relying on him. Too many dreams were laid across his shoulders. He'd had to bulk up to carry them all, gain forty pounds last year alone. There was no room for his own dreams, his tender hopes. He kept his mouth shut, like he'd learned when he was five.

He breathed out, quick exhales like he was at practice, primed and ready for the snap. Watched water drop into the sink. Heard the splash hit the porcelain. He could do this. He could spend the day with Justin, wandering Paris, exploring and sightseeing—just the two of them in the city of love. He could ignore his crush. Bully it away like he'd always done. Focus.

When he closed his eyes, even to blink, he saw Justin's face. Heard his voice, the sharp lilt of his words. Felt the force of Justin's smile smack him in his gut, felt his lungs squeeze as he tried to breathe through the way his skin felt too small and his bones too large. Like he was going to float off the earth every time Justin looked at him with that light in his eyes.

It was probably just the sun. It probably wasn't what he wanted it to be.

And it didn't matter if it was. He couldn't do anything about this.

And... Justin hadn't given any sign, any hint at all that he was anything other than straight. He was cooler than Wes, that was for sure. More connected to the world, more hip, more into things that were en vogue. Wes still shaved with Brut, something he'd picked up from his dad, who'd gotten it from his dad. He drove a twenty-five-year-old farm truck. He hadn't ever been to a concert in his life, much less ballet. Culture seemed to roll off him like water on a duck's back, passing him by without so much as a wave. He listened to the folk and Western music he'd grown up with on the ranch, and there wasn't a radio station at the university that played anything he was familiar with. Justin's phone belted out top 40s alongside classical masterpieces, soundtracks to ballets next to R&B legends. Wes felt all elbows and awkwardness in front of Justin, like he was constantly on the verge of tripping over himself, revealing his hick nature, his country.

Even if Justin was into guys, why would he ever be interested in Wes?

He wouldn't be. He'd want someone fun and bold and hip, someone who knew about dance and pop culture and the world. The world beyond football and ranching. Someone who could talk about something more interesting than what ducks liked to eat.

That pocket full of condoms stabbed at the inside of Wes's eyeballs, rose up like a nightmare to remind him that Justin would tire of him, and soon. He'd be back on the prowl, sliding from Paris bar to Paris bar, or maybe wandering the clubs down on the Riviera or in Monaco, or chatting up a beautiful blond at a winery in the French countryside. Wes wouldn't have Justin's attention for long.

But he had today.

He hadn't been this excited and sick to his stomach at the same time since the scout from the university had come to watch him play back at his old West Texas high school. His phone buzzed in his back pocket, right before Justin shouted through the closed bathroom door, "I just texted you the map."

He wiped his face and pulled his shirt from his waistband, then squeezed himself out of the bathroom. Justin was perched on the end of his bed, tapping at his phone screen.

"Okay, if we start in Montmartre, we can go to the Sacré-Coeur, and then to Saint-Ouen for the market on rue des Rosiers. They say *Chez Louisette* is where to eat while we're there."

Wes's stomach cramped. He'd scarfed down two crepes after their morning run, but he was still hungry. Without the meal plan from the university and extra protein shakes throughout the day, he wasn't getting the ten-thousand-plus calories he needed. But he couldn't afford more than what he was buying. "How much is the restaurant?"

Justin kept scrolling. "I'll buy lunch. You can buy dinner."

Not an answer. But Wes let it go. He stared out the window as he tugged his shirt over his head. He'd like to take Justin out to dinner, someplace real nice with white tablecloths and more than one fork. He'd only ever seen that kind of restaurant on TV. Where he used to go with his dad, it was either a chipped plastic table or, at best, a red-and-white-checked plastic cover.

He'd also like to take Justin out to the ranch, bring him on horseback to his favorite camping spot. Bring down a deer or snare a rabbit and cook a country dinner for him over the open fire, beneath the stars. He'd like to cuddle close in the same sleeping bag, whisper the constellations to him, bury his nose in Justin's neck. Run his hands over that flat stomach, the tautness of his hips.

He'd probably end up buying a couple slices of pizza, or crepes again, from a food truck. It was the cheapest food he'd found so far.

"How do you feel about museums?"

There was a small country museum attached to the gas station two towns over from where he'd grown up. It was a converted Taco Bell, and it was a tourist trap. Its claim to fame was that James Brown "Killer" Miller had blown through town on one of his outlaw sprees. Wes used to wander the two narrow aisles when his dad was buying gas, chewing on sour gummy worms as he stared at the sepia photos taped to the fake wood walls. "Don't think I've ever been to a real one."

Justin pursed his lips. "Thoughts on modern art?"

"Isn't that like gluing a bolt to a Styrofoam cup and calling it a mediation on life? Or painting a white canvas white?"

Justin grinned. "Yes, but that was a mediation on consumerism and the circle of consumption. And white canvases are incredibly popular. The Paris Museum of Modern Art is free. Want to see it this afternoon?"

"Sure. You can educate me." Wes winked. "Or you can try."

Justin rolled his eyes, but he smiled, and he bit his lip as he folded his legs beneath him and pecked at his phone again. "We'll be close to the Eiffel Tower if we spend the afternoon there. Do you want to head over after? Eat dinner on the way? See the park and watch the lights?"

There was probably a food truck or two by the Eiffel Tower. "Yeah. Let's do that."

Justin tapped out a few more notes, dropped a few more pins, and then updated the map he'd sent to Wes. He dropped his phone in his lap and beamed. "All right. Whenever you're ready."

"I'm ready."

Justin's gaze flicked down Wes's body, taking in the university T-shirt tucked into his Wranglers, his Ropers, and then panning back up to his cowboy hat. It was the same basic outfit Wes had worn every day. Justin had a parade of outfits, from oversized plaid shirts to tight polos to trim-fit button-downs. He had a new look every day, from sultry to preppy to clean-cut upper-crust Dallas. Each time, he seemed to look better than the day before. Today, he was back to his skinny jeans, combat boots, and buttoned-up plaid, with the sleeves rolled up to his elbows. His hair was sky high, combed into a straight-back swoosh that showed off his shaved sides. Gel held the whole thing in place. If Wes ever tried to do anything with his hair beyond keeping it short and trimmed, he'd sweat the style away two minutes into a game.

Wes stared down at himself. "Too boring?"

Justin snorted. "You? How could you ever be boring?"

"How could I not be?" He shook his head as he grabbed his wallet. "I'm not like you."

There was a strangled noise from Justin behind his back, something like a cough and a choke and a whimper of pain. He turned, but Justin was grabbing his money and checking his eyes in the mirror, shoving his phone in his pocket, heading for the door. He didn't look at Wes.

THEY TOOK photos of each other at the top of Montmartre, then took a selfie together overlooking Paris. They were a respectable distance apart: friends, nothing more, according to their poses. At Saint-Ouen, Justin found the most ridiculous trinkets and dragged them out to show Wes. Wes was fascinated by the antique clothing

—the colors, the textures of it all—and he fingered every dress and suit and handkerchief they found. There were gadgets and gizmos and antiques neither of them could figure out, and then modern knickknacks and cheap treasures. Justin found an antique print of a Russian ballerina, something smuggled out under Stalin before the censors could erase her and the photograph itself from history, the stall owner said. He bought Wes a black-and-white photo of a cowboy standing in front of the Eiffel Tower in the early 1900s and told him they were going to recreate the picture that afternoon. Wes laughed, but he tucked the photo into his wallet like it was a hundred-euro note.

Chez Louisette was a museum to kitsch, to treasures salvaged from the trash and lovingly strung up with tinsel and blinking Christmas lights. Musicians serenaded the diners as Wes and Justin shared *boeuf bourguignon* and *crème brûlée*. They weren't brave enough, yet, to try the *escargots*. Wes bought them a bottle of wine, despite Justin's protests that he would buy lunch, and after they finished eating, they sat and drank side by side in the tiny plastic booth, listening to a Yugoslavian belt out Edith Piaf to the scratchy wail of his old accordion.

The afternoon was hot, and they wandered tipsily toward the museum before taking the subway when they needed a break from the sun. In the museum, Justin clung to Wes's arm and giggled as Wes gave his uncultured interpretation of each piece of modern art, hamming it up more and more as Justin's giggles turned to snorts and outright guffaws when Wes declared a series of sculptures were mannequins he'd seen at Walmart. Then Justin took over, steering Wes from exhibit hall to exhibit hall, explaining the theory behind the art, what the artist was trying to say.

Wes followed along, mostly, but the best part was how Justin stayed on his arm, leaning against his biceps and his shoulder, whispering into his ear to keep their voices low. Wes felt like he figured he was supposed to on his prom night when Cheryl looped their arms together and pressed her boobs against his side.

Like he was her man and he was protecting her from the world, and he was escorting her through her days and maybe even her nights, maybe even through the rest of her life. He understood then why people walked this way at weddings, why old-time couples leaned together like this. His heart soared, and with every step, his and Justin's bodies moved in synchronicity, like their hips and their thighs and their hands knew the ins and outs and sighs of each other's lives. Like they were a part of each other. That's what it felt like when Justin took his elbow.

They crossed the Pont de l'Alma and turned up the quai Branly, arms still looped together. Justin steered them to the bank of the Seine under the shade of a gnarled tree to watch the ducks and a family of swans. Wes pulled away to pay one euro for two cups of duck feed, and they tossed seed into the water and caused a waterfowl traffic jam. When the seed ran out, the ducks quacked their displeasure and splashed away, leaving a pair of swans behind. Wes tossed the swans a final handful that he'd held back from the greedy ducks.

"Swans mate for life," he grunted. "Once they find their true love, that's it."

"*Swan Lake* is my favorite ballet," Justin said.

"I've never seen a real ballet. Nothing that wasn't done by kindergarteners with glitter face paint. What's *Swan Lake* about?"

Justin chuckled, then sobered. He stared over the Seine, watching the mated swans drift away, side by side. He sighed. "Finding yourself and who you were meant to be, through true love."

"I thought it was a tragedy. Isn't there an evil black swan?"

"It's got everything from a classic fairy tale: a prince, a beautiful maiden, an evil sorcerer. The prince comes across a maiden who, by day, is trapped in the body of a white swan, cursed to float on a lake of her tears forever. At night, she resumes her true human form. The prince sees her then, and they fall in love. She tells him the curse can only be broken if someone who has never loved before declares their undying love for her. But when he is ready to declare his love, the prince is tricked by a sorcerer, who has spelled his daughter to look like the white swan. His daughter is the black swan. The prince declares his love for the sorcerer's daughter, but he finds out he's been tricked, and he runs to the white swan. But it's too late. Brokenhearted, the prince and the white swan drown themselves in the lake of her tears."

Wes stared at the ground, at the gravel beneath the toe of his boot. "He was meant to love the white swan?"

"But he was tricked by the black swan."

"They were together in the end."

Justin tipped his head to Wes. Quirked a tiny smile. "That's why it's a love story."

He didn't know why he did it, but he held out his elbow for Justin. Maybe it was the wine still sloshing in his veins, half a bottle on half a lunch and half a *crème brûlée*. They'd shared a single plate, eating like they were a couple on a date. Everything had been dreamy since, the edges of the world fuzzy, reality blunted, the Parisian evening taking on a warmth and a glow that had him feeling like anything was possible. Even Justin taking his arm again.

Inexplicably, Justin did.

The sun was still up when they arrived at the Eiffel Tower, and they posed for the photos that every tourist snaps: holding up the tower, arms over their head or to their sides. Wes pulled out the sepia-tinted, old-time cowboy photo, and they hunted for the closest spot they could get to recreate the image: Wes in the same pose, with his hat on his head, gazing at the photographer with his thumbs hooked through his belt loops. He beckoned Justin to join him when Justin's laugh burrowed too deeply under his skin, and then they took selfie after selfie, the two of them side by side, Wes plunking his cowboy hat on Justin's head, Justin mugging for Wes and the camera, glaring like he was Clint Eastwood in a dusty old Western.

Eventually, hunger demanded his attention, and he led Justin to a parade of food trucks and told him to pick one. They ate brie-and-ham crepes as the sun set, turning the Eiffel Tower into a torchlit Monet, all the colors of Paris refracting off the old iron girders. They watched the sunset in silence, and then Wes led Justin into the Champ de Mars, the park that unfurled beneath the Eiffel Tower. They had an hour to kill, and he bought two beers from an Algerian barker rattling cold Heinekens their way, opening Justin's for him before passing it over and tucking the bottle caps into his pocket.

Something sang in the space between them, like the sway of their bodies was charging the air, the blood running in Wes's veins, the thoughts running wild in his head. *Take his hand. No, don't risk it.* His eyes slid sideways, watching Justin tip the beer to his lips, watching his throat rise and fall as he swallowed. *He held your arm today. What did that mean? It meant he was drunk.* Park lights were winking on, Victorian-era lamps casting puddles of light across the dusk-hued lawns, the dirt pathways. *He was meant to love the white swan. But he was tricked by the black swan.*

I could fall in love with you, if I let myself.

It was Paris, and it was summertime, and it was the wrong place and the wrong time. He wasn't ready for this yet, wasn't ready for his heart to catapult out of his chest and chase this man, crave him. He wasn't ready to fall in love.

But there was this guy named Justin, and it seemed Wes didn't have a choice in the matter, because he was already on the way.

He led Justin to the front of the park as the hour mark neared. It was dark now, the city lit by streetlamps and the glowing windows of old buildings, and the Eiffel Tower was a dark mass looming above them, shadow against midnight ink. He thought of black swans, and Justin's heat beside him, and his hand in the dark, so close Wes could feel the charge dancing between the backs of their palms.

When the tower lit up, it was as if every star in the sky had fallen in the same spot, winking and dancing for the crowd. Cheers rose around them, gasps of awe, applause. Justin, too, gasped, his eyes so full of joy that Wes's heart ached. Justin smiled —not the smirk, not the playful giggle, but a beaming grin.

In your whole life, there will never be a moment like this again.

Beneath the twinkling Eiffel Tower, in the dark Champ de Mars, Wes stepped forward and cupped his hand around Justin's cheek, and then stroked his football-calloused thumb over Justin's sharp jawline.

Justin's gaze flicked to his. Wes leaned in, eyes open, until their lips were millimeters apart.

Wes waited, counting his breaths. He kept his eyes open. He wanted to see everything: the lights playing over Justin's skin, dancing in the glow of his eyes, falling into the strands of his hair, wild from their all-day sightseeing jaunt around the city. He wanted to see what Justin looked like when their lips met, if his eyes would go wide or if he would smile. Wanted to see, some-how, the lightning they'd created between them arc from his lips to Justin's.

Wes felt Justin's breath hitch, and then he felt Justin's finger-tips brush his cheek, the tiniest fragile touch. A warm glancing wind across his sunburned face. A butterfly landing on his arm. A falling star winking overhead.

"Wes," Justin whispered. They were so close, bodies aligned, Justin seeming to fit into all the nooks and crannies of Wes's over-sized frame. All week, Wes had dreamed of how they'd fit together. How their elbows and hip bones and chests would align.

Perfectly. They fit together perfectly. Like drawing Justin close was something he was meant to do.

"Wes," Justin breathed again. The corners of his eyes crinkled. A single frown line appeared between his eyebrows. "Are you…"

Wes nodded. "I've never told anyone. Ever."

Justin stared, really stared, at him, like he was digging for all of Wes's secrets. Wes let him look, stood and bared himself as he breathed in Justin's smell and rubbed his thumb up and down his jawline, over the hint of stubble just starting to appear.

Panic he'd tamped down rose again. Justin hadn't kissed him. Was he wrong? He stiffened and started to pull away. Dropped his eyes to stare at the dirt, at the trampled edges of the grass, the bottle caps dug into the ground. What had he done? He'd made a terrible mistake.

Justin grabbed his face with both hands and dragged him up to press their foreheads together. Wes's hat tipped back and fell to the ground. He let it go, grabbing Justin's hip and sliding his hands into Justin's hair, the short, shaved strands at the back of his neck.

"Is this really happening?" Justin whispered.

"I hope so." His voice trembled.

Justin's exhale was hot on his cheek, a short bark of shaking air. His eyes were huge, ringed with desire and, inexplicably, fear. Wes ran his hand down Justin's back, pulling him closer. "You're afraid?"

"A little, yeah."

"Of me?"

Justin bit his lip so hard Wes saw the red skin turn white around the divots he created. "I never get what I want," he murmured. "This isn't real. This is a dream. I'm going to wake up and you're getting ready to go on a run, you're tiptoeing around the room, you're putting your earbuds in—"

Wes kissed Justin, pressed their lips together, cut off Justin's breathless ramble. He tasted cherry ChapStick and felt the slide of Justin's slick, soft lips against his own dry, rough pair. Did Justin wish he was softer, that his lips were gentler—

Groaning, Justin hurled himself into Wes's arms. Wrapped his arms around Wes's head, cradled him in the crooks of his elbows, hooked one knee around the solidity of Wes's thigh. He kissed Wes as if he'd wanted to kiss him from the moment they'd met, the moment Wes had walked through the door and seen him in the slanted sunlight. And Wes held him tight, held him like he was precious and perfect and everything Wes had ever wanted.

Because he was. In that moment, beneath the lights of the Eiffel Tower, Paris under his skin and inside his veins, Justin was everything he'd waited his whole life for.

CHAPTER FOUR

HIS BACK HIT the wall outside their hotel room, Justin trying to climb him like a tree. His lips were everywhere, kissing him, sucking on his ear, mouthing his jaw, over his pulse and down to his collarbone. His hands rose over Wes's rib cage, fingers sliding to his back and digging into his shoulders.

Wes groaned, his hat tumbling to the floor again as he wrapped his arms around Justin and hefted him up, trying to drag him closer, as close as he could. Justin wound his legs around Wes's waist, looped his hands behind Wes's head. "Take me to bed, cowboy."

He fumbled with the lock, arms shaking. Was this happening? Was this really happening? Justin in his arms, Justin pressing kisses to every inch of his face. He tried to breathe like he was tearing down the field, like he'd just caught Colton's dump pass and had the end zone in sight. His heart was pounding, harder than it ever had during a game. He carried Justin into the room, kicking the door closed behind him.

Justin's thighs squeezed his hips, hands cradling his face as he gazed at Wes like he wanted to devour him. Wes's throat clenched, and he stumbled as he headed for his bed. He tried to be suave. Gentle. Tried to hide how his hands were shaking as he lay Justin down on his mattress.

Justin was a koala, clinging to Wes even as his back hit the sheets. He never stopped kissing Wes, their tongues tangling as he pulled Wes's shirt free from his waistband. They broke apart for the instant it took to rip it off, and then Justin's lips were back and his hands were on Wes's skin, traveling over his heaving chest, his trembling sides. Justin tugged Wes closer as he spread his legs. Dragged Wes down, wrapping his ankles around Wes's back and rolling his hips up, digging his hard cock into Wes's belly.

Wes made a noise, a grunt, a groan he'd never admit to. His palm landed on the pillow next to Justin's head as his vision went sideways, and he had to close his eyes and hold his breath as Justin's thumbs went to work on his nipples.

Despite the lines of fire sliding through his body, burrowing beneath his skin and into every nerve, his cock was turning shy. *Not now!*

Justin slid one hand down Wes's chest, down his abs, just like he'd imagined that morning, and reached for his fly.

He stilled when he felt Wes's flagging erection. Their lips clung together even after he pulled back a fraction of an inch. Wes tried to chase the kiss, tried to chase Justin. No, no, please. He leaned in, dug their foreheads together. He was shaking.

"Wes?" Justin whispered. He'd popped Wes's fly, and his fingers danced over the bulge of his soft cock.

Why are you doing this now? Now, when this is everything we wanted?

Wes's breath bounced off Justin's lips. "I'm nervous."

Justin's hand cradled his hip. His thumb stroked the arch of bone, the indent of taut skin over his oblique. "No need to be nervous. I don't bite." He smiled. His foot stroked up and down the back of Wes's thigh. "Unless you say please."

Wes chuckled. "I don't know, maybe I'd like that."

Justin grinned. Then blinked. "Maybe?"

"I—" Wes rubbed his nose over Justin's. "I've really never done this before."

"Never been with a guy?"

"Never been with anyone."

Justin's eyes went wide. His foot and his thumb stilled. "Seriously?"

"Yeah. Seriously." Wes shrugged. "It wasn't right with a girl. I never wanted to get close enough to a girl to get this far. And... I've never kissed a guy until tonight."

Justin's jaw dropped. He stared at Wes, into Wes. Sat up slowly, leaning back on his elbows as Wes tipped to his side and crashed to the squeaky mattress. He didn't want to let go of Justin, though, and he kept stroking Justin's thigh, up and down the taut muscle. Justin's cock bulged against his fly. Wes stared at it, wishing he was Superman with X-ray vision and could see right through the denim, that he could get his first glimpse of a cock he was allowed to crave.

"We should slow down." Justin's hand landed on the center of Wes's chest, his fingers pressing into his skin, through the curls of his chest hair. "I didn't know. I didn't think..."

Wes glanced down at his limp dick. Shrugged. "Guess we have to."

"Not because of that." Justin shifted, rolling onto his side and sliding his body against Wes's, legs tangling, hips slotted together, his hand sliding over Wes's heart. "My first time was kind of crappy. It was a rush. We were sneaking. It wasn't special. I don't want that for you."

"You're special." Wes laid his hand over Justin's. His palm was huge, covering almost all of Justin's hand and his long fingers. He pulled Justin's hand up, kissed his knuckles.

"Why?" Justin tipped his head to the side. "Why me?"

If he knew the answer to that... Wes exhaled. He rubbed his thumb over Justin's skin. "I really, really like you. I was coming to Paris to knock out a year of French, but now... You've taken everything over. I can't think about anything except you. Even in class, I'm always sneaking looks at you. I want to hear your voice and see your eyes and watch you smile. I want to listen to you talk all day. French, English—hell, gibberish. I just want to hear your voice. Be around you. And I don't know why. I mean, I do." He fumbled. This was more than he ever spoke at once. "You're… great." *Well said, Wes.* He always had a way with words, his mama had said. They ran from him. "I've never met anyone like you. I'm surrounded by jocks. Football players. Stuck-up athletic trainers. Groupies. I've never met someone so…" *Free.* He wanted to say free. "Independent. Strong. So themselves."

"You don't get out much."

He ran his hand from Justin's hip to his belly, then slipped it beneath Justin's shirt. "You make me feel real."

Justin chewed on the inside of his cheek. "Is that what you want? To feel real?"

"I've always wanted that. But it couldn't happen."

"What's different now? Why are you kissing me?"

"Why does the ball need to be caught?"

Justin frowned.

"Because it's there. Because it's thrown. Why now? Because you're here. Because I waited my whole life for the right moment, and the right guy, and…" Wes smiled. Ran his palm over the taut skin beneath Justin's belly button. "This feels right. Like when I picked up my first football and ran across the yard, all the way down the drive, kept running into the pasture until my dad had to chase me. I knew what felt right. Grabbing that ball and running. Riding my horse as far as I could, to the end of my world. Now you. You feel like the rightest thing I've ever laid my eyes on." He ducked his head. "I didn't know if you would be interested in me. If you were into guys, or…"

"You didn't know I was gay? Seems like everyone knows by looking at me."

"I didn't. I mean, I don't have a lot of experience here, but I just thought you were cooler than I was. More cultured. Smarter."

"Well." Justin smiled. Pretended to be smug. "I try."

"You succeeded. Got me all spun up 'bout you." He laid his accent on thick and heavy, like slow honey under a summer sun.

Justin cupped his cheek and pulled him close, kissing him slowly, and then not slowly, until Wes pushed Justin to the mattress and rose over him again. He kissed Justin's lips, then down to his chin, his neck, bit gently on the edge of his collar-bone. "Can I take your shirt off?"

"Of course." Justin tore his button-down and undershirt off so fast he was almost a blur. He flung the clothing somewhere beyond them, out of sight. He lay back as Wes bit down on his pec, then nibbled his way from nipple to nipple, swirling the tiny nubs with his tongue. Justin tasted like sunshine and a hint of sweat after a long day wandering Paris. Wes brushed his stubbled cheek over Justin's chest. He was close enough to see the goose bumps rise on Justin's skin as Wes's breath caressed it. Was this really happening?

He kissed a slow path down Justin's abdomen. Detoured to his belly button and dipped his tongue inside. Justin groaned, grabbed Wes's head, and dug his fingers into Wes's scalp. His cock was rock hard and tenting his jeans, pressing against Wes's chest.

Wes's heart pounded as he unbuttoned Justin's fly and pulled down his zipper. His hands were shaking. Justin sat up on his elbows, watching Wes, his skin flushed, his lips wet and open, panting. Justin's cock caught on the elastic of his boxers as Wes pulled them down, then shot free, slapping his belly.

And there was his lover's cock, right in front of his face. The first one he could touch that wasn't his own.

His mouth watered, so suddenly, so much, he almost drooled down his chin. Fire burned through him, a coil that went all the way down his spine and settled in his belly. Dropped lower. He'd dreamed of cocks, of getting his hands and his mouth on one, of stroking another man, getting him naked, exploring his body. Kissing his way down a man's stomach and over his hips before burying his face in a man's crotch. Now his dreams were coming true, and, goddamn, it was more than he'd expected. He'd wanted this more than he'd imagined.

Wes wrapped his hand around the thick shaft. Justin's cock head was a deep, dark burgundy. Cut. Justin was about the same size as him, and Wes's fingers just touched when he wrapped his hand around the heavy shaft. Thick. Hot. It felt like he'd grabbed hold of steel wrapped in something delicate. So different from touching himself, holding himself. He squeezed, stroked, and Justin let out a strangled whimper. "Wes."

Wes ran his cheek up and down the side of Justin's cock, then turned and pressed featherlight kisses to the shaft. Inhaled Justin's musk, the masculine aroma of his body, strong after the summer day. He couldn't get enough, chasing Justin's scent all the way to his crotch, to his balls, burying his face in Justin's hip as he jacked him slowly.

He wanted to taste.

He ran his tongue over the crease of Justin's thigh and his body, traced the skin that held his balls. Licked his way back up the shaft until he was at the head. He held Justin's stare as he swirled his tongue there, licking up the precome dribbling from the slit.

Justin stopped breathing.

Wes closed his lips around the purple cock head. And sucked.

He couldn't get all of Justin into his mouth, but he tried his very best. He didn't quite know what to do with his tongue or his teeth, but he opened his throat like he was chugging beer, and Justin's cock slid all the way back, banging against the back of his throat as he hollowed his cheeks and tried to swallow, as he sucked and sucked like Justin was his favorite Popsicle. Justin's legs quivered, and he gasped, cursed, panted Wes's name and clawed at the sheets, gripped them in two fists. "Fuck, where did you learn…"

Wes popped off, wiping his mouth with the back of his hand. He could taste Justin's cock all over his tongue and his lips. "Okay?"

"Keep going," Justin pleaded. "You're a goddamn natural."

Wes stared at Justin as he took him back into his mouth, sucking him as deep as he could before running his tongue up the underside of his shaft, then sliding back, sucking again, going deep. Justin went rip-cord taut, his eyes bulging, lips parted, legs shivering beneath Wes. "Oh my God…"

Wes sped up, his lips a wet seal around Justin's thick shaft. Up and down, Justin's cock head sliding deeper down his throat each time. He grasped the base of Justin's shaft and jacked him in time with his sucks. Saliva dripped from his lips, coated Justin's cock, slicked his hand.

"Wes…" Justin panted. "Wes, fuck. You have— I'm gonna— Fuck. Pull back!"

Wes hummed. Sucked. Refused to pull back.

Justin jerked, curling over Wes's head and grabbing at his shoulders, fingers clawing Wes's back. His cock erupted, hot shots of come slamming into Wes's throat, coating his tongue, filling his mouth.

Wes swallowed, swallowed again, but still, come dribbled out and down his lips as he kept moving his mouth up and down Justin's shaft. The taste made his head spin, made him crave more, again, right now. He licked Justin clean, then sucked one finger after another into his mouth. "Yum. Finger-lickin' good."

"Holy…" Justin grabbed him. Kissed him, hot and dirty, all tongue and teeth, searching for his own taste inside Wes's mouth. Wes braced himself on the mattress and got one hand on his fly, popping the buttons and freeing his cock, finally achingly hard, achingly stiff. Justin batted his hands away and shoved down his Wranglers, then smiled. "Hello, big boy."

Wes flushed. Justin rolled Wes onto his back and slid between his spread thighs, mirroring their position from a minute ago. He kissed his way down Wes's chest, quicker than Wes had on Justin, before wrapping both of his hands around Wes's hard cock. He squeezed, and a drop of precome dribbled out of the tip, ran down Wes's head and over Justin's fingers.

"Oh, I'm going to enjoy this," Justin purred. He looked Wes dead in the eyes as he licked a long, slow path from the root of Wes's cock all the way to the tip, then sucked the head in and out of his puckered lips.

Wes buried his hands in Justin's long hair as white-hot pleasure erupted through him. Justin's mouth, his hot, wet lips, the suction. Wes's cock pushing into Justin's throat, deeper, deeper—

He keened, almost curling into a ball as Justin's throat opened and he took Wes's cock all the way down, until he buried his nose in the curls at Wes's crotch. Justin's eyes rolled up and found Wes's. He'd remember that image until the day he died: Justin's throat around his cock, his perfect lips sealed all the way around his shaft. He'd watched porn like this, had jerked off imagining a guy on his knees—or him on his knees, or both of them blowing each other at the same time—but this, the reality of the moment, of Justin, was beyond anything he'd imagined.

Too much. It was too much, as Justin rocked back and forth, making Wes fuck his throat. He pulled back, sucking the whole way, then dove back down. Suction, scorching heat, then his lips and tongue swirling over Wes's cock head. Justin's hands, jacking Wes's shaft as he sucked.

"I'm gonna come," Wes grunted. He tugged on Justin's hair, trying to warn him. But Justin seemed as greedy for Wes's come as Wes had been for Justin's, and Justin flashed him an impish look as he hollowed his cheeks and *suuucked*, bobbing up and down and up and down.

Wes tightened his grip on Justin's head, fingers tangling in his long strands, and exploded. Come burst out of him, jet after jet filling Justin's mouth. He felt Justin swallow once, twice. "Justin…"

Justin sucked him until he was soft, until he was shivering and flinching and overstimulated and he had to pull Justin off his cock and drag him back into his arms. He rolled, taking Justin with him until they were side by side, foreheads and noses and lips pressed together. He took Justin's hand in his, threaded their fingers together, and brought it to his chest. Held it over his racing heart.

What a pair they made, pants shoved down to their thighs, shirtless, legs tangling together as much as they could.

"Okay?" Justin asked, brushing his nose against Wes's. He seemed almost nervous, the confident sex bomb who'd gone down on Wes and rocked his world, vanished. He watched Wes carefully.

Wes hummed. "Perfect," he sighed. "You're perfect." He kissed Justin's nose, the bow of his lip. His cheekbone. "That was amazing."

Justin smiled, the same wide smile he'd had gazing up at the lights of the Eiffel Tower. "Happy to amaze you anytime."

"*Mmm*, the feeling is mutual." Wes nuzzled him and grinned. "That was so hot. Feeling you come in my mouth."

"I guess I could let you blow me again, since you liked it so much."

Wes laughed and then kissed Justin, smiling. They kissed and never stopped, holding hands, twined together on Wes's narrow bed, as the lights of the Eiffel Tower winked on again, dazzling the city as they got lost in each other.

THE NARROW, squeaky beds were okay for frantic blow jobs and sideways cuddling, but sleeping together was another story. Wes lasted six minutes before his muscles protested, and he was afraid he'd squash Justin or accidentally dump him over the side of the bed in the middle of the night. Instead, he grabbed both of their mattresses and laid them side by side beneath the window, then piled the blankets on top. He shored up the sides with their duffels, trying to keep the mattresses from sliding apart, while Justin brushed his teeth and changed. They slid into their new bed together, wearing boxers and nothing else, and lay curled by the open window.

Eventually, their stroking hands turned more purposeful, sought fevered gasps instead of soft sighs, moans instead of shivers. Wes rolled Justin to his back and slithered on top, pressing them together from lips to toes, kissing him and lacing their hands together as he rocked his hips and his cock against Justin's. Justin arched his back, crying out when Wes sucked a hickey into the skin of his neck, when he tugged their boxers down and resettled on top of Justin, their naked bodies flush together.

It was slower this time, in the shadows and the midnight glow of Paris, their hands sliding through each other's hair and over trembling skin. Justin wrapped his legs around Wes's waist and gripped his shoulders, dug his fingers into the meat of his back as he tipped up his head and breathed Wes's name. Wes kissed Justin's chest, buried his face in Justin's neck, in the ends of his hair, gripped his thigh and held it to his hip as he thrust. He moved on instinct, making love to Justin with his body, their cocks grinding together against their hard bellies. When they came, it was together, Wes's lips pressed to Justin's, Justin's hands in his hair, Wes breathing Justin's name as Justin shuddered and shook in the circle of Wes's arms.

They met again in the middle of the night, seeking each other as if in a dream. Justin was on top this time, Wes's hands around his waist, helping guide Justin's body as they rocked and rolled and kissed, and kissed, and eventually spilled onto each other before they fell back to sleep, wrapped in an embrace so tight Wes couldn't tell where he began and Justin ended. Maybe it didn't matter anymore.

Paris's morning bustle woke them, as did Wes's achingly hard erection. He rolled into Justin's back, kissed his way down Justin's spine, worked his way around to Justin's cock, and sucked him until Justin was shivering and clenching. Wes slipped a finger into his mouth, coated it with spit, and then slid it down and between Justin's taut ass cheeks. He hesitated at Justin's hole.

"Are you sure?" Justin whispered. His hand found Wes's and squeezed. Justin was trembling. "We don't have to."

"I *want* to. I want to do everything with you. But do you want this?"

"Fuck," Justin hissed. He grasped the base of his cock and squeezed. Clenched his eyes closed. Breathed in and out, slowly. Then he spread his legs. "I do. So, so much. I want everything with you, too."

Wes held his breath as he slid his finger into Justin's hole. As Justin's heat closed around him, tighter and hotter than anything he'd ever felt before. He slid in and out carefully, until Justin told him, "Another. Another finger." Wes tried, but it wasn't slick enough, and Justin pawed through his duffel and thrust a bottle of lube at him. "Use this."

His two fingers slid in much easier then, in and out and in and out. Justin clenched on an in stroke and told him to curl his fingers toward his belly button and stroke again, and when he did, Justin arched like he'd touched a live wire, his thighs spreading wider, his fingers clawing at nothing as he silently screamed. Wes did it again and again, until Justin was a trembling mess, his cock weeping precome onto his belly, his legs quaking and spread, knees pulled up to his chest.

Wes kissed the inside of Justin's thigh, the crest of his hip bone, the underside of his cock. He slid his fingers out and wiped them on a worn T-shirt before he crawled up Justin's body and kissed his lips. "Justin?" He nuzzled his cheek. Waited until

Justin's eyes flickered open and he kissed Wes back, soft and slow. "Can I make love to you?"

Justin's eyes went wide. He stilled. "Are you sure?"

"I want my first time to be with you." His first time, his first guy. Maybe, a quiet voice in his heart said, his last guy. His only guy. Some of his friends were getting married or were ready to propose. They'd found *the one*. What if he had, too?

For a moment, there was a flicker of something in Justin's eyes, a shadow of doubt. Wes searched his gaze, tried to find that hesitation again, but it was gone. "Is that what you want?"

"Absolutely, cowboy," Justin purred. He reached over his head for his duffel, then rooted around until he found the pocket with the condoms. Pulled one out. More spilled and littered the floor. Wes eyed them, mentally claiming each. *Mine, mine, mine.* If he didn't screw this up, if he was a good enough lover for Justin, if he could captivate Justin half as much as Justin captivated him, then, maybe, Justin would want to keep him.

He took the condom Justin offered and tore it open. He fumbled a bit, flipping it one way and then the other, and his cheeks burned as he tried to position it correctly. Justin took pity on him and guided his hands, remembering to pinch the tip when Wes didn't, and then rolled it down his hard shaft with a smooth, gentle stroke that left him shivering.

They were all elbows for a minute, getting back into position, Justin on his back, legs spread, a pillow shoved under his hips at the last second. Wes grabbed the lotion and poured way too much onto his fingers. He tried his best to prepare Justin, but all he did was make a slippery mess. He rubbed the rest over his condom-sheathed cock as he lined himself up with Justin's hole.

"Go slow." Justin's fingers squeezed over his biceps. "You're big. I think you're the biggest I've ever had."

"Keep talking like that, and you won't have me. I'll finish before we start." Wes bit his lip and tried to stop the heat from curling around the base of his cock.

Justin smiled. He hooked one ankle around Wes's waist. Rubbed his hand over Wes's arm, his shoulder. "Make love to me."

Wes pushed in.

Heat. A clench, a squeeze tighter than his fist, tighter than he'd ever felt, blazing hot. Wes gasped, almost falling on top of Justin. His arms barely held him up. His vision went white, everything blanking for one moment, all his senses scrambled and overwhelmed.

He heard, though, Justin's hitched breath. His gasp. Saw his neck arch and his chin tip back. Saw his lips go thin.

Only the head of his cock was inside Justin. He froze. "Should I stop?"

"No." Justin squeezed his arms, dug his fingers into his muscles. Curled his leg, beckoning him fractionally closer. "No, just give me a moment. You're good, you're so good. God, Wes…"

He waited, frozen in a pushup, his cock barely inside Justin, all of his senses going wild as he tried to remember how to breathe in and out. He counted off plays, ran passing routes in his mind, replayed drills from practice. Thought of Coach Young hollering at the offense, making them run, and run, and run. Anything except for Justin, looking like perfection beneath him and between his arms.

"Okay," Justin breathed. "Okay, keep going."

He slid into Justin all the way, until their hips were flush and he was balls deep, every inch of his cock inside another person for the first time in his life. He shook, and this time he did collapse, falling onto Justin, burying his face in the crook of his neck. "Oh my God…" He felt Justin's kisses, the touch of lips to his hair, his temples, his forehead, felt Justin's fingernails scraping up his back. His ankles digging into his spine. He chased Justin's kiss, found his lips. Kissed him deeply, like he could pour himself inside Justin and stay with him forever.

Movement. The slide of their bodies together. He groaned and rested his forehead against Justin's as his hips took over. Justin's legs wrapped around his waist, and his arms looped around Wes's neck, and his lips captured Wes's and refused to let go. "Yes," Justin murmured. "Yes, God, yes. Perfect." Justin's words tumbled between their kisses, spilled into Wes like summer rain. He grunted and kissed Justin again. Lost himself to the feel of their bodies merging, Justin surrounding him, holding him. His heart was bursting, so damn gone for this man, gone like he'd made a breakaway and was full speed to the end zone. Gone like he was ready to do this, ready to fall in love with a man, ready to open the door he'd always kept shut and see what lay on the other side. He'd been gone for Justin ever since he'd first laid eyes on him. Every moment they'd spent together, he'd fallen a little deeper, and now here he was. With his first lover. Maybe, hopefully, his last.

Wes shuddered. His first lovemaking was going to be over way too soon. It was too much. Too much heat and pressure and Justin, too much intensity, too much of his heart bubbling over with hope and desire and craving. He didn't want to leave Justin behind, though. He balanced on one hand and reached down, fumbling for Justin's hard cock, weeping precome onto their bellies. He stroked, and Justin went electric, shaking and gritting his teeth as he gasped Wes's name. "I'm gonna come if you keep doing that."

"Good. I want to see it." He wanted to see Justin come apart because of him, spill over into orgasm because of him. Gasp his name and shake apart because of him. He squeezed again, stroked, twisted his hand over Justin's cock head.

Justin cried out as his orgasm tore through him, heat spilling into Wes's palm. His body clenched, and then it was Wes's turn to curse, gasp, almost scream as Justin's ass squeezed his cock, and he thrust in, as deep as he could, and came with a roar.

After, they lay in a tangle of arms and legs and slow kisses, hands laced together, sweat drying on their skin as the sun rose over Paris. Wes played with Justin's hair, ran the honey strands through his fingers. Justin traced the line of his jaw, his stubble, the corded muscles of his neck.

I've fallen so deeply for you, Justin.
But what's going to happen now?

CHAPTER FIVE

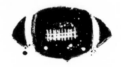

THREE WEEKS WAS A LIFETIME, and no time at all.

Days unfurled before Wes, each one bubbling over with new moments. New experiences. The first time he'd kissed a man, the first time he'd made love. The first time he held a man's hand in public, laced their fingers together and walked side by side down the twisting Parisian cobblestones. He'd tipped his head back and felt the sun, smiling as he closed his eyes.

They were at the Marché d'Aligre, wandering the stalls and eyeing the fresh-baked bread, the wheels and wedges of artisan cheese, the bottles of wine, the produce that looked like still lifes. Everything was brighter, sharper, more alive, as if making love for the first time had unlocked some secret ingredient. Or maybe it was falling in love that made everything seem more incandescent. The world wasn't perfect, but it *felt* perfect when Justin was beside him, his shoulder and arm brushing Wes's, their hips shifting together when they stopped to window-shop at the stalls and booths. Wes stood behind Justin and rested his hand on his hip. He fed Justin a sample, nearly kissing him after he nibbled the caramel-infused cheddar. He couldn't stop smiling.

At the flower stall, he dug out his leftover coins from the

week's budget and spent two euros on a tiny bouquet of wild-flowers tied with twine. The whole thing fit in his palm, and he hid it while Justin had his nose buried in the tulips, then sneaked up on him and teased his cheek with baby's breath and tender lavender. Justin turned into him, and Wes wrapped his arm around Justin's waist, holding him close in the middle of the farmer's market.

Justin tried to pull back. Wes tightened his hold. Justin was so close the brim of Wes's hat shaded his face. Justin's brow furrowed, a small line creasing the center of his forehead. "I thought you wanted to keep things quiet. You're not out."

"Who knows us here?" Wes let him go but didn't release Justin's hand. Instead, he raised it to kiss Justin's knuckles. People were eyeing them as they passed, smiling at them. Wes's heart hammered. "We're just two guys."

"You stand out." But Justin smiled, and he squeezed Wes's hand and didn't try to step away again. He flushed as his eyes landed on the tiny bouquet Wes held in his fingers. "No one's ever given me flowers before."

Again, Wes tickled his cheek with the baby's breath, then slid the sprig of lavender across Justin's lips, a kiss of sun-warmed petals. "I'll have to make a habit of it," he rumbled.

Justin laid his hand over Wes's, squeezing before taking the flowers. He inhaled, grinned, and swayed slightly with his eyes closed, a look of bliss on his face that melted every one of Wes's neurons. Had he made Justin smile that way, look like that? Had he, somehow, made Justin that happy, so joyous he seemed like he was about to float away? Like Wes had to hold on to his hand to keep him tethered to the earth?

He did, lacing their fingers together and holding tight as he set off on an amble down the market's stalls. Artists were sketching the crowd, and a mime entertained a gaggle of children and photo-snapping tourists. Justin twirled the sprig of flowers beneath his nose, smiling at everything Wes showed him, and when he leaned his cheek against Wes's shoulder, Wes's heart skipped a few dozen beats. It only started up again when he wrapped his arm around Justin, and they strolled through the Parisian summer like two interlaced swans, the scent of lavender dancing between them with every step.

Later, Justin eyed him as he wolfed down his third sandwich, one of the half-priced day-old offerings he'd bought from a bakery they'd found.

"You're not eating enough, are you?"

Wes froze mid chew. He looked left and right, then wiped his face with his napkin as he tried to avoid Justin's stare. Justin had a way of peering inside him, like he was picking apart Wes's thoughts through his eyeballs, figuring out the shape of things Wes couldn't find words for. "Um."

"How many calories a day off from your goal are you?"

Justin knew enough about athletics to zero in on the details, ask the question that Wes couldn't evade. He'd played baseball in high school before switching to the drill team, he'd said, and besides, if anyone thought drill wasn't a sport, they'd never sat in a Texas high school football stadium on a Friday night. "About two thousand. Or a little bit more." A lot more. But he couldn't afford to buy more food. Everything was more expensive than he'd expected, plus he hadn't planned for the hit he'd taken to his funds at the airport money changer.

Justin grabbed his phone and started tapping at the screen, pulling up a map. "Okay, there's a *supermarché* a few blocks away. Let's go get supplies."

"Supplies?"

"Yeah. Food for the room. There's a hot plate and a mini fridge, and I saw a few pots and pans. We can cook a few things. Can you cook?"

"I'm okay if we're talking hot dogs or sandwiches. Or if we're cooking over a fire."

Justin rolled his eyes but smiled. "Okay, so I'll cook. Let's get some groceries. I'll buy some, you buy some, and we'll save money eating in the room instead of going out for every meal."

Wes could have kissed him. Justin hadn't said a word about his own finances, but Wes had spied the optional extras catalog with the pages dogeared in Justin's duffel, so money clearly wasn't an issue for him. But he wasn't pushing, nor was he complaining—when he had every right to, considering meeting Wes had basically bulldozed those dogeared Paris plans—and that quiet support meant the world to Wes.

At the store, Wes loaded up on the basics, stocking up on carbs and proteins, and pastas and cheeses, milk and eggs, sandwich meat and bread, fruits and vegetables. Justin went eclectic, grabbing ingredients to make crepes and homemade pizza, baguettes and chicken breasts and simmer sauces. He looked up recipes on his phone and trolled the aisles, adding a mini mountain to his cart, while Wes followed with his more modest selection. At the end, Justin topped off his haul with a jar of protein powder. "Just in case I can't fill you up."

"I think you could give me some shots of protein another way."

Justin went fuchsia, and he turned into Wes's chest, smothering a smile as he ran his fingers down Wes's flat stomach. "I already calculated that into your daily nutrition."

They made dinner that night, a simple chicken-and-pasta dish with garlic bread. For the first time since he'd arrived in Paris, Wes was full—after eating a pound each of chicken and pasta, along with a whole baguette. He was like a bear entering hibernation, warm and sated and happy, enjoying the breeze coming through the window, half a bottle of wine in his veins. And enjoying the sight of Justin across the little bar top they were eating at, his chin in his hand as he swirled the wine in his glass, smiling with the sun on his face.

Wes tried to thank Justin by doing the dishes while Justin typed emails on his phone, keeping in touch with his family and friends. He wrapped a dish towel around Justin's eyes when he was done, then dropped to his knees and gave Justin a slow, sloppy blow job. Justin gripped his short hair and thrust into Wes's mouth, hips shuddering as Wes tried to mimic what Justin had done to him with his tongue and his throat and the way he twisted his lips over the head of his cock. "I'm sorry," Justin gasped after he shot down Wes's throat. "I thought I'd last longer. Jesus, that was too good."

Wes licked his lips. "I'll take it as a compliment."

Justin laughed, pulled Wes up, and kissed him until Wes was dizzy, then put his hands down Wes's pants, jerking him off as they kept kissing and kissing until Wes spurted into Justin's hands and whimpered his name, burying his face in Justin's neck.

They went for walks at night, looking at the sights, sitting at sidewalk cafés to people watch with a bottle of wine or cups of coffee. They went back to the Champ de Mars, where they drank a bottle of champagne and lay on the grass, watching the Eiffel Tower light up every hour. In between light shows, they made out, trading soft kisses as Justin draped himself across Wes's chest and Wes ran his fingers through his hair.

In the mornings, Justin joined Wes for his runs, and, now that Wes was eating enough, he went back to calisthenics, dropping into squats and lunges and stopping for push-ups and pull-ups as they jogged around the park. When Justin held his ankles so he could pump out a hundred sit-ups, Wes didn't count a rep official unless he kissed Justin's lips at the top. Once, Justin lay down beneath Wes when he was doing his push-ups, but Wes only got twenty-seven reps into his set of eighty before he went down and stayed down, wrapping his arms and legs around Justin and kissing him in the dewy dawn.

In class, they only had eyes for each other, and while the rest of the group was going wild over the Riviera or the Alps or gossiping about their trip to Lake Como, Wes called Justin *mon coeur* and *mon amour* and doodled two swans on the pages of their workbook. They sat on the quad to eat lunches Justin packed, watching the ducks and the swans float across the pond until Wes got the feed and they came running. Eventually, the ducks learned Wes meant food, and after that they were swarmed as soon as they tried to picnic.

Every night they made love, and each time was different. Justin rode Wes and held his hands, the lights of Paris dipping into the curves of his naked chest, the planes of his trim, tight muscles. He lay on his stomach and Wes spent a half hour eating him out, exploring his hole with lips and tongue, French-kissing him in a whole new way until Justin was a panting, quivering mess. Wes slid inside him then, kissing his way up his spine and the back of his neck to whisper in his ear, "*Mon amour, tu as mon coeur pour toujours.*"

Other times it was fast and frantic. Too much teasing in class, too much footsie and kissing in the bathroom and holding hands beneath the desk, and when they got back to their room, it was all they could do to get their pants down and shirts off and their bodies together, skin to skin, lips on lips. Wes was an animal in those moments, caging Justin to the mattress or the wall, pushing his body into Justin's, twining his fingers with Justin's as he held his hands over his head and pressed their cheeks together. They'd groan, Justin bucking into Wes's hips, driving himself onto Wes's cock until Wes slid his hands down to Justin's waist and took control. They'd both roar when they came, Justin's seed painting the wall or the sheets or his belly, Wes exploding into the condom. After, Wes always brushed his thumb over Justin's hip. Always hissed as he pulled out, and kissed between Justin's shoulders, over his spine.

An idea grew in the back of Wes's mind, something planted the night they walked back from the school and stopped by the opera house. He had to sneak away during class, duck out to use the restroom and slip down the stairwell to make a call. He fumbled through his questions in French, and the bemused

Parisian on the other end patiently explained to him how much tickets were and which seats were the best in the house.

It took three days to apply for the credit card over his phone and then email customer service to say he was studying abroad and was trying to buy ballet tickets. They'd given him a modest line of credit, but it was enough to buy two good tickets to *Swan Lake*. He spent more than he ever had in his life, but the thought of Justin's face when he'd touched his fingers to the playbill, and the desire in his eyes, made it all worthwhile.

It was the day before their last long weekend at the school, and he waited until they were eating lunch on the lawn before he pulled out the tickets he'd printed from the university's computer lab. He passed the folded sheet of paper, wrinkled from being shoved in the pocket of his Wranglers, to Justin. He didn't know what to say, so he said nothing at all. The tickets would say more than he could.

Justin's eyes boggled as he stared at the printout and then up at Wes. That searching look was back, excavating the deepest parts of Wes, and he wanted to squirm away, but he stayed, let Justin look. Let him see Wes's slow, hopeful smile. "I thought you might want to go."

"Might?" Justin blinked. His hand holding the paper shook. "How did you…"

"I opened a credit card."

"And you want to go to the ballet?" Justin's eyebrows crawled up his forehead, reached for the puff of his pompadour. "That hardly seems your scene."

"I've never been. I have no idea if it's my scene or not. But I know you like it, and I want to take you. Can you show me what it's like the way you see it?"

For a moment he thought Justin was going to cry, and he panicked, thinking he'd miscalculated, done something horribly wrong. He gnawed on his upper lip, trying to come up with an apology. But Justin leaned over and pressed his lips to Wes's, kissing him on the university quad like they had no cares in the world. "Some days, I don't believe you're real, *mon* cowboy."

"I could say the same about you. I didn't think anyone could know me the way you do."

"I think I could spend the rest of my life with you, and you'd still surprise me." Justin's gaze was equal parts searching and adoring, like he was appraising a fine piece of art, a priceless wonder they'd stumbled on in the museum. "I think there are whole oceans inside of you."

Wes smiled and turned his face to the sun. The heat slid under the brim of his hat, warming him to the core. "You can dive into every one."

"Maybe I will."

The performance was Friday night, and Justin spent the entire day an excited bundle of energy. He picked out his outfit at lunch, then picked through Wes's selection of T-shirts and his two pairs of Wranglers before telling him to wear the hunter green Ariat and his darker jeans.

"I'm sorry I don't have anything nicer."

"You look amazing no matter what you wear," Justin said, kissing his cheek as he shaved.

They were the most casually dressed couple at the ballet, mingling in the gilded lobby with women wreathed in silk who hung on the arms of men in suits that were too expensive to even look at. Wes spotted opera gloves and pearls like the flappers used to wear in the Roaring Twenties, and even a real peacock feather in an older woman's hair comb. But no one bothered them, though there were a few raised eyebrows as he led Justin to the orchestra-level seating. Justin clearly knew how good the center-section seats were, and he squeezed Wes's hand so hard he thought his bones would snap.

Wes lost himself in the ballet, captivated by the dancers' muscles rippling and clenching, by their deceptively delicate movements that concealed strength and power rivaling those of the running backs and wide receivers he knew. The ballerinas and danseurs had better vertical leaps than he did, and he'd been considered a favorite for the NFL combine had he chosen to go.

The danseur's skintight leggings that left nothing to the imagination, outlining every shift and curve of his thighs, his ass, and the heft of his bulge, didn't hurt.

Justin's previous bare-bones explanation of the story let him follow along for the most part. The prince and the cursed maiden's love story unfolded through their dance, in breathless touches and the flutter of skin against skin, in how they mirrored one another. *He was meant to love the white swan*. Wes could see it. He could feel it, even.

The best part, hands down, was how Justin looked as he watched the ballet. The light in his eyes, his smile, the way his lips parted and how he was completely absorbed, swaying gently to the music. The way he held his breath, exhaled, gasped along with the leaps and pirouettes and what Wes learned later was called the White Swan Pas de Deux.

At intermission, nearly everyone rose and filed out, heading to the lobby for wine and champagne or outside for cigarettes. Wes and Justin stretched their legs at their seats as Justin raved about the performance, the staging, the music. Wes couldn't stop smiling, watching him.

"I'm sorry," Justin groaned. "I'm being a nerd. I'm talking too much."

"No such thing. I want to hear everything about what you love. And it would be a crappy date if I took you somewhere you hated."

"I love it. I can't thank you enough…"

Wes tugged him close, wrapping his arms around Justin's waist and kissing him quiet. "All I want is to see you smile." Justin did, shy and wonderful and oh so sexy, that little curve of his lips that lit Wes on fire.

Justin cried during the final act, and Wes wrapped his arm

around him and held him close, then laid his own head on Justin's when Justin leaned into his shoulder. Justin was quiet and embarrassed after, wiping his eyes and trying to hide his sniffs, but Wes kissed him and told him he loved it, loved everything about the ballet, and loved taking him. Justin held him so tight he couldn't breathe.

"There's so much to the story," Justin finally said, babbling as they made their way down the block. "The black swan and the psychology she represents. The prince has to confront the evil that cursed his love, but before he can, he succumbs to the black swan and his own fears. He loses everything because he can't face the truth or stand up to the darkness."

He was meant to love the white swan. "He chooses to die with his white swan instead of living without her, though. That's powerful."

"Wouldn't a life together have been more so?"

They wandered to a late-night café and ordered a bottle of champagne, then sat side by side to drink it, holding hands, talking about everything and nothing. Classes they'd taken, stories of past roommates. Wes shared anecdotes about the team, about how they learned to come together, about grueling practices and three-a-day training sessions, workout regimens that nearly broke him. Endless run and pass routes. How it all came together, each brutal moment, every Saturday, when the team moved as one unit, one mind, one body, one soul, and they racked up win after win after win.

Justin told him about how he came out to his parents, and how he'd decided to never come out again after that: the world could think what it wanted and leave him alone. No more waiting for the right time to say, "I'm gay." He lived out and proud and loudly, and screw what anyone else thought. He had the scars left over from people who didn't respect that, who cut him with their words and their hate, but he'd managed to carve out a life for himself, and he was, on the whole, happy. He had his classes, and he had his community dance, a group of friends, and hopes for the future.

"No boyfriend?" Wes asked. He rubbed his thumb over Justin's knuckles.

Justin laughed. "Well, wouldn't it be shitty if I did? If I did, and he had half a brain, I'd be an ex-boyfriend right now."

"I don't need to fight for your hand?"

"No one fights for my hand. I pick my own Prince Charming, thank you very much." Justin sipped his champagne, eyeing Wes. "But I guess you might be at the top of my list of prince choices. I mean, after tonight." He shrugged exaggeratedly.

"I try," Wes drawled. "I'm glad it pleased you, m'lord."

"*Mmm*, keep that up, I *might* decide to please *you* later tonight."

An empty threat, since they made love as many times as they could, until they were both sore and each orgasm stung. Wes was young, sure, and his refractory period was basically a blink and a deep breath, but he was past the years when a stiff breeze got him hard. Well, maybe he wasn't, if that breeze was Justin's breath on his cock. He couldn't get enough of Justin, wanted to love him every way, all the time. Wanted to feel their bodies merge, wanted to slide inside Justin and stay there, wrapped in his arms, forever.

The teasing light in Justin's eyes faded. "What happens next week?"

Next week. Wes racked his brain. They had their French finals, which neither of them was concerned about. They'd planned a big date for Wednesday night, because it was going to be their last night—

Oh.

He hissed. "What are you doing for the rest of the summer?"

"I'll be in Dallas. I told my parents I'd spend the summer with them. You?"

"Going to see my dad out at the ranch. I work with him during the summer. But if I make first string, I'll be back at school in three weeks. If not... I'll be back in August."

"And when we're at school? Does this"—Justin waved his champagne glass in a circle between them—"continue? Or is it a summertime-in-Paris kind of thing?"

Wes gnawed on the corner of his lip. *Swans mate for life.* "I want it to continue," he said. His voice was like thunder, rumbling his own chest. Shaking his own bones. "I don't want to stop. But do you want—"

"I do," Justin said quickly. "I really, really do. But you're not out, and you're on the football team..."

What would his teammates say, if any of them knew? What would Colton—his friend, his quarterback—say? They were closer than brothers sometimes, especially in the middle of the season, when he knew how to read every twitch of Colton's body, every glimmer in his gaze. The half second of eye contact before the snap, and the other half second, when they met each other through a dozen linemen and Colton let loose on the pass, and Wes was there to receive it. They'd made promises in those glances, vows that ran as deep as their blood. *Give me the ball. I'll get the yards. I'll get the down. I'll get the points.* Or *I'll block. I'll pick up the extra from the limping lineman. I'll keep the sack from getting to you.*

I've got you.

What would Colton think if he knew Wes was making love to Justin? If he knew that Wes was gay? How fast would he recoil? How far would he pull back?

How could they ever share those half seconds again if Colton decided he couldn't trust Wes? Trust was an all-or-nothing thing, Wes had found. He trusted the linemen to protect Colton, to open the holes for his rushing or his passing route. If he couldn't trust one of the linemen, the quarter, even the half, could go down the drain. Colton trusted Wes. That's why they were called the nation's best duo, why newspapers called them the next Brady-

Gronkowski duo. They were magic on the field. Unbeatable. Unstoppable.

Unless Colton found out the truth, and that trust, that bond, shattered.

"I can't come out while I'm on the team. I can't upset the dynamics."

"Is that fair to you?"

"It doesn't matter if it is. I'm part of the team. I choose to play. If I don't want to, I can quit." Well, not really, because then he'd lose his scholarship and every dream of his future. Justin would hardly fall for a college dropout with no prospects. No, he knew where his bread was buttered and how he had to play the game. Literally. "While I'm on the team, who I am isn't important. I'm part of a bigger whole. And I'm okay with that."

At least, he had been. Before he'd met Justin. Before he'd known what it was to be with a man, to know and to crave what had only been a formless desire.

"You're saying if we keep this up, we'll have to hide?"

He nodded. "I have to hide, yes." For now, at least. Maybe only two more years. His throat clenched hard, and he tried to clear it, tried to push past the sudden blockage. "If that's not what you want, I understand. You're a lot braver than me and you don't hide anything—"

"I'm not brave. I'm stubborn. I didn't come out to my parents because I was proud or because I was trying to make a statement. I came out because I was sick of their fantasies about my future. Who knows, maybe I would have been a good lawyer, or a good VP of whatever sales, but I'll never know. That's stubborn. Maybe stupid. Not brave."

"I think you're brave. It doesn't matter why you wanted to come out. You did. That's more than I've been able to do."

"Till here, at least." Justin's smile was sad. "How does it feel? Being out, here?"

"Awesome," Wes breathed instantly. "Like a dream. I've imagined holding hands with a guy so many times. Walking down the street with him, kissing him in public. I didn't know if it would ever happen. I didn't know if I could find a guy who wanted me like that."

"Why do you say that? Why do you think no one would want you? Have you looked at yourself?"

"I know what people see when they look at me. I'm big, I'm intimidating, I'm scary. I learned to stay away from everyone, especially at night, and especially girls. They call the police if I get too close. Or, worse, pull their mace out. Guys want to try and fight me to prove something to themselves or to their bros. My professors usually discount me. They figure I'm just a jock and I won't have much to contribute anyway. Or they're starstruck. And I'm a hick from West Texas. I knew how to ride and shoot before I learned how to read, and I'm still more comfortable out on the ranch than I ever am around people. That's what people see when they look at me: big, scary, dumb hick in a cowboy hat."

"Jesus, Wes, that's not at all what I think when I look at you. Not even close. I mean, yes, you're big, but you worked hard to put on that strength. And yes, you're a cowboy, and I can't even tell you how much I don't usually like cowboys, but…" Justin was babbling, his words running together, gesturing with his champagne flute. He shook his head. "You're not dumb. Not at all. You have a full athletic scholarship, and you're not a general studies major. I bet your GPA isn't anywhere close to 2.5."

"3.8," Wes said softly.

"See? That's a lot better than my GPA. And you're not scary. Not at all. Not in any way. You're the gentlest man I've ever met."

Wes shifted. He rolled his champagne flute between his palms. Watched the bubbles rise and burst.

"Hey." Justin's fingers landed on his wrist, squeezing softly over his pulse. "Fuck anyone who thinks that about you."

He set down his glass and grabbed Justin's hand, kissed his

fingertips. Laced their fingers together. "I'd rather only do that with you."

"Well, I'd rather that, too." Justin grinned, but there was a shadow in his gaze again, something that flitted across his features before vanishing as he downed a gulp of champagne. He set the flute on the patio table and stood, holding out his hand. "Take me home, cowboy. I need you to ravish me. Make love to me all night long."

Wes dumped a handful of euros on the table as a tip and took Justin's hand, looping it around his elbow. "Yes, sir."

LATER, Justin lay sprawled across Wes's chest as the Paris night breeze dried their sweat. He tangled his fingers in the fur on Wes's chest, dragging his fingernails across his pecs, dipping into the valleys of his muscles as they caught their breath. Wes had one hand in Justin's hair, the other stroking over Justin's thigh, hiked up and thrown across his hip.

"I meant it," Justin said. He spoke to Wes's neck, his words tickling the sweat that lingered on Wes's stubble. "About how I'd rather you only fuck me."

Wes pulled back enough to peer down at Justin. Gold glittered in Justin's gaze, Paris's eternal reflection.

"I know maybe I'm reading into things, and maybe this isn't more than what it is. Maybe this is just Paris, just a summer fling. And if that's all it is, I get it. I mean, I'll accept it. I'm not going to chase you at school. But—"

"Justin."

Justin's mouth closed.

Wes brushed his lips over Justin's. "There's no one else. I don't *want* there to be anyone else." He kissed Justin again and again.

"Same," Justin breathed. "That's what I was trying to say. I only want you."

Wes rolled over, pinning Justin to the mattress until they were rocking against each other again, and Justin pressed another condom into Wes's hand. He slid back inside Justin with a sigh, resting his forehead, his cheek against Justin's. "You feel like coming home."

He captured Justin's lips before he could reply, rocked his hips back and forth, slid in and out of Justin as Justin's legs wrapped around his waist. Wes thought of white swans, of Friday night lights, of racing down the field, sprinting past the linebackers, juking past the safety, and then nothing but yards of grass and the uprights in the end zone, waiting for him to bring it home.

And there in the end zone was Justin, smiling as the stadium wind ruffled his hair, holding out his hand to Wes.

He'd kissed Justin before he confessed how far he'd fallen, but he couldn't stop the roar of his orgasm, the blaze—the sudden, searing rush—that followed his realization. Love, desire, craving, the run he'd been making his entire life. Eyes on the ball, eyes on the ball, until suddenly there was Justin, and he couldn't look away from the shape of his smile or the sound of his voice. Couldn't look away as he sprinted as hard as he could to catch up with his heart. *I love you.*

He came with a cry, burying his face in Justin's throat as he shuddered and emptied and squeezed his eyes shut. Justin's hands tangled in his hair as he cursed, bucking against Wes, and a moment later, warmth spread over Wes's belly, between them.

I love you.

CHAPTER SIX

TEARS ROLLED down Justin's cheeks despite how he'd sworn, *sworn* he wouldn't cry when this moment came. He scrubbed the back of his hand across his face. Cursed as he rolled his eyes up, glaring at the ceiling.

Wes stood in front of him, staring at the ground, his face hidden by the brim of his hat.

"Fuck," Justin hissed. "I knew this was coming. I mean, I knew for days. Why am I like this?"

Wes shook his head. All Justin saw was the shake of his cowboy hat, the slump of his shoulders. Wes hiked his duffel higher on his shoulder, shoved one hand in his pocket. "How much longer do we have?"

Justin checked his phone. "I have forty minutes until I board. Another two hours until your flight."

After three perfect weeks, this was it. He and Wes were on separate flights to the US. Wes was going back to campus, and Justin was flying to Dallas, where his parents were picking him up and taking him home for the rest of summer.

He was *thisclose* to changing his flight, saying fuck it and going with Wes back to school. But Wes was only going to check in with

Coach—no last name needed; he was the team's god—pick up his truck, and then drive out to the ranch in West Texas, in a town so small Justin had to zoom in and zoom in and zoom in again on Google Maps before he could even see the two-lane road bleeding into the scrub desert and the cluster of buildings that formed his tiny town in the middle of nowhere.

Wes steered him toward the corner of an empty gate, not far from where his flight was waiting to board. The gate area was already crowded, everyone lining up early to try to elbow their way on first. Wes dropped his duffel and took Justin's hands, threading their fingers together as he leaned against the wall. "What are you doing when you get back?"

"Just hanging with my parents. No plans. You?"

"Nothing but working for the rest of summer. Help out my dad as much as I can. Hopefully make some money for the fall." He turned Justin's hand over in his, ran his calloused finger over Justin's smooth palm. "You sure you want to visit? It's a long drive."

"Yes. Absolutely yes. I don't care how long a drive it is. I'm coming."

Wes smiled. He tried to hide how he flushed, looking down and shielding his face with the brim of his hat. "When you come, I want to take you way out to the far ridge. It's a two-day ride by horse. You ever ridden?"

"Boy Scouts. Petting zoos."

"I'll teach you." Wes ran his thumbs over Justin's fingers. The roughness of his hands was grounding, almost a comfort, now. "Out there, when you camp and look up at the sky? It's like the universe is spread out in front of you. Like you can finger paint with the stars. Reach out and pluck one, keep it with you forever. I used to go out there to watch meteor showers, and I swear, one time, I thought the whole sky was coming down."

He could picture it: Wes and his cowboy hat, riding his horse and staring at the stars. He wanted to see it in person, wanted to be a part of that world with Wes.

"We can share a sleeping bag. It gets cold at night, even in summer, but I'll keep you warm."

"I know you will." He tried to be saucy, sexy, but ruined it. Instead of looking cute, his face scrunched up, and he glared at the ceiling again as he blinked fast. Wes's thumbs kept stroking his hands. "When, um. When will you know about the team? About your position?"

Wes exhaled. "Maybe when I get back to campus. Maybe not until later this summer. If I'm second string again, then there's no need to rush back to campus. But if I'm starter…"

"You were hardly second string last year. You had only one less start than the starter. The senior who graduated. What's his name?"

"Watson." Wes smiled. "You googled me."

"Figured I should know a little bit about football if my boyfriend is, like, playing." Justin shrugged, pretending to look annoyed. "Turns out my boyfriend is kind of a big deal. He's made a few touchdowns or baskets or goals or whatever."

Wes's smile melted Justin's spine. He stared into Justin's eyes, those dimples on full display, his cheeks darkening to shades of burgundy, even the tips of his ears going red. "Boyfriend, huh?"

"Well, if you insist." Justin bit his lip. Smiled. "I could be persuaded."

They were in a corner of the airport, off the main path, tucked into an empty gate area, but still. He didn't expect Wes to do anything. Certainly not lean in, cup Justin's cheek in one of his giant hands, and press their lips together. Justin kissed back, trying to chase Wes when he pulled away. He ended up leaning against his chest, tucking his face into Wes's neck. Inhaling. Breathing him in.

The boarding announcement for his flight shattered the moment. He clung to Wes, irrationally afraid to let go. What if this was it? What if, when he turned his back, everything they'd shared evaporated?

What if he never saw Wes again?

Ridiculous. Of course he'd see Wes again. All he had to do was turn on the TV. He could see him every Saturday, and on Sports-Center every week, and on a million YouTube clips. He'd see Wes for the rest of his life, whether he wanted to or not.

But oh, how he wanted to. He wanted to wake up every day and see his face, watch the morning sun wink over his twitching eyelids, watch him come awake slowly, face half buried in the pillow as he fought for those last few seconds of sleep. Wanted to see his eyes roll back in his head when Justin decided to wake him up the fun way. Wanted to kiss him good morning and good night, to cook breakfast and dinner for him, feed him ridiculous amounts of calories, then help him burn it all off with cardio and wild sex. He wanted to watch Wes in the shower, maybe even join him sometime if they ever found a stall large enough. He wanted everything with this man, everything he'd spent the past three weeks savoring, and now it was about to end.

"Text me when you land?" Wes whispered.

"Of course. You, too?" Wes would land first, in New York, and then transfer to his flight to Austin, where he'd take a bus back to campus. Wes nodded. "Let me know about the team. Your position."

Behind Justin, the gate agent started rattling off boarding zones, moving with alarming efficiency. He'd counted on the process being slow, giving him a few extra minutes with Wes. He'd been greedy, wanting every second he could steal.

"I will."

And then the gate agent called his zone, and a minute later, the line of people boarding his flight was nearly gone. They started the final boarding call next, announcing the names of missing passengers. "*Justin Swanscott, please come to gate 29 immediately. Your flight has completed boarding.*"

"Fuck," he hissed. Tears bubbled up again, and he squeezed Wes's hands. "I'll see you soon, okay?"

Wes stared at Justin, his lips thin, eyes wide and shining, as if he, too, was trying to fight back tears. His fingers hadn't released Justin's, and he was holding on like he wouldn't let go, wouldn't let Justin walk away. *Don't let me go. Don't ever let me go.*

He pressed a quick kiss to Wes's cheek, then grabbed his carry-on and turned toward his gate. The gate agent noticed him heading her way, and she waved him on, a plastic smile on her features as she told him to hurry. Then she froze, eyes wide, and stared beyond him.

"Justin." Hands grabbed him and spun him around, and he was face to face with Wes, Wes's body pressed as tightly to Justin's as they'd ever been—closer, even, than when they were making love. Wes's hands slid around his waist, rose to the center of his back. "Justin," Wes rumbled. His eyes darted from Justin's eyes to his lips.

He kissed Justin then, deeper, harder, than he ever had. Nothing, not even their first kiss, was as hungry, as desperate, as the kiss Wes laid on him there, in the middle of the concourse, no longer hidden in a corner and out of sight. There he was, Wes Van de Hoek, one of the top college football players in the US, laying one on Justin like he was trying to give Justin part of his soul, break off a piece of himself and slide it inside Justin for him to keep. Justin dropped his carry-on and threw his arms around Wes.

Their lips brushed as they caught their breath. Justin blinked, the roar of the airport a dull hum behind him, the people and the overhead announcements and the airplanes racing down the runways all so distant in comparison to the feel of Wes in his arms, the taste of Wes on his lips.

That kiss felt like forever. Like a promise. Like a vow. Like everything he'd wished for, all in one moment. He brushed his nose against Wes's. Smiled, and felt Wes smile against his lips in return.

"Mr. Swanscott?" This time, the gate agent came to him, hovering at his side instead of calling him over the intercom. "We need to board, Mr. Swanscott. Everyone else is already seated. Will you be joining the flight?"

"Yes." He pulled away slowly. Held on to Wes's hand as he grabbed his carry-on. Held his hand as he backed away, one, two, three steps, until their arms were extended and only the tips of their fingers were still touching. And then not, and Justin pulled his fingers to his lips and kissed them, then blew his kiss to Wes, who stood like a brokenhearted cowboy alone in a sea of humanity, people rushing around him like water breaking over a rock as he watched Justin walk away.

Justin let the tears fall as he settled into his coach seat. Let them rain down his face and soak his T-shirt while the preflight announcements filled the cabin. A flight attendant slipped him a box of tissue and a little travel bottle of vodka, and he gave her a shaky smile as he squeezed her hand.

He closed his eyes as the plane lifted off. He felt his heart fall free, sink back to earth, stay behind. He'd lost his heart to Wes, and he wouldn't get it back until they were together again. *God, I love you, you big cowboy. I'll see you again. Soon.*

CHAPTER SEVEN

WES WAS a bleary-eyed mess when he finally tumbled off the bus at campus. He hitched his duffel onto his tired shoulders and walked the mile to his dorm. He hadn't slept a wink on either flight. He'd stared out the window for hours, replaying memories of him and Justin, trying to hold on to every second, too afraid he'd forget the sound of Justin's laugh if he closed his eyes. Too afraid he'd fall asleep and wake up sandwiched between two businessmen who wanted to type on their laptops, and realize everything, all of it, had been a dream.

Now he'd give anything for a few minutes of rest.

When he made it to campus, he found his truck in the back of a long-term parking lot and pulled down the rusted tailgate, then threw himself into the bed. He hadn't worried about the truck while he was gone. No one was going to take this clunker. It was more rust than paint, coated in a patina of mud and deer blood from the ranch. Even his teammates didn't want to bum a ride with him. They'd rather walk.

He lay on his back and stared at the sky. See Coach Young. Text Justin. Grab caffeine. He could make it a hundred miles before he needed to pull over and sleep for a few hours at a truck stop. It would cut the trip home tomorrow to only seven hours.

Groaning, Wes hauled himself up, dug out his keys, and dragged himself into the cab. The old rust bucket started up on the first go, and he smiled at the duct-taped dash. "Good girl." It was only a six-minute drive to the stadium, and since it was summer, the parking lot was a ghost town. He passed an athletic trainer and the team doc as he made his way up to the coaching offices and the executive suite, on the same floor as the skyboxes. He spun his keys, his exhaustion replaced with a formless kind of anxiety, a buzz in his bones and a hum that bubbled his blood. He didn't know if he was going to float away or collapse. He'd worked hard his whole life, always achieving everything he'd set his mind to. Always moving up. He'd wanted to be the best in his school, and then the best in his division, and then one of the best in the state. And he was. He'd wanted a scholarship, and he got one. He'd decided to become a starter on the team when he first arrived on campus, decided he was going to be the first-string tight end, and now… he was right on the cusp, the very edge of that dream.

But he also loved Justin. He still wasn't sure how the rest of his life fit in with the truth of that.

In Paris, loving Justin had been effortless. Simple. As easy as breathing, like it was something he was born to do.

But he'd also been born to carry a football, to carry a team. That was why he had such a strong back, his mama had said. He was born to carry his brothers. He couldn't let them down. Not ever.

He spun his keys again, slapping the metal against his palms over and over as the elevator took him up and spat him out on the executive floor. He made his way down the windowed walkway, the hall overlooking the end zone of the stadium. The school's logo stared up at him, freshly painted each week in both end zones and the center of the field.

"Wes!" The bellow hit him before he even entered Coach's office. "I've been waiting for you, son! Get in here!"

Coach Young was a mountain of a man, the only person Wes had ever met larger than he was. He'd played tight end when he was in college, won the Heisman, joined the NFL, won three Super Bowl rings. He took a bad tackle and blew out his knee, and he spent two years fighting his way back before he brought his team all the way to the Super Bowl again. Right before the half, he suffered another bad tackle to the same knee, and it made a crack that could still be heard on the ESPN replays. He'd limped off the field through sheer determination, only to fall to the grass on the sideline. After his quarterback and offensive line carried him to the locker room, he was told he'd never play football again. The team tried to rally and win the game for him, but without Young, they couldn't come together the same way. They lost by three, and the next day, he retired. Became a coach and worked his way up from offensive coordinator to assistant to head coach at a Division III college before making the leap to Division I-A.

Now he was the number-one coach in the nation, with the winningest record under his belt. His program was an NFL factory. He knew how to create professional ball players. His legacy would shape the NFL for the next thirty years, ESPN said.

Coach smiled as Wes walked in. He was perched on the front edge of his desk, a bottle of Johnnie Walker Blue in his hand and two tumblers on the desk. He pointed to one of the leather club chairs in front of him. "Take a seat, son."

Wes did, taking his hat off and resting it over his knees. It was what his dad had taught him to do, and it hid the way his knees were knocking against one another. "Coach."

"Good time in Paris? Did you get the credits you need?"

"I passed the intensive. Knocked out a year of language."

"Fan-fucking-tastic." Coach didn't just speak. He roared, his voice filling the whole stadium, it seemed. "Glad that's out of the way. You are going to need all of your focus for the upcoming year." He raised the bottle to Wes, then poured a healthy two fingers into each glass. He passed one to Wes and held his own up for a toast. "Because I'm looking at the new starting tight end for the number-one college team in the nation—and, if I was a betting man, the next Heisman winner. I'd go so far as to say the next number-one draft pick." He clinked his glass against Wes's. "Congratulations. You earned this. You and your dedication to this team and this organization."

Starting tight end. First string.

He'd done it. He'd actually done it. A smile broke over Wes's face, and he sipped Coach's Johnnie Walker, beaming through the burn. "Coach, thank you—"

"Don't even start. You don't thank me when you put in all the sweat equity." Coach waved Wes's fumbling words away. He downed the rest of his whisky in one swallow and slammed the glass down on his desk. Nodded and then leaned forward, bracing his meaty forearms on his tree-trunk thighs. "Now, we need to talk."

He knows. A river of fear sluiced through Wes. "Coach—"

"Let me talk, son." Coach glared until Wes snapped his jaw shut, squeezed his lips into a thin line. He didn't even sip his whisky. "Look, out of all my starters, you are the only one I really worry about. You know why?"

Wes said nothing. He didn't move.

"You're what some people call a gentle soul, despite being in this game. Seems years and years of this gridiron haven't relieved you of the burden of having a big old heart. Most guys get to where you are through sheer, single-minded determination, and they aren't opposed to throwing some elbows on the way up the ladder. Not every boy who dreams of the NFL can get to the top, you know?" He hesitated, his thumbs tapping together. Coach knew the value of silence and a heavy stare. "Now, I know you're a beast on the field, and there's nothing I or another team can throw at you that can get you off your game or get inside your head. But you've never played at this level before, son. Even last year, when you were trading starts with Watson. You weren't the starter. You weren't ranked as the fifth-best player in the country." His eyebrows rose, and he smiled as the blood drained out of Wes's face. "That's right. Number five in the nation. There's a few weenies from Ohio and Mississippi in front of you, but by the middle of the season, I think you'll knock them down a few pegs. I think you have a few more rungs to climb. When I look at you, I see the best player in the nation."

"Coach…"

"Shut up and listen." He leaned forward, closer to Wes. "You're the top dog at this school, Wes. In this program. And in this sport. I have to ask: are you ready for what's about to happen to you?"

Wes stared, his eyes about to fall out of their sockets. His hand trembled, the whisky sloshing against the crystal walls of the glass. Coach took it gently from him, set it on his desk. Wes gripped the edges of his hat, let the cold sweat from his palms soak into the wool.

"You are going to be under the microscope. Everything about you is going to be turned upside down. NFL scouts will be crawling over your life. They're going to look at your grades, at your girlfriends, at your social circle. What kind of photos you've been tagged in on Facebook. Who you know, and who knows you. Reporters are going to follow you. Dig into your life. Everyone is going to want something from you. You think you've had pussy before? You're about to drown in pussy. Girls will be throwing themselves at you faster than you can blink. Everything is going to change—but all of that, all of that, Wes, is a distraction."

Jesus Christ. Wes's fingers dug into his hat, mangled the brim. Squeezed until he couldn't feel his fingertips.

"Everything that's about to happen is a distraction from what's most important." Coach leaned forward, eyeball to eyeball with Wes. "Remember why you started playing this game. You started, and you stayed, because of the team. Because when you step out on that field, it's not about you, about your glory or the pussy you get or the contracts you might sign someday or the money people promise you. It's about the team. It's about all of you coming together and doing something greater than yourselves. Giving your all to each other so that together, *together*, you can achieve glory. Greatness. So you can all step on that field at the end of the season as champions, and as the best football players in the nation. And so every single one of you can grab those dreams you've had since you were knee-high boys and see them come true. That's why you play, son. For the dream."

Wes couldn't feel his heart. It was either faster than a hummingbird or it had stopped completely. He had no idea which.

"You are going to go pro. I know, I know, you say you haven't decided. But listen. I already have six NFL coaches calling me asking about you. You have the makings of a champion, and I can say that because I've known a few. Hell, I've created a few. You are the best football player I've ever seen. And you—you, Wes—can unite this team, make every one of these boys, who are already great ball players, even greater than they are now. This season is yours to win or lose, and because of that, you can bring all these boys with you, all the way to glory." Coach's eyes narrowed. "Do you understand what I'm saying, son?"

"I... I think so," Wes croaked.

"Lemme break it down really simple for you: keep your eyes on the ball, and you'll have everything you ever dreamed of. And not just you, but the team, your friends, your family. Do you know how much your life can change when you're a first-round draft pick in the NFL?" Coach Young's hand landed on his shoulder and nearly knocked Wes from his chair. "Understand me?"

"Yes, Coach." His response was automatic. His sweat-soaked hands were still doing their best to shred his hat.

"Excellent. Now, you have three weeks off. Get out of here. Go see your father and kiss your girlfriend, and then get your ass back here. We've got a big season and a lot of work to do. We're going to be national champions this year. And you're the team captain."

"Me?" That usually went to a senior, or to the best player on the team—

Oh. Wes flushed.

"Yes, you. I told you. You're top dog at this school. I expect you to act like it. You'll be here first, before practice, and help me and my staff organize drills. You'll stay after, help us review tape. You'll evaluate your teammates every day. You've got your work cut out for you, son. Now might be a good time to switch that major of yours. You've got no free time anymore. All of your minutes are mine. I'm glad you got that language credit out of the way, but let's get the rest out of the way, too. General studies has lots of room, and my classes are always open for one more ball player."

"I'll… think about it." Wes stood slowly. He held his hat to his chest. "Coach, thank you."

"I told you: don't thank me. You earned this." Coach waved, dismissing him as he went back behind his desk. "Now get. I've got work to do, and you've got to go think about your life."

"Yes, Coach." He stuck his hat on his head and strode out.

He made it to the elevator before his knees buckled and he fell to the floor, palms flat on the carpet. He heaved, grabbing the silver trash can by the elevator doors a moment before he lost his burger and fries, fast food he'd scarfed at the airport before boarding the bus.

Team captain… any idea how much your life is going to change… dig into your life. Turn everything upside down.

The whole team is relying on you.

You can bring all these boys with you, all the way to glory.

Remember why you play this game. Remember why you continue to play.

He tipped his head forward, resting it on the cool edge of the garbage can. Smelled the sour wash of his vomit.

You can have everything you ever dreamed of.

Justin.

His stomach heaved again, and he spewed bile into the trash can. Spat and wiped the back of his hand over his burning lips.

Justin.

How many hours had it been since he'd said goodbye? Since he'd kissed him, smack in the middle of the airport, and held him like he was going to make love to him that moment? Like he was going to pick Justin up and carry him down to the church, marry him in front of God and country and declare himself Justin's for all of his life.

There were exactly zero out Division I-A football players. And of the few who came out, none had made it to the NFL.

None had carried their team's dreams.

The team is relying on you.

Remember why you play this game, son.

You can have everything you ever dreamed of.

All the way to glory.

Justin.

They'll dig into your life. Turn everything upside down.

What would it feel like to be outed on SportsCenter? To walk into any bar on campus and see his face on every wide-screen in the joint, fifty different high-definition versions of himself. What would it be like to see his biggest secret blaring from every speaker, every television, every radio?

He hurled again, his stomach empty but still trying to turn itself inside out, shred itself like he'd tried to shred his hat.

What would Colton's face look like if he learned Wes's secret from ESPN? If he read about it online? If he saw pictures of Wes and Justin? What about Orlando and Art? What about Coach? The athletic trainers? What if everyone suddenly knew he was gay?

The stares. The accusations. The disbelief. The broken trust.

Everyone is counting on you.

It would shatter the team if they found out like that. Hell, it would shatter the team if they found out at all. He'd kept this from everyone his whole life, kept it from the guys he'd sweated and bled with, who he'd given all of himself to, day in and day out. Guys who'd traveled this path with him and were counting on him to help bring them the last few yards. Into the end zone. To glory.

And what would happen to Justin if Wes was outed? If he was named as the guy Wes loved? What would happen to his life? He imagined the jeers, the slurs, the hate. Hell, the online attacks he got when he fumbled a pass were brutal enough. What if Wes was outed? What if the world found out that what he wanted most wasn't to catch that shovel pass and make a breakaway for the end zone or to snatch that fade from Colton in the back corner of the end zone and rack up another touchdown on the scoreboard, but that he wanted Justin? He wanted to be on his knees, Justin's cock in his mouth, Justin's hands gripping his skull? To be balls deep in Justin, kissing him until his toes curled, until Justin's ankles crossed behind his back and Wes ran his palm down Justin's smooth thigh, gripped his ass as he thrust in, and in, and in?

Wes could take the heat, the hate. Probably. Hopefully. He already knew the blistering tirades he got from the fumbles and the dropped passes, the missed downs, and he could extrapolate, in a fuzzy way, what that would sound like, look like, if the shouts and curses and death threats, the excoriations to choke on his own jock, drive himself off a bridge, quit the game and wrap his lips around his tailpipe were focused, instead, on how he wasn't a man, he was a faggot, he deserved to die—

Again, he hurled, grabbing the garbage can and curling around it, his stomach screaming.

Once, when Wes was still in high school, a fan had stalked one of the university's quarterbacks. He'd staked out the quarterback's truck at the stadium and waited for him after practice, enraged at how he'd thrown two interceptions in the last game, had blown the lead in the third quarter. The game had been lost to his most hated team, the alma mater of his buddy, who went on to beat him in that week's betting pool.

The fan got up in the quarterback's face, screaming, bellowing, losing his fucking mind. The offensive line came out of the stadium a few minutes behind the quarterback, just in time to see the knife flash.

By the time the linemen got there, the quarterback was on the ground with two punctured lungs and an eviscerated belly bleeding all over the pavement, and his attacker was on the run. Three linemen turned the attacker into a smear on the asphalt, and the police nearly had to shovel his broken body into the ambulance when they finally arrived.

When the quarterback had doubled over, trying to protect himself, the blade had slid into his back and nicked his spine. Paralyzed him from the waist down. All that, because someone didn't like the passes he'd thrown. Because he'd lost fifty bucks on a bet over beer and chicken wings.

What if someone came after Justin? What if Wes loving Justin put Justin's life at risk?

They will turn your life upside down. Are you ready?

He might be able to say yes, but was it fair to Justin to turn *his* life upside down—or worse? Subject him to the capricious whims of football fans, the wild swings of poisonous love and vitriol? Subject him to violence?

What would happen to the man he loved?

Was he willing to risk Justin's life to find out?

God, how selfish was he, even considering it? No, *never*. He could never, ever risk Justin's life, not for football. Hell, he should quit today, march back into Coach's office and tell him thanks but no thanks, he could take the captaincy and shove it, Wes was cleaning out his locker and going home. He wasn't going to play anymore, because he wasn't going to take the risk of the world finding out that—

That he loved Justin.

Swans fluttered on the disquiet waters of his soul, cast ripples across the hollows of his heart. *What price are you willing to pay for your love?* If he didn't play football, his scholarship was gone. If his scholarship was gone, he wouldn't even have enough money to fill up his gas tank to drive back to West Texas. He'd be homeless before the day was over, the money in his pocket—about four dollars and three euros—all he had to his name. And a credit card bill for two grand looming, thanks to Paris and the best date he'd ever been on.

He'd have nothing. Less than nothing. No future. No hope. Everything he'd worked for since he was six years old, gone.

Was three perfect weeks with the man of his dreams enough to outweigh the length and breadth of his lifelong goals? Did loving Justin replace the tears in his dad's eyes when he opened his scholarship letter? His mama had died knowing that when he graduated, football would take him out of their little town, bring him to the wide world, open all his doors. Did loving one man wipe away everyone's hopes for him?

What did he want?

He was made to love the white swan.

Justin. He wanted Justin.

But he couldn't. He couldn't. Not like this. Not with the risks. Not with reporters and NFL scouts and obsessed stalkers and wheelbarrows full of toxic hate. Not with everything, every single thing in his life, on the line.

You can bring all these boys with you, all the way to glory.

Wes squeezed his hands into fists and dug his forehead against the metal rim of the garbage can. Glory had never been what he wanted. He wanted a future. He wanted to see his dad smile as Wes walked across that stage and accepted his college diploma. He wanted to love a man and be loved in return.

He couldn't have what he wanted. Not in this lifetime, it seemed. His shoulders were only large enough to carry everyone else's dreams, not his own. Not in his broken world.

You can have everything you ever dreamed of.

No, he couldn't. Maybe everyone else could. Maybe everyone else could realize their dreams of the NFL, could reach for those elusive stars and grab the future, but Wes had already had a taste of his dreams come true. He'd already held everything he'd ever wanted in his two hands.

Maybe Paris was all he'd ever have. Maybe that was it. One moment in time. One study abroad. One summer love.

Now he had to return to reality. Obligations. Responsibilities. Ties that bound him to others, to something bigger than the cries of his heart. The hunger of his soul.

Justin… I love you.

And I'm so, so sorry.

He dragged himself to his feet and wiped the back of his arm across his mouth. Stuck his hat back on his head and punched the elevator call button. Waited, tapping his foot, forcing his mind to go blank. Blank as the hum of the starting line, the whoosh of his own breath, inhaling, exhaling. Forced the world to narrow until all he could see was the rectangle of the world through his helmet and the bars of his face guard.

He was back in his truck, pointed west on the highway, when the tears started to fall.

CHAPTER EIGHT

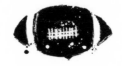

JUSTIN FLOATED THROUGH HIS PARENTS' house, sipping a margarita from the pitcher his mom had made for the three of them. His parents were in the backyard, sunning themselves by the pool, laughing as they grew steadily more tipsy. The sun was sinking through the afternoon sky, and Justin was counting each degree it fell, adding up the minutes like sand in an hourglass. Wes would be back at campus by now. Meeting with his coach. Or finishing up. Justin had no idea how long football meetings went. His entire experience with football coaches was based on Hollywood and highlights from ESPN, middle-aged men bellowing on the sidelines as they mouthed f-bombs on live TV.

Wes would be texting him again any minute.

They'd traded texts when Wes was in New York and Justin was still waiting for his luggage. Wes was exhausted and grumpy, but he'd sent Justin a selfie from his gate, valiantly trying to smile through his baggy eyes and his stubble. *Back on the same continent,* he'd texted, followed by a smiley face.

Just hearing from Wes had been enough to turn his mood around. They were going to see each other again, and soon. He clung to that.

His parents were both wide-eyed and almost speechless when they met him at Dallas–Fort Worth airport. He'd wrapped them both in a giant hug, beaming, joyous about life and the world, about the overcrowded arrivals lounge, about the smell of dirty diapers, about the screaming children at the luggage carousel. He loved Wes, and maybe Wes might love him, too.

When they stopped to eat on the way home, he'd babbled about the trip, about Paris, about the sights and the university and how wonderful it all was. He'd kept Wes out of it, but his dad had given him a wink as he dipped a chip into the queso they were sharing and said, "And tell us about who you met." His mother had slapped his dad's arm and turned away, hiding her face as she wiped her lips.

He'd sucked his frozen margarita dry, cheeks burning, but he was saved by the server arriving with their lunch.

All afternoon, he'd daydreamed of Wes, of when he'd see him again. He'd dumped his laundry from Paris in the wash and mentally cataloged which shirts to repack, what to wear when he went to Wes's ranch. He wanted to look good for Wes, but also like he belonged. Like he could be a rancher's man, wrestle with the elements, hold his own out on the range. Whatever that meant. He'd need more plaid, probably. Maybe better boots. Ropers, like Wes had. Maybe even a, God forbid, cowboy hat.

He dipped his toes in the pool with his parents and listened to his mom talk about her church group. Listened to his dad describe how he'd closed his last deal and brought home enough of a bonus that they were planning their own Paris trip over Thanksgiving. His parents asked him about classes, about his major. What junior year looked like. It was nice, being happy. Seeing his parents happy, too.

Was this what it was like, when you were just… happy with everything? With life?

Justin checked his watch again. Another five minutes had passed. He'd hear from Wes soon. They'd text, and then maybe he'd call as Wes headed for home. They could while away the hours of his long drive on the phone, Justin flat on his back on his childhood bed, staring at the ceiling, his heart pitter-pattering.

His cell phone vibrated, and Justin grinned. He felt the shiver down his spine and danced as he set down his margarita, ice clinking in the glass. His mom's laugh filtered through the screen door. Salt dusted the back of his hand. Sunlight rippled through the kitchen, casting lazy beams over the counters and the walls.

He swiped his screen on and saw Wes's number. Bit his lip and closed his eyes for a moment before pulling up the text. Had Wes made first string? Would Justin be at every game in the fall, wearing Wes's number? Maybe he'd bring his dad to the games. Maybe this was something they could do together. His dad would love Wes, maybe even more than he loved the thought of the bottle blonde cheerleader–slash–sales account manager Justin was supposed to marry. He pictured Wes and his dad tossing a football in the backyard, imagined him bringing them both beers. Kissing Wes, wrapping his arm around Wes's waist. Saw his dad smile at them both.

I'm sorry, his phone screen said.

He kept reading.

He didn't understand.

He dropped the phone. It clattered to the counter, where it slipped on salt crystals and spun, off-kilter.

He needed to breathe, but he couldn't. The words on the screen swam together, blurring into hieroglyphs, algebra formulas he couldn't comprehend. They didn't make sense. Surely they didn't mean what they said.

I'm sorry. I can't do this. Forget you know me. I'm sorry.

Justin's legs buckled, and he sank to the floor, his fingers gripping the granite countertop as he leaned his head against his mother's polished oak cabinets. He smelled her lemon polish, felt the wood grain against his cheeks.

When he was a boy, he'd had a nightmare that he was being

chased by a monster. He was so scared, so terrified that when the monster grabbed him and bit him in half, his vocal cords had been frozen. He'd been screaming and sobbing, but his throat hadn't worked and he hadn't been able to cry out.

Now, with lemon polish in his nose and tequila on his lips, he tried to put sound to the way his heart was tearing in two, the way his soul was shredding down the center.

The screen door slid open behind him. "Justin?" his dad asked. "Justin, what happened?"

I can't do this. Forget you know me.

He buried his face in his palms and tried to scream. Not a single sound came out.

RAIN FELL. He watched the drops smash into the pool, watched ripples form and crash against each other. He couldn't cry anymore, so the world was crying for him, building an external lake of his sorrows. *Thanks, God. Did me a solid on that one.*

Summer rains were sticky things, but they cleared the air, beat the dust to the ground before evaporating into a sweat-slick weight that hung chest-high. Justin hadn't been able to take a deep breath for weeks now. What was another couple of days?

Footsteps splashed across the patio, and his dad ducked under the awning that covered the pool deck. He rubbed his hand through his wet hair, soaked from the ten-foot run from their back door. Justin had come out here be alone, but apparently, his dad had other plans.

"Beer?" A longneck, offered as an opening gambit. Justin hadn't said more than a dozen words to his mom or dad since he'd gotten the text and turned off his phone. He'd spent a week facedown in his bed. For all that, there was a restless energy humming through him as he studied the debris of his broken dreams, the ruins of the fantasies he'd built for him and Wes. The summer they'd planned to share. Fall, and how they promised to try. And what came after. Ever after, even.

He had no idea what to do now. No idea what to think. His thoughts chased themselves endlessly as he berated himself for thinking he and Wes were more than what they'd been all along. What had he done? Taken a study-abroad fling and turned it into dreams of wedding bells?

But what about that kiss at the airport? That had meant something. He'd felt it. That had been a promise, Wes giving Justin something he could hold on to, that he could remember.

No. That kiss had been a goodbye. It had been all the things Wes had been too afraid—too cowardly—to say to Justin's face.

Wes Van de Hoek, now one of the nation's top five college ball players. Justin had wandered into the living room as his dad watched ESPN the night before, and he'd ended up leaning against the couch through the Division I-A news and Southeastern Conference highlights. There was Texas's football team, looping on SportsCenter. There was the quarterback—he knew his name now: Colton Hall. Knew he was Wes's best friend. Knew he ate a box of Froot Loops a day and ran naked across a stadium on a bet to win a PlayStation once.

And then there was jersey number 87, rushing down the field. Justin had walked out of the living room, right as his dad asked him to sit and join him.

Sometime in the next two weeks, a package would arrive on his porch from the university's team store. Inside would be the 87 jersey Justin had ordered. He'd paid extra to have the back lettered, something flirty that could also be explained away. <3 *Van de Hoek*. If he hadn't been so cute about it, he could have given the jersey to his dad. Now he'd just throw it away.

"Justin…" His dad took his silence as a kind of acceptance, a tacit agreement that he could stay. He threw himself onto the chaise lounge beside Justin, sighing as he sank into the cushion. "Weather sucks," he grumbled.

Justin took the beer from his dad. Sipped. It tasted like nothing, but the bubbles reminded him of champagne, and Paris, and splitting a bottle after the ballet. His cowboy at the opera, holding Justin when he tried to hide how he was crying in the fourth act. *I loved you so much that night.*

Every night, every day, all the little ways he'd fallen in love with Wes, again and again and again—

"I, uh. I thought I'd be doing this after your first girl broke your heart."

Weeks without talking, and that's what his dad was going to open with? Justin sent him a scathing stare. Set down the beer and started to push himself up.

"No, wait, Justin. Please. Stay. I'm trying. I have no idea what to do, but I want to help. If this was a girl situation, I'd do what I did with my friends when we got our hearts broken. Get drunk, be stupid, cry it out. Not be alone. I don't know what you need, and I don't know what you want, but if I can help… I want to."

Justin blinked. That might have been more words from his dad at once than he'd heard in years. His gaze drifted to his dad, soaking wet from the rain, sitting beside him, holding out his hand and asking him to stay.

His dad didn't have to be here.

He picked up his beer and chugged, upending half the bottle down his throat. His dad sighed, a tired smile tugging up one side of his face. "College is teaching you all kinds of things."

He could leave. Or he could stay, let his dad try to talk to him, see what wisdom he would try to shovel into Justin. Sighing, Justin sank into the lounge. "I'm going to need more beer if you want to get drunk and stupid."

"I've got more inside." His dad's smile faded. "I bought some for the two of us. Your mom is at a church night with her friends."

"And you stayed to get drunk with your son?"

"I stayed to talk to you."

"So talk, Dad. What do you want to say to me? How I need to

get over it? How I've been moping for a month, and what good has it gotten me? How I'm being ridiculous? That it was only three weeks?"

Silence. Justin gnashed his teeth. Glared up at the awning.

"I knew I wanted to marry your mother five days after I met her." His dad held up his hand, fingers spread. "Five days. I saw her every day for a week, and I knew. She was the woman I wanted to spend the rest of my life with. The woman I wanted to have children with."

Justin squirmed. His eyes slid to the pool, to the raindrops. They'd wanted children, and all they got was him. Something about the pregnancy. His mom couldn't have any more children after him. Sometimes he wondered, if she could go back, have the chance to wipe him away, would she? Would she say *No, not this one, I'll try again next month*? Would another egg and sperm have created an easier, less complicated child? Who led a less compli-cated life?

"I'm not going to tell you that you need to get over something that lasted three weeks, not if it meant as much to you as it did. I saw you happier than you've ever been. Never, not once, have you smiled at us like you did at the airport. Or said that many words to us in one afternoon. Not since you were eight years old. Whatever happened… Jesus, Justin, you were happy. And I'm fucking sorry that you're not now."

"Dad…"

"Here." His dad passed him his nearly full beer bottle. "I'll get more."

He took a sip, and the bubbles, the goddamn bubbles burst inside him, destroying the dam he'd erected over his heart. Memories crashed through him, soaked with champagne and tears. He set the bottle down too hard, nearly toppling it. Nearly spat out the beer, and the bubbles, and the memories.

"That's how it felt in Paris," he choked out. "Like what you said about Mom. It felt like I'd met the guy I was supposed to be with forever. I guess he didn't feel the same way."

"His loss," his dad grumbled, glowering at the rain. "That's his damn loss. If this asshole used you and then dumped you—"

"He didn't use me, Dad. We were…" He swallowed. "I loved him. And I thought he loved me, too."

"What happened?" His dad grabbed Justin's beer bottle and rolled it between his palms, watching the soggy label come apart. "You never said what happened."

Everything was wonderful and then everything was terrible. His parents had had to uncover the clues themselves, pick apart his one-word answers and his weeks-long despondency to put the pieces together. "He told me to forget him." *Forget you know me. I can't do this.*

His dad cursed. Glared at the bottle. "Was he French? Someone you met over there?"

Justin shook his head. *You would love him, Dad. You'd be so proud of me if I brought him home. Maybe it would be weird for a minute, but you'd get over it, because you'd love Wes. He'd be like the son you always wanted. I could have brought him to you, if only.* He made a noise, something between a grunt and a hiccup. Not a yes. Not a no.

"I hope you never see him again."

Justin neck cracked, he looked up so fast, staring at his dad with wide eyes.

"I hope you never see him again, because I don't want him to hurt you any more." Justin's dad shook his head. "I hope he's gone forever. I hope he takes his bullshit and gets lost for good, because you deserve better than that. You do. Understand?"

They'd never spoken like this. His dad had never talked to him about the birds and the bees, or boyfriends, or who he liked and who liked him. His parents had never asked if he was going to prom in high school, much less who with. His mom hadn't wanted to hear about dances after he came out. She'd made a comment, once, about why he'd even go to homecoming if he wasn't going with a girl. For prom, he'd simply taken his suit over to his friend's and dressed there, then stumbled home before dawn, hungover and well fucked.

But when he got back, the porch light had been on for him. Would his dad, at least, have wanted to see him off to prom if Justin had given him the opportunity?

He chugged more beer, let it slide down his throat, let the bubbles pop like the memories inside him. Gone forever… until every Saturday, when number 87, the fifth-best player in the nation, took the field.

Gone forever, except for how Wes Van de Hoek was all over the school's website, the emails, the newsletters. His awards, his ranking, the NFL speculation. His position as team captain. SportsCenter highlights, ESPN reels. Replays, for fuck's sake, of Wes's games, analysis of Colton and Wes and their Brady-Gronkowski magic.

Gone forever, except for how he was everywhere.

Justin sat back and stared at the rain.

CHAPTER NINE

August

AFTER HAULING ten loads from his car to his new room, Justin was done. Most of his stuff was clothes, then sheets and towels, and finally the two boxes of decor he and his mom had bought together, their one mom-and-son date before he drove back to campus. She'd wanted a beach theme for his room after he told her, in no uncertain terms, he wouldn't be putting up anything that had to do with cowboys. Or any mementos from Paris.

He drove down the block and around the corner from his new home, an old Victorian renovated into single-room apartments rented out to students. He'd moved to West Campus, a quaint enclave off the university grounds, full of old homes and narrow, twisty streets. The neighborhood had been the city's original suburb, 150 years ago, and now it was an urban retreat. He parallel parked on a side street beneath the leafy branches of a thick cottonwood. His sedan would be covered in bird shit by morning, but it wouldn't be ten thousand degrees when he got inside, and that was worth more to him than the paint job was.

Justin hauled himself out of the car and sighed. Even here,

buried in West Campus, he could still see the stadium. There was no escaping the double-decker, hundred-thousand-seat monstrosity. It was visible from every corner of campus, every building, as if the stadium were the university's crown jewel. Who was he kidding? It was. How could anyone ever forget that they went to a football school?

And that Wes Van de Hoek was the star footballer on campus.

Wes—a close-up of his focused expression behind his face mask, him running downfield with the ball in his arms, him leaping to catch a pass one-handed—was splashed on every building, every banner that fluttered from the campus light posts, and screamed from every billboard advertising student tickets to the games.

Gone forever, but everywhere.

Justin turned his back on the stadium and locked his car, hitching his backpack on his shoulder. West Campus was a hive of activity, students moving in for fall semester. Cars and trucks jockeyed for position on the narrow streets, loitering outside houses as they dumped students and their belongings on the sidewalks. Justin had never lived in this neighborhood before. He'd lived in the dorms on Southside, the cheap apartment complexes that racked and stacked freshmen and sophomores four and six to a unit. Over the summer, he'd asked if his parents would be willing to chip in to help him live somewhere nicer, somewhere he could have a room of his own and where he wouldn't have to negotiate homophobia and derision from roommates. He hadn't even finished asking before his dad said yes, of course, absolutely.

Here he was, moving into the room he'd rented in a powder-blue Victorian, surrounded by oaks and cottonwoods, a seven-minute walk from campus. Sure, it had a view of the stadium, but where could he go around here that didn't? Where could he go where he couldn't see Wes's face?

Nowhere, that's where. He'd deal. Wes wasn't the only man who would break his heart.

"Dude, Coach is gonna fuck me up at this pace."

"I need to sleep for a week."

"I don't even want to go to the party. I just wanna crawl into bed and cry."

Deep voices burrowed under Justin's skin, coming from behind him. He picked apart the language, the cadence, the vocabulary. Jocks. Of course. And what sport was playing now? Who would be complaining about preseason training?

Football players.

He didn't want to look, but he had to. He turned, tossing a casual glance over his shoulder and peeking over the rim of his sunglasses at the trio of footballers—huge, hulking men with solid biceps, cut triceps, traps like triangles growing from their necks—dressed in sleeveless shirts and athletic shorts, each carrying a water bottle and a duffel bag. One was white, a country boy like Wes, his ball cap flipped backward and his pale shoulders burned red. One was Hispanic, almost as large as Wes was, but heftier. More fluff, less definition. And the third man was Black. Tall, lithe, and strong, all hard muscles cut like diamonds.

Wes's teammates. Maybe even his friends.

Justin cut across the street, ducking between two parked trucks—one absolutely disgusting, more rust than actual vehicle—and juggling his room key between his fingers. He glared, watching the three men amble up the sidewalk in the shade. Why were they here? Where were they going? Why the fuck couldn't he be free of reminders? He jogged up his house's front steps, then stepped back to hold the door for one of his new housemates heading out, buried in a text conversation on her phone.

The footballers turned up the front stoop of the house directly across the street, the hunter green one with the gingerbread trim. They trudged up the stairs and threw themselves across the wide front porch, flopping into shredded wicker chairs and plastic pool loungers. They dumped their duffels and sucked at their water bottles, leaning back like they were there to stay.

Oh no. Oh fuck. No, no way.

He did not move to the other side of campus only to live across the goddamn street from football players. No fucking way.

Justin bulldozed his way inside and up the stairs, practically flattening a housemate's family as he raced to his room. His was on the third floor, a ten-by-ten square with a window that overlooked the west-side fire escape. These homes were technically apartment buildings now, and they had to have emergency exits on each floor. They were rickety add-ons, and most everyone used them as window porches. Justin had a tiny iron platform outside his window, and if he wiggled out to it, he could spy on the house across the street.

Not that he wanted to. At all.

He dumped his backpack on his unmade bed and climbed out the window. Other students were hanging out on their fire escapes, too, sitting cross-legged and drinking beer. One had hung string lights around the railing, even put a potted plant in the corner. Hopefully there'd never be a fire.

Justin grabbed the railing and peered down the block. There was the stadium, rising above all the thick, leafy trees. There was the street, crowded with cars and families dropping off their kids and their toasters and their papasan chairs. And there were the footballers, lounging on the front porch of the house across the street. One rose from his sprawl, and Justin watched him disappear through the screen door and come out with three beer bottles.

Fuck. They did live there.

Groaning, Justin shook the railing of the fire escape like he wished he could shake one of the players. Now he'd have to listen to football bullshit all semester. They would definitely be throwing parties, and there'd be groupies on the block. They'd probably have their football bullshit strewn on the street and in the yard, pads and helmets and balls and whatever crap.

He couldn't ever get away from this. Not from the stadium, and not from the game, and not from Wes.

If not for how restrictive his major was, he'd transfer. Transferring from nursing program to nursing program was next to impossible. He'd have to repeat a year just to satisfy the program's residency requirement. Pushing back his degree by a full year was out of the question. No, he could buck up and deal. Wes didn't define his life. Wes wasn't going to run him off, chase him away from his school or his future plans. Wes, and whatever game he'd played with Justin's heart, wasn't going to ruin *anything*.

A man turned at the corner. Started walking up the block.

From the distance, he was just a dark shape. Someone large—gigantic, really. Defined muscles bursting out of a shirt with the sleeves cut off. He wore a backward ball cap and athletic shorts, carried a duffel over his shoulder and three binders in his arms. He stared at the ground as he walked, his shoulders slumped forward like he had the weight of the world bowing his back. Something about him...

Justin threw himself back from the fire escape until his ass hit the opposite rail.

Wes.

He looked *terrible*.

He walked like a zombie, shuffling like it hurt to lift his legs. He hadn't shaved in Justin didn't know how long. Too long. He'd gone from sexy stubble to wild, unkempt overgrowth. He didn't give off that warm, comfortable, approachable vibe anymore. He was pure strength, raw power, bulging muscles cutting hard edges into his arms, his legs, the glimpse of his abs and obliques Justin saw through his shirt's baggy armholes.

The closer he came, the worse he looked. His eyes were sunken and hollow, black holes in his gaunt face. He looked exhausted. Beyond tired. Like death, not just a nap, was what he needed.

The footballers on the porch called out to him, waving and raising their beer bottles. He nodded to them, then trudged up the same porch steps. One of the players kicked a patio chair toward him, offering him a seat.

Wes shook his head and disappeared inside the house.

Oh no. No no no.

Every one of Justin's bold, strong thoughts fled. It was easy to be strong when he was alone, when he was imagining how, the next time he saw Wes, he'd give him a piece of his mind. How he'd read him the riot act and then leave him broken and miserable as Wes remembered how wonderful Paris had been. How he'd cut Wes with his words, leave him shattered like Wes had shattered him, leave him clinging to the floor and sobbing like he'd left Justin. He'd rehearsed his lines in the shower ten thousand times. He'd imagined himself radiant and gorgeous, maybe with a new man on his arm, looking Wes up and down and saying, "Who?"

Justin sank to his heels, clinging to the railing as he watched the house across the street. Wes's house. Fuck. Fuck.

He bit down on his lip, trying to funnel the pain in his heart to a physical sensation that would ground him. He wanted to be strong, but damn it, he wasn't. He still cried himself to sleep some nights. He still asked *Why* and *What happened* and how did they go from *back on the same continent* and smiley faces to *I can't do this. Forget you know me* in the space of a few hours.

It was football, Justin knew. It was the team. It was Wes making first string. But knowing that didn't change how much it hurt to be tossed aside—not even a second choice, but a nonchoice. Nothing. All those pretty words in Paris, all those promises made over champagne and under the Eiffel Tower. None of it meant anything. None of it was real. Wes was always going to come back and be the footballer, the big man on campus.

And no big man on campus sucked dick. Ever.

Justin wanted to be happy for Wes. Wes had worked hard for

what he'd earned. He'd seized his dreams and made them come true through sheer grit. He was going to be phenomenal. The trajectory of his life was straight for the stars.

It was hard to be happy for Wes, though, when his own heart was so broken. When they'd had hopes and dreams and had started to make tentative promises to each other. *I would have come to every game to cheer you on if you asked me to.*

Fuck. What would his dad say? Well, if he knew Wes Van de Hoek lived across the street, he'd probably ask Justin to go get an autograph for him. But if he knew that the man who broke Justin's heart, who left him a broken mess all summer, was now fifty feet away…

He'd drive down and help Justin pack his shit, move him out, move him anywhere else. And then burn Wes's jersey. In the middle of the street, so Wes could see.

A light winked on in an upstairs bedroom in Wes's house. There were no curtains in the window, and the blinds were raised lopsidedly. Someone hauled the sash upward. A shape appeared: first broad, wide hands, taped at the knuckles. A chest. A wide, square neck and a defined jaw. A grim, glum face.

Wes.

Wes leaned into the open window frame, one arm over his head and resting on the glass. He stared blankly at the street, letting the wind ruffle his T-shirt.

It wasn't enough to live across the street. Justin had to see Wes from his own bedroom?

Maybe he should call his dad. He hadn't unpacked yet. He could move out today.

At least Wes hadn't seen him. And Wes wasn't looking for him, either. Why would he be? Justin was one face among a hundred thousand. He was forgettable, ignorable. He wasn't the great Wes Van de Hoek, celebrated across the entire freaking state of Texas, it seemed. He'd started seeing Wes's face on billboards an hour outside of Dallas.

A trio of girls dressed in spaghetti strap tanks and bandana-tied halter tops sauntered up the street, long, tanned legs gleaming beneath short shorts. The football players on the porch perked up, waving to the girls, and they waved back, called out *Hello*s and *Heys*. One shielded her eyes and looked up at Wes's open window. "Hey, big guy," she called. "How's it hanging?"

Justin's fingers dug into the iron railing hard enough to hurt.

Wes waved, then backed away from the window. The girls bounced up the front steps of the jock house, and they joined the players on the porch for a beer before all six moved inside.

Wes's window was a black hole, and no matter how hard Justin willed it, Wes never reappeared.

Justin stayed on the fire escape for hours, watching, waiting, just in case.

CHAPTER TEN

LAUGHTER BUBBLED UP FROM DOWNSTAIRS. Wes heard his friends' deep guffaws, their loud smack talk. Heard the higher-pitched giggles and cheers from the girls who'd come by. Sandy and Lisa and Julie were sweet, and more than a few of the guys on the team were crushing hard on their All-American charm. They were smart and cute and funny and kind. Everything a Texas boy should want.

He rolled onto his side and stared at the wall next to his bed, at the pictures he'd tacked up. Over the summer, when it was just him in the house, he'd used the printer they'd all chipped in for to print out some generic pictures of Paris he'd found online. The Eiffel Tower, of course. The Seine. The market he and Justin had gone to, where he'd held Justin's hand. The opera house, lit up at night. He'd taped the prints to the wall next to his bed and even put up the old print of the cowboy in front of the Eiffel Tower. When he lay on his side, Paris was all he could see.

The pictures stabbed him through the desiccated remains of his heart, each and every time.

It still hurt so horribly. Still felt like he'd taken a chain saw to his own chest, like he'd carved himself open and torn his insides out. It felt like he'd have that hollow, aching feeling in his chest forever.

His hand drifted under his pillow and squeezed the crumpled photo that lived there. He eyed his closed door, then pulled the photo out and unfolded it. Crease lines and crumples from where he'd balled the photo up in his fist carved white cracks and zigzag lines across Paris's golden glow. The setting sun that night had scattered wildflowers across the evening sky, all the colors of West Texas's fragile blooms above their heads. The Eiffel Tower was like a Monet on fire, glittering even without a single light turned on. In front of the tower, he and Justin mugged for the camera, Wes smiling like he'd found the secret ingredient to pure joy, Justin pretending to look fierce as he wore Wes's cowboy hat. He was gazing at Justin, and it was all right there on his face. How in love he was with the man he'd wrapped his arm around for the first time. How he was thinking about kissing him in a few hours. How he was hoping Justin might be the one.

The colors were blurred where his tears had fallen and soaked through the paper. How many nights had he balled up the picture and sworn he'd throw it away, only to drag it back to his face and whisper Justin's name? He didn't even pretend to throw it away anymore. No, now it lived beneath his pillow, where he held it every night.

Footsteps bounded up the old wooden stairs, and he had just enough time to hide the photo again before his best friend shoved open his bedroom door.

"Dude," Colton said, his eyes raking over Wes. "Come downstairs. The girls are here. We're playing foosball."

He'd heard the frantic spins of the levers, the crack of plastic against plastic. The wild cheers and the stomping of feet. Twelve football players living in an old house was a recipe for destruction. They were going to bust through the floors one day, or the walls were going to fall flat like they were living in a cartoon. And he'd be left in his bed, still curled on his side, still feeling like he wanted to die.

"I'm good," he grunted.

"Dude." Colton slipped into the room. He left the door open, though, so this wasn't going to be when he finally called Wes out. No, this was just one of his regular drive-bys of concern, where he glared and shuffled his feet and then ultimately went back to the girls and the guys and the foosball and the beer. "C'mon, man. You gotta get out of your room sometime."

Wes flopped to his back and sighed. "I'm tired. I'm not feeling it."

Colton gnawed on his lip. He shifted his weight left and right, fingers clenching around empty air like he was searching for the football. Colton was the quarterback, Wes's quarterback, his blood brother. His football soulmate. They could communicate on the field like they were telepathically connected, read every twitch and flinch and wriggle of muscle like they were reading novels about each other in less than a heartbeat.

Why couldn't Colton read him now?

"You've been slamming it in practice," Colton said. "And you're in the gym all the time. I heard the trainer tell you to take it easy. You went beast mode over the summer. Your max lift is higher than the linemen now. How much did you put on— another ten pounds? Fifteen?"

Another sixteen pounds of muscle.

The only time Wes wasn't thinking about Justin was when he was on the field or pumping iron, pounding out reps in the gym until everything in his body hurt as much as his heart.

"You're not taking enough recovery days." Colton shook his head. Glared out the window overlooking the street. One leg jittered, heel bouncing. He was still in his post-practice uniform of cutoff T-shirt, the team's faded logo across his chest, and baggy athletic shorts. He had his ball cap on backward, plunked down after his shower in the locker room. Beneath the brim, the ends of his hair curled over his neck.

"Yeah, so, I'm trying to recover now."

Colton gave him a long look, like he was an idiot for thinking Colton was an idiot. Then he sighed. Lifted his cap and ran his fingers through his long, damp strands. "Whatever, man. Something's going on. I'm not a dumbass. You don't wanna talk about it right now? That's cool. But you're not doing yourself any favors, Captain."

Captain. Colton had started calling him Captain over the summer, after the announcement was made. Was he jealous? Quarterbacks were often captains. Colton was a damn good quarterback, one of the best in the NCAA. Most college quarterbacks were system quarterbacks, and they managed run-and-shoot offenses only. ESPN's archives were littered with profiles of college quarterbacks who seemed destined for greatness, only to collapse when they couldn't adapt to the NFL. Couldn't adjust to the speed, the power. Couldn't take on a new system, adapt to different play styles. Has-been quarterbacks were a dime a dozen.

Great ones, like Colton, were rare. Colton had taken on all the great offensive styles. Air Coryell, Erhardt-Perkins, West Coast. He could run and shoot, and he could flip the script, move to timed option routes or concept plays. He kept defenses not just on their toes but deep in their guts, stressing and spreading the defensive line and the linebackers until they collapsed.

So why wasn't Colton captain? Why wasn't his face everywhere on campus? Why was it Wes's life that had been turned upside down, inside out?

He stared at the ceiling. Hot tears flooded the surface of his eyes. If he didn't move, didn't blink, they'd evaporate.

Colton sighed. "You wanna rest? Okay. Christ, you need it. But we're gonna have to talk about this. You're worrying me."

Going to have to talk about what? How he'd fallen in love? How he'd met the man he wanted to spend forever with? He *loved*

Justin, loved him so damn much, but he'd destroyed what they had, and now there was nothing left. He didn't even feel human anymore. Didn't feel like he could ever love again—or make love again. He'd never find another guy as captivating and wonderful and alive as Justin, someone who would feed ducks with him, who'd listen to him talk about the ranch, who could teach him about modern art and ballet, and who would smile when Wes tickled his cheek with a sprig of lavender and baby's breath.

Fuck. His tears spilled over, racing down his temples. His pillow was half salt by this point, weighed down with endless nights of crying. He didn't move. Tried not to breathe. Maybe Colton wouldn't notice.

Of course, Colton did. "Wes…" Now he did shut the door, and he sagged back against it, head tipped so he, too, was staring at the ceiling. "Something happened over the summer."

It wasn't a question. Wes didn't have to answer. He sniffed. Tried to swallow his snot.

"She really broke your heart, didn't she?"

It wasn't Colton's fault he missed the mark. He had no idea that Wes was gay. It wasn't even in the realm of his possibilities for him. Wes had gone to all the parties, flirted with all the girls. He'd never dated, but the rest of the team chalked that up to his shyness, his aw-shucks charm, his old-school style of politeness. There'd never been even a hint of suspicion, not a single question. It would have been easier, maybe, if there had been.

And anyway, if Colton were faced with a choice—football or a girl—he wouldn't have even blinked before he dumped the girl. Football was Colton's soul in a way it wasn't quite Wes's. Colton wanted the lights and the stadium and the NFL. Wes… The path was there, open and waiting for him, but he wasn't sure if he wanted to take it. But who turned down an easy jog to the NFL?

It was the one rough edge between him and Colton, when they were usually smooth as silk together.

"I just need some time," Wes choked out. Time. He'd need the rest of his life at this rate. The pain was no less excruciating—no less eviscerating—today than it was the day he'd sent those texts to Justin. He hadn't moved on, hadn't moved forward. Not one inch.

"Well, screw everyone else," Colton said. "I have the new Madden. Why don't I bring it in here? We can play."

Wes didn't have a TV or any kind of video game system in his room. He lived like a monk, with a bed, a desk, and his backpack, his books piled on the floor or lined up against the walls. He had an ancient laptop from the librarian at his high school, a gift when he graduated. It took five minutes to boot up.

Why wouldn't he go to the NFL? He'd never have to worry about money again. He could buy a new laptop, a new truck. Hell, he could buy new laptops for every kid in his high school. A new truck for his dad. He could buy a nice headstone for his mom, too, something delicate and pretty, carved with a quote and some doves. Or a swan.

He was made to love the white swan.

Wes's breath hitched, but he scrubbed at his eyes. Forced himself to sit up. Colton was waiting for him, gnawing on his chapped lips as he stared at Wes's pile of textbooks. "Or I'll just hang," Colton said, shrugging. "We don't have to do anything."

It was when he did nothing that everything fell apart. When his memories flowed and the days and nights and the love he and Justin had shared rose to the surface. When everything was right there, so close he could feel it.

His memories gutted him, and every night he ended up on his side, fingertips tracing the printouts of Paris, Justin's photo balled in his tear-soaked fist.

He missed Justin so much.

"I'll go to your room. You don't need to haul your TV in here."

"I'm going downstairs to get a beer. You want?"

"Sure."

Colton grinned again and disappeared, thundering down the

stairs like the elephant he was. Wes heard him tell the guys he was going to hang with Wes, that they were going to chill out without the rest of the losers. The guys started heckling him, teasing Colton that all he was doing was going to watch practice tapes with Wes, that they were going to do some kind of woo-woo shit to increase their psychic bond. Or jack off together to Sports-Center. Wes clung to the railing at the second-floor landing, torn between laughing and crying. He missed his friends. He missed the man he used to be, before he knew about the man he could become when he was in love. He missed messing around and talking smack, falling into the corner of the sagging couch and letting the bullshit flow around him as he sucked down a beer. He missed everything about his old life.

But he missed Justin a thousand times more.

Colton reappeared, taking the steps two at a time with six beers clenched in his massive fingers and a bag of chips under one arm. He jerked his head down the hall, to his larger bedroom near the back. Wes had the smallest room—not even a bedroom, technically. It must've been a coat closet or a secretary's office way back when, but it was the right price and he didn't mind the small space. He didn't have anything to fill it with anyway.

Colton had a large room with a big king bed, a couch, a desk, and a flat-screen TV, and both an Xbox and a PlayStation. They flopped on the couch as Colton called up the game, and, for a few hours, Wes lost himself in digital football, in trying to beat Colton, the house Madden champ. For a few hours, at least, he could pretend to feel normal.

His cell phone alarm went off at ten p.m., though. He silenced the alarm and ended the game, then stood and stretched. "Gotta get to work."

Colton chugged his third beer, nodding. "Come back after if you want. I'm just gonna chill."

The rest of the gang downstairs had settled into watching movies and lounging around. The bass from whatever horror flick they were watching thrummed through the floorboards. Colton never said it, but he didn't like the slasher flick movie nights. He always found something else to do, found somewhere else to be. While Wes was working, he'd most likely bang around his room, play video games, flop on his bed. Be bored. Maybe pull up tapes to watch, like they'd heckled him about earlier.

Wes held out his fist for a bump. "Thanks." He wasn't necessarily feeling better, and maybe he never would, but the hours with Colton had been a distraction from the agony living inside him. And for that, he was grateful.

Colton smiled. "Anytime. Really. And, you know, if you wanna talk about it…"

Wes pulled open Colton's bedroom door. "Catch you later."

"Yeah, bro."

He changed into jeans and the least smelly T-shirt he could find, pulled on his boots, and grabbed his ball cap. He eyed his cowboy hat, sitting on top of his desk, but, like every other day, he left it behind. He caught a couple waves from the mess of his teammates flung across the mismatched couches and love seats and duct-taped recliners in the living room as he headed out the front door.

Wes shoved his hands in his pockets as he slouched down the block. He didn't have time for a steady job during the season, so he took whatever he could get. For now, that was unloading the late-night delivery truck at Daisy Lane, the quirky little café at the heart of West Campus, where slam poetry nights and third dates mixed with study groups and back-room video game competitions. Dance groups practiced on the front lawn under the oak tree, and every time there was a home game win, Daisy Lane turned into the West Campus block party headquarters. The celebrations spilled from the front and terraced back decks up and down the adjoining blocks and into the winding, tree-lined streets. Daisy Lane was open 24 hours a day and was always packed.

He nodded his hello to Miguel, the head cook, and then got to work hauling boxes and crates off the delivery truck and into the storeroom and the walk-in freezer. He carted gallons of fresh milk, tubs of ice cream, hundreds of pounds of flour. Eggs and chicken breasts, fresh vegetables, cartons of fruit. It was amazing how much one restaurant could serve.

He got forty bucks in cash when he was done, and two to-go containers filled with food. His dinner. A double portion of the famous pancakes, eggs, and bacon, and a grilled chicken breast with a salad. He ate both sitting alone on the back steps of the café, in the alley next to the delivery truck and the dumpster. After, he said thanks to Miguel, carried out the trash, washed his hands, and headed back to the house. His forty bucks would be split four ways: food, rent, school supplies, and a small deposit into his meager checking account so he could work on paying off that two-grand credit card balance. He'd barely made a dent in the bill. Who knew interest would rack up faster than he could pay?

Wes got back to the house in the wee hours of the morning. Even though the houses were lit up like beacons and gaggles of students littered the porches and front lawns, West Campus was a peaceful neighborhood. He waved to what felt like every group of guys and girls, nodded his thanks for wishes of a good season, tried to smile at girls who wolf whistled him and told him he'd kick ass. He walked past wide-eyed guys, hearing drifts of "Holy shit, that was Van de Hoek," "Never seen him in the flesh before," and "He's even bigger than he looks on TV."

In the middle of the quietest neighborhood, late at night, he was still recognized everywhere he went.

He closed his eyes. Exhaled. *Justin. You'd hate this so much.* He would hate the microscope, the constant attention. The pressure. Was Wes being polite enough? Was he representing the team, the university correctly? Would his mama be proud of how he walked and how he upheld the Van de Hoek name? If an NFL scout were watching, would he tick the yes or no box?

His life was not his own. Not anymore.

Wes trudged up his front steps, staring at the warped wood beneath his feet. The university flag flapped beside him, put there by Devon last season after one of their early wins. Practice cones littered the porch, mixing with empty beer cans and Nerf footballs, balled-up athletic tape and kicked-off running shoes.

He stilled.

Wes was used to being watched, to being judged and evaluated and measured on the field, off the field, in class, walking down the street. He felt eyeballs on him every day, all day long, deciding everything about him in a single instant.

But that moment, he felt a different kind of stare. A different weight to the gaze that slammed into the center of his back.

He turned. Gazed up and down the street.

Nothing, save for a guy and a girl making out against a car door, unwilling to say good night yet.

Why was his skin on fire, lit from the inside? Why did it feel like someone's eyes were tracing his shape against the glow of the porch light?

He looked up and down the block again before heading inside. He saw no one.

CLASSES STARTED TWO DAYS LATER, and despite Coach's heavy sighs and his cajoling, Wes stuck with his major. Coach looked at him like he was making the biggest mistake of his life. But his dad's tears and his mama's pride kept him on his path, kept him following the fragile dream he'd had since before the NCAA and the NFL dominated his life. College. Degree. Future.

He kept his French class, too. Even though just thinking in French made his chest ache, made his eyes burn and his throat clench, he kept the eight a.m. fourth-year French class on his schedule. The rest of the house was dead asleep, the snores loud enough to shake the walls, but Wes was up before dawn, restless. He jogged for forty-five minutes through the dewy West Campus morning and then showered, started all six coffee pots for the guys, and munched a bowl of cereal, three boiled eggs, two square slices of American cheese, and a protein shake, dutifully notating everything on Google Sheets for the team nutritionist. *Eat more calories*, the nutritionist said. He said the same thing every day. *Eat more.*

Pay me, he wanted to shout at the phone. *If I'm your best player, give me more to eat than just snacks at practice and protein powder to take home.* Colton spent a thousand dollars a week on food. Wes scrounged for every calorie he could find.

That was an old argument, and one he wasn't going to make a dent in. Wes poured a half cup of cream into his coffee, grabbed his backpack, and headed out the door.

Not many people signed up for an eight a.m. French class. There were seven other students, according to his registration, and when he walked in, he spotted six heads scattered at the tables around the room. Wes kept his head down as he slumped in a chair in the back, but he still heard the whispers of his name, saw the sidelong glances sent his way. Even the teacher beamed at him, starstruck.

Less than a minute before class started, the door swung open.

The remains of Wes's heart slammed to a halt.

Justin hurried in, his textbook and notebook in his hands and his eyes down as he headed to one of the empty tables. He slid in right in front of the professor, trying to be unobtrusive despite his last-minute arrival. He was wearing running tights and a baggy long-sleeve T-shirt, and his hair was disheveled. Wes watched him pull the top strands back into a ponytail. The sides were still shaved, but his hair hadn't been long enough to do that over the summer.

Jesus Christ, what was Justin doing in this class? Wes had picked it specifically because it was the worst possible time. He'd thought there was no possible way, if Justin was even going to continue with French, that he'd take this class.

And yet.

Wes slumped in his seat, pulling his ball cap as low over his face as he could. He stared at the table, at his lap, at his fingers as he worried the skin of his thumb. The professor's voice droned as he introduced himself and briefly went over the syllabus, which was already posted in the online class module, before asking everyone to introduce themselves. In French, of course.

Justin went first. He lifted his chin, squared his jaw, and said, in flawless French, his name and his major and where he was from. The professor asked if he had been on the stay-abroad trip over the summer. He had a note in his records indicating he had two students who had attended.

"*Oui*," Justin said, after a long pause. "*J'étais là.*"

"And we have another study-abroad student in this class." The professor, a geeky man built like a string bean, his head like a birthday balloon rising from his thin neck, beamed at Wes in the back corner. "*Monsieur Van de Hoek.*"

Wes saw Justin tense. Saw his spine go rigid and his shoulder blades seek each other, racing for the center of his back. Saw his jaw clench. Wes looked away.

"*S'il vous plaît, monsieur*," the professor said to him, still smiling. "*Racontez à la classe de votre voyage en France.*"

"It was, um."

"*En français, s'il vous plaît.*"

"*C'était bon*," he grunted. "*J'ai beaucoup appris.*"

Yeah, he'd learned a lot. He learned how gay he was. How deeply he could love a man.

Wes had been around guys his entire life, and never had he fallen for anyone like he'd fallen for Justin. He'd tried to tell himself the whole thing was just Paris, just summer, just study abroad. His mind playing tricks on him. The psychology of it all, being away from home. Away from responsibility.

Yeah, sure. Except he loved Justin, and that didn't stop because he wasn't in Paris anymore. He loved him, and he'd always love him.

Even if Justin was sitting ten feet away and projecting so much bitter hate from those rigid shoulders that the university could power the stadium with the force of his emotions.

The professor made it through the rest of the introductions, and then he asked everyone to partner up and to prepare five-minute presentations about what their partner did over the summer to share with the class. "*Oh, s'il vous plaît, Monsieur* Swanscott, *Monsieur* Van de Hoek? Since you both were in Paris over the summer, will you two be partners? You may share with the class what your experience was like and what you learned."

Justin wrenched his head around, staring at Wes like Wes was human garbage. Like he'd murdered Justin's family. Like he was beneath Justin's attention. Wes slumped in his chair. Flicked his pen against his notebook.

Neither of them moved, even though the rest of the class had already scooted their chairs together and started sharing their summer experiences. Wes heaved a sigh and grabbed his books. Justin would not be standing up and moving to join him. The earth would cool, the sun would burn itself out, and the black hole at the center of the galaxy would swallow their solar system before Justin came to Wes. He knew that much. He made his way forward instead, taking the farthest seat from Justin that he could.

"Hey," he mumbled. He stared at the tabletop. Dug his gaze into the plastic laminate. If he looked at Justin, he'd break down. Start begging Justin's forgiveness.

Justin said nothing.

"I can talk about the school, if you wanna talk about some of the extras that were offered," Wes mumbled. "We don't have to talk about anything else."

Silence.

Wes tapped his pen against his notebook. *Tap tap tap tap tap.* Eventually, he couldn't help it, and his eyes darted across the table, over Justin's hands, his arms, up to his face. He looked away again, as fast as he could.

Justin was about to snap his pen in two. His arms were shaking. And his face was set in stone, his lips twisted in a grimace, his pulse fluttering fast above the collar of his T-shirt. He glared at the whiteboard in front of the class.

Up close, Wes could see the sheen of sweat on his skin. The way his hair was slick. The dampness at his neck, a faint discoloration on his shirt. "Were you working out this morning?"

"Rehearsal," Justin ground out. He didn't look at Wes.

"Dance?" He'd looked up the university's dance program over the summer. Ballet, tap, jazz, ballroom, and modern dance. There was a competitive dance team for dance majors and a fun one for anyone who wanted to join.

Justin's jaw muscles bulged as he nodded, once. Strained silence thrummed between them, furious enough to shatter crystal. Wes scratched the back of his neck. "Are you... okay?" He finally whispered.

He could practically hear the creak of Justin's vertebrae, the screech of bone on bone as Justin twisted, turning the full force of his vicious stare from the whiteboard to Wes. He didn't blink. "I'm fine."

Fine. Like a nuclear meltdown was fine. Like the sun about to go supernova was fine. There was so much raw fury in Justin's eyes it made Wes's guts clench.

I'm not fine. I'm very, very not okay. But Wes swallowed. Nodded. *Tap tap tap tap tap.*

"Congratulations." Justin spoke like the words were poison. "Starting tight end. You should be very proud. I know how hard you worked for this." Empty words. An empty voice. "You got everything you wanted."

Wes shrugged. *I lost what I wanted more than anything in the world.* No, he hadn't lost it. He'd thrown it away. He'd destroyed it. He'd destroyed them. He knew exactly who was to blame.

"I never knew you lived in West Campus."

Tap tap tap tap— Wes stilled.

Justin bent the pen in his hands back and forth, back and forth. His lips curved in an ugly grimace. "I used to live on Southside. But I had such shit experiences with roommates that I decided to rent a room in a house this year. Did you know, single rooms in houses are nearly all on West Campus?"

It was Wes's turn to grasp his pen hard enough to break it. "You live on West Campus?"

"I live on Opal Street."

His street. His narrow five-hundred-foot-long street in the middle of West Campus. There were four houses on one side, five on the other. Justin must live within feet of him. The other night came roaring back, the night he'd felt eyes on him, watching him. Justin. It had to be Justin.

"Before you think I chased you or that I'm stalking you, remember: I told you I would never do that. I don't chase anybody," Justin spat. "I had no idea where you lived. All I wanted this year was a fresh start. Imagine my fucking surprise when I realized I lived across the street from a goddamn jock house. Football players." He laughed, bitter and fragile.

Across the street. Jesus, did Justin live in the blue Victorian? The one with the Christmas lights around the fire escape? Wes could see the whole house from his bedroom window.

"I see you're about as thrilled as I was when I found out." Justin's fingers flexed. The pen whined. "I promise, I have zero interest in seeing you ever again, so you have nothing to worry about."

"That's… that's not…"

"To be honest, I'd rather live on the moon than across the street from you." Justin said, right as the pen finally snapped in two. The ink cartridge and a spring went flying in opposite directions, *plink-plink*ing across the tile floor. Justin slammed the broken pen down and scooted his chair back, grabbing his notebook and textbook. "In fact, I'd rather be anywhere than near you. So why don't you tell the class all about Paris on your own? Being on your own is what you're best at anyway, isn't it?"

Justin shoved his chair against the table and strode out of the classroom.

Wes stared at his empty chair, at the negative space Justin had left behind. *He lives across the street. He lives across the damn street.*

"*Problème, monsieur*?" The professor's hand landed on the back of Wes's chair. "Where is your partner?"

"He had an emergency," Wes choked out. "He had to go. But, uh, I can present."

"*Merveilleux*." His professor beamed. "And, can I say, *Monsieur* Van de Hoek, how excited I am for this season, and to watch you play. You will have a fabulous NFL career." He patted Wes on the shoulder twice and returned to his perch behind the podium.

Wes hunched his shoulders and stared at the tabletop.

CHAPTER ELEVEN

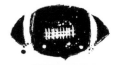

WES'S FINGERS brushed the grass as he bit down on his mouth guard.

Breathe in. Listen for Colton's count.

His heart hammered. Blood thundered through his veins. He felt sweat drip down his forehead, bead on the tip of his nose.

Colton called the snap, and stillness instantly transformed into action, into sound and fury, a violent, vicious rush. He was on a pass route for this play, and he stutter-stepped, juked left, then ran right. The receivers hauled ass on their deep routes, and Wes ran his slant route into the gap behind the defensive line, in front of middle linebacker. He hit his mark and looked back at the line. Colton was in the pocket, eyeing the downfield, looking left, looking right. Wes had no idea how everyone else was doing, what kind of coverage each of the receivers had on them. All he knew was his piece of the action.

Colton's gaze landed on him.

He saw Colton's eyes harden, tighten. Saw the fractional hitch in his throwing shoulder, the little tell Colton couldn't quite get rid of. Wes had never pointed it out because he might be the only person on the planet who knew about that tell. Who else watched Colton as intently, as intensely, as Wes did during the game?

For the tenth time that practice, Colton launched a missile for Wes, and he caught the ball in the basket of his arms, never breaking stride as he started downfield. The linebacker was on him in a hot second, but he spun again and managed another fifteen yards before Coach blew the whistle.

He let his run slow, then peter to a stop. They were at full-speed practice, but it wasn't supposed to be full contact. Plays were blown dead rather than ending in tackles. He and Colton and the starting line were facing off against their own defense, and both sides were kicking each other's ass.

"Take ten!" Coach shouted. "Hydrate! Take a knee and catch your breath!" He moved off to huddle with the offensive and defensive coordinators and the assistants as they made adjustments, formulated their next set of plays and counterplays.

Wes squirted a bottle of water in his face and managed to get half down his throat. Colton appeared next to him, his helmet pushed up. Sweat ran in waterfalls down his ruddy face.

"You finally shaved, huh?" Colton grinned, gnawing on his mouth guard as he tossed the ball one-handed. Colton was never fully himself without a football in his hands.

Wes rubbed his palm over his jaw. He hadn't even realized how scraggly he'd let himself get. But, after French, he'd looked at himself in the mirror and tried to see what Justin had seen. A bruiser, a hollowed-out Goliath, an unkempt monster. He had no right to want to look good for Justin, no business thinking about Justin's eyes on him as he walked up his porch steps.

When he slept, he could still feel Justin's hand on his face. Sometimes he woke up reaching for Justin—in his arms or by his side—or trying to lay his palm over Justin's hand where it cradled his cheek.

"Yeah. I was looking pretty bad."

Colton said nothing. Let the moment pass. "You're on fire out there, Cap," Colton said. "Maybe all that shit you did over the summer was good for you."

Whatever tiny measure of peace Wes had found on the field vaporized. He flinched, nearly buckling, but tried to cover it by dumping the rest of the water bottle over his face. His insides felt like he'd put his guts through a paper shredder. Was it falling in love or destroying that love that made him a better ball player? Or was he fooling himself, and by trying to run from his heartbreak, he was only postponing the inevitable tackle? He'd end up face-first in the dirt eventually.

"You look good, too," he forced out. "But you're not spreading out the passes. Why are you sending everything my way?"

Colton frowned. "Is this Wes asking, or the team captain asking?"

Wes ground his molars. *You'll need to evaluate your teammates every day.* Coach had him glued to his side during nearly all of practice, every day, pointing out the strengths and weaknesses of each player. Even, or maybe especially, Colton.

"You can't rely on one position, or one man. The other teams will pick up on it. You know that."

"No one has managed to stop you, have they? And no one has been able to block my passes. I throw to you because, nine times out of ten, you are who's available. You make the play happen. You want me to throw to the other guys? Get them to make more plays happen." Colton shoved his helmet down on his head. "You know that."

Wes glared at the sky as Colton ran back to the field, where he stretched, jogged in place, kept himself loose and limber. Threw a glare back at Wes before high-fiving the center and one of the tackles, who were taking advantage of the rest break to lay flat out on the field.

Wes's one reprieve, the one place where anything made sense in his life, had always been the football field. When his fingers brushed the grass, when he heard the snap. When he faked out the defender and started on his route. When leather and laces slammed into his chest and he got both hands around the ball. When he saw the end zone and opened up to full speed, chest out, back straight, legs flying.

The gridiron was his zen, his church, his retreat. When he put his pads on, threw on his mesh practice jersey, laced up his cleats, a clarity washed over him, a focus that brought its own peace. Those pads weren't just physical armor. They did something to his insides. On the field, he lived in the zone. He pushed for the margins, always striving for better, better, best. Always pushing, always refining. No matter what was happening in the rest of his life, leather, laces, and pads settled him in the center of his soul.

Not anymore. Was it becoming captain? Shouldering responsibility for the team, on top of his own performance? Trying to cultivate perfection in everyone else, as well as himself? To hone discipline and passion and draw them out when each was needed? How did he inspire everyone to dig deep, find what they didn't know they had to give, and bring it out for the team?

Was he supposed to turn himself inside out as an example for others?

He was damn close already.

Coach called an end to the rest break and had everyone form up on the line of scrimmage again. More play action, more facing off against their own defense.

Across the line, he could see hunger in Trace's eyes. Trace was the defensive captain, the middle linebacker. He wanted to stop Colton and Wes. He wanted to bring Colton, who hadn't been sacked in over two years, down to the grass. Or, since this was just a light-touch practice, he wanted to get his hand on Colton's chest, slap him, wrap beefy arms around him in a bear hug. Lean in and growl, "Got you." He'd done it to Wes many times.

Wes's fingers skimmed the grass again. Sun warmed. Freshly cut. Chewed up from cleats. He breathed in. Pads shifted. Leather groaned. His muscles clenched and released, waiting to fire.

Maybe all that shit you did over the summer was good for you.

Colton was talking about the hours he'd thrown into the gym, the days and nights and evenings and mornings he'd spent on the field, running routes and practicing his footwork in the empty stadium until he couldn't move and he couldn't think and all he could do was lie on his back and try to breathe and, hopefully, for one damn second, not think of Justin's smile.

Justin.

He missed the snap and stuttered over his feet when he tried to recover. In less than a second, Anton, the strong-side linebacker, was on him, up in his face and containing his run. Wes was supposed to be tackled if that happened, but he spun, trying to salvage the play. Anton wasn't expecting the move, and he jerked right as Wes faked left, then grabbed him around the waist and yanked, trying to bear hug him in a soft hold.

Wes planted his foot but stumbled. Lost his balance and felt himself start to go down.

Wes was over two hundred and fifty pounds, and Anton was almost two-twenty. All that solid muscle spiraled around Wes's unstable center of gravity. He tried to go with the motion, but he ended up jackknifing his knee over Anton's thigh before he face-planted on the grass, twisting at the last moment and pulling in his arms to take the hit to the center of his chest and not his wrists. Still, as he hit the ground, he felt a twang vibrate up and down his leg, centered in his knee.

"Oh shit!" Anton was down on one knee right away, holding out his hand and helping him sit up. "You all right?"

Coach's whistle screamed, and he hauled ass across the field, his face red and twisted like a prune as Wes peeled grass out of his face mask.

Wes cringed as he bent his knee. Not an excruciating pain, but a dull ache, a soreness. Damn it.

"The fuck is going on over here?" Coach bellowed. "You two

fucking square-dancing? Why the hell are you on the ground, Van de Hoek?"

"I tripped," Wes said before Anton could speak. "Landed wrong. I think I tweaked my knee."

Coach's expression rippled, concern, fear, superstition, anger, disgust, and anxiety all rolling in one wave across his weathered face. "Get up and get into the locker room," he growled. "Get ice on it right away. Get a trainer to look at it." No one messed with knee injuries. Nothing could bench a player faster. "After practice, you can ice it some more while we review tape in my office."

Anton silently helped Wes to his feet, steadying him as he tested his knee. He could put about half his weight on it. Not too bad, then. It was angry, but ice and heat and he should be fine. Wes limped off the field as fast as he could.

When he passed Colton, Colton slapped the back of his helmet and called him a quitter, and he flipped Colton the bird behind his back. At least they were good. Colton wasn't holding any hard feeling about his criticism earlier.

And, well. At least he'd get practice throwing to other guys.

Wes limped into the tunnel, heading for the locker room, his thoughts circling around and around the moment he'd lost focus, the moment he'd been distracted.

Justin.

What was Justin doing at four in the afternoon on a weekday? Was he in class, or was he at dance practice, or… Was he already doing his placements for his nursing major? What department did he want to work in when he had his RN? Where did he spend his free time? Where did he hang out on campus?

Did he like living on West Campus? Wes had lived on Southside his freshman year, and he'd hated it. It was a rabbit warren of underclassmen who were on their own for the first time and reveled in the freedom with complete lack of responsibility. Wes had hated picking his way past the pools of vomit or trying to sleep through the drunken shouts and late-night parties. He was invited to the jock house on West Campus his sophomore year, and he'd moved in and never left. He liked living with his team-mates, his friends. He liked the tree-lined streets and the peace. There were Buddhist monks who lived a few streets over. They nurtured beehives and had about fifty hummingbird feeders in their yard. Wes watched the hummingbirds every time he jogged by.

Had Justin jogged the neighborhood yet? Had he gone to Daisy Lane? Or found the monks? Did he walk down 24th to campus, or did he drive? Or take the bus?

Wes slumped against the tunnel wall. It was cool there, the sunlight from the stadium barely making a dent in the darkness. He sank down on one leg, favoring his twanging knee, and curled over his helmet. His sweat-soaked hair dripped onto the concrete as he tried to steady his breathing.

Inhale. Exhale. He gripped his helmet until his fingertips turned white and his bones ached.

It didn't matter what Justin was doing, or where he was. He wanted nothing to do with Wes. Not ever again.

Wes tipped his head back and closed his eyes.

———

HE WAS ten minutes late to French class the next morning.

Coach and the trainer had told him to stay off his knee and alternate ice and heat for the next three days. He had a brace he was supposed to keep stuffed with ice packs. He'd slept in the damn thing, then woken up at four to shove the packs back in the freezer and wrap a heating pad around his knee as he tried to read the first chapter of his epidemiology textbook.

He wasn't going to miss an opportunity to see Justin, though, even if all he could do was stare at the back of his head. So he'd strapped the ice brace on and driven the three miles to campus, hunted for a parking spot, nearly pulled his hair out, and finally limped nearly a mile to the humanities building. He kept his head down and tried not to make eye contact, but he still got a dozen questions lobbed his way, grating concern and *Oh no* and *Hope that isn't serious*! He tried to wave it all off with "Just a little twist" and a polite smile.

When he finally made it to class, he was breathing hard and had worked up a sweat, and he was limping even more. The professor's face went from pissed at the late entry to horrified in a single cartoon smear when he took in Wes's injury.

Wes tried to head off his concern. "Sorry I'm late. I tweaked my knee, and I was a little slow on the walk."

"But are you okay, *Monsieur* Van de Hoek? *Pourrez-vous jouer*?"

"Yeah, I should be good. I just need to rest."

"Limping across campus is not resting."

Wes fell into his chair at the back of the room. "I didn't want to miss class."

His eyes skittered to the front row. Justin glowered at him. Well, it was a step up. At least he was looking at Wes. Justin was, again, in running tights and a baggy shirt, his hair pulled back in a sweaty ponytail. He met Wes's gaze and then turned away. Wes's heart twanged like a broken guitar string, just like his knee had the day before. *He looks so good.*

The professor had them partner up again—"same partners, *s'il vous plaît*"—to present each other to the class. Who their partner was, what their major was, what they liked to do.

"You have a very interesting partner to work with," the professor said, clapping Justin on the shoulder as he deigned to sit across from Wes at the back. "I look forward to your presentation on *Monsieur* Van de Hoek."

"What about him?" Wes blurted out before the professor moved on. "Isn't *Monsieur* Swanscott interesting, too?"

The professor blinked. Looked from Wes to Justin and then back. He pasted a plastic smile on his face and said, far too brightly, "*Bien sûr que oui!*"

Justin gritted his teeth as he opened his notebook. "I don't need you to defend me."

"He was being a dick."

"I like being anonymous. Not everyone craves the spotlight, you know."

And there went his heart again, broken string after broken string. Wes drooped, nodding as he stared at his own notebook. Of course Justin enjoyed his privacy. Wasn't that one of the reasons why Wes had ended things? To protect Justin from *exactly* this? If Wes could rewind time, would he go back to being just Wes, the big ole boy from West Texas who worked with his dad on the ranch? What if he could go back and never, ever let himself pick up a football?

Well, then he'd never have met Justin. And, despite the pain, he'd never trade those three weeks in Paris away. Not for anything.

The other groups were already talking softly, getting to know their partners and scrawling notes as they sipped their coffees, kicking back in the most relaxed French class Wes had ever been in. It would be nice, and an easy A, if he weren't paired up with the man he loved.

"What happened to your knee?" Justin finally asked. He wouldn't look at Wes.

"Practice. I tripped. I was distracted."

"Doesn't sound like you. You're never distracted."

I was thinking of you. Wes said nothing.

They made it through the presentation with the least interaction possible. Justin scrawled out a few lines about Wes that he already knew, and Wes, when he tried to ask Justin questions about his life—his dance practice, what he did for fun, what kind of friends he had—was met with an icy silence. Justin stayed at his table, though, for the entire class, and that was something. It was tiny, and it was a sucker's prize, but Wes would take it. He got to see Justin out of the corner of his eye, rake his gaze over the long lines of his legs. Listen to him breathe. Smell him, even, when the air conditioning turned on. His soap, his deodorant, the sweet scent of his sweat.

When class was over, Wes waited for everyone else to file out before standing. His ice packs were all melted, and the brace wasn't supporting him anymore. His knee had started to ache an hour ago, but he'd ignored it so he could stay close to Justin a little while longer.

The only people who were there to see his knee buckle, see him nearly fall, were the professor and Justin, who was gathering his things from the front table after ditching Wes at the end of class without a second glance.

The professor raced to his side, trying to get under Wes's arm and hold him up, but if Wes leaned his weight on that beanpole, he'd snap him in half. Wes politely edged away and leaned against the table as he bent and straightened his knee, trying to work out the stiffness and the pain.

"Where is your car? You said it was a long walk. Shall I call the campus police to escort you back to your dorm? Or should I call for a wheelchair? I can call the campus health office." The professor was babbling, pulling out his cell phone.

"No, no, please. I'm fine. Don't call anyone. I just need a minute."

"Nonsense! We cannot let our star player limp across the school!"

Jesus, no. Him limping into class that morning was bad enough, but being escorted by campus security or taken out of the building in a wheelchair? That would make ESPN, for sure. How many replays would that have on SportsCenter? He waved his hand, tried to stop the professor from calling.

"I'll help him."

The professor started, then turned to Justin like he thought Justin was a piece of the furniture that had just spoken. He blinked. His fingers hovered over his cell phone.

"Thanks." Wes smiled. "I'll be fine, professor. I promise."

The professor eyed Justin and then Wes. "Are you certain?"

"Yes," Wes said. "Very."

The professor pocketed his cell phone, gathered his things, and then held the door for the two of them. Justin got under Wes's arm on his weak side and supported his weight. Wes wrapped his arm around Justin and leaned into him, more than he needed to for his knee. He couldn't help it. Having Justin in, well, one of his arms was like giving cocaine to an addict. He turned his face toward Justin, inhaling, and almost fell again, stumbling as the full force of Justin's proximity slammed into his soul. He trembled, and his arm curled around Justin's shoulders, trying to pull him closer, into his chest—

"I will leave you in this elevator," Justin hissed, "if you don't *stop*."

"Sorry. I'm sorry." He straightened and tried to take his weight back, but Justin didn't let him go all the way. They ended up in an awkward half limp, half wrestle, daylight between their bodies and only their arms touching, all the way to the parking lot.

"Which one is yours?"

"The truck." Wes pointed. There were about fifty trucks in the parking lot. "I mean, the rusted one."

"That?" Justin stared. "That's *your* truck?"

Wes bristled. "I'd buy a better one, but the last big purchase I made was ballet tickets, and it looks like I'll be paying those off for the next two years. I don't have a lot of spare change right now."

He saw Justin's skin flush, felt the heat rising from his neck and his chest. Felt his shoulders rise and fall with a quick inhale-exhale. "I recognize it, that's all," he ground out. "From West Campus. We do live on the same street."

Justin held out his hand for Wes's keys, and when Wes handed them over, he unlocked the driver-side door and then led Wes around to the passenger side. "Shut up," he said, when Wes raised his eyebrows. "We're going to the same place, so it's nothing to drive you there. I get a free ride this way."

Wes shoved four team binders, offensive plays and routes and analyses for the rest of their conference, to the floorboards as he hauled himself into the truck. Water bottles and energy drinks already littered the floor. Protein bar wrappers dusted the bench seat. Athletic tape was balled up and thrown on the dashboard beneath the windshield. The cab smelled like a locker room had died inside. He rolled down the windows quickly, fanning a binder to try to dissipate the smell.

"Too late," Justin said, hopping into the driver's seat. "I already smelled it. You need Febreze."

"Think it's a little beyond that."

"You're probably right." Justin started the truck, threw it in drive, and gunned it out of the parking lot. Wes watched him instead of the road. Justin handled the truck like he did every-thing else: face-first and with no hesitation.

Had Justin ever been afraid of anything in his life? Had he ever second-guessed himself? Wes wanted to fold himself into little squares and disappear. Fly out the window on the wind.

"You'll be able to afford a new truck when you get that NFL contract," Justin finally said, turning onto the main road that led to West Campus. "You could enter the draft after this year."

Yeah, he could, but did he want to throw all his eggs into the NFL basket? Give up on his other dreams? Entering the draft meant no more college, no more degree. What about his parents' dream, to see him walk across that graduation stage?

What about wanting to love a man? There was a single-digit number of out NFL players—nearly all of them retired or inactive —and every one of them had said it was an excruciating, brutal experience to be gay in the NFL. If it were easier, wouldn't more guys have come out?

He sighed and scrubbed his hands over his face. He'd been at the stadium until almost ten p.m. with Coach, reviewing tapes and going over the team roster. They were evaluating the tryouts and the walk-ons as well as running regular practice for the first and second strings. He'd been awake until after midnight, rotating ice and heat in his bedroom before even trying to fall asleep. And when he did manage to sleep, his dreams had been full of Justin. Always, always Justin.

They were on Opal Street a minute later, and Justin pulled up in front of his house and put the truck in park. "Do you need help getting inside?"

"No, I'll be fine from here."

"I'll park in your usual spot."

He squinted after sliding out, peering back into the open window. "You know where I park?"

"Yeah. Right next to me. We both like shade, apparently." Justin tossed him a sardonic grin as he threw the gearshift back into drive. Wes backed up to the porch stairs and leaned on the railing.

Even their cars wanted to be together.

He limped into the house and threw the melted ice packs into the freezer, then hobbled up the stairs to his room. Everyone else was out, at class or at lunch or busy elsewhere, and he had the house to himself. He left his bedroom door open as he face-planted into his bed.

A moment later, he rolled onto his side and stared at his Paris montage. Pulled his photo of Justin out from under his pillow and unfolded it. He sighed, tracing his calloused finger over Justin's smile. "I love you."

He'd said the words a thousand times in his head, had dreamed about saying them to Justin in Paris, in all the perfect days and nights he could have. Or at the airport, before he let Justin go. He'd dreamed he told Coach to pick someone else and then drove to Dallas instead of the ranch, found Justin's parents' house and stood on his porch with his hat in his hand and, when Justin opened the door, told him he loved him and that Justin was worth more than the NFL, more than football, more than everything.

But what would have happened after that moment? When he was broke and futureless and had nothing to his name? What happened after *I love you*? How could he ever hope to keep a man like Justin? He couldn't. Not as a football star—*I like being anonymous*—and not as a loser, which was exactly what he was if he didn't have football or his scholarship.

His cell phone buzzed. Groaning, he grabbed it, shoving Justin's photo under his pillow.

It was a text. From Justin.

The last texts they had exchanged were on the day they flew back to the States. Justin telling him he'd landed, that he missed him so much, that his parents were shocked at how happy he was. That they knew, right away, he'd met someone special. Him, texting a horrible selfie and saying they were back on the same continent. He'd felt like his arm had been cut off when Justin's flight took off from Paris. He'd been anxious his entire flight, desperate to be on the same land as Justin again. Irrational, but he couldn't help it, and he couldn't wait to text Justin when he got to New York. Then his flight to Austin, and then—

I can't do this. Forget you know me. I'm sorry.

Two months later, Justin had finally texted back. *I'm outside with your keys. Do you want me to throw them up through the window?*

He almost smiled, imagining his keys sailing through the open window. *No, come in. The front door is unlocked. I'm the front bedroom at the top of the stairs.*

I know.

He heard the door open, and then the lightest footsteps the house had ever felt danced up the stairs. "In here," he called.

Justin's head poked through his open doorway. He frowned. "This isn't really a bedroom, you know."

"It's what I can afford." He shrugged as he sat up, his heart suddenly racing, his palms going slick, his stomach turning inside out. Justin was here, in his bedroom.

He was all elbows for a moment, trying to straighten his comforter while he was still sitting on it, trying not to jostle his knee, trying not to fall on his face or look like an idiot. He managed none of those, and finally, Justin took pity on him, helping him straighten his blanket as Wes rocked right and left. Justin reached for Wes's pillow to help prop up his knee when Wes tried to bunch the blanket beneath him.

Too late, Wes realized what Justin would find. "Wait, don't—"

Justin froze, pillow in hand. There, in all its glory, was the rumpled photo of the two of them, crease lines, ragged edges, tearstains, and all. Wes grabbed the photo and hid it beneath his thigh.

Justin's eyes closed, and he breathed in. Held it. Exhaled and turned to Wes, giving him the pillow like it was radioactive. His eyes flicked over Wes's shoulder, to the Paris photos on his wall. He frowned, and his gaze skittered away before he turned his back on Wes to wander Wes's tiny room, perusing his desk and running his fingers over his textbooks. Microbiology. Epidemiology. Biochemistry. "Did you have Rajas for biochem?"

"Yeah. She kicked my ass."

"Same."

Justin had a canvas bag over his shoulder from the co-op down the street. After he completed two circuits of Wes's bedroom, he seemed to remember he had the bag, and he started. Stared down at it. Then jerked it off his shoulder and passed it to Wes. His eyes never met Wes's.

Wes pulled open the bag like there might be a rattlesnake inside.

But no, no rattler. Instead, there was a stack of single-use ice packs, the chemical kind that froze when you mixed them up, a couple of elastic bandages, a bottle of painkillers, IcyHot, and a car air freshener in the shape of a Christmas tree. He pulled the air freshener out, smiling, ready to joke about how disgusting his truck smelled—

Whatever he was going to say died when he saw the scent Justin had picked: lavender.

Lavender and baby's breath tickling Justin's cheek. His lips kissing the tender blooms. His eyes, so full of joy, gazing at Wes as he held the sprig of petals to his nose and squeezed Wes's hand.

"Just some stuff I thought you could use." Justin stared at the wall. At his nails. At the floor. He was still in his running tights and his T-shirt, and his hair was still piled on top of his head. Wes wanted to drag him into his lap, bury his face in Justin's chest. Wrap his arms all the way around Justin and hold him close, effortless and carefree like they were in Paris. Tip him over sideways until they were pressed together from head to toe, hands interlaced, noses and lips brushing as they whispered sweet nothings to each other.

Say something. Say thank you. Say please stay. Say I love you. Say something.

"How was dance this morning?" His voice was ragged, like he'd strained his vocal cords through a cheese grater. He wanted to snatch the words from the air and hurl them out his window. Couldn't he come up with anything better to ask the man he loved?

"Fine."

"You, uh, have a performance soon, yeah?"

Justin's eyes narrowed. "How do you know that?"

"I looked it up. Next week, right? At the planetarium?"

Justin's jaw shifted left and right. "It's a space theme," he finally said. "The performance. The dance."

"Cool venue." *Can I come? Can I watch? Would you hate me if I came?* He opened his mouth—

The front door banged open. One of these days, that door was going to fly off its hinges or, more likely, bust through the drywall when one of the guys flung it open like that. Wes rolled his eyes and *thunk*ed his head back, sighing. By the pairs of elephant feet thundering through the downstairs, he guessed at least four of the guys were home.

Justin was like a cat who'd sensed a dog, all stiff and on guard with his hackles up even farther than they already had been. He glanced once at Wes and then headed for the door, calling out a "Bye" over his shoulder. He almost blurred, he moved so fast.

He heard Colton's surprised, "Whoa, hey" on the stairs and Justin's cold, "Just dropping something off for Wes" in return.

"Oh, cool. I didn't know you were Wes's friend," Colton said. Like the women at home would say, bless Colton's heart, he could make friends with a telephone pole.

"We're *not* friends," Justin said. His footsteps pattered down the stairs. "I only know him from class."

Wes closed his eyes and crumpled the photo in his fist.

CHAPTER TWELVE

STARLIGHT WINKED by Wes's head. Jupiter spun inside Saturn's orbit, the two planets twirling on invisible fishing line through a dazzling array of tiny LEDs strung in lazy arcs beneath the dome of the planetarium. The room was dim, the walls lit with a deep indigo glow, the color of crushed sapphires. A small, round stage was set up in the center, and the audience mingled on the outer rim of the circle of seats before the performance began.

Wes clung to the wall by the emergency exit, keeping his head down. He glanced up every minute or so, scanning the room to see if the performance was about to start before staring down at his phone again. He had his ball cap pulled down, and even though it was still warm, he wore his green canvas jacket with the collar turned up. He'd almost gone out and bought a pair of reading glasses to try to disguise himself, give him one evening of anonymity. One night of peace.

His hands were clammy, and he'd already sweated almost entirely through the program. He rubbed his palms down his jeans, then rolled up the program and shoved it into his back pocket. He knew the important details, anyway. Justin was dancing in the second and fifth performances. A duet and then a solo.

The lights dimmed, finally, and the audience moved toward their seats. Wes snagged the closest one to him, still in the back, as close to the exit as he could get. He caught a group of girls looking his way, and he stared at the floor, his hands laced behind his neck, trying to block his face with his elbows, until the overhead lights turned all the way off and only the LED stars lit the stage.

He couldn't follow the story that was supposed to accompany the evening, not without Justin to break it down for him. He gave up a few minutes in and just watched.

The music came from a live string quartet, and it started delicate and airy before dropping into a deep, rumbling bass that quaked the floor beneath his boots. He watched the first dancer, a lithe, muscular woman, leap and spin and arch her way across the stage until she folded into herself on a quivering high note to end her routine. The lights dimmed even further, even the LED stars darkening before the next dance. A vibration from the bass and the cello sent tremors through Wes's bones until every hair on his body was standing on end.

The stars glowed brighter, and there was Justin with another male dancer, wrapped chest to back, necks intertwined, bodies flush. Justin was in a skintight black dance suit, his eyes painted with rectangles of orange that swept up toward his teased and sky-high hair.

Wes's teeth clenched so hard his jaw ached as Justin and the other guy started to move.

He didn't breathe, not through the first half of the dance. How could he, when Justin was writhing and whirling in this guy's arms? When Justin looked like he'd stepped out of the depths of Wes's psyche? Like he was Wes's lust and his pure id made manifest. Wes's heart pounded, and his fingers dug into the denim over his knees.

Justin danced like a man possessed. This wasn't a delicate

dance. It wasn't gentle. He was raw, furious in his power, a counterpoint to his elegant partner dressed in white. Justin's movements were perfect, exacting control balanced on the knife-edge of intensity. When he spun, Wes got dizzy like he'd just twirled the same uncountable number of rotations. Justin tipped out of the spin, bounced off his partner, then tumbled into an easy flip and another spin before arching his spine and lifting one leg, head tipped back.

Wes's fingernails bit into his jeans so hard he bent one back.

Justin fell into his partner's arms and the lights snapped off.

The audience cheered, but Wes couldn't move. Not right away. He had to uncurl his fingers one by one before he could raise his hands and clap. Dizzy, his lungs aching, his vision swimming, he sat back and let the other dancers blur past him until Justin returned for his solo.

This dance was more delicate. The music started slow and dreamy, and Justin's dancing matched it. Airy, with long, languid moves. But the tempo increased, and the bass started sneaking in, and Justin's dancing became sharper. Harder. Full of power. He was showing off a different skill set in his solo. Grace. Flexibility. Good God, flexibility. Wes had no idea Justin was that bendy. And then, passion.

Justin ended up in the center of the stage near the end of his dance, as the music was crescendoing. His gaze locked on Wes, suddenly, his eyes spearing through the center of Wes's soul so intensely Wes reared back.

But no, Justin wasn't looking at him. He was looking at the emergency exit sign over Wes's head. Wes figured that out after Justin started a series of spin moves, rising from the flat of his foot to nearly the tips of his toes in a continuous spiral that Wes swore Justin had said was the hardest move in all of *Swan Lake*. Fouettés, Justin had said, as the black swan had spun and spun and spun. *The dancers pick a focal point when they spin*, he'd told Wes. *They keep their eyes on that point so they don't lose focus.*

Justin ended his solo with a sky-high leap, landed in a lunge, threw his head back, and stared up at the dome overhead. His eyes were scrunched up as agony twisted his face, his arms thrown wide in his final pose. His chest heaved, shoulders rising and falling, and he blinked at the LEDs, their starlight catching the shine of tears at the corners of his painted eyelids. Wes's heart seized.

Then Justin rose and bowed, his face transformed into a careful smile. The audience roared, the applause thunderous.

Wes stayed frozen in his seat. That hadn't been dancing. That was something more than dance, more than fancy footwork and clever choreography. Wes didn't know much about dance, or art, or fine, fancy things, but he knew—knew—that he'd just seen something beyond incredible. Justin had danced his damn heart out. Danced his soul out.

He barely saw the rest of the performance. His mind was replaying Justin's solo. He remembered all that focused energy, and Justin's intensity. He remembered it wrapped around him, and over him, and above him. Remembered Justin and him entwined, closer even than Justin's duet partner had been. Who was that guy, anyway? Jealousy sank through Wes like an oil slick. *He's the guy at Justin's side. Unlike you.*

When the lights came on at the end, the audience rose in a standing ovation, clapping and whistling and cheering. The dancers were in a company line, bowing together, waving and smiling and blowing kisses. Wes, slow to react, slow to stand, spotted Justin as he was taking his third bow.

He saw Justin's duet partner wind his arm around Justin's waist. Lean his head against Justin's, and smile.

"Hey, are you…" A woman's voice shattered Wes's concentration. He blinked, and Justin and his partner disappeared, moving off stage and down the hallway the dancers were using as a backstage entrance. He groaned. Glanced at the woman trying to make her way through the planetarium to his side. She was peering at him, squinting, trying to make out his features in the false twilight. "Are you that football player?"

He shook his head, gave an open-palmed wave, and beat a retreat, scrambling out the exit and through the foyer to the entrance. Head down, stare at the floor. Tuck his shoulders down. Look small.

Yeah, right. He couldn't look small if his life depended on it. People parted before him like the Red Sea, which was great, except that drew attention, and, more than anything, he didn't want that. Murmurs rose to his ears. *Hey, he looks familiar. Is that Wes Van de Hoek? What's he doing here? I wonder if his girlfriend is a dancer.*

He made it outside and jogged around the side of the building, hiding in the darkness between two sodium lights. The parking lot was filling up as family and friends of the dancers spilled out of the planetarium. Cars beeped. Doors opened and closed. Engines turned over, and tires squealed on the pavement. He waited, and the crowd thinned until there were only a handful of cars left.

There was the little white Honda, the two-door coupe that parked next to his rust bucket back on West Campus. He'd scoped out Justin's car for three days, made sure it was his. Like Justin had said, he'd parked next to Justin's little car even when he had no clue whose it was. Now, of course, everything about Justin was imbued with too much meaning. Walking by his white Honda was almost like walking by him, and Wes had to hold back from running his fingertips along the hood of his car every time he passed it.

He hurried across the dark lot, digging the program out from his back pocket and a pen from his front. He scribbled a quick message on the inside, then took the snip of lavender he'd cut from the garden at Daisy Lane and folded it into the center. If he was more sophisticated, he'd fold the program into something cool, like an origami crane, or a swan, or even a heart, but he wasn't that guy. He wasn't cultured, and he wasn't suave, and he didn't know how to do things like that. He didn't know how to dance with Justin like they were making love, and he didn't know how to tell Justin that, no matter what he'd said in those texts, he didn't mean it. He didn't mean a single word.

He tucked the folded program and the lavender beneath Justin's windshield wiper, then turned and strode away.

RAFAEL WALKED Justin to his car after they'd changed and washed their faces, wiping away the makeup and the face paint. Justin's hair was still done up, two French braids tracing either side of his teased pompadour. Rafael's hair was short and razored, sticking up wild after the performance. Justin had never seen Rafael look so casual, in his zip-up hoodie and his dance leggings.

"So…" Rafael said, leaning against Justin's car door. "Did you think about what I asked?" He bit his lip, almost but not quite smothering his smile as he rocked side to side.

"I did."

"And?"

"Yes," Justin said slowly. "I would like to go out to dinner with you."

Rafael hadn't made a secret of his attraction to Justin. He'd been like a shark ever since dance practice started, circling Justin, asking to partner with him in the duet, bombarding him with smiles and questions about his life, wanting to get to know him in every way.

It was… nice. Easy. Comfortable. Rafael was like him, gay and out and happy in his own skin. He was an art major and had an apprenticeship as a tattoo artist. He didn't have sky-high aspirations, and he didn't care about other people's opinions. He hated cowboys, thought hicks were dumb, and couldn't tell a football from a basketball or a baseball. He'd never ridden a horse.

He was funny, and he was smart, and while despite his sharp tongue, and his even sharper personality, he was gentle with Justin. Genuine. He wanted to get to know Justin, not just get into his pants. That slow, tender consideration had worn him down, and he went from tolerating Rafael's curiosity and his flirtations to looking forward to them. They were good dance partners, and he enjoyed Rafael's company.

It didn't feel like he'd felt with Wes, but there probably wouldn't ever be a guy like Wes again. Well, for damn sure there wouldn't ever be a cowboy again, or a footballer, or a football-playing cowboy. He'd known it was a bad idea from the start, and look where he ended up. Brokenhearted and bereft, like a bad country song. All he needed was a train whistle to make it official.

Rafael might not be the one for forever, but he was maybe the one for right now. Justin could dance with him, go out on a few dates. Maybe wind down the nights in Rafael's arms, get his hands on the body beneath Rafael's bodysuit. God knew Rafael wanted to get inside his.

Rafael beamed and dropped a quick kiss to Justin's cheek. "Something casual, I presume? I get the feeling you don't want to rush."

That was another thing Rafael was: perceptive. He'd already dropped hints that he knew Justin was getting over someone, and he hadn't even used that cheesy line about getting under someone else. "Casual would be great."

"Daisy Lane? Meet there tomorrow at… nine p.m.?"

"It's a date."

Rafael smiled again, kissed Justin's cheek as he hugged him goodbye, and headed for his own car. He fished his keys out of his duffel as he went, calling back to Justin, "You danced your ass off tonight, hon. You were the sexiest mofo in there. Hands down."

He laughed, watching Rafael climb into his BMW as he

unlocked his own car. He dumped his duffel in the back seat, then groaned as he caught sight of the paper shoved beneath his windshield wiper. Some Jesus group, probably, taking advantage of a full parking lot to push their pamphlets. He grabbed it, balled it up—

Something fell and hit his foot.

Lavender.

He blinked. Stared at the single cut stem on the asphalt, then at the half-crumpled paper in his hand.

It wasn't a religious pamphlet. It was tonight's program. His performance, his solo, had been circled—and, scrawled in a messy, sideways slant, someone had written *Tu étais magnifique.*

Someone. There was only one person on earth who spoke French and knew what a sprig of lavender meant to Justin.

He picked the lavender off the ground and held the blooms beneath his nose before sliding them down to his lips.

Justin closed his eyes as he sank to his ass, slumping against his car door.

CHAPTER THIRTEEN

FRIDAY NIGHTS, Wes worked a double shift at Daisy Lane, stocking and helping with the trash, the extra crush of dishes, and any other hands-on work in the kitchen and the back of the house. Usually he was hauling empty bottles all night long, or peeling more potatoes for the homemade fries, or taking trash out to the dumpster again and again and again. It was repetitive, but it was work, and he liked being busy. More than that, he liked the anonymity of it. Other than the cooks and Miguel, he didn't speak to anyone, and everyone ignored him. For one night a week, he wasn't the mythical Wes Van de Hoek. He was just a dude hauling trash.

Daisy Lane picked up around eight and was a madhouse until midnight, then had a late-night surge around two a.m. Wes was on his feet from seven p.m. on, hauling, helping, throwing, peeling, refilling, but just after ten that night, Miguel passed him a beer and told him to take a break and not come back until he was done. Wes grinned and headed out to the alley, sipping the cold, crisp brew.

The back deck of the restaurant had been added on in stages, first one level, and then another, and then another, daisy-chaining outward and winding through the trees that made the neighbor-hood so quiet and peaceful. From the alley, Wes could hear the hum and buzz of conversations from the decks above his head. He sat on the steps and leaned back, balancing on his elbows as the conversations played around him.

He heard Justin's laugh first. His loud, wonderful laugh, the one that had run down Wes's spine and fired up every one of his nerves in Paris. The laugh they'd been shushed for at the Museum of Modern Art. The laugh he heard in his dreams almost every night. He *knew* that laugh.

Wes popped up. He could pick out Justin's voice—every fifth word, it seemed. What was Justin doing here?

Wes abandoned his half-finished beer and threaded his way through the kitchen, pushed into the dining room, and slipped out to the back deck. He hovered at the railing outside, near the bussers' dish dump, and scanned the tables.

The place was packed. A hundred conversations hit him, rolling like thunder from tables of six, ten, even twelve. Quieter conversations came from tables of two, people on dates. Couples held hands across the small tables. Two girls fed each other bites of cheesecake. He kept searching, peering at every table—

Justin, though, had already seen him. When Wes spotted him, he was staring at Wes, his jaw hanging open, his face pale, a crimson flush staining his sweeping cheekbones. He was at a table for two, a lit candle flickering between him and another man. Very romantic. Wes's teeth ground together.

Justin's date turned, trying to spot what had spooked Justin, and Wes laid eyes on the man sitting where he so desperately wanted to be: the dancer from the night before, the one who had been so damn intimate with Justin, as if they were having sex with their clothes on in front of everyone.

Of course Justin would be dating him. Of course. He was the kind of cool, sophisticated guy who could attract a man like Justin, who could captivate him, keep him happy.

Wes's fists opened and closed as he stared at Justin and his partner. His pulverized heart buckled like he'd taken a full-force tackle, like all three linebackers had pancaked him at once. Like he was a smear left over after the impact. His vision blurred, and he turned away, pushing through the crowd and the tables, trying to escape from the deck, from this moment, from his own life. He couldn't navigate the narrow spaces, though, and he bumped elbows and spilled wine, jostled cups of coffee and bounced silverware as he tried to thread his way through. *I'm sorry, I'm sorry*, he kept choking out. *I'm sorry.*

I'm so sorry. Forget you know me.

"Wes!"

He couldn't face Justin. Not tonight. Not when Justin was on a date and the last of Wes's heart was turning to dust. He needed to get away, *now*. Needed to get somewhere he could let out the scream building inside him, where he could claw out his own failure, where he could cry, just cry, and whisper Justin's name as he clung to the memories of Paris.

Wes made it through the restaurant and the kitchen and back out to the alley before he exhaled. He ended up braced against the side wall, elbows to the brick, fingers laced behind his neck, forehead down. He sucked in breath after breath. Squeezed his eyes closed.

The back door of the restaurant slammed open and bounced off the alley's wall. "Wes!" A voice hissed. "Damn it, Wes."

He turned, and there was Justin, glaring at him from the steps.

He was lit by the dull puddle of white light around the restaurant's back door. He was in his skinny jeans and a long-sleeve university shirt. The sleeves were pushed up, showing off his forearms, and his jeans hugged every line of his quads and hamstrings. He had on boots like he'd worn in Paris, artfully untied at the top. His hair was pushed back, puffed up and held in place.

He was so damn beautiful it hurt.

"What are you doing here?" Wes tried to clear his throat. He sounded like he'd been strangled.

"That's my line," Justin snapped. "That's what I should be asking you: why are *you* here? Are you following me?"

"What? No." Wes shook his head. "I work here. I unload and I stock. Fridays I help out during the rush. This is my job."

Justin blinked. Some of his vibrating fury faded.

"Are you on a date?"

"So what if I am? What do you care?"

Wes picked at the mortar between the bricks. His lips twisted, and he fought against the burning behind his eyelids. "Is he good to you?"

"*That's* your question?" Justin shook his head, gazing upward. "That's what you ask me? You see me on a date, and that's the first thing you think of?"

"It is a date."

"Yes, it's a date. I'm moving on. It's not like there's any reason for me not to. You ended things."

Justin's words hit Wes like ninety-mile-per-hour football passes. They made his lungs seize, ripped his breath away. "I know—"

"Do you? Because I don't think you do!" Justin marched down the alley to where Wes had tried to hide. "If you did, you'd make more fucking sense. Care to clue me in on what you know?" His head bobbed left and right as he spoke, and his voice was vicious, cutting. "Why do you care that I'm on a date? Why are you leaving flowers on my windshield? Why do you have pictures of Paris up on your wall? Why do you have a picture of us under your pillow?"

He couldn't speak. His tongue was dead weight, useless. He opened his mouth. Nothing came out.

"*You* were the one who ended everything. *You* were the one who said you couldn't do this. *You* were the one who said to forget you exist. I did everything you told me to! I let you go, and

I didn't make a fuss. I never bothered you. I never reminded you about what we had or what we did. And I'm working on forgetting you exist, but, you know, you're making that really fucking hard when you keep showing up."

"I'm sorry—" he croaked.

"Yeah, you're always *sorry*. You're *sorry*, but you can't do this. You're *sorry*, but you changed your mind. You're *sorry*, but you used me because you wanted to see what it was like, walking on the wild side for a few weeks. Look, you got it out of your system, okay? You had your little experimentation phase, and now you can go back to your jock life with your tape and your Monster Energy and your stink."

"What? Justin, no! You weren't an experiment!"

"Oh yeah? Then what was I? What am I supposed to think when you tell me to forget you existed?"

"Jesus, not that!"

"You used me, and you threw me away when you were done—"

"No!"

"Then *what*? What was it that had you running away from me as fast as you could? Because from where I'm standing, it absolutely looks like you're ashamed. You got scared and you decided to leap right back in that closet where it's nice and safe and straight."

He was going to be sick. His stomach heaved. He kept the bile down through sheer force of will.

"And, you know what, I even understand. You worked your ass off for that starting position. I get it." A laugh burst out of Justin, cold and cutting, "I mean, Jesus Christ, you're my dad's favorite player."

"I'm not ashamed," Wes said through gritted teeth.

"No?" Justin threw his arms wide. "Go ahead, Wes. Shout it out. Tell the world what you are."

Wes's lips clamped shut.

Justin's arms fell. "That's what I thought."

Buzzing broke the stillness between them. Cursing, Justin fished his cell phone out from his back pocket. "Rafael is wondering where I am."

"Your date?"

"Yes, my date. Who I just abandoned to chase you."

Wes shook his head. Stared at the ground. "I'm *not* ashamed."

Justin snorted. He strode back down the alley. "Keep telling yourself that. One day you'll realize how ridiculous that lie sounds. Try and remember me when you finally realize. Remember this moment."

Justin was going to walk away, disappear and go back to his date. He was going to leave, and he was never going to talk to Wes again, not after this.

Everything was on the line, suddenly.

Wes started after Justin. He closed his eyes and felt his soul take off, running down the field. The ball was soaring overhead and he was racing it, sprinting as hard as he could to catch up. He was trying to catch up to his heart, and to Justin, and to his life. Run, run, run. What would be there at the end?

How could he know the answer if he didn't take the chance?

"I love you," he called after Justin. "I loved you in Paris, and I still love you. You're everything to me. You're the first thing I think of when I open my eyes in the morning. You're in class with me, you're on the field with me, you're in the gym with me. I talk to you when I'm alone. When I'm driving in my truck. When I'm jogging or working out. You're on my mind every minute of the day. And you're the last thing I see every night. That photo…" He shoved his hands into the pockets of his jeans. "I love you, and I'm not ashamed of that."

Justin had turned to Wes halfway through his word vomit. He stared, not moving, not breathing.

"You're right. I'm scared." Six foot five, two hundred sixty-four pounds, and he curled forward like he was five years old and scared of the dark. "Not about me, or who I am."

There was no possible way to feel worse, he thought, until he saw the devastation on Justin's face. It hit Wes like he'd caught a train in the center of his chest. "I'm gay," he breathed. "I know that. I'm not— That's not—" He fumbled his words, tripped over his thoughts. "I'm not ashamed that I love you. But I don't know how to live with all these different pieces of me." His shoulders rose, stiff and hanging by his ears. "I always thought football was just a tool, you know? I got my scholarship because I decided that was how I was going to get out of West Texas. I thought I'd just play football through college, then get on with my life. I thought, what was four years when I'd have the rest of my life to find someone special?"

His eyes flicked to Justin's, then away. Jesus, he couldn't stand seeing Justin like this. Tears soaked Justin's face, and he was trembling, clenching his cell phone so hard it looked like it was about to shatter.

"But then I met you, and… I didn't want to wait anymore. I wanted to love you—I *want* to love you. I do love you. And I want to be with you, every day, but…"

"But what?" Justin's voice shook.

"When Coach told me I'd made first string, he sat me down and said everything was about to change. He said my life was about to be turned upside down, inside out. That everyone was going to know everything about who I was. They were going to dig into my life, find out everything. NFL scouts, and reporters, and fans, and stalkers, and…"

"And you got scared people would find out about us."

"Yes. But *not* because I'm ashamed."

"Then—"

"Coach also said the whole team was counting on me. I was the one who could take us higher than we'd ever been. And if we have the kind of season he believes we could have, that meant everyone could reach their dreams. Be invited to the NFL combine, or into the draft. NFL contracts." *You can bring everyone to glory. Everyone is relying on you.*

An exhale punched out of Justin.

"What would happen to your dance team if, right before you guys went on stage, you dropped a bomb on them?" Wes asked. "What if you told everyone the deepest secret you ever had, something you knew would throw everyone off their game? Something that would break every bond of trust you'd ever built with each other?"

Justin's eyes squeezed shut, and he shook his hands in front of him, as if that could somehow shake out whatever he was feeling. "What about telling them before the games started? Preseason? During training?"

"The season is our performance. We're on from the very first moment we suit up, from that very first practice. We have to gel on the field, fast. The psychology of it ..." It was Wes's turn to shake his head. "I've played with this starting line for going on three years now. We've bled together, cried together. Hell, we live together. We've seen things inside each other no one else has. The best and the worst. In some ways, I've never been closer to anyone in the world than I am to these guys." Dizziness grabbed him, nearly threw him to the ground. He swayed. "How can I tell them that I'm not the man they thought I was? That I've been lying to them for years about something so huge, so fundamental to who I am?"

"Why do they care? Who gives a shit!"

"People care." The fans would be a mixed bag. Some would be supportive. Others... Hell, he was called a worthless faggot online just for dropping a pass or not breaking through the linebackers. Was told to choke on a dick and get himself fucked in the locker room to teach him a lesson. And that was just from people who signed their comments *#1 fan* and who *didn't* know he was gay.

Maybe the guys would be okay. He didn't think Colton would

disown him. Not look him in the eye because he couldn't get the image of Wes on his knees, cock in his mouth, out of his mind. "It's telling the team the truth now, after so long, will break us apart. All that trust we have in each other will be broken."

If the guys were thinking about how he wasn't who they thought he was yesterday… Everything would be broken, not just their trust in him. Their rhythm, their connection as a team. They'd hesitate, when they'd never hesitated before. Colton hesitating in those quarter seconds before he threw, thinking, even if he didn't mean to, about how gay Wes was. A moment's hesitation here, another there. Linemen a little slow on the block. Eyes sliding sideways to him instead of focused on the ball. Microseconds determined the difference between champions and losers.

"I'm the team captain, and I have to make sure we're all focused on the exact same goal: winning. There's no room in that for me coming out. It's… unnecessary." The word tasted like poison. He wanted to spit it out. "I'd be a distraction. I'd hurt us all if I came out."

And if he hurt the team, he'd be dropped faster than the jobs fled West Texas when the oil prices collapsed. He'd have his scholarship taken from him. He'd lose everything.

Justin wiped his eyes with his fingers, collecting his tears and rubbing them into his palms. He stared at the sky. "You said something like that in Paris." His voice trembled. "But you also said we could figure out the season together. That we'd have to keep it quiet, but that you would. We would. I thought that was the plan. We'd be discreet. I would have," he said, his voice thin. "I would have done anything you asked."

Wes fell into a squat, his hands running through his hair. His vision narrowed, tunneling down to a pinprick as the world went neon. He was going to hurl, and he was going to pass out. He wasn't breathing right. He got one palm on the ground and heaved in a ragged inhale, fighting back the darkness.

Images flashed like fireworks in his mind. Him and Justin in

Paris, walking arm in arm. Him and Justin, kissing beneath the Eiffel Tower. His first-ever kiss with a man. Justin astride him, riding his cock, Wes's hands running down Justin's chest as Justin tossed his head back. Justin wearing his hat and nothing else, winking at Wes as he shook his hips.

Justin glaring at Wes, saying *I like being anonymous.*

Justin surrounded by screaming football fans. Justin chased by a raging mob bellowing and calling him a faggot, a sissy, a cocksucker. Wes tried to get to him, but the mob was roaring at him, too, and keeping them apart.

He saw the mob take Justin down. Saw the punches start to fly, the kicks. Heard the cheers.

Vomit rose, and he couldn't hold it back this time. He fell forward, both palms flat on the ground. Rancid bile, the remnants of his protein shake and the lunch he'd eaten at the dining hall, painted the asphalt. He coughed, his stomach still seizing.

Gentle hands guided his face up. He followed the touch, opened his eyes, and saw Justin crouching beside him. Justin's tears were like diamonds on his skin, fallen stars forming waterfalls on his cheekbones.

Wes spat the last of the bile from his mouth, then melted into Justin's touch. He kneeled on the ground, his cheek buried in Justin's palm. He breathed in the scent at Justin's wrist.

"That's not the only reason why I ended things," Wes whispered. "I'm terrified—petrified—of something happening to you. Because of me. Because of us."

"What do you mean?"

"The fans…" He sighed. Brushed his chapped lips against Justin's pulse, a lightning-fast kiss. "There's so much love for the game, but there's also this ugly hatred. When you're perfect, you're a god. When you're not, there are death threats. People say horrible things. Sometimes they *do* horrible things. We had a quarterback, years ago, who was attacked by a fan because he threw a few bad passes."

"I remember that. He ended up paralyzed, right?"

Wes nodded. "We get so much attention. I thought I was used to it, before, but now… It's a whole other level. I can't go anywhere without being recognized. I don't have a life that's my own anymore. I don't have any privacy. None. And you said yourself, you hate that. You like your anonymity. Your privacy." He cringed. Curled around his aching stomach. *Don't puke again. Puking isn't sexy.* "If someone hurt you because of me, or if someone attacked you—"He couldn't say it.

Justin pressed their foreheads together, and it took every bit of Wes's strength not to break down. He dug his fingernails into the ground. Something came loose inside him, and he grabbed on to Justin, clinging to his elbows.

"Listen to me," Justin said. His voice was, finally, gentle, like Wes remembered from Paris when they spoke to each other at night, their sweat cooling on each other's skin. "No one chooses what risks I take. No one decides for me what I think is worth it. You had no right to make that decision for me."

"But—"

"No buts. If you wanted to end us because *you* wanted it to be over, fine. But if you ended us because you thought you were saving me…" He shook his head. "That's my job. Respect me enough to let me weigh the risks and make the choice."

"But you don't know—"

"You didn't give me the chance to."

"You said you like your anonymity."

"I do. But I liked you a lot, too."

Wes pushed his forehead against Justin's as if he could merge their minds. If only Justin could see and feel his thoughts, all his mixed-up nightmares and breathless, hopeful dreams. "I don't want you to get hurt because of me."

"Let me worry about me, okay? I'm not helpless."

"No, you're not. But I don't want anything bad to happen to you. You don't deserve that."

"Wes, the only person so far who has hurt me because of your football career is you. Why don't you think about that before you go imagining some phantom attacker waiting for me in middle of the night to avenge your lost heterosexuality, okay?"

He wanted to laugh. It was such a Justin thing to say—and, God, he'd missed that, missed his dry humor and his way of cutting right to the heart of an issue, chainsawing his way through the briar patch of Wes's mind. But he also wanted to vomit again, because Justin was right. The only one who had hurt him was Wes. He'd hurt him badly. Maybe unforgivably.

"I don't know how to live with myself," Wes whispered. "I have no idea what to do."

"What are you saying?" Justin asked carefully. "Are you—"

"No. Nothing like that. I just don't know how to put all the pieces of myself together. I don't know how to be the team captain and take care of the guys. I don't know how to be the best tight end in the nation. I don't know how to handle all this attention, the people who think they know me, who want the best for me but are all up in my face all the time until I can't breathe anymore. And I don't know how to live with what I did to you. I don't know how to move on from this. I think about you every moment."

He ran his hands up Justin's arms. Tugged softly until Justin's chest was pressed to his and they were body to body on their knees in the darkness behind Daisy Lane, beneath the overhead deck. A hundred conversations were going on above them, mixing with the live music that washed out the sound of their conversation. Justin's cell phone was still buzzing, but in this tiny pocket of the world, it was just them. "I don't know how to be all those men at once. It's like I have to put on different faces every hour, when the only face I want to wear is my own. The guy I was in Paris. The guy I am with you. Wes, who loves Justin."

Justin's thumbs stroked over Wes's cheekbones, and his fingertips massaged the skin behind Wes's ears, brushed through the short strands of his hair. "You're spread too thin."

"I don't know what to do."

Justin was silent. He brushed his nose over Wes's. His soft lips ghosted Wes's cheek.

"I thought about quitting," Wes whispered. "I thought about telling Coach no, I didn't want it. I thought about calling you, driving up to Dallas. Going to your house. But I can't quit. I'm nothing without this."

"That's not true. You're *you*, and football doesn't define you—"

"I have nothing without football. I don't have a scholarship. I don't have college. I have no path, nothing, if I don't ride this as far as I can. I need football as much as this team needs me. I only have two options: I finish college, or I go back to the ranch. And if I go back, I'll never get out of West Texas again. Living there is like drinking poison water that you can't get out of your body. Once you're in, you're in, and there's no escaping." His breath choked off. He tried to swallow. Couldn't. "I don't want that life. I want to be a man that you'd want to be with," he forced out.

"I don't care what you are. I don't care if you're a footballer or a grocery store bagger or you work at McDonalds or, hell, you're a cowboy."

"You hate cowboys."

Justin almost grinned. "I do. Except for one, apparently. And if you were the biggest cowboy to ever cowboy, I would still care about you. I don't care *what* you do. I care *about* you." His breath washed over Wes's cheeks, his lips. "It's okay to admit that you want this, too. I know you a little bit. I know how hard you worked for this. You wanted to be the best, and you basically are. You should be so damn proud of yourself."

"I'm not. I'm not a good man. I broke your heart. And all I want to be good at is loving you."

Justin sighed. Wes waited for him to say, *Well, that ship has sailed*, or, *You weren't, and we're past when that matters now*, or even,

You're just going to have to get over that, aren't you? He closed his eyes. Braced his soul.

Justin's cell phone buzzed for the eleventy billionth time. He cursed and dug it out of his back pocket. Wes's stomach lurched as Justin swiped his phone screen on.

"Raf? I'm fine." Wes heard Rafael shouting about where Justin had disappeared to, how frantic and upset he was, how he'd feared something had happened. "Something came up," Justin said. "An emergency. Look, I didn't mean for—" His lips thinned, and he closed his eyes as Rafael went off again.

"Raf, I can't do this right now." Justin hung up in the middle of Rafael's tirade. He turned off his phone and shoved it back in his pocket. "There."

"You should go find him. You are here with him."

"Do you want me to go find him?"

Wes's fingers curled around Justin's biceps. He dragged Justin closer, until he could feel the shape of Justin's ribs against his own, feel the heat from his belly and the sharp lines of his hips. "No," he growled. "I really don't."

"I don't, either."

Wes's gaze focused on Justin. There was so much in Justin's tear-soaked eyes: hope and fear and shadows of doubt mingling with curls of anger. Wes leaned in—

"I'm not kissing you. You just puked."

Wes chuffed out a tiny, broken laugh. He still leaned in but moved past Justin's lips until his face was buried in the crook of Justin's neck, his lips on Justin's pulse, his nose in the curve where his shoulder and his neck met and his trapezius fluttered. He could smell Justin's shampoo, the aftershave he'd put on earlier, the scent of his skin, clean and sharp. He breathed in, his arms sweeping up Justin's back, palms molding to muscles he never thought he'd feel again.

"Do you want to get out of here?" Justin whispered.

"Yes."

THEY ENDED up in Wes's truck, screaming out of town on a two-lane country highway, passing the suburbs that had grown up around the city and the university. Past the exurbs and farther, almost an hour out, until they were in the rolling Texas hills, grassland and prairie as far as the eye could see. Wes took the next exit, a farm road disappearing into the black night, a ribbon of black undulating through the hills. As soon as he turned off the highway, the road turned to caliche, and his tires chewed gravel as he bounced a half mile into the darkness.

Justin held his hand the entire drive, both of his hands wrapped around Wes's on the bench seat, holding so tight Wes's knuckles were aching by the time he jerked the truck off the road and threw it in park.

Before they'd driven off, he'd gargled and rinsed his mouth out with a warm bottle of water, spitting into the gutter.

So there was nothing to stop him from sliding across the bench seat and taking Justin into his arms, nothing to stop him from sliding his big hands through Justin's wrecked pompadour, the style ragged after Justin had run his teary fingers through the strands. He pulled Justin almost into his lap, his knee bumping the dashboard and his elbow banging the steering wheel. "You have to tell me not to kiss you," he said. "You have to stop me if you don't want this."

Justin grabbed his T-shirt in both hands and yanked him closer. "You damn cowboy. I never wanted you to stop. Kiss me, damn it, and never stop."

He seized Justin's lips with his own, kissing him deeper than he had in Paris. Their tongues tangled, each of them seeming to try to race into the other, try to make up for the days and nights they weren't wrapped in each other's arms. Justin's fingers dug into the muscles of Wes's chest, and Wes twisted his fingers in Justin's hair.

Justin peeled his own shirt over his head. Wes got his T-shirt down one arm but left it hooked over his elbow. He couldn't bear the separation from Justin, couldn't bear for his hands not to be touching Justin's warm skin. He ran his palms up Justin's sides, over his trembling ribs, around to his back and then down the furrow of his spine. Justin arched against him, pressed his chest into Wes. Wes nibbled across his pecs and bit down on the hard nub of his nipple, and Justin's arms flew around his head, holding him to Justin's body.

He got their jeans open with one hand, got their cocks out and together in his palm. They were both rock hard. Wes hadn't had an erection since he'd told Justin to forget he existed, and now here he was, aching and quivering and shaking as Justin rocked his hips, drove his cock into Wes's tight grasp.

He couldn't last. He whimpered, mouthed his way from Justin's chest up his neck to his jaw, his lips, and poured himself into another deep kiss, trying to tell Justin with his body how much he loved him, how much he'd missed him. He squeezed their cocks together, twisting his grip and stroking his and Justin's precome over their heads. He couldn't hold back, and he whimpered as his orgasm tore him apart, as his come spilled between them, hot over his hand and Justin's cock.

Justin grinned, kissed Wes a dozen times more, and then dipped his fingers down to collect Wes's come. He sucked his fingers into his mouth, licking up Wes's release and hollowing his cheeks. His eyes flashed.

Wes grabbed Justin and spun him, taking him down to the bench seat on his back. He rose between Justin's legs, tugging down his jeans and briefs. He ran his tongue from Justin's balls to his swollen purple head, wrapped his lips around Justin's cock, and sucked him as deep as he could.

Justin keened, and he tried to spread his legs wider. His jeans were still tangled around his thighs, and all he could do was jerk his hips and thrust his cock into Wes's mouth. Wes groaned, and he popped off Justin's cock to say, "Do that again. Don't hold back. Please."

"Jesus," Justin hissed. He slid his hands into Wes's hair and gripped his skull, and when Wes swallowed, Justin thrust his hips up and held Wes in place, sliding his cock all the way down Wes's throat for the first time.

Wes gagged, and Justin tried to back away, but Wes kept sucking. Hollowed his cheeks and went deeper, harder. "Again," he gasped. "Don't stop."

He held Justin's stare as he sucked again, and as Justin started thrusting all the way into Wes's throat each time. Saliva flooded Wes's mouth, trickled from where his lips were wrapped around Justin's shaft.

"You love this," Justin whispered. "You love my cock."

He tried to make some noise of agreement, some whine or grunt or whimper, but Justin's cock was in and out of his throat too quickly, too deeply, and he could only gag and suck, seal his lips around Justin's cock and try to take him deeper. He gripped Justin's hips and squeezed, ran his thumbs into the hollows of his obliques. Held Justin's stare and went down, all the way down, until his nose was buried in the curls at the base of Justin's cock.

"Jesus!" Justin screamed. He threw his head back, holding Wes's head down, thrust once, twice, and then Wes felt Justin's cock jerk. Come flooded Wes's mouth, burning all the way down his throat. He sucked Justin through his orgasm, through the aftershocks, until he was a puddle on the bench seat, lying back with his hands thrown wide, his legs limp and spread.

Wes pulled off and kissed Justin's trembling belly, the rise of his hip bone. He brushed his stubbled cheek against Justin's upper thigh, then kissed the crease where his leg met his body. He caught Justin's taste on the back of his tongue, where Justin's come lingered in his molars. He hunted it, sucked it from his teeth. Cherished it.

Justin's hand drifted down. He got his fingers around Wes's

shoulder and tugged. Wes crawled up his body, skin to skin, holding himself above Justin so he wouldn't smother him. Justin slid his hands over Wes's face. Held him. Stared into his eyes and deeper, all the way inside him. Wes let him look, even though he wanted to hide. Wanted to bury himself and his shame where Justin couldn't see.

"You're a good man."

"Don't—"

"You are. You're always thinking about others and how to take care of them. Even if what you came up with was misguided, your heart was in the right place."

"I'm sorry," he whispered. His eyes slid away.

"Don't." Justin forced his gaze back up. "In Paris, we said we'd figure it out. You told me you weren't coming out, not while you were playing, and I was okay with that. I knew what I was signing up for. I didn't know how crazy it would get when you were named one of the top players in the country, but that wouldn't have sent me running. I was more invested than that. It would take a lot more than that to get me to leave."

"What about stalkers coming after you? What if being together is dangerous—"

Justin kissed him, shutting him up. "No. Not that either. I would have stayed at your side through all of it. If you came out, or if you didn't. If someone found out. If things went horrible. If you lost your scholarship. There's nothing that would have broken me away from you."

Wes's heart was hammering, and warning signs were flashing in his mind. He chewed on his words, ground his teeth together. "You keep using the past tense."

"You hurt me," Justin whispered. "You hurt me like I've never been hurt before."

"I know." Wes did hide his face then, looking down, his chin buried in his chest. "God, I'm sorry. I'm so sorry."

"You didn't even talk to me. You just made up your mind on

your own. And I get it, you were trying to protect me, but… you didn't. And I'm trying, I really am, to focus on the fact that you were trying to care for me, but it's hard. I'm still angry."

"Is there no hope?" He'd thought maybe this was the start of a second chance, forgiveness he didn't deserve. He'd thought this was all his dreams come true, but maybe it was the twist before the nightmare really began. How much worse would it be if he'd tasted his love one more time and then had his heart ripped out again? If Justin hammered the last nails into the coffin that buried their love. "Are you saying we're done forever?"

"I thought you already said that."

All his fears were still there. Nothing had changed. But… "I'd take it back if I could. I wish I'd never sent those texts. I wish I'd quit football."

"You can't quit." Justin slid his fingers through Wes's hair. Cupped the back of his neck. "Promise me you won't quit."

"I would quit for you."

"Which is why I want you to promise me you won't. No matter what. Say it. Say you promise."

It felt like he was grinding his heart beneath the heel of his boot. "I promise," he choked out. "I wish you knew how much I love you. And how much I miss you."

"I've missed you, too." Justin tried to smile, but it came out as a cringe. "Tonight was the first date I've been on since you dumped me. I couldn't even consider it. I'd get sick thinking about any other guy."

"I saw you guys dancing together. You looked amazing. You're so good. You… and him. You were better. I mean, in your solo. That was amazing. Just… amazing." He needed more words. Something better to say. "You were beautiful."

"I got your note on my car. And the lavender."

"I want to keep coming to your dances, if that's okay. But I don't want to upset you. I don't know how to do this, Justin. I don't know how to live with loving you like this. It will fade eventually, right? Because right now it feels like I'll love you for the rest of my life, and I'll just have to learn to live with this hole in my chest forever."

Justin's eyes squeezed closed. He covered his face with his hands as he began to tremble. Behind his hands, a tear slipped free, sliding down his temple and into his hair. "That's how I feel, too. That's exactly how I feel."

"I love you." Wes took one of Justin's hands in his and brought it to his lips. He kissed Justin's knuckles, his fingertips. The center of his palm. Laid Justin's hand over his heart. "I love you, and I would spend the rest of my life proving it to you. Showing you, every day, how much, how deeply, I love you. If you let me." He held his breath. And waited.

Justin crumpled, one hand covering his face and his tear-filled eyes. Wes wrapped his arms around Justin and rolled so that he was on his back and Justin was in his arms, his face buried in Wes's chest as he dug his fingers into his skin like Wes would vanish if he let go.

Wes kissed his hair, his forehead, his soaked eyes. "I love you," Wes murmured. "I love you, Justin."

Now that he could say it, he was going to say it over and over, until Justin believed him. And then he'd still keep saying it, tell him he loved him all the time.

Justin's tears soaked his skin, and his nails left half moons over his pecs. He'd have bruises tomorrow, but he didn't care. Justin pushed himself up, gazing at Wes as wounded-animal noises fell from him, sniffs and broken breaths and shuddering cries. "If I let myself love you, are you going to break my heart again?"

"No." Wes slid his hand through Justin's hair, then ran his palm down Justin's back. He held him against his chest until their heartbeats pounded in rhythm as if they were trying to reach each other. "Never again. I swear."

It was all up to Justin. He wouldn't push. He wanted, so badly, but this was Justin's choice to make. Wes had already made one choice for him, and he'd never be able to take that back. If Justin forgave him, if he gave them a second chance that Wes didn't deserve… maybe he'd be able to survive this season, and the fame, and the constant, relentless pressure. The microscope he'd been shoved under. If he had Justin's forgiveness, then somehow, some way, he'd be able to survive.

Justin's chin quivered. But he reached for Wes, and he laced their fingers together. Brought Wes's hand to his mouth and kissed his knuckles, a mirror of Wes's movements only a few minutes before. "I love you, too. Damn it, I love you, too, and I can't stop."

CHAPTER FOURTEEN

WHEN DAWN SPILLED over the horizon, tipping a paintbrush of marigold and bluebonnet across the eastern sky, Wes was holding Justin in his arms as they lay in his truck bed, watching the stars fade and whispering into each other's ears and lips and necks.

Wes spilled his guts about how overwhelmed he was. Being named one of the best players in the nation was something he'd never expected. Nor was being named team captain, or shouldering the responsibility of making everyone's dreams come true. Coach rode him hard, had him reviewing tape from the other teams in their conference and from NFL tight ends, the greats and the failures. What to do and what not to do.

He tried to describe how his stomach went squirmy every time he was recognized. Every time someone pointed, every time someone called his name or he heard whispers behind his back, as if he were a character in a story for people to project their thoughts onto and not a real, live man with thoughts in his head, feelings in his heart.

And he whispered to him about how he'd stared at Justin's photo every night. How he'd wished on every falling star in West

Texas to turn back time and have a second chance. Another day, even a moment, to tell Justin he loved him.

Justin told Wes about his summer, how he'd swung from the highest high to feeling like his heart had been carved out of him. The yo-yo of agony and anger, anguish and rage. Questions he could never answer. How his dad was such a fan, and how, even when Justin wanted to bury himself away and never see football again, his dad still watched ESPN and SportsCenter and talked about Wes's upcoming season like it was prophesied in the Bible.

"He has no idea it was me?"

Justin shook his head. "I would have told him if you said it was okay, but I never got the chance to ask." He kissed Wes when Wes flinched. "After, it just seemed cruel. To you and to him."

"I hope I meet him someday."

"Play your cards right, and maybe you will."

"I intend to." He kissed Justin, warm and sweet.

"What does this look like?" Justin finally asked. They'd avoided the specifics, but as day approached, there were things they couldn't push off any further. "When we get back to campus. What does us dating, but keeping it quiet, look like?"

A zing went through Wes as Justin spoke. Him and Justin, dating. "What do you want it to look like?"

"I want it to look like I support you," Justin said, his voice sharp. "Stop deflecting. I'm not asking for an impossible answer. I want to know whether I can acknowledge that I know you when we see each other. What are the boundaries when we're in public?"

"Of course you can acknowledge that you know me." Jesus, did Justin think he would keep him hidden away like a dirty little secret? "I want to see you every day. I want to spend every free moment I can with you. I want to meet you for lunch between practices and do homework together. I want to take you on dates and drive out to the country like this. Watch the stars and—"

"Fuck in the truck bed?"

"Make love to you every chance I can. It won't be easy with my schedule, but I want to be with you. Really with you. I'll make time, I swear it."

"People might think we're friends if we do all that."

"Good. I hope they do."

"Oh," Justin said simply.

"Is… that what you want?"

"Yes." Justin cradled his face. Smiled. "Yes, but I didn't know if I'd get what I want."

"You will. I promise."

They kissed until Wes couldn't ignore the forward march of time any longer. "I have to get back," he said against Justin's lips. "I have practice." Justin kissed him again, rolling onto Wes's lap. His long hair fell in a curtain around Wes, shading his face. Wes twirled the strands in his fingers. Brought the ends to his nose and inhaled. "My hat still smells like you, you know. I haven't been able to wear it since Paris because it smells like you."

Justin dropped a chaste kiss on Wes's lips. "You can be ridiculously romantic, you know that, cowboy?"

"It's the truth. I'm just saying it like it is."

Another ten minutes passed before Wes could stop kissing Justin long enough to clamber out of the truck bed, and then another five while they kissed against the passenger door. Justin finally pushed him away, laughing when he came in for yet another tangle of their lips.

There was no way to make it back on time, but Wes didn't care. He didn't even speed. He kept the needle just under the limit, holding Justin's hand as his back twanged and his eyes burned like he'd rubbed sandpaper right over the fronts of both. He was exhausted, worn out all the way to his bones. But he was also so weightless he could fly all the way to campus, spread his wings and soar, take Justin's hand and skip along the tops of the corn they passed by. Swing from the puffy arm of a dewy cloud.

He pulled onto Opal Street twenty minutes after practice started. "I'm sorry you're late," Justin said.

"I'm not." He parked at Justin's doorstep and smiled, suddenly shy. "Can I text you after practice?"

"Yes. Please do."

Wes pressed his lips together. "I'm sorry about Rafael. And interrupting your date."

Justin shoved open Wes's rusted truck door. The hinges squealed, and he slid out, landing on the concrete with a spring in his step. He grinned at Wes. "I'm not."

Wes kept smiling, all huge and goofy, his cheeks flushing as he gripped the steering wheel. He chuckled and shook his head, rubbing his fingers against his temple.

"Go on," Justin said softly through the open door. "Get out of here, cowboy. Before you spend all morning smiling at me, and then you're really late for practice."

"It'd be worth it," he said, shifting back into drive.

Justin rolled his eyes. "Such a cowboy." He slammed the truck door and stepped up to the curb.

Wes watched him in the rearview mirror as he drove away, all the way to the end of the block, and even looked over his shoulder when he made the right off Opal and turned toward the stadium. Justin was still outside, watching him. Wes waved, and Justin lifted his fingers and waved back.

He floated into the empty locker room and dressed in under a minute, humming as he strapped on his pads and laced up his cleats. Justin's smile played on a loop in his mind. He could still taste Justin's lips. Could still smell his hair and his skin.

Nothing could take this feeling from him. Nothing could take the joy from his heart. Justin, despite all Wes's mistakes, still loved him. Justin had beaten some sense into Wes's head, too, straightened out his broken thoughts. Unkinked his spiraling rationalizations.

It wasn't perfect. They would still have to hide, at least for now. But Justin was willing to let Wes back into his life, and he wasn't going to screw this up again. No matter what.

"Nice of you to join us today, Van de Hoek!" Coach bellowed as Wes jogged onto the field. "Did you have something better to do this morning?"

"Sorry, Coach." He squinted. "Won't happen again."

Coach glared. "Start running laps, Van de Hoek. Run until I get tired of seeing you circle me."

Wes grinned. "Yes, Coach." He jogged to the edge of the field as Coach turned to where the rest of the team was still doing warm-up drills. Colton caught his gaze and gave a "What gives?" toss of his hands when the offensive coordinator's back was turned. Wes grinned and shook his head, shoving his helmet down over his smile.

He tipped his head to the sun as he started his first lap.

I'M DONE WITH PRACTICE.

Wes's leg bounced as he texted Justin from his truck. He'd run what felt like a hundred laps, then joined in on offensive drills, and then shadowed Coach as they evaluated scrimmage plays on the offensive and defensive lines. The whole time, he'd been grinning like an idiot, to the point that Coach asked him what fairy had shit glitter in his cereal that morning. He'd laughed but said nothing. Coach had grumbled and told him, "She'd better be worth it," and, "Don't get distracted. I told you you'd be flooded with tits and pussy. Eyes on the ball, Wes."

He had his eyes on what was most important: Justin.

But he'd nodded, said, "Yes, Coach," and tried to keep his joy a little less obvious for the rest of practice.

He'd failed.

He didn't even mind being told to run more laps after practice before joining Coach and the rest of the coaching staff to go over the final roster ahead of the first game next week. The first string was set, but there were a handful of recruits and walk-ons who had shown guts and grit during training camp and the preseason, and they'd earned positions on the second string and the relief. Special teams was still their weakest link, but Coach said he only planned on having special teams on the field for point afters and kickoffs. "We don't punt," he growled. "Your job," he said, pointing his finger at Wes, "is to make sure we never have to."

By the time he was done with all that, the locker room had cleared out and he was able to dump his gear, shower, and change into his shorts and a fairly clean T-shirt scavenged from his duffel. He grabbed his practice jersey before he left, though, and shoved it in his duffel bag. It was still damp with sweat, even after he'd sat in Coach's office for over an hour.

He chewed on his thumbnail as he waited for Justin to text him back. It was midafternoon, and his stomach roared. He'd already digested all three protein bars and the shake he'd thrown down his gullet. The rest of the team spread out and hit the restaurants around the stadium after practice, but he'd munched the bars Coach had thrown at him instead, and now he regretted not taking another three.

The last time he'd felt full had been in Paris. When Justin started cooking for them, and he had all the carbs and protein and dairy he could stuff his face with. And all the extra protein he could swallow, too.

He grinned again, staring out the open window as memories replayed in his mind. Now they were framed in golden sunlight. He could remember Paris and not feel like he was dying.

His cell phone buzzed. *I'm in my room. Took a nap. Someone kept me up all night.*

Wes squirmed, his cheeks going warm, his fingers dancing over the back of his phone case. He pictured Justin lying in bed, sleep-soft and tangled in the sheets. They'd slept naked after that first night in Paris. What did Justin wear when he was on his own? Those tiny briefs? The ones that cradled his ass perfectly?

He texted back. *I should sleep. But I'm too excited to. Too happy.*

Oh yeah? Something happen?

Wes laughed. *Yeah, you could say that. :)*

Justin sent a smiley face back, and then those three dots danced across the screen for a solid minute. Wes waited.

So, what are you up to for the rest of the day? I need to hit the book-store and pick up my supplies for my clinical rotations. You're welcome to join me. Exciting, I know. But after, we could get something to eat?

He couldn't type back fast enough. *I'd love to come. And yes, let's get dinner after. Where do you want to go?*

Shrug emoji. *What do you like?*

Everything.

LOL. Let me think. There are a few places off campus you might like. Anything you can't eat?

Nope. Tho, we never did try escargots in Paris…

Next time.

His heart skipped about ten beats, and Wes bit his lip as he beamed. Next time. Next time they were in Paris together. Because they would go back, of course they would. *Deal.*

Okay, where are we meeting? Do you need to go home?

No, I'm ready. Pick you up?

Sure. Want me to wait on 29th?

The street around the corner from theirs. Off Opal, away from his teammates and anyone else who might start asking questions. Wes sighed. Reality slammed back in, dimming the radiant glow he'd been basking in. *That would probably be smart.*

Justin texted again. *I'm heading out.*

Be there in a few. He shifted his truck into drive and stepped on the gas.

Justin was waiting for him, as promised, on Twenty-Ninth. He was sitting on the brick half wall surrounding one of the side yards of an old gingerbread Victorian. Willow and myrtle branches hung over half of the street, shading the concrete and the line of parked cars. It was still Texas hot, and Justin was dressed in a pair of nylon running shorts and a tight T-shirt that showed off every curve and line of his muscled upper body.

Wes's brakes squeaked as he stopped. He reached across the bench and shoved open the door, grinning as Justin hopped into the cab. "Hey."

"Hey yourself."

He was suddenly shy. Less than twelve hours earlier, he'd been baring his soul and revealing his fears to Justin, ones he hadn't even fully figured out for himself until he was confessing them in hushed whispers against Justin's neck. Now, his tongue seemed to tie itself in a bow.

"How was practice? Did your coach get mad?"

"He made me run. I didn't care." Wes turned off Twenty-Ninth and headed toward campus. The bookstore was on the far side, near the student center and a block of bars and restaurants. "I did have to stay after to finalize the roster and the starting lineup."

"Did you make the team?"

"I did." Wes smiled. Slid his hand across the seat and laced his fingers with Justin's. "How was your morning?"

Justin sighed. "Well, I won't be dancing with Rafael anymore."

Wes stiffened, but he said nothing. His eyes darted from the streetlight to Justin.

"He's pissed, and I understand why. I'd be pissed, too. I couldn't give him a good answer to why I up and ditched him, so he just kept getting more and more frustrated with me."

"I'm… of two minds," Wes said carefully, turning into the garage behind the campus bookstore. "You and he danced real well together. Even I could see you were great partners, and I don't know anything about dance. Without you there to translate, it was a lot of noise and movement to me." He pulled into a space, killed the engine. "Except when you were dancing. Then it made sense. But…" Wes scratched at his forehead. Squinted. "I'd be lying if I said I wasn't a little bit glad he won't be all over you anymore."

Justin's gaze sharpened. His eyes gleamed. "Jealous?"

"I'd like to be the only guy touching you, yeah." He squeezed Justin's hand, then let go. "There's no one else for me. I know I have no right to ask the same of you, but I'd like to be the only man in your arms. And in your heart."

Justin chased him across the bench, looking left and right outside of the truck before he grabbed Wes and pulled him close. "I told you before, cowboy. I don't want anyone else."

"Not even sexy dancers like Rafael?"

"You think Rafael is sexy?" Justin's eyebrows rose.

"Compared to you, he was as sexy as mud." Wes kissed him, intending to keep it chaste, a quick brush of his lips against Justin's, but one touch and he couldn't pull back. He lingered, deepening the kiss, Justin melting into him, Wes's hand sliding around Justin's waist, drawing him closer—

Car tires squealed as someone took the turn around the garage ramp a little too quickly. Justin peeled out of his arms, sliding back across the bench seat as he wiped his lips. Wes closed his eyes, his hands grasping empty air. That was close. But what would it feel like if Justin hadn't pulled away? If they didn't have to hide?

He took a moment to collect himself, run his fingers through his hair and check the rearview mirror to make sure he didn't look like he was just kissing the love of his life. His cheeks were flushed and his eyes were wide, but there was no helping that. He hauled himself out of the truck and joined Justin, who was waiting at the tailgate.

He didn't grab Justin's hand as they walked to the bookstore, but he wanted to. Instead, he and Justin traded sidelong glances, and then, when they caught each other looking, goofy grins. Wes spun his truck keys on his fingers. Anything to keep from reaching for Justin.

Inside, they wandered the aisles, Justin picking out three pairs of black-and-navy scrubs with the university logo on the front pocket, a new lanyard, a textbook, and a clinical rotation guidebook. Wes trailed behind him, turning over odds and ends on every shelf, flipping through the medical textbooks, fingering the key chains.

Justin chose a stethoscope and popped it out of the box, tossing the box into his basket and fitting the earpieces into his ears. He held up the drum, tapped on the bell. Turned to Wes and then pushed the cold end against his thin shirt, right over the swell of his pec. "My," Justin said softly, winking. "What a big heart you have, cowboy."

Wes laid his palm over Justin's hand. He felt his heartbeat speed up. Felt it pound. "Hear that?"

Justin nodded.

"That's because of you." He shifted closer. They were alone in the aisle. "Every time I see you, every time I think of you, my heart goes wild."

Justin bit down on his lower lip. "You might want to get that looked at. Sounds like it could be serious."

"It is." He squeezed Justin's hand, then, quickly, lifted and kissed his fingers. "It's lifelong."

Justin blushed and pulled away, tossing the stethoscope into his basket before drifting down the aisle. He looked back over his shoulder at Wes, and the look in his eyes made Wes's heart do cartwheels. He caught up to Justin and brushed his hand over the small of Justin's back, then moved a half step away as they rounded the aisle to the trinkets section.

A hollow look passed over Justin's face as they passed a pride display. He eyed the rainbow lanyards and pins, the little flags and bumper stickers and T-shirts.

Wes stopped in the middle of the aisle. Justin glared when he couldn't maneuver past him. "Hey, cowboy, you mind?"

"You should get something."

Justin looked at him like he'd just asked Justin to chop his own arm off. He blinked. "That hardly seems wise, considering…"

"You're not in the closet." Wes scanned the pins, then picked a rectangle rainbow flag, something understated and classy. It would look great on Justin's lanyard and stand out against his dark scrubs. He held it out. "You'd get this if we hadn't talked last night."

"Maybe, but if we're trying to be discreet—"

"Don't change for me. I don't want that."

"But I *am* changing, aren't I? And not just for you. For us, so we can, one day—"

"I fell for you exactly the way you are. I like that you're out. I like that you're proud. I admire you for that. Please, if you would have bought this before, buy it now?"

Silently, Justin took the pin and added it to his basket. "One day," he whispered.

One day, I'll buy one for myself, too. "Yeah."

Justin was quiet as they kept wandering, but his pace picked up a minute later, and then they were in the sports section. Team merchandise blanketed the back half of the bookstore. Football dominated, filling multiple aisles with cups and mugs and photo frames, bobbleheads and bottle openers and coozies. Justin traded his plain university-branded lanyard for one with footballs on it, then snorted and giggled at the Wes Van de Hoek bobblehead.

Then came the jerseys.

Justin beelined for them, flipping through the racks until he found the 87s. They were NCAA-official jerseys, and they came in the school colors, and in pink, red, green, and even a wild tie-dye. "Which one is like yours?"

"None of them. These are way too thick." His jersey was mesh, more air in the fabric, lighter and elastic so it would cling to his pads and taper to his body, his waist. These were made for fans in the stands, not for players sweating their butts off on the field.

Justin made a face. "I want to wear your number when I go to the games. Which one should I get?"

"You want to come to my games?"

"Of course. Why wouldn't I?"

"I got the impression you really didn't like football."

"I really don't like cowboys, either." Justin winked, still riffling through the racks. "You know, I ordered a jersey like this over the summer. I mean, when I got back. Actually, I ordered it on the flight home." He shrugged. "I left it in Dallas. It arrived after…"

Wes's heart twanged again, another broken string going sideways. A mom and a daughter were looking at the basketball gear nearby, so he couldn't take Justin in his arms like he wanted to. Instead, he laid his hand over the hangers, stilling Justin's search. He stepped close, his face almost next to Justin's. "I have something better. Something just for you."

Justin moved away from the jerseys. He walked the aisle one more time, laughed at the university-branded lug nuts, grabbed an insulated tumbler, and bopped the Van de Hoek bobblehead. "You'd think you'd get paid for all this."

Wes shook his head. Pursed his lips. "We're not allowed to make money on the sport while we're in college."

"But the university makes…" Justin eyed the jerseys and other merch, so much of it plastered with Wes's face or an image of him leaping for a catch or holding the ball as he faked out a defender. "They're raking it in, thanks to you."

"We're supposed to be grateful for the chance to play. And for the free college."

Justin snorted.

While Justin got in line to pay, Wes waited, spinning a display of touristy postcards next to a rack of bumper stickers. The stickers were the usual mix of university logos and boasting about a son or a daughter at the school or on this or that sports team. Near the bottom, there were brag stickers about academics, too. And then intramurals. He spotted two with the university logo and the word *Dance*, one with a man and the other with woman striking a pose. He grabbed the one with the male dancer.

Another sticker caught his eye: *I <3 my Texas Nurse*, with the heart shaped out of a cardiac rhythm. He grabbed it and got in line behind the mother and daughter.

At the register, he added two bottles of water and a protein bar. Justin waited at the door, eyebrows quirked. Wes passed Justin a bottle of water and smiled, then led him back to the truck.

"Got you something." He fished the dance sticker out of his bag. "Thought you could put it on your car."

Justin's lips parted. He took the sticker and stared.

"What?"

"Nothing." Justin shook his head. "It's just… My parents don't even know I dance."

"Oh. Well, you don't have to put it on your car if—"

"No one has ever understood why I like it so much. Or supported me in it…" Justin interrupted him, tracing the male silhouette.

"But you were on the drill team in high school."

"It's not like my parents put out a yard sign bragging about that. Or a bumper sticker. They didn't like it. They wanted me to keep playing baseball."

"I like when you dance." Wes chewed the inside of his lip. "I really like when you dance. And I liked it when you taught me about the ballet, too. I liked seeing it from your perspective."

Justin turned big eyes up to him, so wide it was almost painful to hold his gaze. Wes smiled. Held out his hand over the cracked leather of his bench seat. Justin took it and squeezed hard.

"I got this one for me." Wes pulled out the Texas nurse sticker. He grinned as Justin rolled his eyes.

"Putting it on your wall by your bed?"

"I was going to put it inside my notebook so I'd see it all day."

Justin's cheeks pinked. "That works, too, I guess."

"Can you pass me my duffel?"

Justin cringed as he pushed Wes's stinky duffel across the energy-drink-strewn floorboard with his foot. Wes laughed as he dug through the bag.

He'd thought this would be cheesy, something they could laugh at. Justin could pin his practice jersey to his wall like a trophy, or laugh at him and shove it under his bed, or even wear it to bed, if he wanted. But maybe... He pulled out his still-sweat-damp, grass-stained practice jersey, clumped into a tight ball, and held it out to Justin. "This is for you, too."

Justin plucked it out of his hand with two fingers. He shook it out, and the stench of locker room mushroomed through the truck. Justin coughed. Wes rolled down the window.

"Oh, Wes," Justin said softly, like he couldn't breathe. "You shouldn't have."

"It's kind of dirty."

"You really, *really* shouldn't have." Justin laughed and picked at a grass stain. "I don't know what to say. You gave me your laundry."

"You can wear it to the games if you want."

"I'd clear the stadium out if I did."

"I mean..." Wes felt heat rise in his face. He rubbed his hand over the back of his neck. "I guess it's been a while since I washed it. It didn't really matter before."

"This is an actual, authentic jersey?"

"As real as you can get, outside of a game."

"That's real grass, from a real tackle? You getting thrown down?"

"Oh, yeah, Anton flattened me like a freight train. I skidded about three yards on that one."

Justin winced. "I think football is human bowling. The return of Roman gladiator death matches. How am I going to watch when you get tackled?"

"I guess I just have to be good enough not to get tackled."

"And then you really will be the best player in the nation."

Wes's stomach twisted. He was caught between a shrug and a nod, and he turned away as Justin carefully folded his sweaty jersey, trying not to touch it too much. He passed Justin his plastic bag from the store, and Justin gratefully slid the jersey inside and tied the bag closed. He left it on the seat between them, his hand on top of the bag like he didn't want to let go.

"Okay, where to for food?"

"Do you like burritos?"

"If they come in pairs."

"These are pretty huge burritos."

"I might need three. I'm pretty hungry."

"Okay, big boy. Head over to Leigh Street, and we'll see what you can fit in that mouth."

Wes faced him, grinning like a Cheshire cat. "I don't remember you having any complaints about what fit into my mouth before."

Justin tipped his head back and laughed all the way to the restaurant.

Wes scarfed two and a half burritos and saved the last half. Justin shook his head as he watched Wes plow through the first, barely stopping to breathe. After, Wes dutifully input the two-point-five burritos and chips into his phone for the team nutritionist. He sighed at the note the nutritionist had left him. *Eat more. Report for weigh-in before Monday's practice.*

After, they went to a park at the end of the block, meandering down the jogging path as kids breezed by on roller skates and bikes while groups of moms power walked and gabbed. More than a few of the women eyed Wes like he was a cold drink of sweet tea, but he kept his gaze averted, focused ahead of him, and eventually the feeling of being on display crawled off his skin.

There was a pond at the center of the park, and ducks floated lazily on the surface. Wes looked, but there weren't any feed stations. "Sorry," he said to the ducks. "I've got nothing for you."

They stayed out until the sun set, then walked back to Wes's truck in the dark. He sneaked a kiss, and then another, and another, against the passenger door, out of sight of the park and the other cars. He wanted more, but they couldn't. Not there. He held the door for Justin and then got in the driver's seat and fired up the truck.

Justin held his hand the whole way home.

They parked around the corner on Twenty-Ninth, Wes pulling in right behind Justin's little white Honda. He carried Justin's bag from the bookstore, along with his stinky jersey, as Justin stuck the dancer sticker to his rear windshield.

"You know, I think we did things backward," Justin said, after Wes passed him his bags. "We met and lived together, fell in love, and now we live across the street from one another. And we're dating."

Wes felt the smile unfurl across his face, like a flag flapping in the breeze. He stared at the asphalt. Dug his tennis shoe into the crack in the road between their bumpers. "Yeah, I guess we did."

There probably wasn't an apartment they could rent that would fit their budget. Wes's budget was pennies, and it wouldn't be fair to Justin to ask him to foot the majority of the bill. Maybe if Wes got a job in spring, and he saved up. Maybe next year.

"It's annoying that you're across the street, too," Justin said, oblivious to Wes's thoughts. "You're maddeningly close. Too close. It's very *West Side Story*, even."

"That's like Romeo and Juliet, right?" Wes squinted.

"Yeah." Justin scrunched up his face. "Is there any epic love story that isn't tragic?"

"Ours." Wes smiled. "It's not gonna be tragic. It's gonna be epic."

Justin rolled his eyes, but he smiled. "There you go, cowboy. Being romantic again."

"What can I say? You bring it out of me."

"*Mm-hmm.*" Justin kept smiling, like he'd never stop. "We could stand out here all night like this."

"I know."

"I should go."

"I don't want you to."

"I know."

They stood there, leaning against Wes's truck, staring into each other's eyes. They could hear laughter on Opal, conversations drifting out of backyards on Twenty-Ninth. Engines humming up and down the cross streets. Birds twittering in the leafy branches overhead.

"Can I walk you to class in the morning?" Wes asked.

"Of course. When do you have practice?"

"Now that school's started, we practice in the afternoons. Two until six. I have to be there early, and I stay late after. All my classes are in the morning. Other than that, all the rest of my time is yours."

"Want to meet for lunch tomorrow? In the dining hall?"

"Yes." And the next day, and the next day, if Wes had his way. Every day. Always.

They stood there grinning, staring at each other, neither one moving. "I'll see you in the morning, then." Justin took a step away—

Wes checked up and down the block. Saw no one. He closed the distance between them and caged Justin between his body and his truck, his palms flat on the tailgate as he brought their bodies together. It was only one second, one moment, but Justin was in his arms, and he brushed his cheek before dropping a lightning-fast kiss on Justin's lips.

He shoved off the tailgate and backed away. If he didn't put distance between them, he might not care about the team or his scholarship much longer. He might throw it all away, just to feel Justin's lips on his again.

"Night, cowboy," Justin said softly. "I'll see you in the morning."

"Sleep well," Wes said. "Sweet dreams."

"They'll be of you."

Wes floated into his house, barely aware of the world around him. There was foosball going in the den, the TV blared Madden, and someone was cooking in the kitchen. He heard his friends talking, laughing. The floors overhead creaked, bodies moving. Someone flushed a toilet. He drifted up the stairs, light as a feather, and wandered into his bedroom. He didn't even bother to shut his door. He fell backward onto his bed and stared at the ceiling, his cheeks aching from smiling so wide.

His Paris tableau tickled the corner of his gaze, and he turned on his side and studied the pictures he'd printed, mentally drawing himself and Justin into each one. Instead of agony, joy spun through him, soaked his veins and his muscles and shot straight to his heart.

His cell phone buzzed in his pocket. He pulled it out.

Miss you already, cowboy.

He grinned. Bit down on his lip. Texted back. *Same.*

I don't miss you enough to wear that jersey though. I put it straight in the wash.

Wes laughed. *You could probably have given it to Rajas. She'd take it to the biochem lab for sure.*

You know, there might have been new lifeforms on it. Too bad we'll never know. Whatever you grew in your armpits is being sterilized away.

I can give you another.

Oh, honey. I love you, but please. One gift of a sweaty jersey is enough for a lifetime.

He couldn't stop smiling. *I love you too.*

Three little dots danced and then stopped. Danced and then stopped. Wes waited.

I didn't tell you this earlier, but I signed up for a ballet class this semester. I needed another credit on my schedule, soooo… Intro to Ballet was available. I signed up because of you.

You're amazing when you dance.

I'm not amazing all the time?

You are. I mean, you're an amazing dancer. You're so good. You were doing those spin things, from Swan Lake, in your solo.

Wow. You really did pay attention in Paris.

Of course I did. It's important to you so it's important to me.

Oh, cowboy. You don't know what you do to my heart.

The same thing you do to mine. <3

Anyway. There's a performance scheduled. It's not important, I mean, it's intro to ballet, so it's like, basically the nursery school version of dance. But it's in six weeks. I mean, if you wanted to come. I'm just letting you know.

He pulled up his calendar and put it in, typing "<3 ballet perform." *I'll be there. I won't miss it.*

I'll see you in twelve hours, cowboy.

He did the math. *Eleven hours and twenty-three minutes.*

But who's counting. :)

I am. I can't wait to see you again.

Same, cowboy. Same. Xoxox

I love you.

Love you too. Goodnight.

CHAPTER FIFTEEN

WES WAS WAITING for him on the street just after seven the next morning, dressed in his Wranglers and a T-shirt and his cowboy hat. It was like Paris all over again, and he fought the déjà vu that ran through him as he trotted down the steps of his front porch. "Haven't seen you wear that yet this year."

Wes smiled. "I haven't. It reminded me too much of you." He touched his fingers to the brim, tipped his head. "Mornin'."

Justin's heart went electric. "Good morning to you, too, cowboy. Shall we?"

They walked together across campus, Wes staying with him all the way to the nursing school, even though his first class was in the sciences hall, a ten-minute walk the other direction. Every other step, it seemed like someone else recognized Wes, called out his name, pointed, cheered, or yelled *Go team* or *Go Van de Hoek*. They could barely carry on a conversation what with how many times Wes had to stop and smile, wave, tip his hat, say thank you. By the end of their walk, Wes was wound tight, his shoulders hunched, his expression taut.

"Sorry about all that." Wes waved behind him as he walked Justin up the steps of the nursing school.

He'd said that he was living under a microscope, but Justin hadn't expected to feel it so clearly at seven-thirty on a Monday morning. "Is it always like this?"

"Some of the time it's worse." Wes looked away. "We have our first game on Saturday, so it will be a crazy week."

"Is there anything I can do to help?"

Wes turned his big smile back to Justin. "You already do. You're you."

That shouldn't send his heart into paroxysms of joy, but it did, and he didn't try to stop it. "When are you out of class?"

"Eleven forty-five. You?"

"Noon. Meet you at the dining hall?"

"It's a date."

He got to the dining hall a few minutes after noon, fighting the herds of students coming and going, the lines snaking out of Starbucks and Panera Bread and Panda Express. He made it to the open area and reached for his phone as he scoped out the tables.

It buzzed as he pulled it out of his pocket. *Your two o'clock.*

He looked, and there was Wes, hunched in a booth with his elbow on the table and his face half hidden by his hand, trying to be the world's most inconspicuous giant. His hat was crown down on the table, and he had an open textbook in front of him, his notebook and another textbook strategically stacked so no one could join him uninvited.

Justin threaded his way through the other students and dropped into the booth seat across from Wes. "It's crazy in here."

"Yeah." Wes smiled. His fingers scratched at the tabletop, like he was holding back from reaching for Justin. "But I get the meal plan with my scholarship, so I try to eat here as often as I can."

"Makes sense. You hungry?"

"Starving."

"Go get lunch."

"Didn't want to leave you stranded."

He smiled. "Go. I'll watch the table."

"What do you want?"

"If they have a croissant sandwich, I'll take one. Chicken salad."

Wes went through the line and scanned his ID card to pay. While he was getting their food, seven different people stopped him, presumably wishing him good luck on Saturday, or tried to shake his hand, or clapped him on the back so hard it looked like it hurt. Justin frowned, watching as Wes tried to shrink inside himself.

He came back with three lunch trays loaded down with food. There was Justin's chicken salad croissant sandwich, along with an apple, a bag of chips, and a bottle of water, and then there were two massive turkey sandwiches on French bread, a plate of spaghetti and meatballs, another plate piled high with steamed vegetables, four hard-boiled eggs, three oranges, and another bottle of water.

"I didn't feed you enough in Paris."

Wes chuckled. "You fed me perfectly. I gained sixteen pounds of muscle over the summer, though. I've got to keep that muscle fed. The team nutritionist keeps telling me to eat more, and I think I've lost some weight. I had to adjust my pads last week. Make 'em tighter."

"Jesus, Wes."

A group of girls passed their table, waving to Wes and wishing him good luck. He nodded. Forced a tight, polite smile, before turning back to Justin. "I'm looking forward to the day when I don't have to do all this." He waved his hand over the four plates of food. "I wouldn't mind being fifty pounds lighter if it meant I didn't have to eat my body weight in protein every day. I feel like a dinosaur some days. All I do is eat."

"And you can't ease up now?"

He shook his head as he finished the first sandwich. "Not at my position. I have to block and receive. I have to be strong enough to tackle and hold the line, and fast enough to run and catch passes, and powerful enough to break through the line-backers and safeties when they try to bring me down. I have to be not just a little bit of everything, but the best at three totally different skills: blocking, catching, and rushing."

"Go Van de Hoek!" Another bro, on the other side of the half wall that divided the dining area, leaned over to hold out his hand for a fist bump. He nearly knocked over Justin's textbook.

Wes bumped his fist and said nothing.

"That sounds intense," Justin said, after the frat boy moved off.

"It can be. It can also anchor the team. If there's great QB–tight end chemistry, the team is almost unstoppable. Colton and I have worked hard to get to that place."

"Colton Hall? The quarterback?"

"Yeah. He's my best friend, too. We met freshman year, when we were both wide-eyed and wet behind the ears. Both of us were real good at our high schools, but here, everyone was real good at their high schools. You had to be better than that. Work harder. Become more. We did, together."

"It paid off." He nudged Wes's boot beneath the table with his shoe. "I meant it when I said you should be proud. Even when I was mad, I was proud of you. You earned this."

"Oh my God, it's Wes Van de Hoek!" This time, the girls didn't approach Wes, but they pointed and stared and watched him eat like he was an animal at the zoo.

Wes dropped his second sandwich onto his plate. "Do you want to get out of here?"

"Yes. I'll get to-go containers." Justin was on the move before he finished speaking.

They ended up on the quad, hiding on the back side of a grove of trees, sitting in the dirt and facing a dried-up creek. Wes finished his sandwich and the spaghetti, then wolfed down the vegetables and eggs as Justin ate his apple.

"Tell me about your clinical rotations," Wes asked. "Where are you working? What department will you be in?"

"University Hospital. I'm in the ER for my first rotation."

Wes frowned.

"I picked trauma. I think I might want to specialize in emergency medicine. I'm looking forward to it."

Wes went quiet as he drank his bottled water. He stared at the dust, at the leaves rustling on the wind, seeming to look inward. "My mom was a doctor," he finally said. His voice was soft. Almost a whisper.

They'd never spoken about Wes's mother, other than when Wes said she'd died, and that it was just his dad and him on the ranch. Justin kept his mouth shut. Waited to see if Wes would keep talking.

"She would drive out to the desert and find people who'd crossed the border. Families, mostly, who'd gotten lost coming over. Or who ran away from the coyotes and the human smugglers. Sometimes she'd find people who were left behind on purpose, if they got sick or hurt during the crossing. She saw a lot of trauma. She came home covered in blood a lot."

"Just her?"

"She and my dad. There were a few others sometimes, but it was mostly her. She'd bring people back to the ranch and patch them up, then send them to her lawyer friend about two hours away. Try and get everyone settled in the right way."

"She sounds amazing. Her and your father both. That's incredible that they did that."

He smiled, but it was sad and faded fast. "She was. She did a lot for people. Out there in West Texas, she was the only doctor in a hundred miles who would see people for free. We never had much, but she said it wasn't up to anyone to put a price on someone's life. She ran a little clinic in town and got some money from the government. I'd help her out after school when I was a kid. Cleaning, stocking. Running errands. Being in the way, usually."

Justin reached for Wes's knee and squeezed.

"But then…" Wes stretched his arms all the way over his head as he inhaled deep and held it. His hands came down, and he laid his palm over Justin's on his knee. "She caught tuberculosis, and it was a bad strain. One of those multidrug-resistant ones. She died seven months later. My dad and I had to take a year-long course of antibiotics, but we didn't get it. Just her."

"Wes… I'm so sorry…"

Wes went quiet again, watching dust float in and out of sunbeams.

"Uh, this explains your major, though. I wondered about it. Public health."

"Yeah. I just…" Wes shook his head. "I watched her die, and it was horrible. Ten million people a year get TB." He shook his head. "She saw it a lot, so I guess it was only a matter of time before she caught it, but…"

"It shouldn't have happened."

"No. It shouldn't have." Wes squeezed his hand again, and, finally, met Justin's gaze. "I never tell anyone about her."

"Not even Colton?"

"Nope. He thinks I'm insane for going into public health. Way too much studying for him. I told him I wanted to fight zombie outbreaks, and I think he believed me."

Justin laughed. "Is Colton a general studies major?"

"Worse." Wes grinned. "He's an ergonomics major."

"A what?"

"It's basically the new underwater basket weaving. For his final last year, he had to make a comfy chair. One that wouldn't strain you while you worked. Know what he made? A bean bag, but with a laptop tray and a cup holder."

He couldn't help it. He tipped forward, burying his forehead against Wes's knee as he giggled. Wes's hand slid through his hair, there and then gone, only a moment's touch. "I dunno, I think Colton may be the smartest one of us. I had to write a thirty-page paper last year. I think I would rather have made a bean bag chair."

They laughed some more, and Wes told him more ridiculous stories about Colton until Justin's sides hurt and he couldn't sit up, and he lay on the ground, almost screaming he was laughing so hard. But eventually, Wes's phone alarm went off. He sighed. "I have to get to the stadium for the pre-practice meeting soon."

"I've got class in half an hour, too." Justin stood and held out his hand to Wes. Wes, to his credit, didn't balk, and he took Justin's hand to steady himself as he rose. "When are you done?"

"Maybe seven, depending on the post-practice meeting."

"Text me?"

"Of course."

WES DIDN'T GET BACK from practice until almost nine, late enough that, even though he said his coach had fed him, he was a little surly on his texts with Justin, a little "Betty White needing a Snickers." Justin ordered him a Jimmy John's sandwich delivered to his house, and Wes sent him a line of heart emojis and a *sorry I was hangry.*

Wes was waiting for him again the next morning, and they walked to class, interrupted again every few minutes. Before they parted, Justin told Wes to meet him by the bookstore at lunch instead of in the dining hall, and to text him what he wanted to eat. "I'll get lunch to go from the dining hall and we can go to that park. Maybe it will be quieter."

It was quieter, and Wes ate his French dip sandwich, chicken Caesar salad, lasagna and garlic bread, two yogurt parfaits, and steamed vegetables in peace while Justin ate a stir-fry bowl and a banana. "I lost four pounds in a week," Wes said, after he finished his lasagna. "The nutritionist was mad yesterday at weigh-in. I'm supposed to eat peanut butter every hour now."

"I didn't get you any peanut butter."

Wes cringed. "If I have another spoonful, I think I'll puke."

"Well, if you need some extra protein shots, I'm sure I could help you out another way. You know, if you want."

Wes sprayed a mouthful of water across the grass, tipping sideways on his elbow as he coughed and laughed at the same time. Justin peeled his banana and took a bite, blinking at Wes with the most innocent expression he could summon.

"We'd have to measure the amount of protein so I could put it on my spreadsheet," Wes said, once he got his breathing back under control. His cheeks, his neck, even the tips of his ears, were dark maroon. "Think you could hold still and aim for a teaspoon?"

Justin feigned outrage. "Please. At least a tablespoon."

When they were finished, and Justin had collected the mountain of recycling and bagged it all up, Wes lay on his side and watched the ducks swimming across the pond as he chewed a long blade of milk thistle, plucked out of the grasses growing by the water. "Oh!" Justin unzipped his backpack and pulled out the gift he'd bought for Wes. "I ordered this for you on Amazon."

Wes looked from Justin to the bag of duck feed and then back to Justin. A smile spread over his face, warm and soft and sweet. "Thank you," he breathed.

"One of my favorite memories of Paris is watching you feed the ducks. There were probably five hundred people at that school, but no one fed them except you."

"Probably because those ducks were jerks after they got fed. Remember when they chased us?"

"Yeah." He smiled.

Wes rubbed his thumb across his forehead. "Always kind of thought I was a little bit of an idiot for doing that. Kind of country boy, hickish. I thought I looked dumb in front of you."

"The opposite, cowboy." He wanted to reach for Wes, cradle his face in his hands, kiss him slowly.

Instead, he stood next to Wes as Wes tossed feed to the ducks, and then they walked around the pond, to the back side and into the shade, where no one went. There, Wes pulled him behind an old oak tree and backed him against the trunk, then tipped his hat back and kissed Justin as softly, as sweetly, as Justin could have imagined. Kissed him so good Justin's toes curled inside his shoes and he clung to Wes's waist, dug his fingers into the skin between his waistband and his T-shirt.

They only stopped kissing when a bicyclist's bell echoed across the pond, and they peeled away from each other, but they still nuzzled each other's noses and cheeks as Wes laced their hands together and whispered his name.

WEDNESDAY, they walked into French together, much to the professor's bemusement, and sat side by side in the back of the class. The assignment for the day was to write an essay in French on their major and their career field, and they spent the class period helping each other look up the specialized vocabularies of nursing and public health, then read each other's essays to double-check everything before they turned them in. The professor gave them both a raised eyebrow, but he spoke only to Wes, wishing him well at the game on Saturday.

Thursday, Justin talked himself into going to Wes's afternoon practice. Some practices were open to the public and some were closed, but Thursday's was open, and he went. He'd never been inside the stadium, and for a moment, he had no idea where to go. He followed the sounds, the whistles and the grunts and the shouts, and wove through the empty tunnels to the lower bowl seating. He ended up near the thirty-yard line, down almost at field level, watching the offense drill play after play.

There was Wes, bursting off the line of scrimmage. Rushing, running a slant route, his hands darting for the ball almost faster than Justin could see. Sprinting, launching into a breakaway. There wasn't any defense set up, so this was all timing practice, working on routes and hitting marks and perfecting the plays.

Wes is pretty damn perfect.

He made the game look effortless. Justin's dad always said that was the measure of greatness: when someone makes the challenging look easy.

If Justin didn't know better—and he did—watching Wes, he'd think he himself could waltz out onto the field and run a route, turn, and catch the seventy-mile-per-hour football Colton launched at him. Pluck it out of the air like he was picking grapes. Dance on his toes as he landed, twirled, and took off at full speed.

For the past week, Justin had stayed up late watching YouTube videos about football. *Football 101* and *Football for Dummies. What Does This Mean in Football.* He'd even texted his dad a few questions. He could feel the shock coming through the texts back, but so far, his dad hadn't asked him why he wanted to know who the greatest tight ends of all time were, or why it was called the strong side when the tight end lined up there.

He could follow along at Wes's practice now, follow what Wes was doing. More than that, he understood it, at least a little bit. Understood how *good* Wes was. Him, and Colton, and the team.

When the coach called a break, Wes tore his helmet off and turned toward the stands. He didn't jog over, but he stared at Justin as he squirted water onto his face and into his mouth. Justin smiled. Didn't wave. He didn't have to. Wes knew he was there.

After the break, Wes played like he'd activated beast mode. He was faster, stronger, moved with even more ferocity. The defense came to face off against the offense, and Wes shredded their plays, easily spun out of tackles, made linebackers and safeties whiff and fly face-first at the grass. He was untouchable, and after thirty minutes, the coach pulled him out and gave him a clipboard and a hearty pat on the back.

Again, Wes looked at the stands.

That was amazing, Justin texted. Wes's phone was surely in his locker, and he wouldn't get the message until way later, but he would get it. *You're amazing.*

He left after another thirty minutes, heading back to his room to finish his homework and wait for Wes's texts.

Around nine, Wes messaged. *I was showing off for you.*

Maybe you were, but you're excellent all on your own.

I'm going to show off for you Saturday, too.

Yeah?

Yeah. I'm going to win this game for you. <3 I'm going to win every game for you, mon amour.

CHAPTER SIXTEEN

BEING in the stadium was different in a million ways from watching the game on TV. When Justin was a kid, he'd hang out, coloring on the floor as his dad watched the Texas game on Saturday or the NFL on Sunday. The TV tried but could never really capture the tens of thousands of roaring fans, the pounding music, the electric energy pulsing with every heartbeat.

He'd never understood people's obsession with football or with going to games. In high school, he'd liked hanging with his friends in the stands more than watching the game. His suburban school had been serious about football, but not so serious they went all out on a bond measure to build a $50 million stadium, like some other towns did. And even the most energetic of away games he'd been to in high school didn't hold a candle to this.

Now, wedged into the student section in the middle of the crowd, the stadium so raucous he felt the pulse and thrum rocking his bones, he got it. Justin was on his feet, shouting and cheering along with the rest of the student section. Three rows below him, five shirtless bros were banging on bucket drums. Another four rows down, four blondes in short shorts and university T-shirts had pom-poms and were leading cheers. The stadium was a sea of university logos and their school colors. Jerseys were everywhere, the ones he'd seen at the bookstore and almost bought.

And then there was his jersey. Wes's jersey. It fit him closely— not skin tight, since it was made for Wes, but it was fitted and looked like the real deal, especially next to everyone else's. He'd put it on over a long-sleeve gray Under Armour, and he'd thought he looked especially badass with his pompadour teased up higher than usual.

"Hey, man, that's an awesome jersey! Where did you get that?"

Apparently other people thought he looked good, too. "Oh, I got it from a friend," he shouted to the frat boy.

"Cool." The guy gave him a fist bump and moved on, downing his beer as he went.

The best part about the jersey? It had Wes's name on the back.

Sure, so did a lot of other jerseys around him. He counted at least twenty Van de Hoeks in his line of sight. But this was Wes's actual jersey. He'd worn it down there, on *that* field. It was like he was wearing Wes himself. *Mine. None of you know, but he's mine. I love him, and he loves me.*

Justin pulled out his phone and took a selfie, and then another, trying to look sexy and happy for the camera, and capture the wild crowd around him. He sent the best to Wes, along with a text. *In the stands and so ready to watch you play. You're going to kick ass. Xo*

He didn't think Wes had his phone on him, but he also had no clue what the team was doing down there before the game. They'd finished warm-ups and run-around drills half an hour ago. According to the countdown clock, there was fifteen minutes before kickoff. Inflatable tunnels were being pumped up outside the team tunnel entrances. Cheerleaders had already taken the field to pump up the crowd. The marching band, a few sections away, was making a racket, more noise than music.

His phone buzzed. Wes. *What section are you in?*

Student section. It was the only one left that had any tickets. The entire rest of the stadium was sold out. Over one hundred thousand people, all there to watch Wes and his team play.

I'll find you.

Cute words, and Justin grinned, bouncing on his toes. No, Wes wouldn't, not in this crowd, but he'd look, and that's what mattered. *I'll be watching you, love. You and your cute butt.*

He got a heart-eyed emoji back, and then Wes texted, *Got to get lined up. Text you after. ILY*

Je t'aime, cowboy. Kick ass!

A few minutes later, the smoke machines started at the Texas tunnel entrance. The music changed to a pounding, anticipatory beat, and then the announcer's voice boomed throughout the stadium. Everyone leaped to their feet, screaming, roaring. The bucket drums went wild.

"Welcome to the field your Texas players, led by team captain Wes Van de Hoek!"

Justin jumped up and down, screaming and grabbing the hands of the frat boys next to him, stomping his feet and roaring with the crowd as the football players burst out of the tunnel through the lineup of cheerleaders. They barreled into the middle of the field, Wes at the very front. The crowd was wild, beyond anything Justin had ever experienced. Everyone was screaming Wes's name, chanting *Van de Hoek! Van de Hoek!*

Wes ran backward. He faced the student section, and as he jogged, he tapped his gloved fist to his chest twice and then pointed to the crowd.

Deafening applause. People leaped to their feet screaming Wes's name, waving signs and posters and cardboard cutouts of eights and sevens. The crowd was so wild that they blocked Justin's view of the field and of Wes.

They thought Wes was giving his love to them, the student body. Their number-one player, the nice guy who never minded when people came up to him and wished him well, who never had an unkind word for anyone. Of course his love was for them.

No, it was for Justin. Wes had done that, in front of everyone, for him. He nearly sagged into his seat, weak at the knees. Wes was about to play his first game of the season, and he'd sent his love straight to the stands, to Justin.

He texted Wes, even though Wes's phone was in his locker. *I love you so much. And so do the fans.* He took a quick video of the wild craziness, attached it to the text, and sent it.

He even texted his dad, sending him a selfie of him smiling in the crowd and wearing Wes's jersey, right before kickoff. His dad sent back a line of exclamation points, and then *Maybe I can drive down and we can go to a game together! :)*

Yeah, Dad. That'd be cool. Up in Dallas, his dad was watching the game, too. About to watch his favorite player—and Justin's boyfriend—dominate.

Wes and Colton won the coin toss and got possession to start. From the very first drive, it was obvious that they, and the team, played a totally different game than the rest of the conference. The university had switched from the Big Twelve to the Southeastern Conference so they'd have more competition and they could play stronger, better, more challenging teams. But from the first snap, it looked like Wes and Colton and the rest of the offense were picking apart a pee wee league, not Florida, last year's top-ranked program in the FBS.

Wes alternated between blocking and slant routes, and the offense marched down the field as if the defense weren't even there, like the game was just another practice and they were executing perfect timing drills. In under two minutes, Colton threw a fade to Wes in the end zone. Wes leaped to pluck it out of the air in between two defenders and came down with an easy triple step for a picture-perfect touchdown. A SportsCenter moment.

The team's defense was equally hot, and they shut down the

Florida offense after only two first downs, forcing a punt. Wes and the offense took the field again, and they were even better than in the opening drive.

Every time Wes came out of the huddle, he turned to the student section. The stadium cameras caught him smiling behind his face mask, and that was the image that ended up replayed over and over and over on the jumbotron. Wes, gazing up at the student section, a wide smile breaking over his face before he turned those big shy eyes back to the game. One of the screaming dots in the student section behind Wes was Justin, bellowing his heart out for the love of his life.

Everyone else watched the game, but Justin watched Wes, even when he wasn't on the field. After his plays, he jogged right to the coach's side, downing water as he mopped his sweat with a team towel. He and his coach compared notes, Wes sharing his thoughts from the field as the coach listened, then gave his insights. Wes listened to his coach and to the offensive and defensive coordinators, and then he would move off. He headed to his teammates and high-fived each, then crouched down to chat. He stood with Colton and mimed throwing the football for him, focusing on his feet. Colton nodded, then laughed. He and Wes giggled on the sideline like the boys and best friends they were.

Justin's heart swelled. He was going to die before this game was over, either from an aneurysm or from overdosing on his love for Wes. It felt like he'd injected pure Wes into his veins, like being in the stadium was stepping into Wes's soul. He'd used to roll his eyes at the football players on his high school campus, so full of themselves, like they were the hottest shit to set foot on the earth. Stuck-up, arrogant pricks. All football players were that way, he'd decided.

Wes was so, so different. So giving. Especially of himself. He was a leader, not just on the field but off. A friend, and a good one, based on the smiles he got from his teammates and the respect in everyone's eyes.

I can't break this team. I can't break us apart. Coach says I can bring them all to glory.

Words Justin had gritted his teeth at and rolled his eyes over. But now, seeing it, feeling it...

He understood.

He was so goddamn lucky Wes loved him and was willing to give their love a chance, even though they'd be hiding. Whatever resentment he might have been feeling, whatever grumbles he hadn't let out of his psyche, vanished with a pop.

By halftime, Texas was up 21–3. Florida's one field goal had been a risky fifty-eight yard attempt, the Florida head coach desperate to avoid the humiliation of a shutout.

The teams filtered into their locker rooms. Wes, Colton, and Florida brought up the Texas rear, stopping by the student section to goof around and shake hands and let the students knock on their helmets for good luck. One of the wide receivers leaped up onto the padded wall, falling back into the sea of hands and screaming fans like he was about to go crowd surfing. He could have, too, but after only a few seconds, he jumped back down, and he, Wes, Colton, and everyone else headed to the locker room. Wes spun around, gazing at the student section as he jogged backward all the way into the tunnel.

Justin texted his dad during the half, comparing their thoughts on the game. Total blowout was his dad's verdict. Proof positive that Wes Van de Hoek was a one-in-a-million player. *You don't see that kind of talent but once a decade, if that. That boy has worked his ass off, and it shows.*

Yes he has.

It's good to see you smiling again. :) I guess you're there with someone?

You could say that.

I hope whoever you're with, he's making you happy. He gets a thumbs up from me if he got you to go to a game!

LOL Dad. Yeah, he's a good guy.

Bring him home. Happy to meet him.

After the half, the team ran onto the field to even wilder cheers and stomps, the stadium even more energized after the phenomenal first half. Wes jogged to the student section for more high fives and handshakes, then repeated his fist to his heart and point to the stands. Justin blew him a kiss, imagined it sailing down to the field and through Wes's face mask, landing on his cheek.

By the end of the third, the game was over. Wes put another touchdown on the board, and then one of the receivers caught a deep pass as Wes helped block, giving Colton the extra time in the pocket to set up the perfect throw. When the fourth quarter started, the second string was in the game, and even some of the third string got time on the field. Florida was so tired, so off their rhythm, they could only put one more field goal on the scoreboard. The game ended 34–6.

The stands went wild as the clock ran out. Wes and Colton crossed the field, shaking the hands of the other team captains, and the coaches met in the middle for a handshake as well. Both teams drifted into their locker rooms, and the crowd finally started to make its way out of the stadium.

Out of the stadium and straight into West Campus. It was an eight-block walk to Daisy Lane, and ten thousand students meandered in that direction. Thirty minutes after the game ended, West Campus had turned into a multiblock street party, headquartered at the restaurant. The old houses were decked out in university colors, with banners and posters and flags in every window and on every porch. Windows were open, and stereos blasted music. Coolers of beer were on almost every front lawn, and students milled in the streets, sat on lawn chairs in their yards, lounged on front porches. It was wall-to-wall humanity, and Justin moved with the currents, eventually winding up on Opal Street.

Where, if at all possible, the party was even more intense, since that was where the starting line lived. Music pulsed, so loud he could feel the air quake. Laughter rang from every direction. He fought his way to his front porch and finally found space to breathe.

His phone buzzed in his pocket. *Told you I'd win the game for you. <3*

You were amazing!!

Did you have a good time?

I loved it. I loved watching you.

He got a heart emoji, and then Wes went quiet for about twenty minutes. Justin people-watched, letting the party vibes flow through him. A frat boy passed him a beer, and he unscrewed the top and shared a cheers. The frat boy told him his jersey was *sick, dude,* and then he moved on, delivering beer to everyone he could, like a beer fairy on a mission.

We're on the way. Where r u?

Back home. This is nuts. Is it always like this?

Yeah. :) It's gonna be more crazy in a minute.

He felt the change when the team arrived. They walked from the stadium, cheered on by the crowds that lingered on the streets. University police cruisers shadowed the players, watching over the party and making sure everyone kept things on the fun side of the line.

When the team turned onto Opal Street, the entire block roared. It was as loud as the stadium had been, as energetic. People close to the players high-fived them and passed them beers. Somewhere, music was turned up. Half the street turned into a dance party.

Justin found Wes first, watching him take, but not open, a beer. He hung with Colton, both of them shaking people's hands, high-fiving, accepting congrats from guys and girls alike. Colton welcomed the attention, basking in it. Especially from the girls. He let them sling their arms around him and wrapped his arms around their waists. He accepted kisses to his cheeks and to his biceps.

Wes was more restrained, shaking hands and tolerating the

hugs, but not returning them. He searched the crowd, scanning faces, searching farther and farther down the street—

Until his eyes found Justin, leaning against his porch railing and sipping his beer.

He beamed at Wes. Raised his bottle in a silent toast.

Wes's expression went from guarded happiness to unbridled joy in an instant. He tried to thread through the crowd, but at every step he was stopped. Congratulated. Fist-bumped. One girl wrapped her arms around his neck and kissed his cheek. Every time, Wes's gaze flicked to Justin, his impatience growing.

Justin smiled.

Wes finally stopped in the middle of the crowd and dug out his phone. He swiped a quick text, then looked up at Justin.

Justin's phone buzzed. *Meet me at my truck?*

Sure.

It took ten minutes to get around the corner, but finally he was off Opal and walking down Twenty-Ninth. There were still people everywhere, but at least the street itself was mostly clear. He headed for Wes's truck and waited, leaning against the rusted tailgate with his shoes up on the hood of his own Honda.

Wes appeared five minutes later, jogging down the street with his head down, ball cap forward, trying to shield his face. It didn't work, and three different groups called out his name in the space of twenty yards. He waved back, then zigged into the gap between their cars, collapsing across the hood of Justin's Honda. He groaned and laughed, rolling his head to the side and peering at Justin. "Oh my God…"

"Your adoring fans love you, m'lord." Justin kept his hands to himself, holding on to the bottoms of his knees. If he touched Wes now, he wouldn't ever stop. "You gave them quite a show in the gladiator arena today."

Wes laughed. He propped himself on his elbow and spread his fingers across the hood of Justin's car as if he were reaching for Justin. "This party is going to go until dawn."

"This is insane."

"Do you wanna stay?"

"Is there another option?"

Wes's eyes flashed. "Wanna get out of here? With me?"

"Oh, with *you*?" Justin pretended to think. Wes grinned, burying his face in his biceps and the metal of the hood as his eyes peeked over the curve of his muscle at Justin. "I guess I could go with you. Where to, cowboy?"

Wes hauled himself to his feet and headed for the driver's door of his truck. "Hop in."

WES DROVE them way outside the city to a country road that led into a state park, the sun setting as they pulled into the gravel lot. "There's a lake about a mile into the park," Wes said, parking. The only other car there was a Subaru, and it had an overnight camping permit taped inside the windshield. "Colton and I used to hike out and fish there last year."

"Not anymore?"

Wes shrugged. "Got too busy." He stepped out, jogged around to Justin's side, and then held out his hand when Justin pushed open the passenger door. Justin flushed, but he took Wes's hand as he hopped out.

Night came quick in the country, and by the time Wes had grabbed his duffel and shut and locked his truck, the shadows were so deep that Wes kept their hands laced together, fingers interlocked. He led Justin into the park, picking the rightmost trailhead that wound into the trees. "Lake is to the left," he said, gesturing behind him. "Usually that's where the campers go."

He turned on his cell phone flashlight and led them down the trail. Justin stayed close, almost right up on Wes. He'd camped before, in Boy Scouts and when he was a kid, but there was some- thing about creeping through the woods in the dark that felt very horror movie to him. There weren't any bears in Texas, and he didn't think there were any chain saw murderers on the loose, but there was still that primeval fear, that little monkey brain that would rather be inside than ducking branches by the light of a cell phone. He squeezed Wes's hand, hard, but kept his fears to himself. Wherever Wes was taking them, he trusted Wes.

Wes led him to a break in the woods that opened up to a field of swaying golden grasses clinging to the last dusky remnants of the setting sun. The tips were tinged in blood orange and marmalade, the stalks already turning silver by the light of the risen half moon. Fireflies flickered in waves all around them. Wes tugged him close, wrapping his arms around Justin's waist from behind. "Gorgeous, huh?"

"That doesn't even begin to describe it."

"I wanted to bring you here and show you. Especially like this, when the fireflies are out." He kissed Justin's neck and took his hand again. "C'mon."

Wes led him into the center of the meadow. He dropped his duffel and unzipped it, then pulled out a bedsheet, a blanket, and a bottle of champagne. "Thought we could have our own celebration."

Justin helped him spread out the blanket, and Wes shook up the champagne before twisting the top off. Bubbles flew everywhere and soaked his T-shirt. He tried to suck the spilled champagne off his fingers, but Justin grabbed his wrist and pulled him down, telling him, "That's my job."

Licking Wes's fingers clean turned into kissing, and abandoning the champagne bottle in the grass, and then Justin peeling Wes's soaked T-shirt off and rolling him to his back on the blanket. He tugged his own shirt over his head, and Wes reached for the button of his jeans. He laid his naked chest across Wes's and slid his fingers through Wes's hair. "Do you have a condom in that duffel, or just champagne?"

"I brought some stuff."

"Thought you'd get lucky, huh?"

"I crossed all my fingers and all my toes. Wished on a lucky star, too." Wes grinned.

"Well." Justin kissed him slowly. "It might end up being your lucky day."

He kissed a path down Wes's body, from his lips to his pecs to his ticklish, quivering belly, and then lower, pulling down the waistband of Wes's athletic shorts. Wes's cock was already hard, already thick and heavy and hot, pressed against his abdomen.

Justin licked a long, wet path from his head to the base of his dick and back up before closing his lips around Wes's cock head and sucking.

Wes groaned, and he gripped Justin's skull, fingers tangling in his hair. He squeezed harder as Justin sucked him all the way down, lips sealed to Wes's shaft until his cock head knocked against the back of Justin's throat. He hummed, sucking in deep pulls. Wes's thighs trembled, and his heels kicked at the blanket.

"Stop, stop. I don't wanna come yet." Wes tugged Justin back up. "I want to make love to you. It's been too long."

They'd been in Paris the last time they had sex. That had been far too long ago. Justin wiped his lips and rolled to his back, shucking his jeans and his boots as Wes dug through his duffel and pulled out a condom and a brand-new bottle of lube. He kicked off his shorts and rolled on top of Justin, caging him between his elbows as he rested his forearms on the blanket. Their hips rolled together. Justin's thighs spread, and he hooked one ankle behind Wes's knee.

Wes splayed his fingers across Justin's cheeks. He rocked against him, kissing his forehead, his eyebrows, his cheekbones. The tip of his nose. His lips, and then his chin. Fireflies winked over Wes's head, flickering in and out like stars that were close enough to grasp.

Justin groped for the lube and dragged it across the blanket. He pumped some into his hand, then reached between his legs and prepared himself as quickly as he could. Wes pushed his forehead against Justin's chest and looked down, his lips open, breath coming in short pants that burned Justin's skin. He grabbed the lube and helped, sliding his thick fingers in alongside Justin's.

Justin tipped his head back and groaned. "I'm ready."

Wes grabbed the condom and rolled it on. His hands shook as he slicked himself. He fingered another pump of lube into Justin's hole, until Justin was trembling and grasping the blanket in both hands. "Wes!"

Wes wrapped Justin's legs around his waist, hefted his ass in one large palm, and lined his cock up at Justin's hole. He exhaled, once, twice, and a third time, like he was in the middle of a game. He closed his eyes. Opened them and stared into Justin's gaze.

"I love you," Wes whispered as he pushed forward.

Justin arched his back and moaned, his fingers clawing at the air, at his own scalp, then at Wes's shoulders. It was too much and not enough, all at once. Wes was big, the biggest he'd ever had, and he felt every thick, hard inch. He was stretched, stuffed, impaled on Wes's cock... and he fucking loved it. His own cock throbbed, dripping precome into his belly button. His ass clenched around Wes. Wes groaned and buried his face in Justin's neck.

He kissed Wes until he could breathe again, then squeezed his legs around Wes's waist and urged him to move. Wes did, slowly, every inch gliding so deep inside Justin it punched the breath from his lungs and left him panting, little puffs of air falling against Wes's lips.

"Je t'aime," Wes whispered, dropping kisses in time with the flickers of the fireflies overhead. "Je t'aime tellement, mon amour."

The warm night, the silvered moonlit meadow. Wes above him, inside him, moving with such sweet slowness he felt like their bodies were merging, like if he rocked back against Wes, he'd fall into his cowboy's big heart and soul. And a week ago he'd thought he'd never feel Wes like this again.

It was all too much, and Justin tipped over into his orgasm without warning. He grabbed Wes's face and clung to him as he smothered his shout with a kiss. Wes followed, gasping as he buried himself inside Justin, his hips thrusting, his arms shaking, his shoulders trembling as his own orgasm burned through him.

After, Wes pulled Justin into his arms, holding him from behind as they sat and watched the stars, wrapped up in Wes's sheet. They drank the champagne that hadn't bubbled over straight from the bottle, passing it back and forth until they were both giggling and nuzzling each other's cheeks and necks and sneaking kisses on every exposed inch of skin they could reach. When the bottle was finished, Justin looped his arms around Wes's neck and pulled him down to the blanket again. He ran his fingers over Wes's face, traced the lines of his jaw and his wide smile. Wes kissed his temple, his shoulder, sucked a hickey into the curve of his pec as Justin laughed and wrapped his legs around Wes's thighs. Their cocks, hot and hard and aching again, brushed together.

Justin bit his lip. Shifted and arched his back. Tried to push his ass against Wes's cock.

Wes twirled Justin's hair in his fingers. "You're the only person I've ever been with." His eyes were like slivers of moonlight caught on the edge of a lake.

Justin's heart hammered. What would the next words out of Wes's mouth be? *I want to experiment. I want to see what else is out there. Maybe I do want to sleep with a girl, see what it's like. Can we open this up? We're not monogamous, right?*

"I get tested every year as part of my physical," Wes said, his voice so soft Justin had to strain to hear him, even though they were less than an inch apart. "I was tested again in August. Everything came back negative."

Oh God. Now Justin's heart hammered for a totally different reason. "I, um. I get tested at my annual physical, too. My last one was before I came back to school. After you and I, in Paris. And yeah. Everything was negative."

"Do you… Could we—" Wes's sudden inhale trembled. "I want to be yours, completely. I want to make love to you without the condom," he finished in a rush. "But if you don't want that, I mean, that's fine. It's okay—"

Justin shushed him with a kiss. "I promised myself I wouldn't do that until it was serious. That I'd use condoms every time, until I was with someone I thought I could be with forever."

A firefly flitted from left to right behind Wes's head.

"I think that man might be you. I know I *want* him to be you."

Wes's exhale nearly blew him away. He collapsed on top of Justin and wrapped his big arms all the way around him, clinging to him, every muscle Justin could feel shaking. Justin stroked his hands over Wes's shoulders, down his arms, up his triceps. "I want to make this work. However we need to, and whatever that looks like."

"So do I." Wes's voice was watery. He hid his face against Justin's neck. "I'm so sorry for what I did. What I said to you. I'm so sor—"

"*Shhh.*" He pulled Wes up and kissed him again. "That's our past. Don't think about it anymore. Think about our future. The next moment, when I kiss you." He did. "And the moment after that, when you make love to me again."

Wes blinked, his breath hot against Justin's lips, his heavy cock brushing against Justin's thigh. Justin was still somewhat slick from earlier, and it didn't take much lube to get him ready again. Wes's hands trembled when he held his bare cock against Justin's hole. "Are you sure?" Wes whispered.

Justin nodded. He hooked his ankle around Wes's waist. "I love you, cowboy."

Wes smiled, and he entered Justin again, easier this time, but so, so different. Skin to skin, body to body, heat to heat. Heart to soul. He slid all the way in, every inch buried inside Justin, and froze. Wes trembled, his hands gripping Justin's thighs, his hips. "Justin." His voice was lighter than the starlight. "Justin, my God."

"*Mon amour*," Justin moaned. There was nothing between them, nothing at all. Wes, the man he loved, was inside him. Touching him where no one else ever had, in a way no one else ever had. Maybe no one else ever would. If Wes was the only man he took inside him like this, he'd be happy with that. Deliriously happy, in fact. *I want you to be* the one. *Please, let us be an epic love story.*

Wes moved more slowly than before, savoring each press and pull of their bodies. Justin rocked with him, moving his hips, his ass, in time with Wes's gentle thrusts. He pushed Wes back and crawled into his lap, sitting on his cock as Wes's big hands wrapped around his back and slid up his spine, holding him tight as they rocked and swayed and kissed until they were dizzy. Eventually he threaded their fingers together, holding Wes's hands to the blanket. He rode Wes with long, deep slides up and down his cock, until Wes was groaning and thrashing, biting his lips and squeezing his eyes closed. Justin wasn't far behind. He let go of Wes's hands and raked his fingers down Wes's chest, bracing himself against Wes's hard six-pack.

"I want to feel you come inside me." He stroked his cock with one hand, leaning forward until Wes's cock dragged over his prostate with each thrust. Lightning sheared through him, and he didn't know if it was the fireflies he was seeing or if his mind was scattering fireworks.

Wes keened. He grabbed onto Justin's ass and squeezed, drove himself up into Justin hard and fast and deep, and then exploded with a long, ragged shout. Justin gasped, his ass filling with a warmth that ran right up his spine. He was slicker than before, too. He kept bouncing on Wes's cock even as Wes whimpered, clenched his fingers into Justin's ass cheeks, tried to speak and only managed broken syllables.

Justin's hand flew over his cock, and he came with a shout of his own, crying Wes's name as he flew face-first into his orgasm. He squeezed around Wes, and Wes curled forward and kissed him as the world faded away.

He came back to himself on his side, tangled in Wes's arms and legs, with the midnight breeze cooling their skin. Wes panted beside him, his hands threaded with Justin's, his lips pressed to Justin's knuckles. He hadn't passed out, but it had been close, and he barely remembered tipping over or Wes wrapping Justin in his arms.

"Wow."

Wes grinned. "There needs to be a better word invented to describe what that was."

"Perfect."

"Still not enough." Wes kissed his wrist, the inside of his arm. "That was more than perfect."

He smiled. "Yeah, it was, cowboy. It was."

CHAPTER SEVENTEEN

FOR WES'S second away game, Justin took a road trip. He didn't follow the buses, exactly, but he left when Wes and the rest of the team did. It was an eight-hour drive to the stadium in Louisiana, and he couldn't text Wes and drive at the same time, so he listened to the playlist Wes had made for him on Spotify. Wes liked Western music, and when Justin asked if he liked Garth Brooks and Florida Georgia Line, Wes had given him a look of horror. The next day, Justin had a Western playlist curated just for him. "Western music comes from cowboy ballads," Wes explained. "Country is that Nashville noise. Western is what they played on the frontier. A guy and his guitar and his horse, sitting around the campfire."

"Which one sings about trains?"

Wes had sneaked a kiss on his cheek as Justin laughed. Listening, he had to admit: the music was very Wes. He could almost imagine Wes singing these songs, if it weren't for the fact that Wes's singing sounded like a camel being strangled. Turned out, there was something he wasn't good at. In fact, he was downright awful.

Justin had made a playlist for Wes, too, so he could listen to something other than a hundred guys farting and snoring and belching on the bus for eight hours. His was an eclectic mix of pop and hip-hop and blues and ballet scores. When they moved in together, they were going to have one hell of a Spotify mix.

He was one of the early birds at the stadium, and he had a tailgate for one in his little Honda. He texted with Wes again for a bit. When they opened the stadium, he found his seat and watched both teams warm up.

Louisiana was supposed to give Wes and the rest of the team a challenge, enough so that the coach had them working extra hard the week before.

I'm not worried, Wes texted. *I promised I'd win every game this season for you. I don't break my promises.*

He was early enough that Wes was able to find him in the stands during the team warm-up. *Now I know exactly where to look.*

Justin texted his dad when Wes and the team headed to the locker room. They'd been texting more and more, sometimes every day. It was nice, and he was getting to know his dad in a whole new way. His dad was funny, and insightful at times, and he really loved his Texas football. He was shocked Justin was at an away game—and, more than shocked, jealous. *I need to meet this guy that has you going to all these games, Justin. He's got to be a huge football fan, and you must be crazy about him. I tried for years to get you interested in football.*

Yeah, but you're my dad. It wasn't cool when you tried.

Of course. Eyeroll emoji. *Well, I need to buy your boyfriend a beer. He got through to you. Football is the best sport of all. And he likes the right team. Imagine if your boyfriend didn't like Texas.* He sent a GIF of a man grabbing his heart and fainting.

Justin grinned. He tried to imagine Wes rooting for another team. Then tried to imagine the look on his dad's face when he showed up at their house one day with Wes at his side.

The only thing I ask of my son is he marries a man who likes Texas football.

Justin laughed out loud. He took a selfie of himself in the Louisiana stands, in Wes's jersey, with a Texas beanie on his head and a Texas scarf around his neck. *Meet your approval, dad?*

You make me so proud, son. Crying emoji. *Hey, why don't you ever send a picture of your boyfriend and you together?*

He's shy.

I don't bite.

There was nothing he could say, so he powered off his screen and tucked his phone back in his pocket. Only ten minutes to kickoff, anyway.

Wes and Colton lost the coin flip, and the Texas defense took the field first. Louisiana pushed hard, but the defense rallied and held them to a field goal after stopping a drive on the two-yard line and batting down two attempts at the fade pass to the end zone. The offense came on after a kickoff return brought them out to their own thirty-eight.

Colton started with a short pass, getting a feel for the churn and grind of Louisiana's line. Wes had taught Justin, one night when they were watching the stars in the bed of Wes's pickup truck, that great football wasn't made in the showy plays, the Hail Marys and the breakaways. Greatness came in the half seconds between the play action and the tackle. In the inches fought for between the two teams. Offensive and defensive lines fighting to open and close routes for their side to barrel through. A leap for a catch between three defenders, and the scramble to set and run after the screen pass. A hitch, the juke, and the spin for an extra yard.

He watched Colton launch the ball at Wes. Wes caught it in the center of his chest, turned, planted his feet, and ran right into the arms of Louisiana's middle linebacker. Justin heard the crunch of pads on pads all the way in the stands. He covered his eyes as the play was blown dead. Held his breath. But Wes hauled himself up and trotted back to the huddle, and they were only two yards off a first down.

The first half was a grind, like Wes had said. The Louisiana defense stuck to Wes like stink on shit. It was more than man coverage. It was like eight on one. That opened up some deep routes for passes, and Colton started targeting the wide receivers more as Wes shifted into a blocking role, or spun off for dump passes when Louisiana pressed hard. By the time the half was called, the score was tied, 10–10, and Wes's uniform was a kaleidoscope of grass stains and a long streak of blood from when he ripped the skin of his forearm on a sliding tackle in the second quarter.

For the first time, Justin got a text from Wes at half. It was a picture of him with an IV in his elbow, his forearm wrapped and bandaged. *You would have done it better.*

Why do you have an IV!?!?!?

Hydration. I was starting to cramp.

Oh. Jesus, he'd been about to tear out of his seat, run right to the locker room and burst in, never mind their secret. *Christ, you scared me.*

Sorry. I was a little woozy from the lack of fluids. I feel a lot better now. Just wanted to hear from you, though.

He sent back a line of hearts. *You're playing great.*

We're going to come out strong in the next half. We have good adjustments we can make. We're going to win. Promise.

The second half started with Texas in possession, and Wes was right. They exploded out of the tunnel as if the entire offense had been given cocaine and sugar water. He almost texted Wes to ask what kind of elephant stimulant had been in that IV.

But no, this was all Wes. Justin could see the adjustments he'd texted about: the way he tightened up his movements, dug harder on his plants and pivots. Colton launched his passes faster. The offensive linemen held back the pass rushers more. Wes joined in blocking about half of the time. Even Justin, who'd watched a dozen of Wes's practices, couldn't figure out what play was being run next, whether it would be a rush or a short pass or a deep route.

He was exhausted watching, clinging to his scarf and screaming his heart out. The Louisiana defense, trying to contain Wes and Colton and the team, looked like they were sucking wind by the start of the fourth.

And, in the fourth, Wes scored a touchdown that broke the grinding back-and-forth tie, and on the next play, Louisiana threw an interception that brought the Texas offense back onto the field. They were tired, but they rallied, and Wes blocked for Orlando, who rushed a breakaway sixty-yarder for another touchdown, and they were up fourteen over Louisiana.

After another grueling seven minutes, Colton took a knee to wind down the clock, and Texas put up their seventh win of the season, making them one of only two teams in the league that were still undefeated.

Wes turned to the stands and blew a kiss to the Texas fans. They roared, cheered for him, chanted his name and waved their posters and their 87s.

But Wes was looking right at Justin when he did it. Justin closed his fist around the chilly Louisiana air and brought it to his lips. He kissed his fingers, as if he were kissing Wes's hand, and sent the kiss right back.

Congratulations, cowboy. You were perfect.

Told you I'd win for you. <3

See you back at home?

Drive safe, mon amour.

"DUDE, SCOOT OVER."

Halfway through the drive back to campus, when the rest of the team was snoring, Colton appeared at Wes's side, shoving him to make room on the two-seater row Wes had claimed for himself.

"What's up?" he asked, pausing Justin's playlist and pulling his earbuds out. He tucked his phone into his hoodie and scooted over for Colton's massive frame.

Colton spun a football in his hands. They were at the late-night portion of the drive, out on the stretch of I-10 that was a whole lot of nothing. Inky darkness filled the windows. Only a few scattered phone screens lit the inside of the bus. Colton was more shadow than man, what little light there was lost in his hoodie and track pants and skirting the rounded edges of the football.

"I know something is going on with you."

Wes froze. He couldn't see Colton's eyes, not in the dark.

"You're seeing a girl. It's obvious."

He let out a whoosh of breath, straightening his legs to try to hide how much they were shaking. "I don't know what you—"

"Dude. You changed overnight. You went from a broken-hearted mess to practically skipping down the sidewalk. She's got to be something special if she's got you like this."

"Like what?"

"Happy." Colton spun the football faster. "I've never seen you this happy. Ever. So, what gives?" There was a wounded note in Colton's voice. "Why didn't you tell me?"

He had no idea what to say. He couldn't find the words, couldn't scrape together anything that sounded plausible.

"Where did you guys meet? In class? Or is this the girl from over the summer? The one you were so broken up about? She someone you met when you did that study-abroad thing?"

"Yeah. Yeah, we met over the summer. In Paris."

"Does she live overseas? Is that why you never brought her around?"

It was an easy out, but he couldn't speak the lie. He chewed on the words. Stared at the football in Colton's hands, spinning, spinning, spinning. "No. Local."

"Well, why haven't I met her, then?"

He kneed Colton's thigh and tried to laugh. "Yeah, right. Like I'll let you go all horndog."

"Man…" Colton shook his head. "Not this time. I can tell she's something serious for you. I've never seen you like this. You never date, and if you hook up, you're super chill about it. You've got that classy gentleman cowboy vibe that the chicks just swoon for."

"What are you talking about?"

"All the chicks that are always trying to get your attention! Dude, you're a pussy magnet. Especially in that ridiculous hat."

He barked out a laugh as his cheeks flushed, heat racing through every vein and soaking his muscles. "Whatever, man. I'm not interested in all that."

It was the first true thing he'd said to Colton since the conversation began. Part of him flinched. They'd been so close two years ago. Like brothers the year before. Now he was lying to Colton, hiding the biggest parts and pieces of himself. Hiding the most important person in his world. His stomach cramped, and the tacos the team had eaten before the drive home threatened to come back up.

"Yeah, I know you're not, especially not anymore. This chick is serious for you. Think you might end up going all the way? She might be the one? College sweetheart follows you into the NFL?"

"Maybe."

"Tell me about her. What's her name? What's she look like? Can I see a photo?"

"Why are you so interested all of a sudden?"

Colton caught his football in both hands, stopping the spin. "It's not all of a sudden, dude. I've always wanted you to be this freakin' happy. Why are you being so cagey about it? You ashamed to bring her around?"

"What? No!"

"You're not, like, too good for the rest of us all of a sudden? With your real major and your big science classes?"

"Stop." He lunged for the ball, trying to strip it from Colton.

Colton twisted away, elbowed him in the stomach. Wes glared. "That's not it at all."

"Then what gives?"

He blew out another harsh breath and threw his head back against the bus seat. "I—we—want to keep things private. It's insane, man. All the stuff this year? All the attention?"

Colton slumped in his seat, the tension in his arms and legs evaporating. He flopped his leg into the aisle and spun the football on the flat plane of his stomach. "It is pretty crazy how much attention you're getting. I mean, you deserve it. You do. But yeah, man. It's wild."

"I feel like I can't even take a dump without someone trying to follow me in and get a photo of it."

Colton snorted.

"This, what we have? It's not in the media, and it's not something I'm hounded about. We're not hounded about it."

"Think she wouldn't like the attention? Or wouldn't be able to deal?"

"It's not that. It's… it's the only thing that's mine right now. And that's special to me." *Justin is special to me.*

Colton was quiet. He stared at his football, spinning it, his lips pursed. "You're not even going to show me a picture?"

He shoved Colton, pushing him out of his row and into the aisle. Colton squawked, waking up Orlando and Art. Orlando threw his empty Monster can at Colton's head.

Colton held up his hands, surrendering. "All right, all right!" He kicked the Monster can back to Orlando's row, and Orlando flipped him off, grunted, rolled toward the window, and went right back to snoring. "Look, I just want you to know, I'm happy for you, 'kay? I can tell that you're freaking gone for this girl. I do want to meet her and make sure she's good for you. But." He held out his fist for Wes. "I get what you're saying. Just know I'm rooting for you guys."

Wes bumped his fist against Colton's and smiled. "Thanks. I appreciate it. And… one day."

Colton sauntered back up the bus. He flopped down, stretching out across an entire row, his legs stretched across the aisle with his heels up on the opposite seat. He kicked off his sneakers, and one of the linebackers groaned. "Gross, man. You need some fucking Odor-Eaters."

Wes rested his forehead against the window and stared out at the darkness. His thumb brushed over his phone screen, turning it back on. He reread the text Justin had sent him when he stopped for gas: *Still thinking of your arm. I can take a look when you get back?* and a selfie of him sipping his coffee before he started the last half of the drive.

It is serious, Colton, he wanted to say. *It's the rest of my life. Justin is everything I ever wanted.*

What would Colton's face look like if Wes said Justin's name?

His stomach lurched again, and he hunched in his seat, head between his knees. Cold sweat beaded on his skin, across his forehead and down his spine. He swallowed hard. Squeezed his eyes closed.

How did he bring all these pieces of himself together? How did the Wes who caught footballs and had stadiums packed with fans leaping to their feet, screaming his name, roaring as he made touchdown after touchdown, live with the Wes who loved Justin? How did the two men coexist inside of him?

Trick question. They were all him. He was only one man, but he was being pulled in too many different directions, and he could feel the fissures forming in the center of his soul. He was one man, with one heart—and that heart belonged to Justin, while the world wanted it to belong to football. But it didn't, and he couldn't force it. He didn't want to. He just wanted to love Justin.

If the world ever found out…

The loss of his scholarship would be the least of his worries.

He ran his thumb over Justin's selfie. *Who am I when you love me? Who am I when I fall in love with you?*

He shoved his earbuds back into his ears and pressed play. Justin's playlist started again. Wes pulled up his hoodie and laid his head against the window, watching the yellow line on the center of the asphalt roll on and on and on.

CHAPTER EIGHTEEN

JUSTIN STARED into the mirror overlooking the ballet classroom and wrung his hands. Why had he thought this was a good idea? He was an idiot for inviting Wes. What the hell was he thinking?

His ballet class was a group of thirteen freshman girls, two other gay guys who had hooked up, had a spat, and now weren't speaking or even looking at each other, and him. Their little performance was nothing more than a series of abbreviated solos, three minutes max for each dancer to perform for whoever they'd invited to crowd around at the back of the room. Most of the people watching were moms.

And then there was Wes, buried so far in the corner in his cowboy hat and his Wranglers he looked like he was trying to merge into the wall. Every mom in the classroom was eyeing him up, long, lingering once-overs of the famous cowboy footballer trying to look inconspicuous in the ballet studio.

Tracey finished her three-minute solo, and her *Nutcracker* music cut out. The instructor strode out in front of the tiny audience to announce the next dancer. "Next up is Justin Swanscott, a junior, who will be performing Odette's entrance from *Swan Lake*."

He saw Wes stand up straighter. Fold his arms over his chest. Shift his hips and try to look like he wasn't suddenly as focused on the dance floor as he was at his own games. Even behind the dance partition, Justin could feel the force, the intensity of his stare.

He heard the music start and took a breath. Three minutes. *Think of Paris.*

He closed his eyes and danced the movements he remembered by heart. This was an intro class, but he wasn't a beginning dancer, so he didn't stumble or drop a leg lift. He hit each position cleanly, and his lines were long, and, even though he wasn't dancing *en pointe*, he got to his toes and reached for the ceiling. When three minutes were up and his music tapered off, he opened his eyes and looked first at Wes.

Wes stared, his jaw hanging open, lips parted, pupils blown wide. He'd lost his rigid stance, and it looked like a single breath could knock him down.

Justin looked away quickly, in case one of the mothers figured out Justin and Wes were connected. They'd arrived separately and hadn't said a word to each other, and most of the gossip was focused on whether Wes was crushing on or dating one of the freshman girls.

He bowed as the studio applauded. He thanked the audience and then scampered back behind the partition. His instructor kissed him on both cheeks and told him he was phenomenal and that he had to take Ballet II next time. He thanked her, threw on his warm-ups, grabbed his duffel bag, and slipped out the back door.

Wes met him around the corner, jogging to where Justin had parked in an out-of-the-way spot far from the streetlights. He ran right up to Justin and grabbed him, took both of his shoulders in his massive grip, and backed him against the car.

Wes pressed their bodies together so Justin could feel his erection, achingly hard against his belly. "That was the hottest thing

I've ever seen," Wes growled, right before he captured Justin's lips with his own.

They kissed in the darkness until they heard tires rolling on the pavement and broke apart right before headlights swept over them both. Justin wiped his lips and steadied himself, and Wes braced his forearms on the roof of Justin's car and bowed his head.

"I can't think," Wes croaked. "All the blood in my body is in my cock. I've never been this hard."

Justin jerked open his car door and pushed the front seat forward. "Get in the back. Now."

Wes barely fit, but they made it work. Justin crawled in after him, kneeling on the floorboards and pulling Wes's cock out so he could get his mouth on him, swallow Wes down. He sucked him deep and hard, and played with his balls. Pressed his finger against his perineum, massaging the smooth skin until Wes's thighs quaked and he dug his hands into Justin's hair. He kept going, pressing until Wes thrust his cock all the way into Justin's throat and erupted with a hoarse cry. Wes came so much, so forcefully, Justin couldn't swallow it all, and some dribbled down his chin. Wes leaned forward and kissed him, licking his own spilled come. Another car passed by, but the windows were fogged, and they didn't try to hide.

"Jesus," Wes breathed. "You were incredible."

Justin patted his lips daintily, like he'd just finished tea with the Queen. "Thank you."

"Not that." Wes held his hand. He was slumped half in Justin's backseat, half falling to the floorboards, one leg shoved between the two front seats over the center console, the other bent up like he was squatting. "That was epic, too. You need to keep dancing. You're gorgeous."

"I'm nothing special."

"You remind me of the danseurs we saw in Paris."

Justin laughed. "They are some of the best on the planet!"

"You remind me of them," Wes insisted.

"Thank you. That's very sweet, cowboy."

"I mean it, *mon amour*."

Wes began the arduous process of disentangling himself from the inside of Justin's car. When he finally bear crawled out onto the pavement, Justin said, "Congratulations. You've just been born again."

"That's exactly what it felt like." Wes stretched and popped his back. "Let's take my truck if we ever need to go on a road trip. That's not a car. It's a jack-in-the-box."

"Deal."

"Do you have plans later tonight?" Wes asked, almost shy.

"Wes, you're my plans. You're my boyfriend. I don't do anything without you. I don't want to do anything without you."

Wes bit his lip and grinned. "Okay. Then get in your jack-in-the-box car and follow me."

He was curious, but he did what Wes said, getting in and waiting for Wes to pull up beside him in his truck. He expected to head out of the city, and he wasn't disappointed when Wes turned onto the county highway. But he was surprised when Wes pulled off only twenty minutes later, turning into the parking lot of a Holiday Inn that catered to truckers. Wes parked by the back door and waited for Justin.

"I wanted to do something special for you." He took Justin's hand. "Close your eyes."

He let Wes lead him into the hotel, down two hallways that smelled of cigarette smoke and carpet cleaner. Air conditioners rattled, and HBO blared from behind one of the room doors. They came to a stop, and he heard Wes slide his keycard into the lock. Heard the door open. Wes guided him a few steps into the room. "Wait here. Keep your eyes closed. No peeking." He heard a lighter flick on.

"Okay… You can open them."

Candles were the first things he saw. A dozen tea lights scattered on the laminate dresser. The flickering glow reminded him of Paris, of the Eiffel Tower, of their first kiss. He smiled and stepped forward, to where Wes was waiting—

His steps faltered. White rose petals carpeted the bed. A bundle of lavender and baby's breath, the biggest Justin had ever seen, rested on the pillow, tied with twine, like the little bundle of buds Wes had bought him in Paris. His breath hitched, and he turned to Wes, gasping.

Wes pulled a single red rose from behind his back. He twirled it in his fingers and smiled. *"Tu es mon plus grand amour."*

You are the love of my life.

CHAPTER NINETEEN

"HEY, WES?" Colton poked his head into Wes's bedroom. "Oh. Hey. You're… Justin, right?"

Justin sat at Wes's side on the floor. Both of their backs were to Wes's bed, and their textbooks were spread around them.

Wes's heart sped up as he turned to Colton. "What's up?"

"We're going out tonight. You wanna come?" He arched his eyebrows at Justin. "You're invited, too, if you want. I mean, if that's your scene?" Colton's voice trailed off, his eyebrows crawling toward the backward brim of his ball cap.

"Where are y'all going?"

"Frat party. Beta Theta."

Wes frowned. "Those guys aren't jocks. They're way too smart for you."

"Yeah, they are." Colton laughed. "They're pretty cool dudes, though. And the chicks really dig those Beta Theta dudes, so there's gonna be a lot of girls there. Maybe even your girl." He grinned. "Might have to actually introduce me."

Wes turned to Justin. He tried to keep his expression neutral. "Want to go?"

Justin tipped his head back against Wes's mattress, looking at Colton. "I'm down for meeting some cool chicks. What time?"

Colton's face scrunched up, tilted almost on its side like he was a dog who'd heard something he couldn't quite make out. "We're heading over around ten."

"Cool. Enough time to finish and change." Justin grimaced at his scrub pants and undershirt.

"Cool." Colton pasted a grin on his face. "See you guys there."

Wes waited until Colton's footsteps faded down the hall before he buried his face in Justin's shoulder and let out a snort. "Down for meeting some chicks, huh?"

"I'm always up for networking." Justin brushed his lips over Wes's forehead. "He can take that however he wants. I know what I meant."

At ten, Wes, Justin, and the rest of the offense—Colton, Orlando, Art, Devin, Quinton, Josh, Patrick, Austin, and Cesar— wandered to Beta Theta's frat house. They could hear the party before they arrived, the thump of the bass reverberating through the pavement. Lawn chairs were set out on the front yard, and beer pong and foosball tables had been placed in the backyard under an oak tree strung with globe lights. People mingled, clutching beer cans and red Solo cups. Four kegs squatted on the back porch. A few people were dancing in the living room, but most of the party was, like all frat parties, loud noise and guys and girls trying to figure out how to talk to each other and not make fools of themselves.

Wes grabbed beers for him and Justin and steered them to a corner of the living room. The rest of the team scattered to the game tables or other parts of the backyard, where most of the single girls were hanging out. Colton found the frat president and handed him a bottle of tequila.

"The quarterback showing up to your party is a pretty big deal," Wes said, sipping his beer. "Beta Theta has done some good things on campus, and they've stayed away from a lot of the crap that gets frats in trouble. This place is going to be flooded once it gets out that the team is here."

"The team? Or the great Wes Van de Hoek?"

Wes shot him a look. "Notice the dark corner I'm in."

"*We're* in." He nudged Wes. "It's cozy. I like it."

Wes eyed him as he took another sip. His gaze raked down Justin's body. Justin had changed into skinny jeans and a plaid button-down, and he looked like he had in Paris when they went out that first weekend and Wes had finally kissed him. How long would he be able to hold out tonight? How long until he couldn't wait another second?

Colton appeared, dragging them to the beer pong table, where he challenged Wes and then Justin to a game. Wes held his own. Justin was terrible, and by the end, he was tipsy and leaning into Wes. Wes guided him back inside as two girls congratulated Colton on his victory, both of them kissing his cheeks at the same time.

"You okay?" Wes asked, lifting Justin and sitting him on a counter in the frat's out-of-the-way kitchen. He got Justin a glass of water, and Justin downed it, then a second one. His face was flushed, his pupils dilated.

"I'm good, cowboy." His fingers curled in Wes's waistband. "I'd be better if you were naked, though."

Wes stiffened.

Justin pushed his lips against Wes's ear. "There's got to be a bedroom somewhere in this house."

Wes brushed their cheeks together briefly, his stubble catching on Justin's, before he leaned back and searched Justin's gaze. Justin bit his lip. Ran the toe of his boot up Wes's calf again.

He grabbed Justin off the counter and spun him around, guiding him through the house, standing so close behind him they were almost walking in perfect sync. In the living room, Wes had a choice to make: front door or stairs? Go home? Or…

Justin's hand snaked behind his back. His fingers brushed over Wes's bulge.

Stairs. Wes hurried Justin up, passing two girls going down and one of the frat brothers monitoring the landing. The brother looked Wes up and down, then shifted his gaze to Justin. "Guys okay?"

"Yeah, he just needs a place to rest for a minute. Beer pong did him in." Wes shrugged. Kept Justin close, trying to hide his wandering hands.

"He going to be sick?"

"Nah. He just needs a cooldown. Someplace quiet for a bit."

"I got ya." He pointed. "End of the hall. Bedroom there is nice and private."

"Thanks." Wes practically shoved Justin down the hall, squeezing his fingers tight to keep them from unzipping Wes's fly. How did Justin end up with so many damn hands when he was tipsy?

He got them into the dark bedroom and the door shut before Justin turned and flew into his arms. He tasted like beer, and he giggled when he kissed Wes.

"How drunk are you?" Wes asked, peppering Justin's lips and cheeks with kisses. "I don't want to do this if you're drunk."

"I'm tipsy, not drunk," Justin said. He pantomimed a field sobriety test, perfectly touching his nose and balancing on one foot. Then he wrapped himself around Wes. "I miss you all the time. I want you all the time." Justin moved his body against Wes's like they were dancing, or like Justin was dancing, at least.

Wes stood stock-still, not knowing how to move or what to do. "God, I want you all the time, too." It was like an itch he could never scratch, a thirst he could never quench. He ached for Justin, and no matter how many times he jacked off thinking about Justin, or remembering being inside Justin, he still couldn't calm himself down. He was like a live wire, a gun ready to fire, every moment. One look from Justin and he was half hard, right in the middle of campus.

"We've been so good, haven't we?"

"I think so."

"We're at a frat party. Don't people hook up at frat parties? Sneak off and fuck in bedrooms?"

"I don't know. I never have."

"Neither have I." Justin reached for his fly. "Let's do it together. What do you say?"

He guided Justin backward until his knees hit the mattress. Justin plopped down, grinning and undoing Wes's fly as Wes undid Justin's. They moved fast, almost frantic.

He peeled Justin's jeans down his thighs, then pushed his legs straight back so he could bury his face in Justin's ass. Justin covered his mouth, trying to stifle his moans as Wes French-kissed his hole until it was soaked with his spit. He fingered Justin quickly, trying to push more spit inside him.

"Nightstand," Justin gasped. "Lotion."

God bless frat boys. He grabbed the bottle and squeezed way too much into his palm, then ran it all over his cock and fingered some into Justin. He got his pants down and crawled onto the mattress. Maneuvered Justin's legs, still tangled in his jeans, together over his right shoulder.

"This is going to be quick," he warned.

"I'm ready." Justin cock was hard and leaking, purple in the dim light of the bedroom. "I can't believe we're doing this. I'm already about to come."

"Me, too." Wes lined up and pushed, and he slid inside Justin with lotion-slick ease. Justin grabbed his biceps. His calves tightened. Wes kissed his denim-covered leg, buried his face against Justin's knee. "Tell me when."

"Now. Give it to me."

It was hard and fast, Wes pounding Justin harder than he ever had. The mattress squeaked as Justin's ass bounced up and down on his cock. Justin's mouth opened in a silent wail, and he reached for his own cock, stroked once, twice, and then came, curling over himself and biting his lip as he tried to muffle his moan. Justin's quick orgasm sent Wes over the edge, and he buried himself inside Justin and exploded. He tipped forward, almost falling on top of Justin, bending him in half.

Justin kissed him, hot, wet, and slow, as Wes softened. He panted against Justin's lips.

"I can't believe we did that." Wes brushed his nose against Justin's. He pulled out gently and grabbed a tissue from the nightstand for Justin. Justin wiped himself off, then pulled up his briefs and his jeans as Wes tucked himself back into his Wranglers.

For a moment, it felt like they were just a normal college couple, like they didn't have to hide. Wes's heart lurched. In the bedroom, they could pretend to be normal. He could kiss Justin and hold his hand, savor the naughtiness of sneaking away. But as soon as they walked out that door…

What if he just kept holding Justin's hand?

No, he couldn't. But that didn't mean he didn't want to.

He and Justin were balancing on the knife-edge of discretion. They blurred a few new lines each week, it seemed. But no one ever guessed they were more than friends. Close friends. But nothing more.

He walked Justin to class in the mornings, and they'd eaten lunch together at the park until Justin's clinical rotations had begun. They squeezed in dinners together, eating in Wes's truck or driving to the park. Then they started eating on the porch of Wes's house. Wes came up with the bright idea to do homework together, and that led to them sitting on the floor in Wes's bedroom together. They'd have their textbooks spread on the floor, their notebooks open, laptops in their laps… and hold hands between their legs, out of sight of anyone who might barge into Wes's bedroom. There was no privacy in that house.

"Where did you guys meet?" Colton asked Wes one day in the upstairs bathroom, halfway through shaving.

Wes was brushing his teeth, and he spat toothpaste on Colton's whiskers left behind in the sink. "French. We've had a few classes together. He's cool. Real funny. And crazy smart."

"Is he friends with your girl?"

"They know each other."

Colton had nodded, like he'd finally figured out why Wes was even talking to a guy like Justin. He'd gone back to his shaving, then paused again. "Is that why you're taking so much French? For this girl?"

"I might want to use it one day."

"You don't need French in the NFL."

He'd ignored Colton, walked out and turned the light off on him. Colton called him an asshole and then never brought up Justin's name again. Had he forgotten the whole thing? Forgotten, so easily, the man who meant everything in the world to Wes?

What if he'd told Colton the truth?

His secrets clawed at his insides, made his guts ache.

He wanted to see Justin all the time, but they couldn't be together as often as he, or Justin, wanted. And to hook up, they had to sneak away: cuddling in a sleeping bag under the stars in the back of Wes's truck way out in the boonies, or, one memorable evening, going at it in the locker room when Wes purposely stayed way late after practice and Justin sneaked in. Justin had watched Wes shower and then made Wes give him a blow job in front of Wes's locker. After that, Justin rode him on the locker room bench until Wes's fingernails bit into his hips and he came shouting Justin's name.

They were trying to be discreet. Keep their love hidden. But it was hard. Wes wanted Justin to be a part of his life, in every way possible. Wanted to spend the night with him, like the other guys had girls stay over in their rooms. Wanted to wake up in Justin's arms, wake Justin up with Wes's mouth around his cock. He wanted to hold Justin's hand as they walked to class. He wanted to carry Justin's backpack and his books. Take him out on real dates, not just to drive-throughs and parking lots where they could sneak a make-out session.

He could feel the rents in his soul growing. Feel the pieces of himself slide farther apart.

Who am I when you love me?

He only felt complete when he was with Justin. He was the man he was meant to be when they were together.

And he didn't want to ever let that feeling go.

Wes helped Justin to his feet and kissed his forehead. "Wanna get out of here?"

"Yeah. I don't think I'm going to find the girl of my dreams at this party."

Wes laughed, and he guided Justin out of the bedroom and back down the hall past the frat brother, now deep in conversation with a leggy brunette and her blonde friend. They thundered down the stairs and burst into a living room choked with people. College kids were wall to wall. The stench of beer and sweat hit them like a truck. Wes took Justin's hand and led him through the crowd to the front door.

Outside, he reluctantly let go of Justin's hand. It was a ten-minute walk to Opal Street, and they detoured to a late-night coffee bar on the way. By the time they got back, Wes was buzzing, caffeine and Justin and the crisp autumn air hitting his veins. He eyed his house as he walked Justin up the front steps of his blue Victorian.

Justin seemed to read his mind. "Why don't you come up to my room?" He slid his ID card into the door lock. "Most everyone clears out on Friday nights. It should be pretty empty inside."

Dangerous. If he went to Justin's room, he might not leave. But… He bit his lip. Grabbed the door and held it open for Justin. "After you."

They jogged up the three flights of stairs as quietly as they could. Justin's neighbor was in his room and, according to the noise, having a party—or an orgy. Justin shut and locked his door, and when he turned around, Wes was there, pushing him against it. Kissing him and grinding his whole body against Justin's.

"This is a bad idea," Wes whispered.

"I know."

"I won't want to leave."

"Then don't." Justin ran his thumbs down Wes's cheekbones. Nibbled on his chin. "Stay tonight."

Groaning, Wes lifted Justin into his arms and carried him to his bed. He set him down in the center and peeled his shirt off, tossing it aside. He reached for his belt and his fly. "If we have all night, I'm going to use every single minute to make love to you."

CHAPTER TWENTY

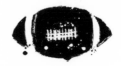

THE LOCKER ROOM was so loud he couldn't hear himself think.

Couldn't line up one thought with the next. Everything was a mishmash, a jumble of color and sound. It was almost like he'd taken a helmet-to-helmet hit, but he hadn't. The game had been easy, in fact. The number-three-ranked team in the FBS was practically a joke. They'd fallen apart early in the second quarter as Wes and Colton picked apart their defense. Devon, Quinton, and Orlando had made phenomenal plays that would end up on SportsCenter all week long.

Wes's body buzzed with restless energy, even though he wanted to close his eyes and lean his head back. His heels bounced, and he batted his cell phone back and forth from palm to palm.

He was desperate to text Justin. It was a hunger that crawled inside him. A need swimming in his veins. Everyone else had texted their girlfriends already. They were already winding down into that postgame buzz, relaxed after their showers, bullshitting each other as they waited for the official release.

But he couldn't. Not yet.

The reporter from ESPN was still making her rounds.

She'd started off making a beeline for Wes, but he'd demurred when she asked him how he'd won the game that day. "It wasn't me. It's the entire team. Colton is a phenomenal quarterback, and Orlando is one of the league's best running backs. Devon and Quinton are the best receivers I've ever played with. And none of us could do anything without Art, Josh, and Patrick on the line. How about asking them how their games were today?"

She'd spun off toward Orlando, who was an absolute clown and lived for the spotlight, and he entertained her camera for a good twenty minutes before turning it over to Colton. But she was coming back to Wes soon, and he had to wait until she did.

He closed his eyes and leaned back on the stool in front of his locker, imagining Justin. His smile. The sound of his laugh. The way he looked when he danced, every one of his muscles taut and tight. How he looked when he was arching in orgasm, head tipped back, mouth open, panting Wes's name. The look in his eyes when he took Wes's hand, or when he told Wes he loved him.

He squeezed his cell phone, his lifeline to Justin—his lifeline to his own soul—so hard the plastic case creaked.

"So, Wes Van de Hoek."

He opened his eyes, and the first thing he saw was a pair of long legs wrapped in a tight suit skirt. A silk blouse neatly tucked in, encasing her voluptuous chest, and waves of blonde curls tumbling over her shoulder. She smirked when his eyes met hers, as if she'd caught him eyeing her up.

He cleared his throat and stood, taking a step back and putting space between them. This was part of the game, part of the deal. He had to talk to the media. As the team captain, as the school's representative. He had to put on his mask and smile for the cameras, be the man who loved football, who was born to play football, who was going to shake up the NFL because he was so damn good at football.

She shoved the microphone into his face before he was ready. "It's been an incredible year for you, Wes. You're leading an undefeated team with a major shot at winning the national championship. At the start of the year, you were ranked the fifth-best player in the FBS, but now, everyone is saying it's pretty clear you're the best player in the league. Maybe the best in your generation. You've always been good, but this year, you seem to be on fire. What do you credit your incredible success to over the years, and what has changed this year in particular?"

Justin. I play my heart and soul out for him. "You know, I just always worked hard. Football is a job like any other, and I put in the work."

"And this year? What's put you over the top?"

I fell in love. He flushed. "Just hard work, ma'am. Putting in those hours at practice. Always staying focused on that end goal and keeping your eyes on what you want most." *College. Graduation. Justin. A life together.*

"In two weeks, you play the only other undefeated team in the league. Any nerves heading into your Thanksgiving showdown? Anything you're specifically focused on as you prepare for this game?"

"I'm going to sound like a broken record, but it's the same hard work, ma'am. Show up, every day, for practice. Give it your all. Give everything you have to your team. That's what got us here, and that's what will get us the win in two weeks."

"What makes this team so special?"

"How tight we are together. We're more than a team. We're brothers. I know everyone says that, but it's different here. We're connected, off the field and on, and that connection and love we all have for each other makes us unstoppable. I'd do anything for them"—his voice choked off—"and I like to think they'd do the same for me."

There were noises in the background, grunts and *Hell yeah*s from his teammates.

But was it true?

"You said you were keeping your eyes on what you want most. The NFL, I'm assuming. A professional career. Seems almost guaranteed for you at this point. Are the rumors about you possibly tossing your name into the NFL draft at the end of this season true?"

"Nothing is guaranteed in this life. And those are just rumors. I haven't thought about the NFL draft at all this year. I'm focused on this team. These guys are my priority."

"You seem to have it all. A promising start to a stellar career, the skills and drive to go as far as you want in the sport, fans who love and adore you. What about a girlfriend? Any special lady in your life?"

He ducked his head and pressed his lips together, trying to force a smile. "That's a little personal, ma'am."

"So you don't kiss and tell?"

"No, ma'am."

"You're a good guy, Wes." She reached for him, squeezing his biceps, then turned to the camera to end her segment. Once the camera was off, she turned back to Wes. "I'd love to buy you dinner tonight. I could tell you all about the NFL and line up some conversations with coaches I know. Just a few friendly chats between them and you about the league."

The locker room went silent, the bustle and hum of conversations dropping to a hush as everyone pretended to be busy with their locker junk. Folding shirts they'd never folded in their lives, or wiping nonexistent stains off their helmets. Behind the reporter's back, Colton stood with his eyes as wide as dinner plates, white running all the way around his irises. He nodded, comically huge, and gave Wes two big thumbs up.

"Thank you for the offer, ma'am," Wes said, stepping back. "But I'm sorry, I've got plans tonight."

He saw the shock in Colton's face, in Orlando's, in all the guys' stunned looks and dropped jaws. No one turned down a beautiful woman like that. And no one who wanted to play in the

NFL turned down the opportunity to meet and greet with the league heavies.

"Well, congratulations on your win today, Mr. Van de Hoek." She held out her hand and he shook it. She gathered her bag and walked out of the locker room, not looking back.

He was swarmed in under a second, Colton and the rest of the guys shoving him left and right, asking him what the hell was he thinking. What the hell did he have to do that night that was so much more important than networking with her? "Dude, I know you got your girl, but man—" Colton said.

"You got a girl?" Orlando jumped in. "Whoa whoa whoa! When did you get yourself a girl?"

"Who has a girl?" one of the linebackers boomed from the next row of lockers.

"Wes!" Art shouted. "But he's been keeping her a secret!"

"Why are you keeping her a secret?" Quinton asked. "Bring her around!"

Wes shot Colton a look as he stripped off his jersey and unhooked his pads. He'd stayed suited up for the interview because it played better, according to the media relations people at the university. He'd had to read a whole manual before the season began about what to say, how to act, how to represent the university. What would get him fined and what would get him suspended or expelled.

"Who is this girl, man?" Orlando wouldn't drop it. "Where did y'all meet?"

He peeled off his pants and threw everything in his locker, then wrapped his towel around his waist. Everyone was crowding him. Smothering him.

He'd made love to Justin right there, where Josh was straddling the bench.

He shoved through the offensive players he loved like brothers. "I gotta shower."

"Wes, don't be like that!" Art shouted. "Why you hiding from us?"

"We just wanna know if she's pretty!" Patrick hollered. The guys busted up laughing, catcalling and whistling as Wes retreated.

Wes waved his hand over his shoulder and headed for the showers.

CHAPTER TWENTY-ONE

JUSTIN SMILED as he saw Wes heading for the truck, but then hesitated when he saw the strain lining his love's face.

Wes threw himself through the passenger door, flopping sideways on the bench seat and groaning. He rolled his face against Justin's thigh and kissed his denim-covered leg. "I'm so glad to see you."

"You okay?" Justin slid his hand into Wes's hair. It was longer now, shaggier. He hadn't cut it since the season began.

Wes squeezed his eyes closed. "Headache."

"I heard your interview."

Another groan. Wes dug his face into Justin's thigh. Spoke into his jeans. His voice was muffled, and Justin had to strain to hear what he said. "She asked me out to dinner tonight. Said she could hook me up with some NFL coaches."

"Do you want to go?"

Wes rolled onto his back, glaring up at Justin. "What? No way. Are you kidding?"

"If you have a chance to network with NFL coaches, wouldn't you like to?"

"Now you sound like the rest of the guys." He scrubbed his

hands over his face. Wes reached for Justin's hand and kissed his fingers, then cradled his hand against his chest. "The rest of the team thought I was crazy when I told her no. But I want to be with you tonight. No one else."

"It is a little bit crazy." Justin leaned over and kissed his nose. "But I'm not complaining." He dragged his long hair over Wes's face until Wes grinned and chased him for another kiss. "Where am I taking you?"

Instead of meeting outside their homes, Justin had started waiting in Wes's truck at the stadium after home games. It was easier to head out together directly, rather than fight the crowds and the fans and the parties. It was colder now, and the streets weren't quite so packed after a game. But the thrill of an undefeated season and having a superstar player had energized the school and the city. The entire state of Texas.

"Somewhere quiet. Somewhere I can hear myself think." Wes curled his face into Justin's thigh again. "Somewhere I can be with you."

Justin turned the key in the ignition and shifted the truck into drive.

Half an hour later, Justin killed the headlights as he headed for the back of the state park's parking lot. There were no other cars in the lot this time. They were alone.

Gravel crunched beneath the tires. Wes hummed, closing his eyes as he exhaled. "Love that sound."

Wes hadn't sat up for the whole drive. He was still sprawled across the bench seat, one leg down on the floorboards and the other bent up at an angle. He'd kept his face against Justin's stomach and his eyes closed, and when Justin parked, Wes wrapped both his arms around Justin's waist like he was Wes's pillow.

Justin cracked the window. Crisp autumn air flowed into the cab. An owl hooted nearby. Branches creaked, their leaves rustling together. Country noises. Night noises.

Wes's shoulders loosened, and his breathing began to slow. Justin ran his fingers through Wes's hair again, down the back of his head and up his neck. In minutes, Wes was snoring, his lips parted and pressed into the skin between Justin's jeans and his sweatshirt. Soft puffs of air blew over Justin's belly. He smiled, curled over Wes and kissed his temple, and then leaned back and closed his eyes.

HOURS LATER, Wes kissed him awake. "I'm sorry I fell asleep."

"You needed it." Justin kissed him back, his eyes not open yet. "You're exhausted."

Wes sighed. He sat up, his body pressed against Justin's from their knees to their shoulders. "This season is way more than I expected. Every week is punishing. Every defense tries to take me out. Every school wants to be known as the one who took us down. And then there's the media, and the attention…"

"And us."

"That's not exhausting."

"Well." Justin smirked and winked. Wes snorted. "I meant the secrecy," Justin said. "Making sure no one finds out."

"Sometimes I think about quitting," Wes whispered. "Sometimes I want to. Because even with all this, the chance at an undefeated season and the national championship? All the publicity and the craziness? All I want to do is take your hand in the middle of campus. Kiss you before a game, like the guys do with their girlfriends. I want to give you a family ticket and have you sit with the rest of the VIPs." He traced Justin's fingers, the lines of his palm. "I thought it would be easier to keep things separate. But I feel like I'm shredding apart."

"Do we need to take it slower? Maybe cool down for a bit?"

Wes grabbed his hand, squeezed so hard Justin flinched. "No, please. Anything but that."

"I didn't mean take a break, or break up. I just meant maybe cool off how much we see each other—"

"Seeing you is the only thing that's keeping me together."

"But…"

Wes took Justin's face in his hands and pushed their foreheads together. "Not that. Please. Anything but that."

"I'm not going anywhere."

Darkness fell over Wes's gaze, and his eyes slid away from Justin's. "I don't feel like I do enough for you. You come to my games, and I take you to parking lots in the middle of nowhere."

"But I love that." He cupped Wes's jaw. Felt his muscles trembling. "Hey. I do. I love watching you play, and I love when we do this, or when it's just you and me sitting on the hood of your car eating Wendy's. I love everything we do together."

"You deserve more."

"I want what we have." Wes still looked like he'd been kicked in the kneecaps. He still wouldn't look at Justin. "We knew exactly what this was going to look like while you were playing," Justin said, dragging Wes's chin up until their eyes met. "I don't want anything else. I only want you."

"I want more," Wes mumbled. "I want to be with you. Really with you. Out and in the open. I want the world to know I love you." He turned into Justin's handhold and kissed his palm. "It kills me that I can't right now. I wish I could have told the guys about you. Or told that reporter that I was seeing my boyfriend tonight."

"I know." He stroked Wes's cheek. Ran his fingertips over Wes's stubble. "You give so much to your team. I know it hurts now. I feel it, too. But I tell myself, what's two years when we have forever together?"

Finally, Wes smiled, so big and wide Justin felt Wes's dimples form beneath his palm. "Yeah. Forever sounds pretty good."

They drove home holding hands, Wes with his head tipped sideways on Justin's shoulder. He was quiet, more so than usual, and Justin rubbed his thumb over the back of Wes's hand as he took the long route back to campus.

"What are you doing for Thanksgiving?" Wes asked when they hit the outskirts of the city. "Are you going back to Dallas?"

"I hadn't decided yet. What are you doing? You have a game on Friday."

"The biggest game of the season. Two undefeated teams going head to head. Betting is already off the chain in Vegas. It's a home game, so it's going to be insane. People are coming back to campus early. Alumni and major donors are flying in."

Justin squeezed his hand. "Does the team go home that week? Or do you stay and practice?"

"We stay and practice. We have a team Thanksgiving on Thursday. I liked it in the past."

"In the past?"

"I'd rather be with you this year."

"If I stay in town, I can pick up some extra clinical rotations over the holiday. That would advance my placement, and I could have an easier schedule later on. More free time to spend with you."

"Do you want to stay, though? Working over break sounds like no fun."

"I'd rather be here with you, working, than up in Dallas without you, moping around."

Wes was quiet. "Will your parents be okay with you not going home?"

"I'm a big boy. They know I make my own decisions. We had that argument when I was eighteen." He sighed. "They'll miss me. And I've gotten closer with my dad these past few months. I want to see him. But when I do, I want to have you with me."

The rest of the drive was silent apart from the hum of the tires on the road and the click of the turn signal. When Justin pulled into Wes's usual parking spot and killed the engine, Wes lifted his head from Justin's shoulder. "I don't want to leave," he said. His voice was almost fragile. "I don't want to let you go."

"Come spend the night with me again?"

Wes turned his big eyes to Justin's. "I shouldn't. We shouldn't."

"You're right. We shouldn't." Justin shook his head. "I'm sorry—"

Wes kissed him, slowly, like they weren't parked around the corner from the jock house, like there weren't still parties going in the houses around them. Like they couldn't be seen at any moment, spotted by a fan or one of Wes's teammates or even one of Justin's housemates. Justin finally pulled back, and he stopped Wes from chasing him for another kiss. "Not here. Jesus, we're trying to be less risky. Come with me, even if it's just for a little bit. You can climb out the fire escape if you need to."

Wes followed him into his house, tiptoeing up the stairs and past the rooms where parties were raging. Across the street, Wes's home was lit up like a parade float.

Justin led Wes to his bed, stripping him as he went. He pushed Wes to the mattress and straddled him. "Let me take care of you, cowboy."

CHAPTER TWENTY-TWO

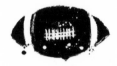

CAMPUS WAS a ghost town Thanksgiving week.

The dorms were closed, and the university kicked nearly all of the students out. Only the ones on West Campus, or students who lived in their own apartments, were allowed to stay. At least until the weekend, when everyone was told to come right back and cheer on Wes Van de Hoek and the rest of the team in their biggest game of the season.

Justin checked the line in Vegas. The odds were ten to one for Texas. Everyone believed Wes would smoke Mississippi, never mind that they were also undefeated. *Van de Hoek mania*, some sports writers called the bets. *But is it mania when Wes Van de Hoek is the greatest player of his generation?*

Wes Van de Hoek mania, and not a single person on the planet, other than Justin, knew who the man really was.

I think about quitting. I just want to be with you.

I feel like I'm being torn apart.

It wasn't fair to Wes to make him feel like he had to choose: football or himself.

What would the world say if Wes walked away from it all,

turned his back on the NFL and millions of dollars? Moved in with Justin and started playing gay house?

Justin shoved those thoughts away, focusing on his clinical rotations. Hospital shifts. Trauma nursing. He shadowed the charge nurse and prepped an IV, then took another patient's blood pressure and updated their chart.

Wes had to decide for himself what he wanted from his life. Whatever that decision was, Justin would be there at his side. That was Justin's choice.

For now, they were going day by day. They'd built up weeks together. Months. They were over two-thirds of the way through the season. This was the tenth game, with the highest stakes. Wes and the team were definitely heading for a bowl game, but would they be playing for the national championship? That was the question on everyone's lips, and the Mississippi game would be a big factor in deciding that.

The regular season was ending in two weeks. After January, the bowl championships would be over.

And then Wes could breathe a little easier.

He'd take Wes somewhere in spring. They could drive to the coast, disappear on a beach where no one knew them. Though, after this season, how likely was it that no one would recognize Wes Van de Hoek? Where could they go where he wouldn't be seen and known right away? He wasn't exactly inconspicuous, and, thanks to ESPN's wall-to-wall coverage all season long, he was a household name.

Maybe they'd go off the grid. Wes would like that. Camping, or out to some cabin hideaway. Just them and nature. Gravel roads. Long, dark nights. No electricity. Maybe they could go horseback riding, or Wes could teach him how to fish. Show him all those country things Justin only ever saw on TV.

He racked up his clinical rotations while Wes practiced with the team. Without classes, the team was back to two-a-days. Justin and Wes texted all day long, before practice and at lunch and through the afternoon.

And, after practice, Wes slipped across the street to Justin's house. Only one other student had stayed there over the break, an IT major who worked nights at the university lab and slept all day. They could hear him snoring behind his bedroom door on the first floor. He was easy to avoid.

For three days, it was like they were living together again. Justin cooked dinner in the house's shared kitchen. He made Wes chicken and pasta, hamburger sliders, and seared steak and rice. Wes steamed vegetables and shook up protein shakes, gulping them down alongside hard-boiled eggs and spoonfuls of peanut butter. After, they drank wine in Justin's bedroom, Justin's laptop balanced on their legs as they held hands and watched Netflix. And when Wes had digested his five-course dinner, they made slow, sweet love, whiling away half the night in each other's arms.

It was, for three days, perfect.

Colton texted twice on the first day, asking where Wes had gone after practice and if he was coming back to the house. Wes said something vague, that he was staying somewhere else, and Colton told him not to exhaust himself with his girl, that he needed to be ready for the game on Friday.

Tuesday, Wes texted Justin and told him all about the bullshit the guys gave him in the locker room. That they'd bought boxes and boxes of condoms and stuffed his locker full of them, taken some out and blown them up like balloon penises and taped them all around his locker door. They bought horny goat weed and the knock-off Extenze pills that seedy gas stations sold. A couple packs of Monster Energy. "Don't wear yourself out, man!" Orlando crowed, flicking him a packet of male enhancement powder. "In fact, I want a sexually frustrated tight end on Saturday! Someone who is gonna pound the shit out of Mississippi's defense!"

"Oh! Maybe that's the secret!" Art wagged his finger at the rest of the line. "Maybe Wes is so damn good this year because he's been getting good pussy on the regular."

"Maybe we should all look for good girls, then. Damn. Your girl got friends, Wes?" Orlando hung off the locker next to Wes, batting his eyelashes. "I wanna be just like you, Captain. Show me them magic pills you swallow."

The team howled, and Wes let them run wild as he went nuclear fuchsia, blushing so deep he felt it scald his bones. They teased him mercilessly as he suited up, strapped on his pads, and laced up his cleats. He left them snorting in the locker room as he jogged out to the field to run off his nerves.

Thursday, they had a half day of practice, perfecting their plays and running drill after drill after drill. At lunch, everyone came together for the team Thanksgiving. Wes sent Justin a picture of the buffet spread: twelve massive turkeys, five hams, platters and platters of stuffing and green beans and mashed potatoes. Sweet potato casserole by the pallet. A full pumpkin pie for each player.

Wes made two to-go containers and brought a second dinner home for Justin. They ate on the back porch out of the Styrofoam, feeding each other bites off of plastic forks as they shared a bottle of cheap wine in Solo cups.

Wes relayed the speech Coach Young had given to the team, repeating the sections that had gotten stuck on a loop in his mind. Trust and fidelity. The bond they shared. The strength of their love for each other, and how that strength drove their game. How their trust in each other made them unstoppable. The absolute faith they had in their brothers. And in their captain.

Everyone had shouted and stomped their feet and chanted for Wes to give a speech after that, but all he managed to choke out was a thanks to everyone for trusting him to guide them that season, and that it wasn't him who made the team, despite all the crap on ESPN. It was all of them together. He was nothing without all of them. And he loved them all like brothers.

"That was a good speech," Justin said, rubbing Wes's big, broad back. He could feel the tension coiling through Wes's muscles. "The team is very lucky to have you. Most college stars are in it for themselves."

Wes shook his head. "Aren't I in it for myself? I don't want what everyone else wants. I don't want the fame or the glory. All I wanted was a college education. Hell, I should have joined the military for that."

"Then we wouldn't have met." He nudged Wes's hip with his own, playful with a half bottle of wine inside him. He rested his head on Wes's shoulder. "I don't think you're in anything for yourself. You're staying in the closet for the team. Everything you've done, all year long, has been for someone other than you. For me, for them, for the fans. You even brought me Thanksgiving lunch today. You couldn't be selfish if you tried."

Wes tried to smile, and he laid his head against Justin's. Laced their hands together. Downed the rest of his wine. Justin snapped a selfie of them, tipsy and smiling at the camera, heads together, hands interlaced. "I should send that to my dad."

"Do it. I'm fine with it."

"No, I want him to meet you. I want to see his face when he sees that I'm dating you."

"I can't wait to meet him." Wes kissed Justin's temple and wrapped his arms around him. "Want to head inside?"

"*Oui*, cowboy. Take me to bed." He held out his hand, and Wes helped him to his feet. They walked inside arm in arm. Justin's housemate was still snoring.

At the bottom of the stairs, Wes scooped Justin into his arms. Justin yelped but threw his arms around Wes's neck and tipped his head back. "Oh, cowboy, are you going to carry me to bed?"

"Of course." He grinned. "Gotta practice, you know?"

"Practice?"

"To carry you over the threshold the day I marry you."

Justin pulled him down for another kiss. "Presumptuous?" he breathed, laughing after kissing Wes to within an inch of his life.

"Just trying to make your dad proud."

He laughed, loud enough to interrupt his housemate's snores. Wes charged upstairs, taking the steps two at a time, Justin still in his arms. He got the bedroom door open one-handed, walked inside, and then kicked the door shut with his toes. He carried Justin to the bed and laid him down, then crawled right on top, biting his T-shirt and dragging it up his chest. He buried his face in Justin's belly, flicking his tongue in and out of Justin's navel before undoing his fly and pressing his face to Justin's crotch. "I'm going to love you all night long."

"Remember what your—*oh*—team said." Justin gasped as Wes's lips closed around his cock. "You can't be exhausted tomorrow."

Wes sucked him deep, hollowing his cheeks, and then popped off his cock. "That's my secret," Wes said. "The key to my success this season has been you."

"Well, then." Justin spread his legs and dug his fingers into Wes's hair as Wes's lips closed around him again. "Time for your protein shot, cowboy."

They descended into giggles, Wes falling to his side in the middle of the blow job, Justin curling around him as he howled. Laughter turned to sighs, and then into moans, and then they didn't say anything more for the rest of the night.

FRIDAY MORNING, their perfect world imploded.

CHAPTER TWENTY-THREE

A Cowboy in Paris:
The Secret Life of Wes Van de Hoek
By SportsWorld Staff Writer Geoff Brady

IMAGINE THIS:

You're one of the best college football players in your generation. The buzz around you is incredible. The NFL circles you like bees around honey. Your school is begging you to stay in the program. You're their star player. Your face is plastered on billboards across five hundred miles. Fan mail arrives at the school in ten-pound sacks every day. You're the hottest man in the entire state, and, according to the internet, you're single.

Until one wayward photo blows everything up.

See that? That's a picture of the Marché d'Aligre. It's a Parisian marketplace famous for its amazing variety of produce, trinkets, and street entertainment. This photo was snapped in June, when a vacationing family took a picture of a street mime.

Did you catch the guy in the background? The one in the cowboy hat? Holding the hand of the guy next to him?

That's Wes Van de Hoek, holding hands with his boyfriend, right in the center of Paris.

CHAPTER TWENTY-FOUR

WES WOKE late Friday morning to the clatter and buzz of his cell phone vibrating on Justin's nightstand. He groaned and shut it up, then folded himself around Justin again. He didn't need to be up until at least nine. But his phone was blowing up before eight, and that was a crime after the night he and Justin had had.

His phone buzzed again. And again.

"Answer it," Justin grunted. "It might be important."

He sighed and reached over his head, fumbling for his phone and dragging it by the charging cord over his shoulder and into the bed. He swiped on the screen.

One hundred and seven text messages. He blinked. "What the…"

"What?" Justin rolled in his arms and propped himself up on one elbow. He yawned, his hair sticking up. "Everything okay?"

"I don't know." He unlocked his phone and pulled up his texts. Fifty were from Colton. Had he gotten drunk the night before?

Dude. DUDE.

What the fuck. What the ACTUAL FUCK.

You've been lying to me for years! You've been lying to us!

"Oh my God…" His heart began to pound, heat and ice racing through him in dizzying swells. "Oh my God, Justin…"

How could you let us find out like this?

How could you keep something like this from us?

Are you actually, for real, gay?

Is that guy, Justin, your boyfriend?

You let me believe you were dating a girl!!

You lied to me!

How long have you been lying to us all?

What the fuck

What the fuck dude

"Justin, they know. Oh my God, everybody knows. Everybody knows."

"What? How?" Justin scrambled up, grabbing Wes's phone and turning it to him. He saw Colton's texts, then swiped back and pulled up the other texts, from Orlando, Art, Devon, Quinton, Josh, Patrick, and even Coach Young. Coach's text was a link to an article.

He clicked, and a full-page image of the Marché d'Aligre loaded. And there they were, in the background, in perfect, damning clarity. Justin had the lavender and baby's breath to his nose, and they were standing far too close to explain away.

More pictures, scattered throughout the article, sealed their fate: two more from Paris, holding hands, arms around each other's waists. Pictures of them on campus. Wes gazing at Justin like he was smiling up at the sun. A grainy picture of them sitting inside Wes's truck, talking intently. Wes holding the door open for Justin at the nursing school. Wes coming down the fire escape outside Justin's window.

There were quotes, too, from students on campus. One from a Beta Theta fraternity brother, who described Wes and Justin coming to a party and disappearing into a dark bedroom together, reemerging fifteen minutes later, disheveled and sweaty. Students who had seen them together around campus. "They're close. There's definitely something there."

"Oh my God…" Wes dropped his phone. His thoughts raced in a thousand different directions at once. Everybody knew. And they had found out in the worst possible way. Not from Wes, but from the media. From an investigative reporter. *They will turn your life upside down. Inside out.*

Well, they had. They had dug and dug, until they stumbled on pictures of cowboys in Paris and found Wes. And found Justin. And then they'd found their secret.

Justin's phone started to buzz. He lunged across Wes, grabbing it off the nightstand. It was an incoming call, and the caller ID said *Dad*. Justin sent the call to voicemail. His dad called again. And again. Justin turned his phone on silent.

Colton's texts to Wes had gone from confusion and shock to pure rage.

I don't even know who you are. I don't know anything about you. You fucking lied to me. You fucking looked me in the eyes and lied to me. Fuck you.

You're with him right now, aren't you? Jesus, you've been with him all season. Every time you stayed out. You were with HIM.

He dropped his phone like it was molten lava. It landed face-down on Justin's bed, Colton's words finally blocked out. He scrubbed his hands over his face, screamed into his palms.

It was over. It was all over. Football. His friendship with Colton. His scholarship. Everything he'd ever dreaded, everything he'd feared, had arrived at sunrise on a Friday morning, on the biggest game day of his career. Well, not his career anymore. Not after this.

He pitched sideways, falling into Justin's lap as he screamed again, as his tears started to fall.

Justin wrapped his arms around Wes and held him as his heart shattered, and the tattered pieces of his soul ripped fully apart, and the crushing weight of failure rolled over him like a wave, sweeping him out to sea.

HE HAD no idea how to do this. No idea how to take those steps, walk the hundred feet into his own locker room. Three years he'd been on the team. Waking this walk, from the parking lot to the stadium. Today, he didn't know how to summon the courage to take the first step.

Justin sat beside him, holding his hand. He kept apologizing, kept saying he was sorry, so sorry. They'd wept together in Justin's room, clung to each other. ESPN had picked up the story, and so had three major news networks. Everywhere they turned, it seemed, there was Wes, holding Justin's hand. Kissing him. Their private love, on display.

Wes had taken his phone with him into the bathroom at one point. After he'd locked the door and made sure Justin couldn't see, he'd checked the message boards and Twitter and found exactly what he'd feared: vitriolic hatred. Shock. Disgust.

Threats. Threats against Wes, which he could shove down, push away. Threats against Justin, which made him see red, made him ball his hands into fists and slam them into the tile wall until his knuckles split. Promises to come and find him, find Justin. Show them what faggots deserved. He'd buckled, screaming into the bunched-up fabric of his sweatshirt until he couldn't breathe, until he was gasping, choking. It was so, so much worse than he'd feared.

Three hours before the biggest game of his life, there he was, sitting in his truck like a coward. Those threats ran on a loop in his mind. He didn't want to let go of Justin's hand. What if something happened while he was in the stadium? What if he couldn't get to Justin in time? What if someone took Justin from him? What if he lost *everything* today? Not just football, not just his friends, or the team, or his scholarship. What if he lost Justin, too?

"You need to go in." Justin's voice was small and broken. So unlike him. "You have to talk to Colton."

"I don't think Colton wants to talk to me."

In fact, he knew Colton didn't want to talk to him. Colton's last text messages had told him to fuck off forever, that Colton didn't know him, had never known him. That Wes was a liar. A fraud.

"This is your team," Justin whispered. "This is your game. These are your friends."

"Not anymore."

Justin buried his face in his palms, his arms braced on the dash. His hair fell forward, and Wes brushed it back behind his ear before pulling Justin across the bench seat, into his arms. "We knew this was the risk."

"We should have been more careful," Justin gasped. "I shouldn't have pushed you at that party. I shouldn't have played beer pong. I shouldn't have—"

"You didn't force me to do anything. I was right there with you. I wanted it all."

Justin leaned into Wes's chest as his tears soaked Wes's T-shirt. Wes's own eyes were dry now, and there was a hollow sort of finality inside him, along with a formless, aching dread at the thought of walking into that locker room.

"Go," Justin choked out. "Go. Or you never will."

"I don't want to leave you—"

"Go." Justin pulled out of his arms, dragging in deep, shuddering breaths in a valiant attempt to calm himself that Wes saw right through. "I'll be here after the game. We'll figure this out. But you need to go. Now."

He nodded. Gripped his duffel. Exhaled.

And then he lunged across the seat and grabbed Justin, kissing him deeply, like Justin was the only thing tethering him to the world anymore. Maybe he was. He kissed him one more time, and then he threw himself out of the truck and slammed the door quickly, before he climbed back in and drove him and Justin straight to the middle of nowhere and stayed there forever.

Every step felt like he was walking to his end. He trudged forward, his clammy hands sliding up and down the strap of his duffel. Fans had already started to tailgate, and when they spotted him, the jeers and the heckles began. They were a roar of static, the background noise to the collapse of his life. The wind billowing off the freight train that was headed right for him. He was standing in the center of the tracks, his feet cemented to the railroad ties. Nothing to do but face his end.

He felt eyes on him with every step he took into the stadium's depths. He passed janitors and groundskeepers, security guards, university police. Every one of them stared at him like he was suddenly completely different from the man they'd high-fived and laughed with the day before. Shared a Thanksgiving meal with. He gritted his teeth and looked straight ahead.

He nearly faltered at the door to the locker room. Nearly turned tail and walked out. *Justin.*

He dug down inside himself, to the same place where he'd grabbed the courage to kiss Justin for the first time, the same place he'd reached for when he told Justin's retreating back that he loved him, that he'd always love him, and that he'd made a terrible mistake. He touched that space inside himself, the part of his soul that belonged to Justin, and pulled open the locker room door.

Every conversation stopped. A hundred pairs of eyeballs swung to him.

Orlando was up front, wrapping his wrists in athletic tape. He shook his head and turned his back on Wes. Threw his tape into his locker like he was pitching a fastball. It bounced off the back wall with a hollow *thunk*, rolling out and spiraling across the carpet.

He grabbed his helmet and stormed out. Art followed, not even bothering to look at Wes or acknowledge his existence. Art led the offensive line like a parade, Josh and Patrick and Cesar walking silently to the field. Every one of the guys Wes had played with for three years turned their backs on him as he dropped his gear at his locker and started to change.

"So you showed up."

Wes hissed. He yanked his Under Armour over his head and tucked it into his uniform pants. Tied the laces at his waist. "I did."

"Course you did. You need your fucking adulation, don't you?"

"What?" Wes turned. Colton was furious, all dark lines and rage, scowling as he strangled the football in his hands. Wes frowned. "What are you talking about?"

"All your bullshit yesterday. All that fucking bullshit about us being a team, and you needing us, and you being nothing without us. That's fucking bullshit! All you care about is yourself!"

"That's not true! I love this team!"

"You have a fucking funny way of showing that."

"What did you expect me to do? Announce my first day of training camp freshman year that I'm gay?"

Colton hurled the football into the concrete wall at the end of the row of lockers. It ricocheted off, landing with a hurdy-gurdy bounce in the second-string defense locker bay. "You knew you were gay freshman year?"

"I've known I was gay since I was nine."

"And you never told me!" Colton roared. "You never told any of us!"

He kept his mouth shut. No, he never had. Because this was the reaction he'd feared. This was exactly the reaction he'd feared.

Colton ran his hands through his long hair. He was half dressed, like Wes, in his pants and his Under Armour but missing his pads and his jersey. He paced away. Kicked a locker so hard the metal buckled. "You treated us like we're goddamn pawns in your fucking show-off game."

"Colton—"

"Three years. Three fucking years, and you didn't say a fucking thing."

"Why would I? When this is what happens?"

"It's not that you're gay!" Colton roared. "It's that you lied to us! Fuck, yesterday we were talking about your girl! Right here! Right fucking here! You let us all believe you were head over heels for some perfect girl you met in Paris! Not fucking *him*!"

"Don't you dare say anything about Justin," Wes growled. "You can hate me all you want. You leave him out of it."

"He did something to you. You say you've always been gay, but you've never been like this. What the hell did he do to you—"

"Shut your mouth!"

"Or what? You'll lie to me again?"

He turned away, grabbing onto the sides of his locker.

"I asked you to your face, on the bus, what was going on. I *asked* you." Colton shook his head. "What is it about him that made you turn your back on us? That made you lie to us? To your team? To *me*? Was his mouth that fucking good? Did his blow jobs rock your world that much—"

He didn't remember moving. He didn't remember pulling back his fist or letting it fly. He blinked, and Colton was on the ground, holding his jaw, glaring up at Wes with shock in his eyes.

Colton laughed. It was an ugly, horrible sound, and it made Wes's skin crawl. "You should see your face, man," Colton said. He spat blood on the locker room floor. Pushed himself to his feet. "You look like you just punched your best friend. Newsflash, jackass: I'm not your fucking friend anymore. I'm not friends with people who lie to me. Or who use me."

"I didn't use you—" He tried to reach for him. Colton ripped his arm away. "I'm sorry," Wes choked out.

"You think punching me is so bad? How could you possibly do anything worse than what you've already fucking done?" Colton shook his head. He grabbed his pads and his helmet and turned his back on Wes, striding out of the locker room and leaving Wes alone in the wreckage of his life.

WHEN HE JOGGED out onto the field, a ripple went through the stands, through the fans already in their seats two hours before the game. He heard the boos, the jeers. His skin crawled. He wanted to jump out of his skeleton.

Coach looked right through him as if he wasn't even there. He spoke to some distant point over Wes's shoulder, even though Wes was standing right in front of him. "You have made a grave mistake."

"Coach—"

"This is not the time for your lips to be moving. The time for you to open your mouth was months ago. Maybe even years ago. You put a bomb at the heart of this team and played with the detonator, and now you're shocked and shaken that everything's fallen apart, huh?" Coach shook his head. Glared at the scoreboard. "I warned you, Wes. I warned you what would happen."

"It's my private life—"

"It's not!" Coach pushed right up into Wes's face, finally looking at him. "I told you they would turn your life upside down. Turn you inside out. You want a private life? A secret boyfriend? Then you keep that shit private! You don't go flaunting it all over Paris or all over this campus! At the very least, you should have come to the team, or to me, with this. Given us a goddamn heads-up that this was a possibility. That one morning we might wake up to some news. We'd be able to handle it together, then. But no, that's not what you decided."

He paced away from Wes, shaking his head. "You think you're paying for it, but it's not just you. The whole team is about to suffer for your decisions."

This was what he'd so desperately wanted to avoid. Everything he'd done, every choice he'd made, he'd thought it had all been for the team. For them.

How wrong, how horribly wrong he'd been.

"I'm ignoring ten calls from the NCAA. I can't ignore them much longer. It looks like there's going to be an investigation. No one really understands what you've done. Did you misrepresent yourself? Make false statements? Cause the university to earn more money than they would have if you'd been out? There's going to be an inquiry into your life. Into the choices you made and didn't make."

Wes looked away, staring at the brittle blue sky over the scoreboard. It was a perfect day for football. A bite to the air, the open sky so pure and wide it felt like the lid had been lifted off the world. Not a cloud in sight. Slight breeze, just enough to tickle the skin but not to interfere with any passes. The perfect day for the end of everything. No more football. No more scholarship. No more college. No more future.

He tried to keep his chin from quivering. "I understand, Coach."

"I don't think you do. Not yet." Coach took a step back. "You'll warm up on your own before today's game. Run, Wes. Run until I say stop."

He set off around the field. He tasted salt with every ragged inhale.

When he and Colton walked out for the coin flip, half of the stadium booed as his name was announced. Colton ignored him, wouldn't even look at him. Wes kept his helmet on to hide his swollen, red-rimmed eyes. He turned away when the cameraman tried to zoom in to his face.

They lost the coin flip. The captains of the other team only shook Colton's hand. They left Wes hanging, his hand in the air, as if he didn't even exist.

Mississippi elected to receive, and in under two minutes, they marched up the field for an easy touchdown, putting seven points on the board with barely any effort.

The sideline around Wes was deathly silent. No one spoke. No one joked around or tried to rally any excitement. Clusters of Wes's teammates sat in stony silence.

He trotted out onto the field with Colton and the offense as the stadium erupted into a mix of weak cheers and deep, thunderous booing. Never, in his whole time at the school, had their team been booed. Shame ran thick and hot in his blood as he set up on the line.

"Hey fag." One of the Mississippi linebackers leaned over his defensive end. He blew Wes three kisses. "Coming for you, fag."

Colton called the snap late, and the play was doomed from the first quarter second. The offensive line was slow. Colton didn't have good pass protection. He was under pressure too soon, and he couldn't set up for a deep pass. Orlando was under coverage, and he wasn't an option for a dump pass. Wes was on a slant route, the third bailout option for Colton.

He was open.

Colton's eyes flicked to Wes's. Wes saw the moment Colton decided not to throw, to keep the ball even though the offensive line had crumbled and a linebacker was coming right for him. He looked away from Wes, curled over the ball, and took the sack, hitting the field with a sick crunch, pads on pads. Half a second later, Wes was tackled from behind, technically a late hit, but so close to the end of the play it would never be called. He hit the dirt hard, his helmet digging into the grass deep enough that his face mask ripped it up. He grunted, tried to throw his tackler off.

"Like that, fag?" The same linebacker. He thrust his hips against Wes's ass, once, twice. "I'm going to fucking destroy you." And then he was up, clapping his hands for the television cameras, trying to pump up the crowd as he ran back to the defensive huddle.

Wes pushed himself up slowly. Ten yards behind him, Colton was doing the same. Art helped Colton to his feet. No one helped Wes.

He was a ghost in the huddle. He was never chosen as the pass receiver. When he blocked, he was left all alone, isolated, and the defensive guards tag teamed him, steamrolling him to the ground and leaving him choking on dirt.

By the end of the first drive, it was clear: the team had collapsed. Nothing worked. Not their plays, not their rhythm. Not their drive. None of the strength Coach had talked about the day before was there. None of the love they had for each other was on the field. Maybe it was gone forever.

The sideline was a seething mass of fury. Colton hurled his helmet to the ground after being sacked for the sixth time. The offensive line was fighting each other, throwing blame left and right. Orlando screamed at the offensive coordinator until he got his pads grabbed and he was thrown down to the bench to cool off. The defense was a broken bunch of lost souls, watching the offense collapse and feeling the ebb of failure suck their confidence like water racing away from the shore before a tsunami. They were raw tempers and naked fury, exposed nerves and hair triggers.

It took nothing at all to strike the match that lit the fuse.

Orlando shoved Wes in their locker room at the half. "Are you fucking happy?" he roared. "Happy with what you did?"

"I'm not playing like crap out there!" Wes snapped back. "I'm open! But Colton isn't throwing to me!"

Colton snorted. He wouldn't even look at Wes, hadn't looked at him since he'd made the decision not to pass to him. He shook his head. His lip was split and swollen, and he was flexing and unflexing his throwing arm. Bruises were blossoming along his side from all the tackles he'd taken.

"Man, he can't throw to you!" Art snapped. "You've got a damn target on your back. You can't take a single step without getting your ass thrown to the ground."

"Maybe if I had some coverage, I'd get somewhere!"

"Oh, *now* you want our help?" Art bellied up to Wes, flanked by Josh and Patrick. "*Now* you need us? Now you want us? That's not how it works, motherfucker!"

Wes shoved Art hard, and then all four linemen got into it, throwing Wes back against his locker and shouting in his face about what a fucking liar he was, what a goddamn hypocrite. How he broke the team he claimed to love. The rest of the team joined in, and the locker room descended into the beginnings of an all-out brawl.

"Hey!" Coach's voice roared over the melee. "Get back! All of you!" He hauled on pads and pulled bodies apart until he got to Wes and Colton, who had death grips on each other's pads like they were linemen battling in ankle-deep mud.

He got one hand on each of them and hurled them to opposite ends of the locker bay. "Knock it off!"

"Coach!" Colton started.

"Shut your mouth!" Coach roared. He whirled on Wes. "*You*," he seethed. "You fucked your team, Van de Hoek. You wanted to get fucked this year? Well, congratulations. You fucked everyone here instead!"

"That's not what—" Wes shouted.

"That's exactly what you did! You wanted to have it all! You wanted your boyfriend and you wanted to be a star, and you were willing to step on everyone here to do it!"

Wes roared. He flung his helmet as hard as he could, and it sailed clear across the locker room and slammed into the back wall of the showers. Tiles shattered, and when his helmet crashed to the shower floor, the faceplate and the right side were cracked and broken.

Silence filled the locker room, save for the heavy, wet sound of Wes's near-strangled breathing.

"What the fuck did you think would happen when this came out? In the media, on the morning of our biggest game of the year?" Coach shook his head.

Wes reached under his jersey and unclipped his pads. He hauled them over his shoulder and threw them into his locker. Grabbed his duffel and his cell phone.

No one moved. No one tried to stop him. No one said a word as he stormed out of the locker room. It was as still and silent as a tomb, rank with the stench of failure.

He couldn't see as he stumbled through the underground tunnels. Tears formed in his eyes. Snot dripped down his face. He let it run. He had to get out of there. He had to get away, as far as he could. He had to get to Justin.

"Wes!"

There, running toward him, was Justin, a security guard trailing after him like Justin had talked his way into the stadium and was being escorted to the locker room.

He slammed into Justin, both of them moving at full speed. Justin's arms wrapped around him, and his arms wound around Justin, holding him close, as if he could pull Justin inside his soul. He buried his face in Justin's neck, finally letting out the sobs he'd leashed since his fight with Colton, since he'd jogged around the field, since the team had fallen apart around him, because of him, and there was nothing he could do about it because he'd already made the wrong choice, so many wrong choices, and he had no option but to feel his way through the failure and the shame.

All he could do for the team now was walk away and try to take the pain with him.

"It's over," he breathed. "It's all over."

"I was listening on the radio. I convinced them to let me in. I thought…"

"Get me out of here. Please."

Justin took his hand and led him out of the stadium for the last time.

CHAPTER TWENTY-FIVE

THEY LAY SIDE BY SIDE, facing each other, holding hands. Fore-heads pressed together so hard Wes would probably have a bruise when he finally pulled away. One of his legs was twined between Justin's, and Justin's thigh was hitched over his, his foot tucked behind Wes's knee. They were as close as they could get, sharing each other's breath.

"I'm supposed to go to the hospital tonight," Justin whispered. "I traded my shift with Michelle for the game today."

Wes's slow exhale trembled.

"I'll call out. I'll tell them I can't."

"No, you should go." He kissed Justin's salt-crusted lips. Tasted his tears. "One of us should have a decent future. You're doing great with your clinicals. You're going to be a great nurse."

"You still have a future—"

"I'm going to lose my scholarship. I'm going to have to go back home." And then he'd never leave. He and his dad made ends meet, but they never had extra. Not for something as expensive as tuition. This had been his chance. He'd known it, ever since he was nine years old. *Play real well, son*, his dad had said. *And you can have a bigger life than this.*

What would his dad say when he found out? Did he already know? News traveled slower way out in West Texas, but his dad had alerts on his phone for news with Wes's name. He couldn't always get somewhere where Wes's games were broadcast, so the Google alerts filled him in on the score and Wes's plays. Had he woken up to an alert about his son hiding his gay love affair? And then read all about the destruction Wes had left in the wake of his choices?

Would he even have a home to go back to?

"I'll come with you," Justin said. He tugged Wes's hands, pushed himself more firmly against Wes's body. "I'm not giving up on us just because you don't have a scholarship or you have to go back to West Texas. I'm coming with you, wherever you go."

"Justin—"

"We said this was for life, right?"

Wes dropped his eyes to Justin's lips. Failure soaked his bones. Was he going to pull Justin down with him? "Are you sure—"

"Don't even finish that question. Don't you dare ask me if I'm sure I want to be with you. Nothing has changed how much I love you."

He kissed Justin, squeezing his hands until his arms shook. He didn't deserve Justin's love. It wasn't fair to uproot him because of Wes's failure and shame. It wasn't fair, but he wasn't strong enough to tell Justin no. He needed Justin, now more than ever. He'd thought he could have it all, but he was wrong.

But as long as he had Justin, that was what truly mattered.

"Go tonight," he said, nuzzling Justin's cheek. "I'll be okay."

"Are you sure?"

He nodded. "I'll wait here."

They'd fled to the Holiday Inn on the highway. Justin had booked them a first-floor room near the back entrance, and Wes pulled his truck around and parked behind the dumpster.

Justin's dad had been calling. Wes had seen the string of texts before Justin turned off his phone. *We need to talk, Justin. Pick up your phone. Call me back. Justin, please talk to me.*

They kissed for another twenty minutes before Justin climbed out of bed to get ready. Wes hovered as Justin washed his face and tied back his hair. Suddenly he wasn't so sure about being alone. He'd been brave a few minutes ago. Now he felt like a scared little boy who desperately wanted Justin to stay. "When will you be back?"

"My shift ends at midnight." Justin poked at his eyes. It was clear he'd been crying for hours.

He was still so breathtakingly beautiful to Wes.

"Okay." Six hours. He could last six hours. With nothing but his thoughts and his memories, and his teammates' words rattling around in his skull. Their hatred, so sudden, so searing. He closed his eyes. Exhaled.

"I'll text you every moment I can."

He kissed Justin and then walked him to the hotel room's door. They'd have to figure out next steps soon. Where would Wes live after today? He couldn't stay in a hotel for three weeks, until finals. He didn't have that kind of money. Would he move in with Justin? Live across the street from the guys who hated him? And after finals, then what?

Questions for later. He squeezed Justin's hand and held the door for him, then watched him walk away. Justin walked backward, holding Wes's gaze all the way to the back door. Wes tried to smile. Justin blew him a kiss.

And then he was alone.

But not alone. Colton's voice echoed inside him. *You lied to us! Three years, Wes.* Art's voice joined in, layered on top. *That's not how it works!* Orlando, too. *Are you fucking happy?*

I'm not your fucking friend anymore.

How could you possibly do anything worse than what you've already fucking done?

His heart jackhammered. His chest ached, his lungs seizing

every time he tried to breathe. He paced, his hands fisting in front of him over and over. The only thing louder than his teammates' words was the roar of his own blood, the pounding of his heartbeat.

He grabbed the remote and turned on the TV.

ESPN came on at full volume, and Wes went rigid, unable to shut it off. His smiling face was splashed across the screen, his NCAA promotional shot. The picture changed, and there was his team, collapsing on the field. Colton getting sacked, over and over. Passes being intercepted. Wes running his passing route. Turning too slow, his footwork sloppy. Colton ignored him and tried to shovel the ball to Orlando. A moment later, Wes was creamed from behind.

Like that, fag? I'm going to destroy you.

The sportscaster kept up a running commentary, incredulity straining his voice. "What a stunning collapse today. An absolute blowout by Mississippi against Texas, who were visibly rocked by the publication of an exposé of their star player, Wes Van de Hoek."

His co-host chimed in. "That wasn't just a collapse, Sam, that was a demolishment. Mississippi thrashed Texas. It was like they were playing a high school team out there."

"Not high school. Middle school."

"Or even younger. I mean, this was an absolute, total disaster. And the team has only one man to blame for that."

"You're talking about Van de Hoek?"

"Absolutely. Look, we've been talking all year long about Texas's magic. They're all top-level players at that school, but a big part of that magic comes from how tightly bonded those boys are. Most of that starting line has been playing together for years. They've got an almost psychic connection on the field, and we've seen how well that works. Now, remember your shock this morning, when you saw those pictures? Imagine how Van de Hoek's teammates felt."

"But doesn't Van de Hoek, if what was printed is true, deserve a little bit of a break? Doesn't he deserve a private life?"

"Sure, but he wasn't trying very hard to keep this private. If you're in the public eye, you need to be more careful."

"Jerry…"

"Come on, Sam, sneaking off to have sex with his boyfriend in the middle of a college party? What was Van de Hoek thinking, if he wanted to keep this secret? He wasn't thinking, that's what."

"No one would care if it was his girlfriend."

The announcer spread his hands. "That's not the world we live in. People care. And it's not even about that. Look, I don't care if Van de Hoek likes guys or girls or Martians. He's a damn good football player. Damn good. But he's that much *better* of a ball player because of the strength of that team. He's supposed to be their captain. If he knew there was something in his life that could blow the team up this badly? That could shatter their bond, break them apart and cause this much of a collapse? He owed it to his team to be up front with everyone from the very beginning."

"If he'd been up front from the beginning, maybe he wouldn't have gotten this far in the game. As you said, people do care about this kind of thing. There are no—none—out gay footballers in Division I football right now."

Another shrug. "Is it about you, or is it about the team? That's the question every player has to ask himself. Who are you playing for? Your own glory, or what you can accomplish together? We thought Van de Hoek was playing for his team, but it looks like maybe he wasn't. Unfortunately, Texas completely crumbled today, and this may be the end of their hopes for a national championship."

"All right, turning from college ball to the NBA now…"

Wes sank to the bed. He thumbed off the TV and dropped the remote. Buried his head in his hands.

Coach's growl filled the ensuing silence. *You think you're paying for it, but you won't be. The whole team is about to suffer for your decisions.*

He'd thought he was protecting the team, but everything he'd done had made things so much worse.

There was too much coursing through him. His teammates' voices mixed with his own bitter recriminations. Failure was red hot, fire licking the inside of his skin. Shame was ice, wrapping like ribbons around his bones. Desperation sliced at his organs, turned his stomach and his guts into empty, aching pits.

He wasn't made to sit still. Since he was six years old, he'd run. To make the catch, to make the block. For yards. For touchdowns. For his team. He ran, and he pushed, and he made his life happen.

He couldn't sit in this room.

He grabbed the room key and stormed out the door.

It was dark, which was good, because it meant no one could see his face when he got out onto the road. He pulled his hoodie up and took off, jogging down the farm road toward the pitch-black horizon. The road wound for hundreds of miles through rolling hills and empty fields where ranchers let their cattle roam. Small towns popped up here and there. But for now, it was just him and the road and the empty night.

Wes ran until his body cramped up, until sweat poured down his face and soaked his hoodie. He took it off and tied it around his waist. He still had on the university Under Armour he'd worn beneath his pads and jersey. He still had the team's logo, the team's name, across his chest. His numbers were still on his back.

Finally, after an hour, he couldn't hear his teammates. He couldn't hear Coach. He couldn't hear the sportscasters. He couldn't even hear himself, the constant echo of *failure, failure, failure* with every heel strike. He couldn't even feel the shame anymore, not over the way his muscles were burning and his lungs were aching and his skin was so cold and soaked in sweat it felt like needles were stabbing his hands and his legs and his flushed cheeks.

Wes doubled over, sucking down deep breaths as he fought down his queasy stomach. The world was fuzzy on the edges. Wavering. He was dizzy. He hadn't drunk enough before the run. He'd walk it off, though. It wasn't the first time he'd overexerted himself. He started walking back to the hotel with his hands laced behind his head, opening up his chest to drag in more air. God, how far had he run?

Headlights painted the asphalt, coming up fast behind him. His shadow stretched in front of him, a giant in the middle of the road. He turned his head away from the street, not looking at the driver as they passed.

Tires squealed. Rubber burned as brakes locked. A truck, a King Ranch edition dually, slid out on the highway, coming to a jackknifed stop across both lanes.

"Hey!" The driver hollered. Wes couldn't see his face. He was lost in the shadows behind the shine of his brights. "Hey, you Wes Van de Hoek?"

Wes swallowed. He kept walking.

"Hey! I'm talking to you!"

He said nothing.

Another voice joined the first. "Looks like that faggot."

"Let's get a closer look."

Doors opened. Two big guys stepped down from the front of the truck. Boots hit pavement and strode across the asphalt. They were in Wranglers and plaid button-downs, open to show off their stained T-shirts underneath. Both had on cowboy hats.

"You are that faggot!" the first one—the driver—shouted. "Jesus Christ, you're him!"

Wes whirled on him. "Say that again!"

The man hocked a huge wad of spit at Wes's face. "Faggot!" He bellowed. "That's right, I said it. That's what you are. You're nothing, boy! Ya hear me? You thought you was something, but turns out you're nothing!"

Wes roared, but he turned away. Forced himself to take one step and then another. This wasn't anything worse than he'd read online.

"I had fifty bucks on your fucking game today!" the second guy shouted. "What, you wanted to suck a dick more than play football?"

Wes gritted his teeth, molars scraping hard. One foot in front of the other.

"I wanna see what kind of guy made you suck his dick!" the driver shouted at his back. "What kind of fucking fairy shook his gay ass and made you think that was better than a sweet, juicy pussy and twenty million NFL bucks!"

Wes spun and charged back toward both men. "Shut your fucking mouth!" Spit flew from his lips, and his voice cracked with his rage.

"Or what?" Both men stepped forward. Wes was big, but so were they. Big country boys like him, who worked hard on a ranch and were fine-tuned with real strength.

Two on one. He could take them. "Don't talk about Justin like that."

"Justin! Is that your bitch's name?"

Wes stepped forward. Got into the driver's face. "Shut your fucking mouth."

"Know what?" The driver's voice was like cut glass, sliding up Wes's spine. "I'm gonna find this Justin and sample his sweet ass myself."

Wes roared. He grabbed the driver and threw him down, got one hand in his shirt and raised his fist. The second man tried to tackle him around the waist, but Wes had been breaking tackles since he was eleven years old. He shook him off. Brought his fist down on the driver's face and felt a crack when knuckles met jaw.

"You motherfucker!" More voices came from the truck. More doors opened, more boots hit the pavement. "Get him!"

He looked up in time to see three more big country boys running at him. Farm boys, ranch hands. Cowboys. Guys who'd gone somewhere to watch the game the day after Thanksgiving, their day off, and were heading back to their bunkhouse full of piss and vinegar because their team had lost. No, not just lost. Their team had imploded. And Wes was to blame.

Five on one. Wes threw the driver down and backed up. He raised his fists. One of the men pulled brass knuckles from his pocket, and another undid his belt and pulled it free. He gripped the buckle and the worn end of leather in each of his hands.

Better me than Justin. Better me than him.

He bellowed as the five men charged him in the middle of the highway.

CHAPTER TWENTY-SIX

"JUSTIN?"

He started, sliding his phone into his scrubs pocket. Why wasn't Wes answering? Had he fallen asleep? Maybe that would be for the best. He needed a year of sleep to recover from the past few months. And then another year to recover from this day. But Justin still wanted to hear from him. Get a text back. Connect, just a little bit. Recenter his world. The only thing that mattered anymore was Wes. Them, together.

He turned to his supervisor, Tammy, the charge nurse for the emergency department, and pasted a smile on his face.

"You haven't been a part of a Life Flight transfer yet, have you?" Tammy asked, rubbing hand sanitizer into her palms.

"No. None have come in while I've been on."

"We've got one coming in now. A John Doe transfer from Blanco County. Hit and run. Pedestrian versus vehicle."

"Ouch."

"Yeah. Trucker called it in to the state police. Found him lying in the middle of the highway." Tammy passed him a surgical gown, goggles, and a pair of gloves. "Come observe. There's a lot of moving pieces in these, but when it comes down to it, Life

Flights are the same as ambulance admissions. They just arrive on the roof and not in the parking lot."

He followed Tammy and four other nurses into the elevator. Tammy briefed the team as they rode to the roof, and when they got there, they waited with Dr. Williams in the arrival bubble, a glass-encased vestibule. The landing pad was painted with a giant white cross, a red H in the center. Lights ringed the cross, and a wind cone flapped in the night breeze.

Justin bounced on his toes. He hung back, staying out of the way of Tammy and her team. As they waited, his thoughts drifted back to Wes.

Behind him, the radio built into the wall crackled. The pilot, announcing his final approach. Justin craned his neck as Tammy confirmed she had a visual on the helo coming down.

"All right, let's roll." Dr. Williams led the team out to the edge of the pad, ducking when the chopper touched down.

It wasn't as fast as Justin thought it would be, based on Hollywood. This wasn't the military, though, and it wasn't combat. The crew chief helped power down the helo, and the flight nurses on board prepped their patient for transfer. Tammy and Dr. Williams guided the team forward, then conferred with the flight physician as the nurses transferred the patient. Justin held the gurney steady as four nurses huffed, hauling the backboard out of the helicopter.

Whoever the patient was, he was huge. His feet hung off the bottom of the backboard. He was shirtless, and his bare chest and tree-trunk arms were covered in smears of blood. More dried blood caked his hands, almost up to his wrists. Bruises littered his torso. His eyes were swollen shut and ringed in bruises. His face was cut, lip split, flesh torn open across his cheekbone. His neck was wrapped in a cervical collar, but there was some deep bruising under there, a wide band that ran all around his neck and up under his jaw.

Justin held the gurney as the nurses carefully slid his backboard up, until Justin was gazing down into the patient's battered face.

Everything stopped, like someone had pressed pause on the world. The humming helo engine, still turning over on standby, faded to a dull buzz. The wind, the rotors, even the people slowed around him. "Wes?"

It couldn't be.

It couldn't be Wes lying in front of him. It couldn't be, because he'd left Wes in the hotel room, and Wes was going to stay there and wait for him. "Wes?" His voice rose, panic shredding his vocal cords.

Wes hadn't responded to his texts for hours.

"Justin? You know this man?" Tammy appeared at his shoulder. Her hand was steel on his shoulder, trying to pull him back.

He didn't budge. He ran his hands down Wes's bloody cheeks, brushed his thumbs over Wes's swollen eyelids. "This is Wes Van de Hoek." He gasped as every broken part of Wes's body came together in front of him. He'd been looking only at the injuries before, cataloging cuts and bruises. He hadn't been looking at the man like he was someone Justin knew, someone he loved.

Tammy yanked, both of her hands on his shoulders as she dragged him away from Wes's gurney. Dr. Williams took over, running down a quick assessment. "His breathing and his pupils are sluggish, and his pulse is low. Has he regained consciousness at all since he was brought in?"

The flight physician shook his head.

"Where's all this blood coming from? Anyone see any active bleeds?"

"We couldn't find any," one of the flight nurses said.

"Wes…" Justin pleaded. He tried to reach for him, tried to fight against Tammy's hold. Wes looked so broken, so fragile. His chest rose and fell in fractional shudders. His hands dangled off the sides of the gurney, fingers limp and curled toward his palm.

"He might have internal bleeding. We've got to get him into

the CT, now." Dr. Williams nodded to the other nurses. "Let's get him down to the ER. Michelle, page radiology as soon as we're down. Tell them we have an emergency CT and X-ray coming to them. I also want neurology downstairs in twenty minutes. I want to know what kind of head trauma we're looking at. Prep ICU, and have surgical on standby. All right, let's move."

They jogged for the vestibule, rolling Wes away. Justin tried to follow, but Tammy held him back. "You can't be involved, Justin. You know the patient."

"That's Wes!" He fought against her, trying to shake loose. His vision was blurring, and his cheeks were wet. His throat, his lungs wouldn't work. He wanted to call out to Wes, but he couldn't make his brain and his vocal cords work together, couldn't form the words he wanted to say.

His knees gave out and he sagged in Tammy's arms, dragging her down with him as he sank to the concrete. Why? How? What had happened?

"You said that was Wes Van de Hoek?" Tammy crouched next to him, one hand on his wrist, holding on. "How do you know him?"

"Did you read the article this morning?"

"Is there anyone in this town who hasn't?"

Justin cringed. "I'm his boyfriend."

Tammy said nothing. She turned and stared into the night, over the cluster of office buildings in the center of their tiny downtown.

———

HE ENDED UP IN THE NURSES' lounge, torn between crying and wanting to flip the furniture. Tear the metal lockers apart with his hands. Break a chair over his thigh and hurl the pieces against the wall. He paced instead, unable to keep still as he waited for information.

Wes went into and out of radiology, into and out of the CT scanner and the X-ray machines. It became clear, quickly, that Wes wasn't hit by a car. That his injuries came from *someone*. Or several someones. That he'd been attacked.

The university police were called. Justin knew the procedure. Wes was photographed and stripped, his clothes bagged, and swabs were collated from his knuckles and under his nails. He pictured Wes motionless on the hospital bed, eyes swollen shut, hands limp, his broken body dressed in a hospital gown that was too small for him.

"You're done for the night," Tammy told him. "You're in no state to be dealing with patients." He hadn't even tried to argue. "Do you have someone to drive you home?"

"I'm not leaving," he'd growled. "I'm staying here. I'm staying with Wes."

Tammy had eventually gone back to work. Once Justin was alone, his thoughts tumbled, turned, grew thorns. Questions he didn't have answers to rose in waves. What-ifs circled like sharks smelling blood. What if Wes was permanently injured? What if something irreplaceable had been taken from him?

What if he didn't wake up?

After two hours without answers, Justin pulled out his cell phone and called his dad.

"Justin." His dad picked up before the first ring ended. He sighed, a great woosh of air rushing over the line. *"Jesus, Justin, why didn't you pick up earlier? I've been so worried about you. That article—"*

"Dad—" He couldn't speak, couldn't get any words out of his clenched throat. "Dad," he tried again. His fingers dug into the wall as he struggled to stand. "Dad, it's Wes."

"What about him?"

Justin crumpled to the floor as his dad tried to talk him through his gulping sobs.

"*Justin, breathe. Breathe. Talk to me. What happened to Wes? Where is he? Where are you?*"

"I'm at the hospital," he forced out. "He was brought in by Life Flight—"

"*What happened to him?*"

"I don't know! I think someone attacked him!" He screamed, covering his mouth with his hand. His eyes squeezed closed. He pitched forward, his face against his knees. "Dad, he hasn't woken up…"

"*I'm on my way. I'm driving down. Right now.*"

CHAPTER TWENTY-SEVEN

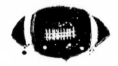

STEADY BEEPING WAS the foundation of Justin's world.

He breathed in rhythm with the beeps. His dreams played out in time with their cadence. His thoughts took shape alongside the beeps, formed into checklists and to-dos that he scratched off as the machines kept time. Hold Wes's hand. Smooth his hair from his forehead. Kiss his temple.

Breathe in. Breathe out.

No one had any answers for him.

All the doctors could tell him was what they didn't know: they didn't know if Wes had long-term brain damage. They didn't know if he would remember what happened, or where he was, or even who he was, when he woke up. They didn't know whether he'd have full use of his arms or his legs. "We don't really know what happened," Dr. Williams said. "We don't know how long he was lying in that road. We don't know what kind of trauma or brain swelling might have occurred before we got to him."

Someone had wrapped a belt around his neck and tried to strangle him. There was a two-inch-wide black-and-blue band around his throat, riding up on both sides and under his jawbone, like someone had stood behind him and yanked. The doctors said

Wes's size and strength had protected him. His throat was more than half swollen shut when he'd been brought in, but he'd never stopped breathing.

Wes was lucky, they said. No major organ damage. Bruised ribs. Bruised kidneys. He was black and blue and putrid green from the roots of his hair to his toes, more bruises than healthy skin. But he was alive.

No one could tell Justin when he would open his eyes, though.

Justin's dad slept on the couch behind him, in Wes's private ICU room. He'd made the five-hour drive from Dallas in just over three hours in his Porsche, had flown into the hospital and wrapped Justin in his arms like he was four years old and he'd fallen off his bike. Justin had cried in his dad's arms, his face buried in his chest, and his dad had held on to him until every tear was out and until he could stand on his own wobbly feet again.

They talked over Wes's bed, after the doctors and nurses finally checked Wes's medical release information at the university and saw Justin was listed as his local emergency contact. Wes had made an offhand comment about putting Justin on his paperwork, swapping Justin in instead of Coach Young. "I'd rather have you there if I break my leg than him," he'd said. They'd laughed about it, imagining Coach Young trying to comfort Wes with his leg in a cast and a sling.

There wasn't any laughter now.

"I saw the game," his dad had said.

"He wasn't trying to hurt anyone." There was too much to say, too many factors that had gone into Wes's calculus. Too many variables in his decisions and in the vectors of his life. Every path had spiraled like a football, a pass thrown with no receiver in range. How was he to know how everything would play out? How wrong everything would go? Life wasn't lived with the benefit of hindsight.

"His team was pissed. You could feel their rage through the

TV." His dad sighed. "Someday, you'll have to tell me how this all happened." He held Justin's hand over Wes's blanketed thighs. Ran his other down Wes's arm, until he gripped Wes's wrist above the IV. "You and Wes Van de Hoek?"

"It was Paris," he'd whispered. "We met in Paris."

"He was the guy?" Justin's dad had scowled. "I wanted to kill that guy. You never told me it was him."

"Because he's your favorite player, Dad, on your favorite team. I didn't want to ruin the game for you."

"Fuck the game. You're more important than football, Justin."

He'd smiled, sadly. "What about how all you wanted was for me to marry a Texas fan?"

"All I want is for you to be happy. Happy, safe, and healthy. That's all a parent should ever want."

Justin was quiet as he squeezed his dad's hand. He managed a tiny smile, after a long moment. "I mean, I did do good, though, huh? Not just a Texas fan, but your favorite Texas player."

"He's only my favorite player if he treats you right."

"He's perfect, Dad. He's perfect for me." His voice went thin, and he buried his face against Wes's thigh. "I love him so much. We said we'd be together forever, Dad, and now—"

"*Shhh*. You'll have that. He's going to wake up."

Justin counted the seconds and then the minutes and then the hours, collecting time like he was a hoarder. Each revolution around the clock was another revolution that Wes didn't stir. Another moment he didn't open his eyes. His dad peeled away when the sun rose, falling into the couch and closing his eyes. He was snoring before the morning nurse came to check on Wes.

Justin slid his chair right up next to Wes's bedside. He laid his head on the mattress beside Wes's. The nurses had wiped Wes's face clean, but they hadn't been able to wash his hair, and it stuck together in clumps, matted with blood. Justin tried to finger comb the strands as he whispered to him, told Wes he loved him and that he was there, he was right there, and he wasn't going anywhere. He held Wes's hand and told him his dreams for their future. How Wes could teach him how to ride horses, and they'd go out to that ridge Wes told him about. They'd camp together, somewhere Wes could hear the country and let his soul fill up all the empty spaces the world had hollowed out of him. Justin could get a job nursing anywhere, and he would. Anywhere Wes wanted to be. All that mattered was them, together. And he was right there, and he would be right there. He wasn't going anywhere.

Inhale. Exhale. Beep.

Justin laid his forehead against Wes's bandaged cheek and let his tears fall.

CHAPTER TWENTY-EIGHT

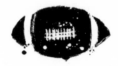

AT 10:28 A.M., someone banged so hard on the front door of their jock house it nearly came off its hinges. The glass rattled in the old panes, and the warped wood leaped in and out of the frame. *"Open up!"* A deep voice hollered. *"Open this fucking door!"*

Colton threw himself off the kitchen counter and slumped past his roommates to the foyer. They'd been up all night bickering, snapping left and right, throwing attitude in each other's faces. Now they slouched in the living room and den, angry stares boring holes in the faded wallpaper. Melancholy soaked the rank air, thickened by a grief they couldn't name.

He ripped open the front door. "What the fuck do you want?" He glared at the middle-aged man on their porch, who had his fist raised and was getting ready to hammer on the door again. "Who the fuck are you?"

The man shoved him, driving him backward into the house and throwing him against the paneling in the foyer. His forearm pushed up against Colton's throat, holding him in place.

The rest of the team was on their feet and racing for Colton and this wild man who'd appeared in the middle of Saturday morning in his dad jeans and his tennis shoes and his golf shirt. Cries of "What the fuck?" and "Who the fuck are you?" and "Get the fuck out of here!" bled together.

"Shut the fuck up!" the man bellowed at them all. "I'm Nick Swanscott! Justin's dad! Wes's boyfriend. I'm his fucking father!"

The team faltered. Orlando came to Colton's side, but he held back from getting in Justin's dad's face. He hovered next to Colton. "Yeah? What the fuck do you want? Wes isn't fucking here. You want to go fuck him up, you have to find him somewhere else. He didn't come home."

Nick's eyes flashed. "Anyone Justin loves, I love, and that means Wes is like a son to me. Do you fucking understand?"

He grabbed at Nick's arm. He was fucking strong. "What the fuck do you want?"

"Did you fucking hurt Wes?"

"What the fuck are you talking about?"

"Did you hurt Wes? Are you the reason he's in the hospital?"

"Wes is in the hospital?" The urge to fight faded, replaced by the emptiness Colton had felt since yesterday morning, when he'd woken up to Orlando's text messages blowing up his phone, and then Art and Josh and Patrick banging on his door, and then that fucking article about Wes. Reality had shifted ten degrees to the left, leaving him hovering on the edge of a black hole. It was like being sacked and falling forever, never hitting the ground.

"Wes is in a coma!" Nick roared. "Someone beat him half to death." He dug his forearm into Colton's throat. "Was that you?"

"No! Jesus fucking Christ!"

"Anyone else?" Nick shoved off of Colton and faced the rest of the team. He was maybe one-eighty, just under six feet, but he squared off against them like he was three times Wes's size. "Are any of you the reason why my son is crying over Wes's unconscious body right now?"

Silence. Feet shifted against the old wooden floors. Orlando turned to Colton, his big eyes asking a question Colton couldn't answer.

Nick pushed past them. He took the stairs two at a time, stomping up to the landing. Colton drifted after him. "Wes's bedroom?" Nick growled.

Colton pointed.

Nick grabbed a duffel from under Wes's bed. It was the bag Colton and Wes had been given their freshman year when they joined the team. The year they met and became best friends. Nick threw Wes's clothes into Wes's old duffel, sweeping his laptop and his textbooks and the few odds and ends on his nightstand into the ratty bag.

"What are you doing?"

"Moving Wes out. He obviously can't stay here anymore."

The rest of the guys hung behind Colton in the hall. They'd talked about this last night. What the hell were they going to do about Wes in the house? Colton's mind stuttered and rewound, still stuck on Nick's earlier shout. He shook his head. "Why is Wes in the hospital?"

"I told you. Someone beat him half to death."

His friend. His best friend. The guy who had kept pace with him at freshman training camp, even though he could easily have run farther, faster. The guy who caught all his passes, even his shitty ones, and made him look better in front of Coach Young. The guy who told him he was going to be great at the university level, even though he was only a good quarterback from a decent school in Houston and suddenly he was surrounded by players who were just as good as he'd ever been—or better. He and Wes had spent days and nights on that field, practicing routes and passes and plays, running drills, putting in time after practice until they were a clock that ticked the same time. A heart that beat the same beats. Wes worked with him over the summer when he wanted to learn a new offense. Did it again when he wanted to learn one more.

Why hadn't Wes said anything? Why hadn't he ever sat down and looked Colton in the eyes and told him, "I'm gay." He'd had a million opportunities, a million moments he could have said the words.

Why hadn't he trusted him?

Didn't Wes know Colton would've been there for him? If any motherfucker had ever said a fucking thing to him, Colton would've been the first one to beat their face in. The whole campus, the whole world, would have known, Colton Hall was there for Wes Van de Hoek. No one would have said a fucking word to him unless they wanted five hundred pounds of pain raining down like righteous wrath.

So why was Wes in the hospital?

The raw stink of failure unfurled inside him again. They had all been huddled in failure since the game, wallowing in rage. The collapse of their team. The collapse of their brotherhood. His failure as a quarterback.

Someone beat him half to death.

Now, his failure as a friend.

He sagged against Wes's doorframe and ran his hands through his hair, threaded them behind his neck. How many times had he stood right here, talking to Wes and tossing him a ball as they bitched about Coach and practice and homework? He could still see the shadow of his friend at his desk, smiling at him and wearing that ridiculous cowboy hat. "Is he going to be okay?"

"They don't know. They don't know when he'll wake up."

He heard his teammates curse behind him. Heard Art stomp down the hall. Heard a door slam and then a fist go through the drywall once, twice, three times. Josh and Patrick turned away and gripped the landing's banister so hard the wood creaked. Orlando, beside Colton, cursed a blue streak, shifting back and forth like a chipmunk on cocaine.

"Where were you last night?" Nick growled. "In my mind, you

all are the best fit as suspects in this. The entire country could see how much you hated Wes yesterday."

"I don't hate Wes." It was reflex, it was automatic. It burst out of him before he'd even thought about the words. He'd felt them, and they fell out without his mind's permission.

Nick snorted. "You could've fooled me." He zipped Wes's duffel closed and threw the strap over his shoulder.

"Wes is my best friend."

"Sure looks that way." Nick pointed to Colton's split lip and then shoved past him, his shoulder slamming into Colton's on his way out the door.

The look on Wes's face when Colton had insulted Justin, and then after he'd laid Colton out, had stayed with him throughout the game. It was all he saw when he looked at Wes, and later, all he saw when he closed his eyes. Not the linebacker flying at his face, or the scoreboard memorializing their blowout. It was Wes's face, looking down on Colton like his whole world had shattered, like everything had come undone. Like Colton had broken something he could never fix.

That's what it had felt like when Colton had read the article about Wes, too. His best friend. The guy he loved more than he loved his own brothers, his own mother.

Nick stomped down the stairs, taking the remnants of Wes with him. If he walked out that door, Wes would be gone forever, erased from the house and the team like he'd never been there.

Other than the hole in Colton's soul and the empty clutch of his heart, searching for the one it was supposed to beat in time with.

You didn't work for years to synchronize your existence with someone only to rip them out of your life in a single moment.

Of course, you didn't lie to that person, either.

Why had Wes lied to him?

How had he missed the truth, though? He'd seen how gone Wes had been this season, how head over heels in love he was.

Why didn't he see that the person Wes loved was right in front of him—literally? Justin, and not Jessica or Jennifer or Julie? Justin.

"Wait," he called out, chasing Justin's dad. "Wait!"

Nick hesitated at the base of the stairs. He didn't turn around.

"Take me to the hospital. Take me to Wes. Please."

CHAPTER TWENTY-NINE

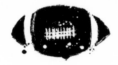

IF HE CLOSED HIS EYES, it was almost like they were lying in bed together. Like his cheek was pillowed on Wes's chest and they were drifting off to sleep in the bed of Wes's truck, wrapped in the sleeping bag that smelled like campfire smoke. Or they were in Justin's bedroom, on one of those stolen nights. Or they were in Paris, where he'd fallen in love with his football-playing cowboy.

But when they were together before, Wes's arms were always around him. Wes always held on to him, cradled him against his big chest. He held Justin like he was precious to him, like he loved him. Because he did.

Now, Wes's arms lay limp. He wasn't holding Justin, even though Justin was curled against his side, their bodies fitted so perfectly it was like they were made to be together. And that constant beep drowned out the heartbeat Justin wanted to hear, the steady thump deep in Wes's chest that always soothed him right to sleep. No matter how much he wished it, this wasn't another night. And things weren't okay.

He clung to Wes, his face pressed to Wes's shoulder. He couldn't stop crying. It was like all the blood in his body had been replaced with tears, and his broken heart was hemorrhaging out the sorrow in his soul.

"Wes…" His breath hitched. His snot pooled on the thin fabric of Wes's hospital gown. He squeezed Wes's arms, digging his fingers into the meat of his biceps. "You have to wake up. You have to come back. *Please*."

Wes was power and strength wrapped in a human body. His bones were his convictions, and his muscles were his promises, and his soul was made out of his dreams. He was the strongest man Justin had ever met, in body and mind. This couldn't be his end. This couldn't be their end.

"Please," he whispered. "Please come back to me."

He'd talked to Wes for hours, all night and all morning, whispering his dreams for the two of them as he stroked Wes's hair. He reminisced about his favorite moments with Wes, all the way back to when Wes walked into their shared room in Paris and looked at Justin with those big blue cowboy eyes. That first bus ride and how devastatingly polite Wes had been. He'd rocked Justin's world from that first day.

And Justin had fallen for Wes so fast. There was never a choice between Wes and the Riviera, or the Alps, or Vienna. He'd watched Wes scatter duck feed into the pond, his muscles rippling beneath his faded T-shirt, and he'd gone all in. To hell with common sense. What was the point of being common, anyway? He was going to chase the wild beat of his heart, spend all his free time with Wes. Go to the market and the Sacré-Coeur and the Museum of Modern Art, and if it was agony at the end, when Wes's eyes turned to some gorgeous French girl, well. He'd have had a beautiful day with a gorgeous man to remember.

But Wes had kissed him beneath the Eiffel Tower, and there went the rest of his life.

"I can't pinpoint when I fell in love with you," he whispered. His fingers traced Wes's heart, over his chest and down his side, then up his arm before starting the circuit again. "It was just there one day, inside me. I didn't want to be without you. And then I *couldn't* be without you. That's when I knew you were the love of my life. You'd become a part of me, and my life was incomplete without you." His lips brushed over Wes's jaw, the stubble on his chin. "You're it for me. *Tu es mon plus grand amour." You are the love of my life.*

For a moment, it seemed like there was a hitch beneath him. Like Wes's breathing had shifted. Justin stilled. Stared at Wes and willed him to move.

Nothing.

It had probably been his own body shaking. Justin smothered an open-mouthed cry as his fingers dug into Wes's chest. "*Je t'aime de tout mon coeur.*"

Stubble grazed his forehead. Lips ghosted over his hair. "*Tu es mon plus grand amour…*" Wes's voice was broken, fractured and catching on his words, but it was there. His shaking fingers curled around Justin's hand. "Justin…"

Justin screamed. Screamed for the doctors and the nurses, screamed Wes's name. Grabbed Wes's hand and squeezed, then kissed each of his fingers. Ran his hand down Wes's bruised cheek and kissed him right over his split and torn lip. Wes's eyes were still swollen, only one able to partially open. But Justin saw a sliver of blue—lake blue, moonlight in a meadow blue, the blue of a Paris summer sky. He smiled, finally, trembling as he cradled Wes's face and smoothed Wes's hair back.

When the doctors and the nurses were finished examining Wes, they told him he was one lucky, strong son of a bitch. They asked what happened, and Justin's tears rained down as Wes recounted the details. His voice was ragged, his throat still swollen and bruised. But he spoke, and he didn't falter, not even when he told them about the brass knuckles or the man with the belt, how he'd stood behind Wes with it wrapped around his neck as the rest of the men took turns beating on him.

"They tried to kill you," Dr. Williams said. "But they didn't

even come close. You're way too strong for five guys to take out."
He smiled at Wes, then tilted Wes's chin up and gently examined
his neck. "You're going to recover, Wes. You're going to be all
right. We'll get you back on that playing field."

Wes didn't say anything to that. Eventually, the nurses
followed Dr. Williams out, leaving Justin and Wes alone again.
Justin peppered firefly kisses on every inch of Wes's skin he could.
This time, Wes held his arms out for him, and Justin crawled right
into his hold. He kissed Wes softly, pressed their foreheads
together. Cradled his face and stared into his eyes, whispering in
French and English how much he loved him. Wes tried to speak,
but Justin kissed him quiet. "Don't talk. Let your throat heal. I'm
here, I've got you, *mon coeur*." Wes smiled, and he threaded their
fingers together–

The hospital room door opened. His dad walked in, followed
by Colton, and then Orlando, and Art. All the rest of Wes's housemates. Most of the starting line, offense and defense. All there,
suddenly, watching them kiss in Wes's hospital bed.

His dad dropped a duffel on the sofa beneath the window and
came to stand behind Wes and Justin.

Colton went pale as he came closer and saw the extent of
Wes's injuries. The rest of the guys followed, eyes wide, Art and
Orlando cursing under their breath. "Dude," Colton whispered.
He hovered a few feet from the bed, his hands grasping the air
like he was searching for a football. "What happened?"

"Fans," Wes choked out. He squeezed Justin's hand. Justin
could feel him trembling. Wes hadn't shown an ounce of fear
when he was retelling what happened to him out on that dark
road, but now, facing Colton, he was quaking. "I ran into some
guys who were pissed about the game. And me." His voice was
thick. He turned his face down, pressed his cheek against Justin's.
Closed his eyes.

"Wes…" Colton shook his head. His broad shoulders rose and

fell as his hands tangled in front of him. "Fuck," he hissed. "Jesus Christ…"

"I'm sorry." Wes's eyes opened. Tears spilled down his cheeks and fell onto Justin's. He tasted the salt of Wes's sorrow. Tried to fight back his rage. He held on to Wes, trying to shore him up with love. "I didn't mean to hurt you guys. I never meant to hurt the team. I was trying to hide it. I was trying to keep it a secret."

"You can't hide how in love you are." Colton looked like he was going to be sick. "And you shouldn't fucking have to. Damn it, no one cares that you're gay. No one."

"I was trying to protect the team," Wes said. "I thought if no one knew, nothing bad could happen."

"Something bad did happen!"

"I know. I failed you guys—"

"No, man!" Orlando snapped. "No!"

"Someone attacked you! That's what happened!" Colton's face twisted, and he bit down on the corner of his lip. "Someone fucking attacked you, and we weren't there. We weren't there to fucking pound whoever it was into the fucking ground—"

His voice died, and he turned away, paced to the wall, and threw his fist into the tile. He roared, then flung himself forward, bracing himself on his forearms as he bowed his head. "Fuck!"

Justin's dad squeezed the railing of Wes's bed.

"Help me sit up," Wes whispered. His arms shook as Justin helped him move, and he bit back a whimper that only Justin heard.

There was a heart and a soul to every football team. Wes may have been their captain, but he was only one half of the team's heart. Even Justin, who knew nothing about football, had figured that out, watching Wes and Colton at the practices and the games and hearing Wes talk about him. The bond between them was the soul of the team. Their friendship, and how they'd trained and perfected their game until they were the best in the league. How much they gave and gave and gave to each other, how deeply they trusted one another.

The team's heart and soul had shattered when Wes and Colton did. If there was going to be a way forward, it had to start between them.

Wes was still catching his breath, his hands gripping the bed rail and Justin's leg, but he squared his shoulders and looked up at his friend. "Colton."

Colton's shoulders shook. He faced Wes, his jaw clenched, his hands shaking as they formed fists at his side.

"I never told anyone I was gay until I kissed Justin in Paris. I thought I could bury this until I got out of college. I never planned on coming out, or dating, or anything, not as long as we were playing. That's why I never told you. Because it wasn't a part of my life." His gaze met Justin's. He tried to smile, a quiver of his cheek and a pull of his split lip. "Until it was."

"Wes—" Colton's voice was wrecked. He stared at the ground.

"I never meant to hurt you or lie to you. And I never wanted to use you. I never wanted my life to touch you guys or be a problem."

"Your life isn't a problem, man." Orlando looked like someone had kicked his puppy on Christmas morning. "That was never the issue."

Wes's gaze dropped to his hospital bed. "I'm sorry."

Colton shook his head. He kept shaking it until his whole body was shaking, and he stumbled to the foot of Wes's bed. He fell forward onto the mattress, his face buried in Wes's hospital blanket as he grabbed onto Wes's bandaged hand. "I'm sorry," he choked out. "I'm sorry, Wes. Jesus, I'm so fucking sorry."

ONE HALLMARK MOMENT did not a recovery make, though.

There was still tension in the air, between the team members.

No one knew what to say to Wes, or how to say it. There was hurt in their eyes, resentment that slid onto Justin when their gazes flicked from Wes to him and then back. Most of the guys hung around Wes's hospital room for a few hours, grabbing chairs from wherever they could and crowding around his bed. But eventually they drifted away, heading back to the house to finish homework or essays, or to the gym to work off emotions they hadn't yet been able to verbalize.

By the evening, Wes and Justin and Colton were alone in the room. Even his dad had stepped out, saying he was going to find food for them.

Colton sat at Wes's bedside, and for a while, they did nothing but reminisce, revisiting memories of training camp and drills, of riding the third and then the second string, of being good enough the year before to have a handful of starts and more than a handful of finishes. Wes was a good player on his own, but he was great with Colton. And Colton had worked his ass off, but Wes made him look phenomenal.

Through it all, Justin stayed glued to Wes's side.

"Come home," Colton said to Wes, out of a moment's quiet. He jerked his chin at the duffel on the couch. "Justin's dad packed up all your stuff." His eyes flicked to Justin, then away. "I mean, you can go wherever. You can move in with Justin, I guess. But you could come home, too. I want you to come home. We all want you to come home."

"I don't know if I'm eligible to live there anymore. You need to be an active player, and I don't think I am."

"Why not?"

"Coach said the NCAA was going to investigate me."

"Bullshit. What are they going to do? Fine you for having a secret? They don't even kick people out who drink and drive or beat their girls. They're not kicking you out over an article. You didn't do anything wrong."

Wes didn't look convinced. "Coach said they're investigating if

I misrepresented myself to enhance the program. You know the NCAA only cares about money."

"Dude, I'll walk if they do anything to you."

"Colton."

"I will. Fuck that. I'm not letting that happen." He ran his fingers through his hair. "You're not alone, dude. You're not. Okay?"

"Even if the NCAA clears me, I don't know if I'm still on the team. I haven't heard from Coach."

"Yeah, me either." Colton scrubbed his hands over his face. "I kinda got the feeling he was letting me figure this out on my own. He wasn't so... up in my face about it. Like he usually is, you know? He's probably giving you the same space."

Wes shrugged.

"Look, we've got a bye week, and then we've got the final game of the season. You'll heal up by then. I've seen you shake off tackles that are worse than this." Colton's eyes kept skittering off Wes's throat, tracing the strangulation marks and then sliding away. "We need to win that last game. If we do, we go to the championship. We can't win without everyone, so, yeah, you're playing." Colton hesitated. "I mean... you wanna play, right?"

Justin's gaze fell to the floor. He squeezed Wes's hand but said nothing. Hadn't that been the question Wes had been wrestling with all year? Football or being true to himself? *I think about quitting*, he'd said. *I just want to take your hand in the middle of campus.*

Now they were holding hands in front of Colton.

Now the world knew.

What did Wes want, now that there were no secrets left? Justin ran his thumb over Wes's knuckles and waited. *Whatever you decide, I'll be beside you,* mon amour.

"I think I do." Wes's voice was quiet. Almost a whisper. It was still breaking in places, his vocal cords bruised and mangled. "If it came down to a choice between football and Justin, it's no contest. I know what I'll choose every time."

Colton's jaw clenched. "You don't have to make that choice, though. You never did."

"I felt like I had to."

"Fuck that. You don't."

Wes was quiet. "I never imagined the possibility of both. Football and loving you?" He turned to Justin.

"I thought about it." Justin ran his hand down Wes's bandaged cheek. "I thought about what it would be like if people knew you were blowing a kiss to me, not to your adoring fans."

Colton coughed, his cheeks darkening.

"Oh, you just realized that?" Justin grinned. "I was at every game. All those kisses to the stands were for me."

He and Wes smiled as Colton's flush grew. Wes tipped his head sideways, resting against Justin.

"I didn't think this was how it would be," Justin whispered. He traced the bruises on Wes's face with the tips of his fingers. "I never imagined anything like this would happen."

"I was afraid of it, but I was afraid they'd come after you."

"If they did, I'd be dead. I couldn't survive what you did."

"Don't say that." Wes pulled him closer. Hid his face and his shiver in the crook of Justin's neck. "Don't ever say that."

Justin held him through it, stroking his back as Wes trembled. Colton waited, watching. He reached out and laid his hand on Wes's thigh.

Wes pulled back and rubbed his snotty nose on his arm. "I'm not sure everyone wants me to come back."

"Like who?" Colton asked.

"The fans, for one. That was a lot of booing at the Mississippi game. And…" He gestured to himself, to his neck and his face.

"Fuck the fans," Colton growled.

"Colton—"

"I'm serious. Fuck them. Fans"—he spat out the word like it was diseased—"did that to you. Fans booed us for walking on the field, before we even made a bad play. Boo me for throwing an interception. Boo me for calling a bad snap. Boo me for playing like shit. Don't boo me, or you, just for being there. So, yeah, fuck the fans."

They lapsed into silence, memories of Friday morning tumbling around them. "What about the rest of the team?" Wes finally asked.

Colton blew out a long, slow breath. "I think you should talk to everyone and lay it all out there. Why you thought you had to do what you did. Everyone thought you were using us, you know? You had your own world that no one knew about and that you didn't trust us with, but you sure as shit were fine with us catapulting you into stardom. When I read that article…" Colton's jaw moved left and right. "I thought, Jesus, I'm only good enough to throw you sweet passes. Give you touchdowns, give you yards, get you some good stats and wall-to-wall ESPN highlights. But apparently I wasn't good enough to really know you. Like I was just someone you put up with to get what you needed. That I— none of us—were really your friends."

"That wasn't what it was at all."

"I know that now. And the guys know it, but there's a difference between knowing and feeling. I think if you talked to them, they'd get it. They'd understand. And then we'll be good. Listen, no one—and I do mean no one—cares that you're gay. Fuck, we'll paint the locker room rainbow if you want. Orlando has already texted me a link to order everyone rainbow sweatbands. Like, that's not an issue, at all. I swear."

"Please don't paint the locker room. That's a horrible idea."

"What are you talking about? It's a great idea."

"No way, dude. Come on."

"I'm texting Orlando. He'll get the paint today. We are so doing this."

"Colton!"

"It's done, man. It's happening." Colton pulled out his phone and texted, grinning like an idiot. Wes made a weak grasp for it, but he didn't have the reach with his bruised ribs. He ended up leaning into Justin as he held his hand over his side, laughing and wincing at the same time.

Colton shoved his phone back in his pocket and grabbed Wes's hand, holding it like they were making a warrior's vow. "We're gonna get through this, okay? I swear, we're gonna get through this. I'm going to help you with all your recovery and shit. And I'm going to find whoever did this to you, I swear to God—"

"The police are investigating. They'll handle it."

"Whatever. No one fucks with you and walks away. No one." His eyes shifted, landing on Justin. "Or you. No one fucks with you, either. The team will kick anyone's ass for both of you guys. Got it?"

Justin nodded. Wes squeezed Colton's hand, and they seemed to communicate through white knuckles and trembling forearms for thirty seconds, holding each other's stare until Colton finally looked down.

"So... come home? We've got a lot to do. And we're here for you." He stood, stumbling over his feet, over the chair. He looked like a drunk horse instead of the league's best quarterback. "And, uh, Justin? You should come, too. I mean, Josh's girl spends, like, four nights a week in the house. No reason why you can't be with us."

CHAPTER THIRTY

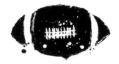

IT WAS time for lights out on the ward before Wes, Justin, and Justin's dad were all in the room together, alone. The nurses and the doctors had finished their night exams, and Wes was declared both on the road to recovery and damn lucky. He would stay through the week for observation and to make sure he was truly on the mend.

This wasn't the ideal way to meet the father of the love of his life, but Wes was nothing if not stubborn. After being stripped and prodded and examined, after his catheter was removed and he was helped to the toilet and then back to bed, after he fell back against the pillows and clung to Justin while he remembered which way the earth spun, he caught sight of Justin's dad trying to disappear on the corner of the couch. He was burning holes into *The Economist*, trying to look as if he was reading.

Wes took a few deep breaths, squeezed Justin's hand, and hauled himself—slowly, delicately—into a sitting position. He squared his shoulders. "Mr. Swanscott?"

"*Hmm*, yes?" To his credit, Justin's dad acted like he'd just been greeted in an airport lounge and all that mortifying examination business hadn't happened. "Wes. How are you feeling?"

Wes tried to smile. Half his face still felt like it was falling off. Brass knuckles had knocked on his cheekbone a few times, but that guy had eaten them in the end, when Wes flung him off and put him in the dirt. "Mr. Swanscott, this isn't how I wanted to meet you," he said. Was his voice shaking? "I imagined something very different. But…" He picked at the thin hospital blanket. "Thank you for being here. It means a lot to me that you are."

"Please, call me Nick. I'm here as long as you need me." A frown crossed his features before it smoothed away, a practiced move. "Will your dad be here soon? It's a long trip from West Texas, so I know he can't get here as quickly as I could."

Wes shook his head. "He's on the cattle drive right now. He and a bunch of other ranchers move their herds from West Texas to California for the winter. Out to those feed lots in the Central Valley? I couldn't even tell you where he is right now."

"Does he know?"

"I sent him a text. Told him I was hurt and gonna be a few days in the hospital, but that I was going to be fine."

Nick arched an eyebrow at him. "That's not a comprehensive assessment of the situation."

He had that caved-in feeling again, like his ribs were crunching around his heart. "He can't afford to make the trip. And I am going to be okay. I don't want to worry him."

"Your dad is going to worry about you no matter what. That's the job." Nick sat on the end of Wes's bed. "You are going to be okay. You're right about that. But I think your dad will want to know what's happened."

He fiddled with the edge of the blanket. He cleared his throat. "I um. I wanted to tell you about me and Justin, Mr. Swanscott—"

"But I wanted to see your face when you saw who he was, Dad," Justin said, interrupting. "Wes wanted you to know."

"It's all right." He clasped Wes's ankle through the bedclothes. "I understand. You boys had a lot going on this semester. You didn't need the stress of meeting a parent on top of that."

"I want you to know, Mr. Swanscott, that I love your son. I'm in love with him, and I'll love him for the rest of my life. Hopefully he lets me love him for the rest of his life, too."

Justin grinned. "That's the plan."

"Wes, I've watched you play football for three years. I thought you were pretty damn incredible before my son fell in love with you. Now Justin has told me stories about the two of you together, and if I thought you were a good guy before, that doesn't compare at all to how I think of you now. You treat my son right. Hopefully he's treating you right, too." Nick winked. Wes chuckled, and Justin squawked. "I don't think I could imagine a better man for my son than you." He covered Wes's hand in his own. "It pains me to say it, but even if you were an Aggie, I'd be proud to know you."

High praise indeed. The Aggies were Texas's most reviled rival. "I can count to ten, Mr. Swanscott. I promise, I'm not an Aggie."

Justin's dad laughed. "I hope you both are happy with each other for a long, long time." Nick let go of Wes's hand and smiled at them both. There was an echo, though, around him, something Wes caught hold of. It reminded him of his dad after his mom died, the way he'd bounced around in a life made for two, suddenly become one.

Later, after he'd lain back and closed his eyes, and he was hovering in the twilight of sleep, Justin's fingers threading through his hair, he heard Nick ask if he could talk to Justin, alone.

———

JUSTIN'S DAD shut the hospital room door behind him and smiled at Justin. It was stilted, though. Pained. "Can I buy you a coffee?"

"Sure." He followed his dad down to the cafeteria, then sat

across the table from him and wrapped his hands around a mocha. This wasn't what he'd expected their relationship to look like. If he'd had a pair of binoculars to peer into the future with when he was sixteen, he would have laughed and laughed and laughed.

But now that the future was here, and he and his dad were friendly—even friends—it was… nice. More than nice. It was great. Knowing his dad as an adult was so different from knowing him as a child. His dad was smart and funny and kind. He'd probably been that way Justin's whole life, but Justin had been too wrapped up in himself to notice.

He was beyond thankful his dad had picked up the phone when he called. Beyond thankful his dad had gotten in his car and set a new land speed record coming down from Dallas. He'd dropped everything to come to a hospital in the middle of the night and hold Justin as he bawled.

His dad had taken Wes in immediately. And what he'd said to Wes—that whoever Justin loved, he loved, too? Justin had nearly started crying again.

He wanted to know what had happened when his dad disappeared and then showed back up with all of Wes's teammates in tow. There was a story there. But for now, this was good. This was more than good.

His dad spread his hands on the laminate tabletop. His fingers were splayed, as if he could reach all four corners with just a little more effort. "Look, there's no good way to say this, so I'm just going to come out with it. Justin, your mom and I are getting a divorce."

Justin froze, his paper coffee cup jerking in his hands. "What?"

"I'm sorry to drop this on you now, with Wes in the hospital and finals coming up. It's terrible timing, but there's never good timing with something like this. I especially hate that it's happened when you and Wes are starting your lives together. I want you guys to focus on how happy you both are. Keep that love alive, and you'll be together forever."

"What happened? I thought you guys were happy together. Over the summer, you both looked…"

His dad sighed. "Life happens. Sometimes you can love someone for years, and then something happens, and you realize you love someone else more."

The coffee he'd swallowed soured. Had his dad met someone else? On a business trip, or in Dallas? He flicked the plastic lid of his coffee cup. Tried to push back the sudden anger.

"I thought we were happy over the summer, too. But…" His dad squeezed his eyes closed. "Justin, I don't know how much of this you want to hear."

"Tell me, Dad," he snapped. "Just spit it out. Please."

"It's her church. I can't put up with it anymore. At first, it was just a social group for her. She'd go out to lunches and to Bible studies. I never agreed with their teachings, but I thought she was just making friends. But…" He breathed in. Held it. "After you came back from Paris, and it was obvious you'd met someone you were over the moon for, she… I don't know, she couldn't handle that." He sighed. "I loved seeing you happy. I loved seeing you in love. I wanted to know everything about what was going on with you. Cynthia… didn't. And then, after—after you and Wes broke up, it was like she thought that confirmed all of her worst thoughts. That you could never be happy being who you are." His face fell. He stared at the table.

"You were never really open around us before. You always kept that part of yourself closed off, and I'm not sure now if that's because you knew, maybe subconsciously, how she'd react, or… I don't know. I don't know why you were distant when you were younger, or why you decided to be more open after you came back from Paris. I loved seeing you open up."

He had no idea what to say. No idea what to think. He couldn't even begin to form a thought.

"Cynthia started coming home with all sorts of hateful, horrible ideas. That you were broken and needed to be fixed. That you needed to go somewhere so the church could fix you. I told her she was way out of line, that I wouldn't put up with that crap. I wouldn't hear it in the house, and I wouldn't let her talk about you like that. That the only person who was wrong was her, and her damn pastor."

Justin's eyes rose, but now his dad wouldn't look at him. It was his turn to play with his coffee cup, avoiding Justin's gaze.

"And I can't—I won't—put up with that. I can't listen to anyone saying my son is—" He didn't finish his sentence. "I told Cynthia I wasn't going to stick around if she believed any of that trash. I won't put up with anyone thinking that of you. Not even her." He blew out a long breath. "So, what happened? Sometimes you can love someone for years, and then something happens, and you realize you love someone else more. I love my son—you —more than I love the woman she's become."

"Dad…" Justin reached across the table and grabbed his father's hand, prying it from the cardboard coffee sleeve he was peeling apart piece by piece.

His dad clung to him, squeezing his hand so hard the table rattled.

"I'm sorry to dump this on you. I'm sorry this happened. I'm sorry she's lost, and that she got brainwashed by those people. I don't know if you'll hear from her, to be honest. And if you do, it might not be the greatest conversation. I wanted you to hear this from me, and sooner rather than later. Cynthia and I agreed to call it quits, and I'm in the middle of packing up. I'm looking for places to live now, and—" Finally, he met Justin's gaze again. "With my job, I travel so much that I can be based anywhere. I was thinking about moving down here to be closer to you, and to Wes, now that I've met him. But only if you want me to. If you don't, I understand."

Justin's mind spun, and he squeezed his coffee cup like it was an anchor to the world. "I'd love it if you lived here," he whispered.

"He's good to you? Really?" His dad peered at him. "I know what you said, and I know what you've told me. It sounds like you guys were made for each other. But I also know what happened over the summer. I can't forget how brokenhearted you were."

"That was both of our fault. Yes, Wes broke up with me, but… I had a lot of pride, and I didn't reach out to him to ask why. Maybe if we'd talked about it, we could have figured out a few things sooner than we did."

"As long as you're happy, I'm happy. If he ever makes you unhappy…" His dad trailed off, letting the promise linger between them.

"He never will. We were made to be together. He's the love of my life."

"You guys have a real love. Something that goes deep. I can see it, and I've only been here a day."

"Thank you, Dad. For… standing up for me. Loving me."

"Never thank me for that. You're my son. I will always love you."

CHAPTER THIRTY-ONE

MONDAY MORNING, at the crack of seven, Colton showed up, waking Wes and Justin. They were sleeping together in Wes's bed, and if Colton was shocked or horrified by that, he didn't show it. He'd brought coffee and bagels and Muscle Milk, and he fed the two of them as he took up a position in the chair next to Wes's bed.

"Don't you have classes?" Wes asked. "It's finals next week. Don't you have stuff to do?" Wes's eyes were ringed in black and blue, like he was wearing a cartoon robber's mask. The bruises on his cheeks and his jawline were fading to a poison-orchid violet and bile green, save for the still-black belt loop around his throat. Justin's heart broke a little every time he looked at him, anguish for the pain Wes had suffered and bone-melting gratitude that he was still here, that he was going to be all right.

"Dude, I'm an ergonomics major." Colton snorted. "And the rest of my classes are with Coach. So no, I've got nothing going on."

"What's your final for ergonomics this semester?"

"Making a better mouse pad." Colton winked. "I've got the best idea: a waterbed for your wrist."

"I think they figured out wrist support a few decades ago," Wes said.

"But have you ever seen a waterbed on a mouse pad? Or one for your arm?"

"You're duct-taping a hot water bottle to a mouse pad, aren't you?"

"It works great. I'm telling you. After a game, when you're tired as hell, but you gotta get that Call of Duty in."

It was strange to all of a sudden be fine with being out in front of Colton. Justin was used to hiding his and Wes's relationship, to sliding away, to sneaking around. He wasn't used to Wes's hand gliding up and down his back as he lay against Wes's side and the two ball players went back and forth, laughing like they hadn't broken each other's hearts three days ago. Poking fun at Colton's major turned into talking about the team and then the conference standings going into their bye week.

Nothing was the same, but everything that mattered to him was the same. Him and Wes. Their love. Their foundation.

Wes and Colton were rebuilding their foundation, too. Justin could still sense the strain, feel the tendrils of hurt curling off them both. See the way their eyes lingered when they thought the other wasn't looking. But every hour strengthened them. Every shared memory, every quiet laugh. Colton was as much a part of Wes as Justin was. Wes couldn't excise his best friend and the game they shared, just like he couldn't excise Justin from his life after Paris. Wherever their future lay, Colton would be a part of it. Maybe football would be a part of that future, too.

Justin was okay with that. More than okay, in fact. If Wes was happy, if Wes could have everything he dreamed, all the different people and moments that made him smile, that was a good life. The best life.

After lunch, the nurse told Wes he needed to get up and move, to get out of bed and walk up and down the hallway at least once. Colton reacted like he was born for that very moment. He cracked his knuckles and grinned. "Are you ready to recover, bro? Cause I am so ready to work you."

Colton and Wes limped up and down the hospital's long hallways for an hour. Wes started off leaning most of his weight on Colton, but by the end of the first lap, he was standing on his own two feet, and he stayed that way for a full up-down of the hallway before he faltered and had to lean against Colton again.

Justin watched from Wes's door, cheering every success.

When Colton brought Wes back, he was sweaty and shaking, and he needed both of their help to get back in bed, but he was smiling as wide as he could. Happiness shone through the bruises and the scabs. His ribs were sore, he said, and he was wiped out from the exertion, but he was happy. He passed out for four hours, leaving Justin and Colton alone with each other.

For the first time, they spoke one-on-one. Colton asked about the two of them. How they met, and where. What had happened over the summer and why they split up. Why Wes looked like someone had taken an ice cream scoop to his heart. Why they came back together, and how.

And what did Justin want from Wes? What did he imagine for their future together?

Justin asked questions in return, about Colton and Wes and how they became best friends. What Wes was like his freshman year. What it was like to play football, to be on the field in the middle of the play, a hundred things happening in a split second. Needing to make a snap decision that could make or break the game.

Colton said it was easy when he and Wes were together. Together, they could do anything, and they were going to prove it. They were going to show the world what they and the rest of the team could really do.

Eventually, the heart-to-heart descended into playing cards, and they ran through three rounds of poker before Justin pulled out his laptop and they turned on Netflix. When Wes opened his eyes, Colton and Justin were slumped side by side on the couch with Justin's laptop balanced between their knees, giggling along with the stand-up comedian they were watching.

Colton took Wes for another hallway walk after dinner, urging Wes to keep going, keep pushing. The nurse finally threw him out just before ten p.m., but he was back the next morning, bagels, coffee, and Muscle Milk in hand. He got Wes out of bed and walking before lunch, and then again in the afternoon, pushing him to do another half lap of the hall. And then another. Just to the next doorway. Just one more step. Now give me another. He pushed Wes until Wes was trembling. But he was moving better every time.

They spent their days in a jumble of hospital walks, Wes's naps, and Netflix. By day three, Wes was walking on his own up and down the hallways. Up and down the stairways, even, Colton following him and cheering him on.

By day four, he was jogging. Colton ran backward in front of him, facing Wes and urging him to keep going. Another ten feet. Another step. Another doorway. Keep going. Just a little bit more. Don't quit. Push. Keep pushing.

Dr. Williams discharged Wes two days later when he stepped out of the elevator and found Colton and Wes in starting-line positions at the end of the hall, counting down to one. They took off, both men sprinting for the nurses' station as patients cheered them on. Two nurses had a banner of paper towels stretched across the hall, like a ticker tape finish line for them to barrel through.

Wes was still more bruises than unblemished skin, but his bloodwork was good and his kidneys and spleen were no longer swollen. He said his ribs were sore, but that wasn't unusual during the season. Hell, he said, Jason Witten played with a lacerated spleen, and Ronnie Lott lost his finger on the field. Jack Youngblood played with a broken fibula throughout the entire post season. And Drew Brees threw a touchdown pass with eleven cracked ribs and a partially collapsed lung.

Justin knew Wes. A little physical discomfort wouldn't make him quit. Not when he was all smiles, holding Justin's hand as Colton yapped about Orlando's latest antics in the house or told Wes about another of Art's failures as he tried to teach himself how to repair drywall.

"I know how to do that," Wes said. "I can help him."

"Dude, he'd be so thankful. He's at the 'Fuck it, just cover the holes with duct tape' point."

"How'd he get holes in his walls?"

Colton flushed and looked away. "Uhh, he got a little mad."

"At me?"

"Dude, no. When we found out you were here. That's when we all got really mad."

Wes signed his discharge papers as Colton grabbed his duffel, and the four of them—Wes, Colton, Justin, and Justin's dad—headed down to the parking lot.

"So," Colton asked, after they loaded Wes carefully into Justin's dad's Porsche. He fiddled with his own car keys, shifted from left foot to right. "Where are you headed?"

"Home." Wes smiled. "See you there?"

CHAPTER THIRTY-TWO

THE WHOLE STARTING LINE, offense and defense, was packed into the jock house. Guys were crowded on the couches and perched on the recliner arms. More guys had dragged chairs in from the kitchen and the front and back porches, or hauled desk chairs out of bedrooms. Everyone sat together in the living room, in as close to a circle as they could get. At the top were Wes and Justin, holding hands. Opposite them was Colton.

Wes closed his eyes as everyone settled in around them. His heart pounded. His palms were clammy, cold sweat soaking the skin between his fingers. Justin's hand slid against his own, but he didn't let go. Wes wrapped both of his hands around Justin's and lifted his fingers to his lips. He kissed Justin's knuckles as his friends, his teammates, quieted.

"All right, we all know why we're here," Colton said. He had a football in his hands again, was twirling it like it was a fidget spinner he couldn't set down. "We've all got thoughts and opinions on what happened. Most of us were fucking wrong about what we thought. We don't know what the fuck happened, and we can't keep acting like we do. So, here we are. We're going to listen to Wes." He nodded across the circle.

Wes breathed in. Justin squeezed his hand.

"I was never going to come out," he started. His voice was thick, but it didn't break. "Not in college. Maybe after, if I met someone. But I wasn't going to come out while I was here. You guys know where I'm from. Being gay out there…" He shook his head. "I knew a few things by the time I was in high school: I wanted to get out of West Texas. I wanted a different life. And the only way out was to go to college. But to go to college, I needed a scholarship. I've been running a football since I was knee-high on my dad. I'm not the smartest guy in the world, and my grades weren't good enough for an academic scholarship. But I knew I had a chance at a football scholarship if I gave it my all…"

His breath shook as he exhaled. He rubbed one sweat-slick palm down his Wranglers. "I've got nothing without my scholarship. I don't have enough money to pay for college on my own. If I lose that, I'm out. I'll be back home in West Texas, and I'll never get out again. This scholarship is my one chance for a different life." He turned to Justin. "A life I really, really want."

His teammates shifted. He heard chairs creak. Cushions sigh. Throats clear.

"So I worked hard, from day one. From that first day of freshman training camp, when I met most of you guys." He grinned. Saw grins reflect back at him from some of his teammates. "To hold on to that scholarship, I had to give this everything I had. And because of that, I told myself I'd bury that part of me. I never dated in high school, because I was too focused on getting that scholarship. I wasn't going to date here, either. I was going to stay focused on football. Finish my degree. What was four years, I thought. I stuck to my plan. Until…"

Again, he looked at Justin. Justin smiled softly. *He was made to love the white swan.* "I fell in love," Wes said. "I didn't expect to, but I did. And it couldn't have happened at a worse time."

Silence. No one moved. He didn't even hear his teammates breathe.

"Coach sat me down over the summer, when I got back from study abroad, and told me about my rank in the league. That I was suddenly a pretty big deal." His gaze fell, and he stared at the floor. "He also told me that I was responsible for the team this year. That I could elevate the team, and if I did, all of us could see our dreams come true. If I played my heart and soul out and made sure we had a good season, everyone would get what they wanted. NFL scouts would be at all the games. We'd all be in the draft. If I stepped up. 'You can bring them all to glory,' he said."

"Damn," Art said, in the silence that followed. "He put that on you?"

"He wanted you all to have what you wanted. Have your dreams come true. And I do, too. I want it for every one of you. You all deserve to play in the NFL. You're all eligible after this year, and if we put up those numbers... I decided I was going to do exactly what he said. I was going to have the best season of my life for you. I was going to bring you guys to where your dreams came true. And I knew, if we were going to have that kind of season, there couldn't be any distractions. No surprises. Nothing that disrupted our rhythm on the field or in the locker room, or got between us. It wasn't the time to come out. Not with everything on the line."

"You hid," Josh said. He glowered, but Wes couldn't tell if he was scowling at Wes or at the world. Patrick, next to him, folded his arms across his chest and glared at the floor.

"Yeah. I was trying to give you guys the world, and I didn't want my life to get in the way of that."

Silence. Colton stared at Wes across the circle, his face so full of heartbreak it hurt to hold his gaze. Wes looked away. His gaze went blurry as he stared at the line of their coffeemakers, the giant tubs of protein powder he and the guys shared crowding the kitchen counter next to twelve boxes of cereal and five boxes of Pop-Tarts.

God, he loved these guys. And he'd been so afraid of them

finding out about him that he'd pulled back and pulled back, until the distance between them was the size of the Grand Canyon. No wonder they thought the worst of him. They didn't know him anymore. He'd been isolating himself for months.

There was so much pain in that room. Battered, bruised trust, and the wreckage of his secrets.

He wanted to play foosball and beer pong with them again. He wanted to stay up all night on a Madden tournament, heckling Colton and trying to make him lose, even though Colton never lost. Grill in the backyard with the guys and throw the ball around in the street. Bitch in the locker room about Cesar's snoring or Colton's stank feet. And then walk out on that field together, like they were meant to. He wanted to feel them come together in that perfect way, feel them become extensions of each other, like Colton and he were making the play happen in the heartbeat they shared. Or he and Orlando were setting up the rush, and he was blocking as Orlando was on the move, and they flowed together like they could read each other's mind, but no, they were just that in sync, that well tuned to each other.

He *missed* that so much. He missed his friends, his teammates. His brothers. Tears spilled over his eyelashes as his chest shuddered. Justin's hand gripped his, and he wrapped his other hand around Justin's and held on tight. He'd get through this, and afterward, Justin would be there. He'd known, from the very beginning, how it would end. He fell in love, and like all epic love stories, there was a price to pay. He was made to love the white swan, after all.

"Damn, bro," Orlando finally said. "Damn."

"Coach shouldn't have put that on you," Patrick grunted. "That's fucked up."

"We had a good season, though." Wes tried to smile through the pain. "Until I screwed it all up. But you guys definitely got seen by the scouts. ESPN has highlight reels of you that make some of the NFL players jealous. You guys got great time in front of the league. You'll all find your next home in the NFL. I know you will."

"Man, the season isn't done yet." Art frowned, looking at Wes like he'd said that the Aggies were the best sports program in Texas. He shook his head at Wes. "What, are you quitting *now*? We've got another game to play."

Wes looked at Colton and then back to Art. "I don't want to hurt you guys any more. I don't want to hurt the team."

"You don't," Josh blurted out. "You belong on the field with us. We're a team, like you said."

Cheers and *Hell yeah*s echoed around the crowded room.

"We started this season together. We end this season together," Quinton said. "I don't even want the NFL looking at me if they're not looking at you, too. It's all of us, man. It's not just one of us, or a few of us. It's all of us."

More clapping. More *Hell yeah*s. A few *Fuck yes*es.

Colton rose. He gripped the football between his hands and crossed the circle, then stopped in front of Wes.

Wes stood.

"Come back. We all want you with us. We all miss you." His jaw clenched hard, the muscles around his neck bulging. "*I* miss you. It's not the same."

Murmurs of agreement, and his teammates nodding in the background, falling in and out of blurry focus behind Colton. His teammates smiling at him. Waiting for him.

What world was this, where everything shattered and then they put it back together? Was this only a figment of his imagination? Was he still in a coma, dreaming of everything he wanted but couldn't have? He tried to inhale, but his muscles were clenching and his ribs were aching and all he managed was a ragged, broken gasp. He stared at Colton.

"I'm sorry," Colton said. "I'm sorry for everything that happened. What Coach put on you, and what the world put on you. The fans, and their fucked-up shit. I want to kill those guys who jumped you, man." His teeth clenched, and his hand squeezed down on the football until it deformed. "And I'm sorry I reacted like I did. You were trying to talk to me in the locker room, and I didn't listen to you. I had no idea all that other stuff was driving you." He held out the football. "Can we make this right again?"

Wes grabbed the football with one hand and Colton with the other. He dragged his best friend into a bear hug, clinging to him like he was a life ring and Wes was lost at sea, like he'd been treading water for days and days and days. It felt like he had been. The agony of not knowing where he was going, wondering what would happen. He'd been so terrified of the collapse that he hadn't thought of the after, and he had no idea how to find his way through the wreckage.

Wes felt Justin's hand on the back of his thigh, grounding, supportive. He buried his face in Colton's shoulder as the rest of his teammates joined them. He felt hands on his own shoulder, on his back. Hands covering his where he clung to Colton's shirt, fingers clenched hard in cotton and muscle. Colton clung to him, too, whispering promises into his ear. Promises to be there for Wes. To be there for Justin. To never, ever leave him alone again. That he'd never let another piece of shit lay their hands on Wes. That they'd never lose a game again, not when they were together, like the brothers they were.

Eventually, he came out of Colton's hold. With Justin at his side, Colton in front of him, and his team all around, for the first time in his life, all the parts and pieces of the man Wes was came together. He took a deep breath and felt whole. One man. The man he was meant to become.

The man he'd always wanted to be.

"Yeah, okay," he said, nodding. His voice was breaking again, but this time not from pain. "Let's go get that national championship title. Together."

THE BALL ARCED, soaring, soaring. Wes's lungs burned as he sprinted. *One, two.* He held out his arms—

Thunk. Colton's pass slammed into the center of his pads, right between his numbers and into the basket of his arms. He caged the ball, juked, evading an imaginary defender, and jogged out of the route.

"Great job!" Colton shouted. "That was faster." Murmurs and claps rose from the right, where some of the team had come out to watch him and Colton drill. Practice didn't start for another half hour, and most of the team was still in the locker room getting ready. But his roommates and the rest of the starters were all there.

"Want me to give you a real defender?" Anton jogged out to Wes and Colton, passing Wes a water bottle. "I can put some pressure on you if you want to check your footwork."

Colton arched his eyebrows at Wes.

He was the one coming back from the hospital. He was the one who had to decide when to break and when to push. He was drenched in sweat, and his muscles were burning, screaming after being unused the past week. He was breathing hard, and his sides ached with every inhale. But he was out in the sunshine, and the air was crisp, a hint of bite in the early December afternoon. There wasn't a cloud in the sky, and when he looked up, all he saw was the football, Colton's pass coming his way. When he ran, the pain was a reminder he was alive, that he was back on the field. The weight of his pads across his shoulders was welcome, as were the smell of the grass and the crunch of his cleats in the dirt.

Wes nodded. "Let's do it."

Anton took up position opposite Wes on the thirty-yard line, their pretend line of scrimmage, setting up as the middle linebacker. Colton called the snap, pulling the ball back from between the imaginary legs of his imaginary center, and then dropped into his pocket. Wes took off, sprinting down his route. *Inhale. Exhale. One, two, three. Pivot.*

Colton looked left, right, and then their eyes met. He fired off his pass, a missile coming right for Wes.

Wes lifted his hands. The ball slammed into the center of his palms. He brought it down, tucked it against his side. Turned.

Anton was there, putting pressure on his movement. Wes juked and spun to the right, and left Anton behind when Anton committed to the left block. He jogged out of the play to the claps and cheers of his teammates.

"Nice." Anton clasped his hand in a high five, then pulled him in for a quick chest bump. "Nice job, man."

"Want to try a deeper route?" Colton asked as he met Wes back at the thirty-yard line. "How you feeling? Need a break?"

"No, I'm good. Let's push it. Yes, deeper routes."

Colton's gaze flicked past him. Wes saw his shoulders rise and tense. Saw his jaw go stiff, his muscles clench. Wes turned.

There was Coach, crossing the field and heading for them. His face was blank, his eyes hidden behind dark sunglasses. His lips were pressed in a thin line. Wes's teammates slowly stepped forward, surrounding Wes and Colton.

Coach walked right up into their faces. He peered at Colton first, then turned to Wes. He peeled off his sunglasses and eyed the fading bruises on Wes's face and neck. They were deep in the bile and putrid lime stage, and he looked like a child's bad face-painting project. His neck was still purple, that wide belt band vivid. It looked worse than it felt, though. Wes held his ground as Coach looked him over.

He slid his sunglasses back on. "Well," he said. "You two finally decided to show up for practice, huh?"

"Yes, Coach," Wes said.

"Good. Seems to me like you've got a few people to prove wrong. Some people need their own shit shoveled right back at them. And there's no better way to do that than to win."

Wes's heart squeezed. "Coach, the NCAA. Am I still eligible?"

"That horseshit." Coach waved his hand like he was swatting a fly. "I talked those weenies off their little panicked cliff edge. They dropped the investigation. There wasn't anything there to begin with."

Colton sagged into Wes, a relieved laugh bursting from him as he buried his forehead against Wes's pad-covered shoulder.

"Are you playing, Van de Hoek? You still on this team?"

Maybe this was all the apology he'd get from Coach. A welcome home, with open arms. No questions. "Yes, Coach. We want that title."

"Then you guys will earn it. Together." Coach took a few steps back. The rest of the team was jogging out of the tunnel to the field. He checked his watch, then put his hands to his mouth and started hollering. "All right, let's move! Let's move! Hurry it up, gentlemen! You've got a goddamn national championship to win! Let's get to work!"

CHAPTER THIRTY-THREE

"WHAT DO you think about this one, Dad?"

Nick poked his head into the second spare bedroom, then crossed to the sliding glass doors that led to the balcony that ran the width of the entire apartment. The unit was in an ultramodern high-rise downtown. From the balcony, he could see Sixth Street and the bars and music halls, and the river and the greenbelt beyond. At night, the city would spread out like glitter, surrounded by a river of midnight as the landscape turned to country and rolling hills.

"I like it."

They'd looked at apartments all morning, from suburban complexes near the train line to units just outside downtown. This was the only one that actually was downtown. It was totally different from anything else they'd seen, and different in every way from the house that Nick had shared with Cynthia, the house Justin had grown up in. No granite counters or shiny wood floors. Here the floors and walls were expanses of polished concrete, and stainless steel counters and cupboards lined the kitchen.

The rental agent gave him the pricing details again, then stood back and let him poke into closets and open and close drawers in the bathrooms and kitchens. Could he live here? It would feel empty when he was alone, but maybe Justin and Wes would come over for a break from their dorms. He was looking for a three-bedroom apartment specifically so they'd have a place to stay, if they wanted to. And when they weren't over, he could sit on the balcony and enjoy the view. Or he could go out himself. Walk to the bars or the live music lounges. Maybe, one day, he'd even meet someone.

That thought was too new, too raw, to hold on to. He let it go, focusing instead on Justin and Wes coming to visit. He could grill on the balcony. Maybe they'd watch football on Sundays. Justin and he could finally enjoy a game together. He'd wanted to have that father-son moment with Justin since Justin was old enough to toddle around after him.

What did Justin envision? What did he want from Nick, now that they were actually building a real relationship?

There was so much he didn't know about his son that he desperately wanted to. What did Justin do for fun? What filled up his days and his weekends? Why had he picked nursing as his major? What did he imagine his life would look like?

This was the closest apartment to campus—a ten-minute walk. It was the most expensive he'd looked at, but what did that matter if it meant Justin and Wes could stop by, pop in, hang out? If he could see Justin more, it didn't matter what the place cost. He'd empty his bank account in a heartbeat.

"I'll take it." He smiled at the rental agent, a young brunette with a gorgeous smile and a body he'd have had a hard time dragging his eyes away from when he was younger. "When can I move in?"

"You can move in today, if you'd like." She smiled. "Let's get you the keys to your new home, Mr. Swanscott."

After he signed the lease agreement, Nick took Justin to lunch. Before Nick could bring up how close he was to campus, Justin did himself. "I could walk to see you. You know, if you wanted me to."

"Come over anytime." He smiled as he poured ketchup on the plate for his fries. "In fact, why don't you and Wes set up the third bedroom as your own? I got it so that you guys could come over whenever you wanted."

Justin grinned. "Can I help you decorate the rest of the place, too?"

"You like interior design?"

"Dad, I'm gay." Justin gave him a look before he bit into his club sandwich. "It's in my DNA."

He laughed. "Well, I'm not bringing any furniture down. I was going to start over with everything brand new. I was just going to swing through Ikea, but—"

"Please. No. We can do better than that."

Another laugh. "All right, let's do it. You can teach me a few things. Or you can try. I might be too old."

"Hardly." Justin rolled his eyes playfully. "You're never too old for good taste. First step, redo your apartment. Second step, redo your wardrobe." He arched an eyebrow. It was, Nick noticed, perfectly sculpted.

"I'm game. I'm up for new things. And I want to spend more time with you and get to know the things you like. Fashion? Interior design? What else?" He munched a handful of fries as Justin's eyes widened.

"Uhh... Just stuff, you know."

"I don't. I don't think I know you that well. I want to fix that. Tell me: what do you like? What do you do for fun?"

Justin set his sandwich down and wiped his fingers. He took his time answering, sipping his beer and then straightening the bottle on the table. "I dance, still," he finally said. His voice was soft. "I was doing modern dance, but... Wes took me to the ballet in Paris. He told me I should try it myself. I signed up for a ballet class this semester."

"You've been dancing since high school?"

"Yeah. I never stopped after drill team."

"I never knew that."

"I know," Justin said softly. "That wasn't an accident."

Nick stared down at the ketchup slowly separating on his plate. Why hadn't Justin wanted him to know? His son was, in some ways, a stranger to him. That thought hurt, like someone had reached into him and seized hold, closed a fist around his heart and wrung it out like a sponge. He cleared his throat and forced a smile. "Tell me about this ballet class. What do you learn?"

"Well, ballet," Justin said slowly. "The positions. Ballet is a series of positions and movements, and you have to learn how to execute each of them crisply before you can put it all together. I was more advanced than the other students because of the other dance I've done, but it was still a different focus. It's just an intro class, but my instructor said I should try out for a local dance company. And Wes thought I was pretty good when we had the little class showcase, but his opinion doesn't count." Justin tried to laugh. It fell flat.

"Of course his opinion counts."

"He loves me. He's always going to like what I do." As soon as the words were out, Justin cringed. He looked away.

Nick reached across the table and laid his hand on top of his son's. "Yes, the people who love you are going to support you. And they will always think you're special. But that doesn't mean that you're not."

Justin's jaw clenched.

"Are you going to try out for the dance company?"

"It's not a big deal. At best, I'd be a backup dancer—"

"It *is* a big deal. It's a big deal because you enjoy it. If you want to do it, then go for it. Backup dancers become lead dancers all the time."

"Dad…"

"I'm sorry I missed your class performance. What did you do?"

"I danced Odette's intro from *Swan Lake*." Justin's gaze fell to his lap.

"Did anyone record it?"

"I don't know. Maybe. I can ask the instructor if she did."

"Please check? I'd like to see it." He squeezed Justin's hand and sat back. "And I'd like to come to your next performance, if you want me to be there."

His son was quiet. Then, "What is all this? Why are you doing this?"

"Because I love you, Justin. I don't just love the new football fan part of you, or the part that's dating Wes, or the part where we don't talk about anything you like. I love all of you, and I want to know all of you. You've held back a lot from me, and I'm not sure why or how that started, or how we got to where we are. I know I should have been more tuned in, and I'm going to be, from here on. If you're afraid I'm going to pull back and think something you like is too much, or too gay..." He shook his head. "That will never happen."

Justin's eyes were watery when he looked up, and he blinked fast, wiped his fingers beneath his lashes, stared at the restaurant's ceiling. "You remind me of Wes sometimes," he said, sniffing. "Or maybe Wes reminds me of you? I don't know. Maybe there's something to that whole daddy issues thing. One thing I love so damn much about Wes is how kind he is, how supportive he is. He's all in when he loves someone, and I'd never felt that before. I didn't think anyone loved me unconditionally until he did. But now you're here, and you are saying all these things, and..." He cupped his hands over his face and set his elbows on the table. His shoulders shook.

"Of course I love you unconditionally. I'm sorry you didn't know that. I'm sorry I wasn't a better father to you. I'm sorry you didn't know I supported everything you wanted. I mean, I wasn't too thrilled about the underage drinking, and some of your friends in high school were a little wild. But all I've wanted for you, since the day you were born, was for you to be happy. You have to know: there's nothing about you I don't like or that I want to change."

"Then why didn't you and Mom support me when I joined the drill team? You had the baseball team yard signs and bumper stickers up for years after I quit. That didn't really fill me up with confidence and acceptance."

Nick's eyes slid closed. "Your mother didn't want to take them down. I thought... I thought I was helping her. I thought..." He shook his head. "I thought if she had time, she'd accept you. You didn't exactly come out the easiest way possible."

"I'm sorry about how I did that," Justin mumbled. "I just had to stop the expectations. The pressure. I swear she was already planning my wedding and had picked out names for my kids."

"We always wanted to have more kids, and we couldn't. Maybe she turned all that hope and expectation onto you. I don't know, because she and I never talked about it, and maybe we should have. I should have seen how what she was doing was affecting you. There's a lot of things I did wrong."

Justin was quiet for a long time. Then, he said, "You could still have more kids, Dad. You're young."

He snorted. "I'm not young."

"You're not old."

"I have a perfect son, Justin. I got everything right my first try." He winked, trying to lighten the moment. "Why mess with success?"

Justin laughed. He grabbed his napkin and dried his eyes. "I'm not perfect. I was kind of a bitch when I was a teenager. I'm sorry about all of... that. Being with Wes, and going through this season, taught me a lot about patience. And priorities. You know, I told myself once I'd never date a man in the closet?"

Nick snorted.

"Obviously, that didn't stick." Justin grinned. "Though I have to say, I'm glad we don't have to hide anymore."

"Wes is good for you in a lot of ways. I can see it, and more than that, I can feel it. You feel more grounded. More certain of yourself."

Justin nodded. "A lot of that is from loving him, and from him loving me. But part of that also comes from having a better relationship with you."

He beamed. "I'm glad we're here right now, reconnecting. I'm glad I'm going to be able to spend more time with you now."

"Even though—"

"Yes." He cut off Justin's question before the anxiety could take over his gaze. "This is the right choice. It's hard to dissolve a marriage, but… the only other time I was this certain in my life was when I held my newborn son and knew I loved him more than life itself." He nudged Justin's foot under the table. "Okay, we need to change the subject. We're going to Wes's practice after this, and if you look like you've been crying, Wes is going to be mad at me. Tell me about the ballet Wes took you to. Which, let me say, that's about the most romantic thing anyone could do. The ballet in Paris? Jeez, Wes, go ahead and make the rest of us men look bad, will ya?"

Justin tipped his head back and laughed, and Nick's heart soared.

He was making the right choice.

CHAPTER THIRTY-FOUR

"WATER BREAK! TAKE TEN!" Coach blew the whistle and called the rest of his coaches together as the team took a knee. The linemen all rolled to their backs, spread-eagle on the grass, to catch their breath. Colton tried to squirt water into Art's and Patrick's mouths, but most ended up splashing on their faces. Josh grabbed Colton's ankle and told him he'd put him in the dirt if he tried it on him. Colton laughed and then crossed the field to Wes.

Wes flipped through the team's playbook, reviewing notes the coaches had scribbled during each run-through. "Hey," he said when Colton jogged over. He took the water bottle Colton handed him. "Look at this. I think we need to tighten up the line on these plays. There's an opening for the defense to chip their way through."

"Huh. I didn't see that before." Colton peered over Wes's shoulder.

"I could feel it on the line. I think we need to work on a few of these plays some more."

"Yeah, I also want to do some more pass routes with all the receivers. I think we can tighten up timing there, too."

"Definitely, but we've got to get the line solid or you won't have the time you need in the pocket to get the ball thrown to anyone."

"Makes sense." Colton grinned. "Good eyes, Captain. Oh, hey, look who's here." He waved to the stands.

Wes turned as Colton launched his football into the bleachers, right at Justin and Nick as they came down the steps to the fifty-yard line. Wes saw Justin's eyes go wide right before Nick stepped in front of him and plucked Colton's pass out of the air with both hands.

"All right!" Colton threw his arms up. "Not bad for an old man!" He held his hands out for Nick to throw the ball back.

"Nick isn't old. And Orlando said he almost kicked your ass."

"What?" Colton stumbled, glancing between Nick and Wes as Nick launched the ball back at him. He had to run to make the catch. "Dude, he didn't kick my ass." Colton spun the ball in his hands. He nodded to Nick, who waved and sat beside Justin, stretching out his long legs and leaning back. "I mean, he was kinda intense. He busted into a football house and was trying to throw down. That takes some fucking balls. I thought Patrick was going to dribble him into the street."

"He's a good guy. I like him."

"I fucking hope so." Colton snorted. "Considering you're probably gonna marry his son."

Wes grinned. "Think Justin will say yes when I ask?"

"Does a bear shit in the woods?"

Wes laughed, and he jogged to the bleachers to meet Justin, who was coming down to the railing overlooking the sideline. "Hey."

"Hey yourself." Justin ran his fingers through Wes's sweaty hair. "How's practice?"

"Great. We've got a good rhythm. We're finding our timing together again. It feels good to be with everyone out here."

"You look good. How are you feeling?"

"Tired. A little sore. But it's a good sore."

"Good sore, huh? Sounds like me after you make love to me." Justin winked, and Wes felt himself flush. "I'll have to give you a massage after practice, cowboy."

"You going to come home with us?"

"I was planning on it." Justin's breath hitched. "If that's still okay?"

"More than okay." Wes grabbed the railing and pulled himself up, then leaned forward and laid a kiss on Justin's lips. "I can't wait."

Justin grabbed his face and kissed him again before Wes dropped out of his chin-up. "Go kick ass, cowboy."

Wes backed away, his smile so wide it made his cheeks ache. "I'm going to win the game for you, *mon amour*."

"Promise?" Justin grinned.

"*Oui*. I promise."

AFTER PRACTICE, Justin showed up at the jock house with a duffel and a case of beer. Colton opened the door for him, beamed, took the beer, and then hollered up the stairs, "Wes! Your boyfriend is home!"

Ten heads appeared over the railing. Wes's teammates waved down at Justin. It was weird to see them all without their helmets and their pads.

Wes came thundering down the stairs to take Justin's duffel and lead him back up. The rest of the team was still there, hanging around and pretending to all be doing something on the suddenly-crowded landing. Wes introduced Justin to everyone officially, and he shook their hands as they scoped him out.

"Welcome to the house," Orlando said. "We made Art clean up."

"*Pfft*," the big guy named Art said. Justin knew him as Ramirez, the center. "Nah, man, we made Patrick do his damn laundry. You had shit in there that hadn't been washed since last season, bro."

"Man…" Patrick, one of the linemen, shoved Art. "How are those holes in your wall?"

"Wes is gonna help me fix those. Aren't you, Wes?"

"Yeah, I will." Wes guided Justin into his bedroom. "But not tonight."

That set everyone off, and the house filled with catcalls and wolf whistles, cries of *Ooooo* and *Daaaamn*. Wes shook his head and tried to salvage what he meant, but Justin grabbed him and hauled him into his bedroom. Orlando made a show of putting his earbuds in, and down the hall, someone turned on a stereo and turned up the volume.

Justin laid Wes belly-down on his bed and massaged his back and his shoulders, then his arms and legs, until Wes was boneless and then asleep. Justin laughed as he poked at Wes's shoulder. Totally out, so unconscious he was drooling onto his pillow. So much for the wild sex the other guys were ribbing them about. But Wes was relaxed, so Justin counted that as a victory.

He washed the lotion off his hands in the bathroom down the hall, and as he did, he heard voices from downstairs, guys chatting in the kitchen about finals and the game. He headed down, grabbing a beer from the fridge and taking a seat at the kitchen island—and nobody blinked. Colton asked him about his finals, and he told them about his nursing clinical exams and his advanced pharmacology final coming up. He left out his and Wes's French final.

They had to give a thirty-minute presentation to the class on a topic that was meaningful to them both, and they'd struggled to come up with one. Wes didn't want to do football, because that wasn't something they shared equally. He suggested ballet, but Justin vetoed that for the same reason. In the hospital, they'd finally decided on their topic: how they'd fallen in love, and what it had been like to have to hide all semester. It was an undeniably sentimental presentation, full of "*mon amour*" and "*mon coeur.*" It was probably going to end up on YouTube by the end of the week. Wes said he didn't care, and he'd held Justin's hand as they walked to the stadium together afterward.

Austin and Josh came in and said they were going to start dinner. Justin said he'd help, and he joined in with the linemen as they made spaghetti and meat sauce for twelve football players. Twelve pounds of ground beef, twelve full boxes of pasta. Justin made the chicken Caesar salad and garlic bread for the sides. The salad was over five pounds, and he used five loaves of French bread.

The team grabbed their dinner buffet-style and then spread out in the living room, huddled over the coffee tables or eating from their laps. Patrick and Art ate out of mixing bowls, spaghetti and salad all in one big pile. Justin sat on the floor next to Colton with his modest plate.

"I guess Wes didn't work you up into a big ole appetite?" Orlando teased.

"Y'all were in there for about an hour." Quinton shoveled pasta into his mouth and winked.

"Actually, Wes is the one who passed out," Justin speared a bite of chicken and lettuce. "Guess I worked him out too hard."

The guys lost it. Colton almost sprayed pasta across the room, and Patrick needed a back slap when his beer went down the wrong tube. Orlando gave Justin a fist bump and a nod, and Art said, "Respect, man. Respect."

Everyone descended into giggles when Wes appeared, his hair sticking up in all directions, eyes still sleep-soft and pillow lines crisscrossing his cheek. "Any food left?" he asked, rubbing his belly.

"I put a plate in the fridge for you," Justin said.

Wes headed for the kitchen and reappeared with a plate piled high with pasta. He sat next to Justin and leaned into his shoulder. "Thanks."

Justin held up a piece of his chicken salad for Wes. "*De rien*, cowboy."

"All right, what we watching tonight?" Art grabbed the remote and turned the TV on. "Wes, move your big ole head, you're in the way. You and Justin come sit against the couch."

The team argued for half an hour about what to watch. When they finally decided on a slapstick comedy, Wes laid his head on Justin's shoulder and took his hand, dragging it into his own lap. "*Je t'aime*," Wes whispered into Justin's neck, lips grazing Justin's skin.

He kissed Wes's hand. "I love you, too, cowboy."

HE HAD a final in the morning, and Wes and the team had practice, and it was a mad rush in the house bathrooms. He brushed his teeth in the hall and then spat and rinsed while Orlando showered. Blenders were whirring downstairs, and toasters were popping every minute, firing out Pop-Tarts by the boxful. Wes made him his own fruit smoothie and offered him a Pop-Tart. Justin took the smoothie and let Wes keep the Pop-Tart. They kissed on the porch as the team hurried past. "C'mon! We're gonna be late!" Colton called from the street.

"Go kick ass, cowboy."

Wes kissed him again and then jogged after his teammates.

Justin finished his last final on Wednesday and then went to the stadium to watch practice. Wes and Colton were conferring on the sideline with Coach Young, who was nodding along with whatever they were saying. After a break, the team ran drills again, and both Wes and the offensive coordinator came in to make adjustments. Later, Wes had his own one-on-one with the offensive coordinator and Coach Young, then made his own adjustments as he ran route after route with Colton throwing him the ball.

The team showered and changed, and Wes and Colton came out from the locker room first. They got into Justin's car, and then Justin suggested a stop at the grocery store, where they ended up buying so much food they filled the trunk and every available inch inside. Wes and Colton had to get in the car and have Justin pile groceries on top of them. He couldn't even see out his windows on the drive home.

The three of them cooked burgers for everyone, making smash patties on electric griddles in the kitchen. Each of the guys ate three, some of them four, and Justin understood why they bought bread by the truckload. Justin, Wes, and Colton ate together at the kitchen island, drinking beer and demolishing a bag of chips as Wes and Colton reviewed tape from practice on their phones. Justin sat on Wes's lap so he could watch, and Wes pointed out what they were looking for on each video so he could follow along.

Later, Wes and Colton ended up in Colton's bedroom playing Madden, and Justin cheered Wes on. For the first time in the history of ever, Wes beat Colton, and he whooped and hollered and jumped up and down. Colton wallowed in his defeat, and Justin pulled Wes in for a kiss as the rest of the team showed up at Colton's door to see what the hell was going on.

They made love late at night, when everyone drifted off to bed. Wes lit a candle he'd bought and set it on his desk, and he stripped Justin slowly before laying him on his bed. He took his time, worshipping Justin's body with his lips and his tongue, kissing the swell of his thigh and the inside of his knee, the curve of his calf and the bottom of his foot. He worked his way back up Justin's legs and took his cock into his mouth. He blew Justin, sucking every inch as deep as he could, all the way down his throat. Justin smothered his moans in Wes's pillow, and he had to fight back his shout when Wes moved down to rim him and finger him open.

Wes shuddered when he pushed inside, and he kissed Justin's

leg, resting atop Wes's shoulder, and then rocked his hips. His cock slid deeper, all the way inside Justin, where only Wes could reach. Justin curled his toes and gripped Wes's arms.

The candlelight flickered across Wes's body, the golden glow dipping in and out of the curves of his muscles and the planes of his stomach. Justin's hands roamed over his skin, over the scars left behind after the scabs had fallen off. He loved this man so much. Loved all the ways Wes came together, all the parts and pieces that made Wes himself. Loved how much he loved Justin, and loved football, and loved his friends. Loved his dedication, the way he gave every bit of himself to who and what he loved. It still left Justin breathless sometimes, how the love of his life had simply waltzed into his life in the middle of Paris. He'd gone around the world to find adventure, and he'd found a football-playing cowboy who stole his heart and ran away with it.

Well, Wes could keep it. He could keep it for the rest of his life.

Wes pulled out and guided Justin on top of him. Justin tipped his head back and groaned as he sank down on Wes. Wes filled him up so perfectly, every single time. His skin tingled, and he took Wes's hands in his as he started to ride, to grind up and down on Wes's cock until Wes was panting and gritting his teeth, and his fingers were squeezing Justin's, and his arms were shaking and his thighs were trembling. "Justin," he breathed. "I'm close."

Justin grabbed his own cock, rock hard against his belly, and stroked. He loved coming with Wes, loved feeling Wes erupt inside him as his own orgasm made his body clench. He leaned forward, kissing Wes, and Wes grabbed his ass in both hands as he pistoned his hips, driving his cock in and out. Wes gasped against Justin's lips, and Justin felt it, felt the heat and the fullness inside him. He went right over the edge with Wes, cursing as he spilled over Wes's abdomen. His ass milked Wes so hard a groan punched out of Wes, loud in the silent house.

Justin held his hand over Wes's mouth as they both went still.

Justin giggled silently, twisting as he tried to hold his laughter inside. They waited, frozen, listening.

Someone, somewhere in the house, let out a long, low wolf whistle.

Justin buried his face in Wes's neck and laughed.

———

FRIDAY'S PRACTICE didn't start until the afternoon, and everyone slept in. Except for Justin.

He slipped downstairs and started making pancakes and eggs and bacon, and he fired up all six coffee makers. The smells drifted upstairs, and he heard the guys start to rise and shuffle downstairs. It was different, seeing all these guys he watched on the field and saw on ESPN now with their bed head and boxers and sleepy faces. He smiled as they made their way through the kitchen, grabbing coffee and plates of breakfast and grunting their thanks. Art kissed him on the cheek and said, "Bless you," and Josh, with his mouth stuffed full of pancake, tried to tell Wes he'd picked a good boyfriend. It came out a carb-stuffed warble and ended with a yawn.

The first few hours of practice was a closed team meeting, so Justin spent the afternoon with his dad, shopping for furniture and decor for his new place before stopping for drinks downtown. They walked to the stadium for the end of practice and watched the team scrimmage, offense against defense. Both were on fire, and each managed to hold the other in place. They all took a knee after, and Coach Young told them to go home and get some rest and prepare for the game tomorrow.

Justin saw Colton smack Wes on the arm when Coach Young said to rest. He felt his cheeks flush, and then flush harder when his dad picked up on what was going on and cleared his throat. His dad looked away, smothering his own embarrassed grin.

Saturday morning broke brisk and beautiful, with a clear blue sky overhead and a light wind. Perfect football weather, crisp enough that little clouds of breath puffed in front of everyone in the stadium. Justin and Nick watched from their seats at the fifty-yard line, dead center in the front row on the Texas sideline. Nick had bought resale tickets online, and he wouldn't tell Justin how much he spent. "It doesn't matter," he said. "I want to watch my son's boyfriend with my son beside me. There isn't a price to put on that."

They clapped and cheered when the team ran on the field, leaping to their feet and screaming along with the crowd. There were no boos this week. Coverage on ESPN leading up to the game had been nothing but positive: reports that Wes Van de Hoek was back on the team, that the team was back in sync, that they were united again.

There was nothing about Wes's attack, though. Wes had asked to keep that out of the papers, and the hospital and the team administration agreed to respect his wish for privacy. The police were still searching for the guys who'd attacked him, combing hospital admissions across the state for anyone coming in with fight-related injuries after that night. "It will be enough to win," Wes had told Justin, late at night, holding each other in bed. "To shove their faces in it. To prove that they tried to put me down, but they couldn't. That we came back as a team, and we won together."

"They need to go to prison," Justin had said, tracing his thumb over the bruise beneath Wes's jaw.

Wes had kissed him, and that was the last they said about it that night.

Now the whole state seemed to be waiting to see what would happen. Was this going to be a win, or another collapse? Could a team shatter and reform, return to the heights of glory that they had touched together? Justin could feel the expectancy inside the stadium.

"What are they wearing?" Nick asked as they watched the team flood the center of the field. "What's on everyone's wrists?"

Justin's heart stopped, and he grabbed his dad's arm. "Dad, they're wearing rainbow sweatbands." Every one of Wes's teammates had a rainbow sweatband on his wrist, big and bold and bright against the white of their uniforms.

Wes broke off from the team and headed for the stands. He ran right to Justin and Nick and held up his hand, reaching for Justin. Justin reached back. Wes brought Justin's hands to his lips and kissed his fingers. "I love you, *mon coeur*," Wes shouted over the roar of the stadium. He pounded his chest and pointed right at Justin as he backed away, running to his team as they huddled up.

The entire thing had been captured by fifteen television cameras and played over and over on the jumbotron. Wes kissing Justin's fingers, Justin gazing at him, his love for Wes obvious from a single glance. How had they ever hid anything, if that's how he looked at Wes? Heart emojis surrounded the image on the big screen, and the kiss cam logo appeared in the corner.

Wes and the team were jumping up and down on the sideline and psyching themselves up. Wes got in the center of the huddle, facing his teammates, his friends, and shouted, "Are we gonna do this? Are we gonna win? Are we gonna show the world who we are?" Each time, the team roared back, "Yes!"

He and Colton walked out for the coin toss. Vanderbilt's head captain shook Wes's hand, then Colton's, and smiled at them both. Texas won the coin toss and chose to start with the ball, and after the kickoff, Wes, Colton, and the rest of the guys took the field.

On the opening play, Colton fired a missile to Wes running a crossing route, and Wes one-two stepped, spun, and broke away from the linebacker and the safety. He had nothing in front of him but open field, and he sprinted down the sideline as the Vanderbilt defense tried to catch him. He ran the ball all the way into the end zone as the stadium went wild. Horns blared, and the marching band roared out the school's fight song. The student section bellowed, chanting Wes's name as bucket drums and cymbals clashed with the stadium's touchdown music. In the end zone, Wes spread his arms wide and stared at the sky, then turned and pointed down the field to Colton and the rest of his team, cheering for him at the line of scrimmage.

On the sideline, the team all clapped Wes on the back—except for Colton, who body-slammed him in a ferocious bear hug. A television camera got up in their faces, trying to capture the moment for ESPN, and Colton turned right into the lens, shouting, "Texas is back, baby!"

By late in the second quarter, it was over. Texas had put thirty-one points on the board, and Vanderbilt had three. Wes was pulled from the game just before the half. He was given a headset and a clipboard and he glued himself to Coach Young's side. When the teams came back after halftime, Colton was next to Wes, both of them watching the game and their own team, taking notes on plays and where they could make adjustments going forward. By the end of the third, the rest of the first string was out, resting and letting the second and third strings get in good play time. Vanderbilt toughed it out and put a touchdown on the board, and the game ended 38–10.

Wes and Colton shook the Vanderbilt captains' hands after the game as the rest of the team and the stadium exploded into celebration. Wes ran back to Justin and Nick, hauled himself up onto the railing, and kissed Justin right on the lips. "We're going to the national championship!"

Justin cradled his face and beamed as every camera in the stadium turned to them. "You going to win that one for me, too?"

"*Bien sûr, mon coeur.*" And then Wes kissed him again.

CHAPTER THIRTY-FIVE

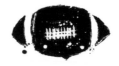

WES FLEXED his fingers inside his gloves. The locker room was quiet, only the sounds of athletic tape and the snapping of pads filling the air. Every breath Wes took was choked with tension, with the collective anxieties and nerves his teammates had carried within them all the way to this moment.

Colton slid onto the bench beside him. He leaned his shoulder against Wes's and held out his fist. Wes bumped it, then leaned back against his friend. They said nothing.

Coach Young came out of the office set aside for him in the Kansas City locker room. "All right, everyone, gather around," he called to the team. "Bring it in, bring it in." He waited as the players shuffled forward.

"This is it," he said, once everyone was near. He never minced his words. "This is your moment. This is what you worked all season for. The national championship title is yours, if you go out there and do what exactly what you have every single week you won: Believe in each other. Trust each other. Love each other."

The team nodded. Eyes flicked to each other, then over to Wes.

"I know you're nervous," Coach said. "I can feel it. But you need to let that go right now. The team that is about to walk out of here and face off against Mississippi isn't the same team that took the field against them over Thanksgiving. You were broken that day. Well, that's changed. You are whole again. And you are more than a team. You are a family."

*Hell yeah*s and scattered claps rose.

"You boys are the best team in the entire nation. Mississippi took something from you on Thanksgiving, and it's time to go get that back. So you're going to run out there, and you're going to win. Not for me. Not for the university. Not for the NFL scouts watching you. Not for the glory. You're going to go out there and win this game for *you*." He pointed to individual players, naming them. Finally, he got to Wes. "You're going to win this game today because this is what you were all born to do together."

Coach let the silence grow and let his conviction, his faith in them, fill the room and seep into each player, push out all those unspoken nerves and anxieties, the fears and the hesitations. Wes closed his eyes and felt Colton's hand on his back. Felt Art slap the back of his head. He grinned.

"All right!" Coach clapped his hands. "Get your helmets and get ready. Let's go play football!"

They roared, and they grabbed their helmets and lined up in the tunnel. Wes and Colton were right up front, and they started jumping together, staying loose. Their teammates behind them joined in, a few more at a time, until everyone was jumping. Colton turned to the team and started chanting something Wes couldn't quite make out over the roar of the stadium outside, but the rest of the team picked it up. Suddenly, ESPN and the other broadcast cameras surrounded them, capturing the shot. Wes turned to face the team, and what they were chanting hit him square in the chest.

They were chanting his name.

He grabbed Colton and shoved their helmets together. ESPN was right there, watching. "I love you, brother," Wes grunted.

Colton grabbed his helmet. "I fucking love you, too. Let's go win this."

The team roared out of the tunnel, fireworks shooting off around them as they tore out to the fifty. Wes spun, trying to orient himself. It was so different in the stadium now, with the fireworks going and the lights dim, only the neon lights and the flash of fifty thousand flashes lighting up the field. But... there. He turned to the Texas sideline and looked up at the VIP box where all the families of the starting-line players were seated. He put his fingers to his face mask and blew a kiss up to the box. "I love you, Justin," he shouted, right as the ESPN camera swung around him for a close-up.

He imagined Justin blowing him a kiss back. Closed his eyes and breathed in. This moment was theirs. It was the team's, yes, but it was also his and Justin's. He was the only out NCAA Division I-A player now, and he was leading his team as they played in the national championship. A hundred news organizations wanted to interview him. Nick was acting as his manager-slash-bulldog for now, and he'd said time and again that he wouldn't make any public statements until after this game. No one needed to know anything about him other than what he left on the field with his team. Everything else was a distraction.

But Justin... Justin was his life. He was a part of Wes, all the way down inside, so deep he was inside the atoms of his soul. When Wes played this game, he was playing not just for him, and not just for the team. He was playing for, and with, Justin, too.

He and Colton stayed loose on the sideline while Mississippi came onto the field, and a choir sang the national anthem as a flyby buzzed overhead. Colton took his hand in a warrior grasp and brought Wes to his chest, then said in his ear, "No fucking around this time. If they don't acknowledge you, I'm starting shit."

"Don't get ejected from the game."

Colton's eyes flashed. "Then they'd better shake your fucking hand."

They walked out for the coin toss together, and Colton didn't extend his hand until both Mississippi captains shook Wes's. Then he held his out, but the handshake he exchanged with the defensive captain looked painful, like they were trying to crush each other in a test of strength. The referee eventually separated them, eyeballing each for a long moment.

Mississippi won the toss and chose to kick, so Texas started with the ball.

Nerves thundered through Wes, electrifying his muscles and his veins. In the huddle, his breath shook. Everything was so bright, so vibrant. The grass had never been so green beneath stadium lights. The crowd had never been so loud. He watched Colton's lips to hear the play over the roar.

After they lined up and set, one of the linebackers came up, leaned over his defensive end, and called out, "Hey, fag. Remember me?" He blew a kiss to Wes.

Josh, set on the offensive line and next to Wes, roared. He lunged across the neutral zone, trying to tear his way through the Mississippi defensive line to get at the linebacker. Mississippi's players shoved him back, and then Patrick, Art, and Quinton were there, shoving Mississippi players off of Josh.

Whistles blew. Flags were thrown. The refs came running, and they hauled players from both teams off each other by the backs of their jerseys. The line ref pushed Josh back ten yards when he wouldn't stop shouting. Colton took the head ref aside, and Wes watched as he tried to explain what had happened. The head ref shook his head.

"False start," the ref called, reciting Josh's number. "Five-yard penalty. Repeat first down."

Colton called a huddle again. He looked at Josh and Wes. "What was that?"

"That fucking linebacker," Josh spat, "said some fucking bull-shit to Wes!"

"He was saying it all last game, too."

"Are you fucking kidding me?" Josh spun out of the huddle, grabbing his helmet. He came back, cursing so hard his face was purple. "I didn't fucking hear it last time. I'm sorry."

"It's fine—"

"It's not fine." Colton ripped his helmet off. "Look at me. We teach these motherfuckers a lesson, right now. No one says shit to us, or about us. Any of us. Fuck the play. When I call the snap, fucking blow them away. Orlando, take the handoff and run it out. The rest of you?" Colton grinned. "Bring the fucking pain." He clapped to end the huddle, and they all trotted out to the line again.

Wes's heart hammered. The entire defensive line was blowing kisses at him and Josh, wolf whistling and making sex noises, grunting and groaning and moaning, just soft enough so the refs couldn't hear. Wes could feel his teammates clench. Colton counted off the snap, far too quickly.

He breathed in, eyes locked on the linebacker who'd given him shit.

The linebacker grinned. Blew him another kiss.

"Hut!" Colton shouted. He took the ball from between Art's legs and bounced back. Passed it off to Orlando in a flash of white and orange. Then he roared and charged.

The entire line exploded upward, two thousand pounds of raging linemen moving as one, thundering right through the Mississippi defense. They put each defender in the dirt, toppled them on their asses, and then kept going, charging the linebackers. The linebackers and the corners froze. This wasn't a play from any playbook, and they had no idea how to react to it, to an all-out offensive charge. They shifted left and then right, trying to track the ball as the full fury of Wes's teammates bore down on them.

Wes ran with Josh, and Colton appeared beside them, and all three of them ran down the middle linebacker and hefted him up, then brought him to the dirt as they heard the whistle blow.

"Listen up, you fuck," Colton growled into the linebacker's face mask. "We'll fucking take you out every play if we have to. Until you shut your fucking mouth."

"Man, get off me!"

"You just got tackled by the fucking quarterback." Colton put his hand on the linebacker's helmet and used it to push himself up. "Enjoy that replay on ESPN."

Hands grabbed Wes's pads and hauled him up. He spun, but it was just Art, grinning at him. He had grass stuck to his face mask, and his arm was bleeding from a six-inch scrape, but he was smiling ear to ear. Wes held out his hand for Josh, and they jogged back to the huddle.

The defense was still picking themselves up out of the grass. One player looked like he was about to hurl. Substitutions were running out onto the field. On the Texas sideline, Coach Young was staring at his clipboard with his play card over his mouth. Wes could see the crinkles around his eyes, though.

"Well done," Colton said. He called the next play, giving the ball to Wes.

Wes caught Colton's pass and ran for twelve yards before one of the linebackers brought him down. Not a single one of Mississippi's players opened their mouth.

They fought for each down, grinding out yards in a series of first, second, and third downs, then fought for another first down. By the time they made it to the red zone, close enough to make a play for a touchdown, they were all sucking wind in the huddle, their hands on their knees. Colton called the play, a diamond sweep, and locked eyes with Wes. "Get to the end zone," he said, panting. "I'll put it in your hands."

When the ball snapped, Wes burst off the line, running flat out before fading to the right and the back corner of the end zone. He had three defenders on him, jostling him, shoving him out of sight of the refs. He turned and saw Colton launch the ball.

He breathed in, felt the beat of his heart. Imagined the ball soaring through the air. Saw the pass from Colton's vantage point. He counted, and then leaped. His hands rose over his head, fingers spread wide—

The ball slammed into his palms, and he squeezed, pulling the football down to his chest as he let gravity take over. He and all three defenders went down to the painted grass inside the end zone. Whistles blew, and he saw refs throw their hands up. Heard the stadium go wild.

Touchdown.

He got to his feet, bellowing as Colton and Josh and Patrick came running for him. Orlando and Art slapped his helmet, and they screamed nonsense into each other's face masks. He turned to the VIP box and blew another kiss. *For you, Justin.*

"Fuck," Colton said on the sideline, pouring water over his face as they watched special teams set up for the point-after kick. "That was the hardest six points we've ever earned." He grinned. "But also the best."

Their defense fought hard and held Mississippi to a field goal, and then they were back on the field. They ground through the end of the first and into the second quarter, and they got three first downs before they had to call for special teams to come out and try for a field goal.

Wes and Colton moved from player to player, crouching down and checking in with everyone in between plays. What did they need, and how were they holding up? Josh and Patrick were sucking wind, and Josh said he was afraid he was slowing down. Wes said he'd share the load with him, and Colton made adjustments on their next possession, giving Wes more blocking plays so he could stay at Josh's side and shore him up.

Two minutes before the end of the second quarter, Mississippi was up by three, and they needed to make something happen to take the lead going into the second half. They ground their way down the field, fighting all the way to the two-yard line before the Mississippi defense shut them down.

After the third down, Colton took a knee in the huddle and said, "All right. We can call special teams out and they can tie it with a field goal. Or we can bust this open and take the lead. What's it gonna be?"

Josh and Patrick were almost on their knees. Art was heaving great, deep gasps. Even Orlando looked tired, and he never looked tired. "We run it," Josh said. He breathed in. Held it. "Fuck it, we score now." He turned to Wes. "Block?"

Wes nodded, and he and Josh fist-bumped. "All right," Colton said. "Hammer push, right side. Wes, you and Josh. Orlando, with me. Ready?" He waited, giving them as many seconds as he could to catch their breath before breaking the huddle.

Colton lined up under Art. He looked left. Looked right. Wes caught his gaze. Colton winked.

Wes and Josh moved together at the snap, bursting off the line and shoving the defense back, blocking for Colton and Orlando. Orlando rolled right and then made for the hole Josh and Wes forced open through the defensive line. Wes saw Orlando fly by him, then slam into a wall of Mississippi linebacker. Roaring, he got behind Orlando and shoved, pushing him through and, finally, moving him forward.

Orlando came down with his arm over the line, the football inside the end zone. The whistles blew, and the refs ran out, arms over their heads.

Touchdown.

JUSTIN WAS FAR TOO nervous to eat anything from the buffet laid out for the families. His dad was having the time of his life cheering Wes on. Justin just played with his bottle, batting it back and forth between his hands as he hunched in his seat.

He took a walk at the half, wandering through the upper hallways and trying to calm his heart. His hands were shaking, and they wouldn't stop. He stopped by the elevator and bent over, his head between his knees as he breathed.

The elevator dinged. Justin pushed himself up and tried to look presentable. The only people who came up the private elevator were players' families or heavyweights from the university. He'd already met the university president and the director of athletics, both men saying, "Oh, so *you're* Justin Swanscott. We've read so much about you in the news."

He chewed on the inside of his lip and was starting to turn toward the glass balcony, away from the elevator, as the doors parted.

A man who looked like Wes had stepped into a time machine and emerged thirty years in the future walked out. He wore Wranglers and Ropers, a pearl snap-button Western shirt, and a jean jacket. He had a cowboy hat in his hands, and he was playing with the brim, the same way Wes played with his when he was nervous.

Justin stared.

The man looked right at him. His tanned face was creased, deep lines etched into his brow and around his eyes. But they were laugh lines, not frown lines. His blue eyes were set in deep sockets, and he looked at the world like he hadn't been surprised in over two decades.

He stepped in front of Justin. "Mr. Swanscott?"

Justin swallowed. "Um. Yes?" Mr. Swanscott was his dad. He was Justin, just Justin.

The man held out his weathered hand. "I'm Graham Van de Hoek. I'm sorry I'm late. The bus can be awful slow from West Texas. I've been listenin' to the game on my phone. We just took the lead?"

Justin nodded. He couldn't breathe.

Wes's dad smiled. "Can you show me where we can watch my boy play?"

"Of course." He stumbled forward, suddenly dizzy, and Graham caught him and steadied him. He looped Justin's hand around his elbow and left it there as they started walking. They went arm in arm down the hallway, back to the VIP suite. His dad was outside waiting for him, texting, and he looked up when Justin approached. He frowned when he saw Justin arm in arm with another man. Then his eyes widened and he stepped forward, hand outstretched. "Hi, I'm Nick Swanscott. Justin's father."

"Graham Van de Hoek." Graham shook his hand. "It seems our boys are in love."

His dad laughed. "They are very much in love." He gestured toward the door to the suite. "The second half is about to start. Join us?"

"I'd love to. Thank you." Graham tipped his head like he was tipping his hat, exactly like Wes did. Justin's heart squeezed.

His dad led Graham to the front row of the box, to the seats that overhung the mezzanine, and they started a play-by-play run-through of the first half, reliving the good parts and the belly-clenching ones. Justin grabbed three beers and brought them back, then sat on the other side of Graham. He tried to smile as he handed Wes's dad a beer.

Graham peered at him for a long moment. Whatever he saw must have satisfied him, because he clapped his hand on Justin's arm and chuckled.

Justin couldn't take a single sip of his beer during the second half, either. He was too focused on the game, on watching Wes move on the field. And on Graham, and how he was watching Wes just as intently, following his son's every movement up and down the field and on the sideline. He and Graham weren't following the football like his dad was. They were following Wes.

Watching Wes on the sidelines. Watching Wes talk to Colton. Watching Wes grab his helmet and jog back onto the field.

By the end of the third quarter, the game was tied again, and it was getting rough. Tackles were harder. Players were thrown to the ground and were chewing dirt when they came up. The Mississippi defense, after the half, had found a way to contain Wes, and Colton wasn't able to pass to him as much throughout the third. Colton focused instead on running plays and on deep passes, but it wasn't enough to break the deadlocked score.

Justin was a mess by the middle of the fourth. He was sitting forward, his elbows on his knees and his face half buried in his hands. He couldn't take his eyes off of Wes, not for a single moment. His heart was going to explode before the game was over.

Graham's hand landed on his shoulder. It was solid, and firm, and as weighty as Wes's was. "My boy will bring them home," Graham said. "He always does. You just wait. You'll see."

On the next drive, Wes lined up in the backfield, in the fullback position behind Colton. When the ball was snapped, Colton faked a handoff to Orlando, then spun and scooped it to Wes. Wes took off, hauling ass through a hole that appeared between Josh and Art, then juked right and spun out of a diving tackle from the middle linebacker. He danced forward, almost falling, but kept his footing. Quinton appeared in front of him, motioning him forward, and Wes put on a burst of speed. He and Quinton tore down the field, right up the sideline, and all the way into the end zone.

Justin and his dad leaped to their feet, along with what felt like everyone else in the stadium, and bellowed Wes's name at the top of their lungs. Everyone save for Graham, who stayed seated, though he was beaming from ear to ear. He lifted his hat on his knee and bounced his heel up and down. "That's my boy," he said. "That's my boy. You show them, son. You show them who you are."

Justin broke down and cried as Wes's entire line chased him to the end zone. Colton leaped into Wes's arms, and Josh and Patrick hoisted Wes into the air. Quinton and Devin and Art clapped him on the shoulder, and he jogged off to the sidelines to a hero's welcome from the rest of the team and his coaches. He still had the ball in his hands, the one he'd scored with, and he held on to it as he sat on the bench, spinning it in his hands. He turned his gaze up to the VIP box.

I love you, Justin mouthed, even though Wes couldn't see him. *I fucking love you.*

Justin took Graham's hand in his for the point-after kick, and then he didn't breathe for the next seven minutes. Every play by Mississippi made his heart stutter and stop. He fell sideways against Graham's shoulder, gasping when Mississippi lost first one and then two down attempts. Mississippi managed a third-down conversion, though, and Justin clenched his fingers on Graham's hand so hard his arm shook.

Graham held on, through every brutal minute. "Don't you worry, Justin," Graham said. "This game is already won. Wes won it. His team won't let him down now. You watch. Those boys are playing for more than a title right now."

Mississippi had one more chance. They needed a touchdown to send the game into overtime. It came down to one play, one attempt by the Mississippi offense, and the biggest stop of the Texas defense's life. Justin held his breath. His dad leaned forward, body taut.

Mississippi snapped, and the quarterback dropped back, searching for an open player. They had all their receivers running deep, hoping for a long pass and a breakaway, a deep Hail Mary. But Texas was blitzing, sending every man at the quarterback instead of downfield after the receivers. It was risky on both sides. Justin almost closed his eyes, afraid to watch the pass.

But Anton got through the line. He came over the guards and flew at the Mississippi quarterback.

Justin watched as the quarterback buckled and folded in on himself. He watched him go down to the dirt as Anton's arms wrapped around him, sacking him ten yards behind the line of scrimmage.

And that was the game. There was still a little over a minute on the clock, but the stands were already erupting, Texas fans and the Texas sideline going wild as Colton and Wes jogged onto the field. Colton led the offense in a victory formation, taking a knee after the snap to run the clock down.

Wes's teammates stormed the field as national champions.

Justin pitched forward in relief. Big hands stroked his back. Graham's hands. Someone else guided him up, and he saw his dad's face.

Wes did it. After everything, he'd done it. He brought his team to glory.

A stadium rep appeared at their VIP box and led everyone down to the field. Out of view of the cameras, Justin wiped his eyes and downed a bottle of water. His dad checked him before they went on the field, and he took a napkin and wiped Justin's face again as Graham watched and smiled.

They came onto the field and into a cacophony of noise and bedlam. Players were screaming, running to the stands for handshakes and high fives with the fans leaning over the lower railing. Confetti twirled in the air as balloons clung to their ankles and tried to trip Justin with every step he took. It seemed like a million people were on the field: the players, the families, the coaching staff, the dignitaries. Justin pushed through the crowd. He had to find Wes.

There he was, in the center of the field, jumping up and down with Colton and Art and Josh and Orlando. They were screaming at the tops of their lungs, arms wrapped around each other, heads tipped back in pure relief, pure rushes of adrenaline, and pure, unbridled happiness.

"Wes!" Justin shouted.

Wes turned, and his eyes landed on Justin. He grinned even wider, and he pulled away from his teammates.

Wes started running, and so did Justin. Wes flung open his arms and Justin leaped, flying into his hold, yelling his name as he wrapped his legs around Wes's waist and his arms around Wes's neck. He pressed his forehead to Wes's, smiling, crying, too many emotions thundering through him at once. "You did it, *mon coeur*."

Wes held Justin tight. "I did it for you. I won for you, so the world could see how much I love you."

Justin cradled Wes's face in his hands as he leaned down and captured Wes's lips. He meant for it to be a sweet kiss, something ESPN could replay, but Wes deepened it, and then deepened it again, even though the cameras were circling and zooming in. Colton and Josh started batting the cameras away, and the rest of the team surrounded Wes and Justin, clapping and cheering.

Eventually, Justin broke the kiss and pushed their foreheads together again. "Wes, there's someone here to see you." He dropped down to the grass, took Wes's hand, and turned.

Graham Van de Hoek was right there, his hat on his head, his smile as big and wide as the Texas sky as he stood in front of his son.

Wes stilled. "Dad?"

Graham grabbed Wes, rocking him in his arms, his cheek pressed against his son's. They were mirror images separated by time and the sun.

Wes curled into his dad's hold, and Graham held him, wrapping his hand around the back of Wes's neck as he whispered into his ear. Justin saw the shape of his lips, saw Graham tell Wes he was so proud, and that he loved him, and that Wes had grown into the man he'd always dreamed Wes would be. And again, that he was proud, so damn proud, of who Wes was.

Wes came out of his father's hold and wiped his eyes on the bottom of his jersey. Graham kissed his forehead and stepped back, smiling at Justin. Justin wrapped Wes up again, letting Wes hide his face from the cameras for a moment.

Colton appeared, tapping Wes on the shoulder and handing him a football. He waved the entire team over, and they leaped into action, forming a circle around Wes and Justin as if they'd been waiting. Colton made room in the circle for the two fathers. Justin eyed Colton and then Wes, standing in front of him.

Wes took the football in both of his hands. He faced Justin and breathed in. "This is the ball I scored the last touchdown with." He held it out. Justin wrapped his hands around it, cradling it like he was touching Wes's beating heart.

Wes dropped to one knee in the grass. "I promise you, Justin, that I will love you and cherish you as hard as I play this game. Harder, even." He grinned. "I want to spend every day for the rest of my life loving you. What do you say? Can I be yours? And will you be mine?"

He dropped to his knees in front of Wes and kissed him. "*Bien sûr*, cowboy," he said, beaming. "Forever."

EXCERPT FROM THE MURDER
BETWEEN US

Please enjoy this excerpt from
The Murder Between Us
A Noah & Cole Thriller, Book 1
available at Amazon and on Kindle Unlimited.

———

It's Vegas. This city was built for people to come and shake out all their bad decisions. All their… curiosities.

Noah wove his way through the casino hall, sidestepping for a waitress balancing an overloaded tray in one hand. He smiled. She smiled back.

His friend James spun and watched her walk away, whistling as he stared at her long legs encased in sheer black stockings. Her skirt ended at the tops of her thighs. More than a few guys were breaking their necks to watch as she sashayed down the casino hallway amid the whirs and jangles and frantic chimes pouring out of the rows and rows of slot machines. Even some of the guys at the blackjack tables turned to look at her.

She glanced back and met Noah's gaze again. She winked. A slow smile unfurled over her perfect face.

"Dude!" James grabbed at Noah's arm and almost walked backward into one of the pillars lining the hall. Noah grabbed him with both hands, steadying him before he fell into a crowd of Japanese tourists. "She smiled at you, man. Go back there! C'mon, go on. You definitely have an in!"

Noah shook his head. The rest of their group slowed to a tipsy halt, forming a loose bubble around Noah and James. They were practically carbon copies of each other: seven guys lurching toward middle age with mostly flat stomachs and most of their hair still on top of their heads. They were all dressed the same, even: khakis and a polo, but some of the guys had left behind their sport coats before dinner. They were the ones wearing the fanny packs around their waists.

"Go on!" James tried to push Noah after the waitress who had simply smiled at him, a gentle flirtation after he'd stepped aside to ease her way.

He wasn't kidding himself. There was no way a woman like her—gorgeous, with a perfect body, and young enough to make him uncomfortable—would ever want him chasing her down.

"I think the night is over," Noah said, spinning James and propelling him toward the elevators. The group laughed and followed, the just-past-drunk, ambling stroll of men at midnight in Las Vegas. "We've got an early morning. C'mon."

James groaned. "Why do they have this conference here?" He threw his head back and trudged toward the elevator bank. "Why can't they have this conference in…" His eyes slid sideways. He grinned. "In Des Moines. Somewhere boring." Noah knuckled his friend's hair as James laughed.

All one thousand of them were there, spread across the tenth through twenty-fifth floors of the hotel. God bless the government and its bulk room discounts. Where should the Federal Bureau of Investigation put the special agents who attended the largest annual FBI conference? All together, like sardines in a can. No one could quite figure out whether the conference was a mini vacation or a horrible tease. Agents had to attend a week's worth of sessions, lectures, and breakout workshops, each of them putting together their own thirty-hour-long conference schedule. Nights were theirs… as long as they badged in every morning on time. More than a few agents overslept each morning, hungover and destroyed from a night out on the town. If an agent was late two days in a row, they were sent home, and from there, it was a short trip to the doghouse—or worse. Maybe the whole conference was a test of character.

Whatever it was, the conference was Noah's week away from home—Des Moines, Iowa—and a chance to reconnect with his friends from the academy. James had been his roommate way back when, and now he was chasing bank robbers in Southern California. Gary was running the white-collar crime squad out of Philly, while Pete and Carl were chasing right-wing terrorists in Seattle.

Everyone else was in a major field office, while Noah had somehow landed in the Des Moines resident agency—a satellite of the larger Omaha field office—and stayed, like a farmhouse dropped by a tornado. He was the assistant special agent in charge of Des Moines now. Technically, that meant he outranked all of his friends. Even if it was only Des Moines.

Everyone had done well. Everyone was at that comfortable point in their careers: close enough to the middle to settle in, far enough from the beginning to have shaken out the kinks and the nerves. Far enough away from retirement for that to still be a distant thing, something relegated to when the knees began to act up and the gray hairs were multiplying.

The elevator doors slid open, and the guys piled in. They leaned against the mirrored walls, laughing about the evening, reminiscing over the dinner they'd spent way too much money on, remembering the women they'd seen out in the casino and on the Strip. Everyone's eyes were glassy. Their shoulders were starting to droop.

Noah's hands shook inside his pants pockets. One foot tapped silently against the carpet. *It's Vegas. You waited all year for this.*

He'd chickened out for the past two nights, heading back to his room when everyone else did and pacing for an hour before watching the neon glow of the Strip from his window. Eventually, he'd turned on CNN and listened to the warble of the news anchors as he face-planted in bed, hoping the drone of their voices would force out the thoughts that kept circling around and around his mind. *Coward. You'll never know. You'll never know if you don't try.*

The elevator started spitting everyone out at the eleventh, fourteenth, and seventeenth floors, until it was just James and him stepping off on the twentieth. Their rooms were across the hall from each other.

James leaned back against his door, key card in one hand, sport coat crumpled in his other. His holster was out and visible now—a violation, but it was midnight, and they were alone. Who was going to write him up?

"I'm telling you, man," James said, in the languid drawl of the inebriated. "You should go back down there. Maybe she's not the one for tonight, but she definitely would be willing to flirt with you if you happened to run into her again. How long has it been since a pretty woman smiled at you?"

Noah's eyes fell to the carpet as he dug his shoe into the wool fibers.

"I know you've been focused on your career, and…" James trailed off with a sigh. "I know it's been a while. That can eat at a man, you know? You deserve to be happy. God, out of all of us, *you* deserve to be happy." James smiled, a lopsided, tipsy grin. Despite wolf whistling at the waitress, James was all set to pour himself into bed and call his wife, whisper sweet nothings to her as she recounted every moment of her day with their three young daughters. James had been texting her throughout dinner, sending her pics of the appetizer and then his entree, and of his ridiculous drink.

James was a man who had certainty. He had the love of a great woman, three amazing daughters, and the satisfaction that came from knowing his place in the world.

Jealousy seared through Noah. Certainty. What a thing to be jealous of. To know yourself and what you wanted.

"Breakfast tomorrow?" James pushed off and shoved his key in the lock. It beeped, and he shouldered open the door before tossing his jacket into the darkness.

"Meet you in the restaurant." Noah nodded, waiting for James to head inside.

His friend, despite seeming to be the inebriated fool, was still a federal agent, and he could still put the clues together. He looked Noah up and down, eyes narrowing as his smile shifted, turned almost salacious. "Tell me 'bout it in the morning," he said, disappearing into his room. "Have fun!"

The door shut. Noah heard the deadbolt turn.

It's Vegas. You're supposed to do this in Vegas. You're supposed to let loose. He tipped his head back. Sighed. *Go down there. Just for a few minutes. Just look.*

Yeah, okay. He could do that. He could look. Looking wasn't anything permanent.

First things first. He pushed into his hotel room and unholstered his gun, locking it in the safe. If he was going to head back out, he might as well freshen up a bit. Change out of the clothes he'd worn all day. In the bottom of his suitcase were a pair of black jeans, snugger than he ever wore in Iowa, and a slim-fit button-down he'd accidentally bought along with the regular ones he preferred. It was way too tight to wear to the office, and he felt ridiculous when he put it on. In the slim cut, he felt like he was playing dress-up as Hollywood's idea of a special agent. But he had to admit the shirt showed off his flat stomach and his broad shoulders, the taper he'd built in high school and college through intramural sports and kept up thanks to turning to the gym whenever his frustrations started to boil.

Might as well run his fingers through his hair, too. And brush his teeth. Should he shave? Why not.

Half an hour later, Noah stared at himself, eyeballing the tall, dark-haired, shit-scared man in the mirror. He was just a guy. Just a guy going down for a drink. Nothing more. "It's Vegas," he whispered. His fingers curled around the sink's edge. "Let yourself look."

He never had before.

Noah grabbed his wallet and his room key and forced himself to walk out the door. He left his badge and gun behind. He wasn't a federal agent tonight—or at least, not for the next hour. Or, hell, the next ten minutes, if he was truthful with himself about how long his courage was likely to last. He'd rather be back at Quantico than let go of the hotel room door and go down the elevator.

The hallway was empty, not a soul in sight up or down its cavernous length. It was that in-between time for Vegas. Too late for families, too early for the partygoers. All the people who weren't going out were in for the night, and those who were still going were going to last all night.

But not him. No, he was just going to have one drink. One look.

One, two, three steps. Noah shook out his arms, rolled his shoulders. Strode down the hall. He could do this.

He couldn't do this. What had he been thinking?

The casino, if possible, was even more packed than earlier. The floor was brighter, louder. The slots were screaming, electric jangles and digital bells roaring. Neon and strobe lights slammed into him. Men and women, couples and groups, surged. Laughter and shouts rose from the gambling pit, the cocktail tables, the crowds by the slot machines.

He was adrift in a sea of humanity. No one else was alone like he was. Everyone he saw had someone. Friends, a significant other, a partner. Someone they were with. Except him.

The bar was dead ahead, a giant circle of raised marble in the center of the casino floor. He beelined for it, sliding into an open space and leaning on his elbows. He squeezed his eyes closed. What was he doing? He should go back to his room and turn on CNN. Again.

"Hey, honey!" A slim hand landed on his shoulder. Noah jerked, twisted—

It was the waitress from earlier. Her name tag, pinned low on her breast and drawing the eye to her cleavage, said *Rachel*. She leaned into his side, beaming, and one of her stocking-clad thighs rubbed against his leg. "Uh—" he stammered.

"Ditch your friends?" Her gaze flicked down, taking in his change of clothes. Her eyes seemed to ignite, and her smile, when she looked up, was different. Hungrier. "Hanging around for a bit, sexy?"

Noah swallowed hard. "I… I don't know." He shook his head. He couldn't think. She was too close. Her breasts were pushing against his arm. As gingerly as he could, he shifted away, putting centimeters between his body and hers. "I only came down for one drink."

As quickly as she'd lit up, she became completely uninterested. She shifted away and flicked her hair, sending her long, black tresses over one shoulder. "If you're here for a drink, Philippe will get you one." She caught the bartender's eye and jerked her chin to Noah, then pushed back from the bar top. "Enjoy your night."

"Have a good night, too," Noah tried to say, but he was speaking to her back as she strode away, smiling at new people, taking drink orders effortlessly and batting her eyes at the men with the tallest stacks of chips in front of them at the blackjack tables.

"What'll it be?" a gruff voice barked. Philippe, behind the bar, was six feet of solid muscle. He had long hair pulled back in a ponytail, and his black T-shirt wasn't just tight, it was stretched so thin Noah could almost see the individual fibers struggling to hold on to their atomic bonds. Philippe glowered down at Noah, rubbing his hammer-sized hands in a bar towel.

"Whiskey, please. Jameson on the rocks."

Philippe nodded and poured his drink silently, then slid it across the bar top. "Twenty-four dollars."

Jesus. He didn't know which to be more confused by, the outrageous price or Philippe's hostility. How had he pissed off two people in less than a minute? *You're not in Kansas anymore.* Or Iowa, even. He opened his wallet, thumbed out thirty dollars, and slid the bills to Philippe. Philippe pocketed the cash and walked off.

And then Noah was alone again, sandwiched between two groups of businessmen who had passed tipsy an hour ago and were howling at stories that were being told louder and louder. Elbows jostled him, and a man in a blue sport coat backed into his hip, barely grunting an apology before Noah spread his arms and tried to stake out his territory a bit better. Maybe he should take his drink and go. Walk. Find somewhere else to be. Hell, he could sit in front of a slot machine and get ignored by Rachel and have a better time.

Or he could go back upstairs.

So much for his big try.

Sighing, he slumped forward, head down, fingers twirling his glass on the marble bar top. Ice sloshed and slipped in and out of the amber liquid.

This wasn't him. He wasn't this uneasy, this out of his element. He was forty years old, not fourteen. Too old, maybe, for this. He gave himself a silent toast—*Hey, you tried, have a participation trophy*—and downed the rest of the whiskey.

He caught sight of a man staring at him across the bar. An attractive—*Jesus, he was really handsome*—man. His blond hair shone under the bar's lights, and his head was tilted to the side, just so. A tiny smile played on his lips as if he was laughing at some inside joke he and Noah shared.

Lightning sparked down Noah's arms, electricity zinging beneath his skin.

He froze, whiskey half down his throat, glass to his lips. He nearly inhaled the Jameson, almost ended up spraying whiskey over the backs of the obnoxious sales guys crowding him on his right. His eyes watered, and he set his glass down too quickly, nearly losing it as his hand slipped on the condensation. He couldn't have looked more undignified if he tried. Heart pounding, Noah peered across the bar, trying to spot the blond man again. His breath hitched, caught, as Philippe paced in front of him—

The blond man was gone.

Disappointment knifed through him. He dragged in a slow breath as his fingers clenched around his empty glass. One look. One glimpse. One skip of his heart. Jesus, if this was the reaction he got just from making eye contact with a good-looking guy, then…

Well. It's not like he really wondered anymore. He pretty much knew. But there was a difference between thinking, and wondering, and pretty much knowing and… *really knowing.*

Of course, to know, he'd have to work up enough courage to do something about it, and considering his track record…

It wasn't so bad, being alone.

Besides, that guy was probably looking at someone behind him. One of the sales guys, or, more likely, Rachel. Or any other attractive person, male or female. Who in this casino would pick him out of the crowd, drinking alone at the bar, to smile at?

Well, he'd had his drink, he'd seen a guy who made his heart race, he'd nearly dropped his drink, and now it was time to head back to his room. Noah batted his glass between his palms on the bar top: once, twice, a third time. He nodded. He'd done what he said he would. Time for another year of thinking about it, thinking he might be—

"Can I buy you another one?"

The voice that spoke was honeyed whiskey, amber and gold sliding down his spine and burrowing beneath his skin. Warmth flowed from Noah's chest, slid up his neck, and grabbed the back of his skull. A hard body leaned into him, just like Rachel had, but instead of cleavage and soft curves, a sculpted chest wrapped in a dark suit slid against his side. A knee brushed the back of his.

The impulses to jump and to melt crashed inside Noah, and he did both and neither at the same time. Jerking, he twisted, losing hold of his empty glass in the process. He lunged for it before it slid off the bar top.

The man beside him caught it one-handed, as if Noah had pitched it to him on purpose.

Jesus. Noah flushed from the roots of his hair to his toes. His eyes flicked down, and down, and then up, quickly. It was him. The blond man who had smiled at him was right there, one leg behind Noah's, elbow on the bar top, holding Noah's glass. He was close enough that Noah could feel the heat coming from his skin, see his chest peeking out from beneath the top two buttons of his shirt, undone and open.

He was tall, as tall as Noah, able to look him in the eye as they stood practically inside each other's shadow. Up close, Noah saw a distinct lack of fine lines and crow's-feet, the signs he'd come to recognize in the mirror as he hit the big 4-0 and that he saw creeping onto the faces of his friends. Deep brown eyes, like old leather and cognac, stared back at him. His stomach flip-flopped.

The sales guys behind Noah roared again, laughing at yet another story told too loud. One of them backed into Noah, this time not even bothering to mumble an apology. Noah turned, glowering. "Hey. Back up, please. No need for that."

They were drunk enough to be happy, and the group shifted six inches down the bar. When Noah turned back, the blond was studying him, that hint of a smile back on his lips, as if he was appraising what Noah had just done.

"Sorry." Noah gestured to both the sales guys and his glass—still in the blond's grasp—at the same time. "It's a little crazy here tonight."

"This isn't your normal scene."

"Definitely not." Noah chuckled. "I uh, wasn't planning on coming out tonight."

Noah felt the blond's eyes rake down his body. "I'm glad you did."

He flushed, as if the sun had turned its entire focus on him and him alone. His vision blurred, and there were suddenly two blond hunks in front of him until his eyes snapped back into focus. He coughed, looked down. Ran his finger over a seam in the bar's marble as he fought a slow smile. "When in Vegas." He shrugged.

Silence. He felt studied, like a lab rat. He looked back up and met the blond's gaze. The lights from the bar dipped in and out of his facial features, curving around his angled cheekbones and the square lines of his jaw. Across the bar, he'd been eye-catching. Up close, he was breathtaking. Noah's chest squeezed.

"Is this your first time?" The question was quiet, the man's voice soft. Gentle.

He barked out a quick laugh and looked away, squinting at the bottles of top-shelf liquor. He was going to jump out of his skin. "Is it that obvious?"

"Well, I saw you shoot down the waitress—who, I might add, a hundred other guys would give just about anything to get a smile from. I thought I might have a better chance with you than she did, but… now I'm thinking I might be the first guy who has ever asked to buy you a drink." His eyes peered into Noah's, searching.

Noah swallowed. Lifted his chin. "You are."

"Was my offer unwelcome?"

It was an off-ramp, a way to escape this conversation. Escape the question, escape his own question, escape his search for answers. "No. It was welcome. You're right, though. I've never done this before. I'm not sure what I'm doing."

"What did you come here for?" The man was still staring at Noah. The rest of the bar faded away: the shouts, the jingle of the slots, the electronic chimes and whirs. Even the sales guys and their boisterous, drunken laughter. Everything disappeared except the two of them and the inches that separated them. The heat of the blond's knee where it brushed the back of Noah's.

"I was…" He was what? Coming down here to look at men? How did that sound, when he said it outside the four walls of his hotel room? He sounded like a creep, like someone he would investigate and expect to find a string of sexual complaints behind, maybe some Peeping Tom activity or stalking. It hadn't sounded that ridiculous before. *Let yourself look. Let yourself pretend you're allowed to.*

God knows he'd wanted to.

He'd imagined meeting a man so many times, dreamed it and yearned for it and hungered for it, the skin of his hands itching from wanting to reach out and…

He wanted to know what it was like. Was the reality anything like the wanting?

"I was giving myself permission," he said.

Smiling, the man held out his hand. "My name is Cole." His smile made his whole face light up, turning the strong angles into gentle curves. "If you'd like, I'll buy the next round and we can chat for a while."

He has kind eyes. Whirlpools of warm wood, dark velvet and starlight. Cole's eyes went right through Noah. That clench he'd carried for years was back, a constriction in his chest like his heart couldn't beat right. "I'm Noah." He took Cole's hand. His skin was warm, smooth. His fingers were long. Jesus, he was gorgeous. "I'd love to have a drink with you."

Cole beamed.

Grab your copy of The Murder Between Us today!

It was just one night.
It was just one mistake.

FBI Agent Noah Downing had questions about his sexuality that a single night in Vegas should have answered. But dawn finds him on a plane back to Iowa, back on the trail of a vicious serial killer who disappeared six years ago and has suddenly resurfaced. There's nothing like a murder investigation to escape an existential crisis.

FBI profiler Cole Kennedy is still reeling after finding a heart-stopping connection with a seemingly perfect man, only for him to vanish. When he's sent to Iowa to profile the killer terrorizing America's heartland, he finds more questions than answers - both about the murderer and about Noah, the last man he ever expected to see again.

A twisted secret stretches between Cole and Noah, tangled with questions they both have about each other. But now, thrown together, they'll have to unravel the killer's profile and follow his trail... back to the very beginning, to where everyone's questions are answered once and for all.

STAY IN TOUCH!

To never miss a release, sale, or special, sign up for my <u>newsletter</u>!

If you liked this novel, please leave a rating and / or a review.
Thank you!

You can find my other novels here!

Follow me on Facebook,
and visit my Facebook reader's group!
Follow me on Instagram!
Follow me on BookBub!

Check out my website at www.talbauerwrites.com

Who is Tal?

Tal Bauer writes breathtaking, heartfelt, and often action-packed gay romance novels. His characters are head over heels for each other, and fight against all of the odds for their happy ending. Nothing stands in the way of love. Tal is best known for his romantic suspense novels, including the *Executive Office* series, *The Night Of, The Jock*, and the Noah & Cole thrillers, including *The Murder Between Us* and *The Grave Between Us*.

facebook.com / talbauerauthor
instagram.com / talbauerwrites
amazon.com / author / talbauer
bookbub.com / authors / tal-bauer

ALSO BY TAL BAUER

The Noah & Cole Thrillers:

The Murder Between Us

The Grave Between Us

The Sean & Jonathan Mysteries:

The Night Of

MM Sports Romance:

The Jock

The Executive Office Series:

Enemies of the State

Interlude

Enemy of My Enemy

Enemy Within

Interlude: Cavatina

The Executive Power Series:

Ascendent

Stars

The D.C. Novels:

Hush

Whisper

Stand Alone Novels

Hell and Gone: Gay Western Romantic Suspense

A Time to Rise: Gay Paranormal Romantic Suspense

Splintered: Gay Paranormal Romantic Suspense

Soul on Fire: Gay Romantic Suspense

His First Time: Gay Erotic Short Stories

ACKNOWLEDGMENTS

Thank you to Maria, Alicia, and Lindsey for your help with this novel.